For my wife… my love, and my muse.

The Watch Maker

By
L. E. Gay

"Until we have seen someone's darkness, we don't really know who they are. Until we have forgiven someone's darkness, we don't really know what love is."
- Marianne Williamson

Chapter One

The air was alive with electricity. Making his way past the staggering hordes of Bourbon Street, the dark figure sought out familiar avenues he once called his own. He permitted his mind a stroll through ancient memories; images long buried suddenly clawed their way to cognizance. Each reflection layered onto the next, a grand crescendo in a symphony for his soul. Titillating scenes of light and shadow flashed across his mind as his olfactory senses restored them to vivid color. Hobbling through the crowd, the old man stopped often, breathing deeply, savoring the smells of authentic Creole cooking and aged whiskey. Even the foul odors of soured garbage and vomit were comforting to his spirit. They smelled like home.

Welcoming a departure from the neon glow, the old man turned his eyes to a familiar, darkened side-street. A sting shot through his arthritic, crippled knee as he stepped from the curb. Pain barked a warning with each step as he crossed the intersection then bit firmly as he stepped back to the sidewalk and limped his way down Ursulines toward Chartres. He delighted in his nocturnal stroll despite the screaming protest of his aged body. Driven by enthusiasm he could not explain, he pushed on, taking in all the sights, sounds, and smells his senses could hold. Each memory produced a sigh of elation to once again be roaming the Quarter – owning it. Besides, he thought, the pain would soon be gone.

Tapping his cane determinedly along the sidewalk, he scanned the street for activity. The area was unusually bereft of stragglers, though there appeared to be some movement in the next block. With the glow of Bourbon behind him, his eyes adjusted quickly to the darkness. Turning them toward the distant sky, he watched between the buildings as lightning illuminated the outlying clouds. He could smell the rain; it was not far off. A brisk, chilly breeze whipped down the street catching him stoutly in the face, urging him to gather his overcoat around his chest and protect his spindly frame. The sudden wind would have easily unseated his top hat, were it not pulled down firmly across his brow.

As he approached the intersection at Royal, the old man slowed his pace, yielding to a tour group shuffling up the walk like sheep behind their shepherd. He loathed tourists, but respected their place as a necessary evil. For an instant, the irony of his silent judgment stabbed him like an ice pick. Here he was, walking the Quarter, feeding off its aura just as they were. Perish the thought! He belonged here. He was home. Though his travels kept him away far too long, New Orleans was in his very blood.

He lingered quietly on the outer edge of the group, intrigued by the commanding timbre of the tour guide's voice. For such a young man, the guide had a keen knowledge of the area and its general history. He was obviously well-studied and held the group's attention admirably. Though his dusty Panama and beige safari shirt offered him little distinction from his camera-happy tourists, the guide was surely a native. The absence of a jacket, however, screamed of either ill-preparedness or lack of concern for the approaching weather.

The old man listened as the guide pointed to a haunting structure on the corner and recounted the story of Jacques Saint Germaine, an infamous New Orleans resident of the 1920's. A thrilling, multilingual conversationalist and musician with a flare for hosting extravagant parties, St. Germaine held a striking similarity in character to the Comte Saint Germain of France circa 1700. Though he entertained the elite of New Orleans on many occasions with lavish dinners, Jacques was never seen eating a bite, only drinking his wine.

"One night, a panicked woman ran screaming to the police, having jumped from the second floor gallery of this building," said the guide in a sobering tone. "Claiming a narrow escape after being attacked by St. Germaine, the woman insisted he attempted to bite her neck and convinced police to investigate. Upon searching his residence," the guide continued, gesturing again to the building behind him, "The police found that St. Germaine had vanished, but a thorough search of the premises uncovered evidence of strange and macabre practices. Police found several large bloodstained tablecloths and dozens of bottles of wine mixed with human blood."

The old man silently scoffed at the gasps from the crowd as the tour guide suggested St. Germaine was a vampire who might still walk the Quarter to this day. "Tourists and their pop-culture fascinations," he thought with mild amusement. He watched their eyes feverishly scan the night, clearly hoping to catch a glimpse of some silly sparkling entity. He listened as long as he could, chuckling to himself at the absurdity until he was politely asked to move along out of respect for those who "paid good money" to participate in the tour. Without a word, the old man politely tipped his hat and continued on his way as lightning once again split the horizon.

He could still hear the commanding voice of the guide as he limped his way to Chartres Street and turned right. His other knee soon joined the first in painful protest. Cursing his mutinous joints, he paused to massage the tender spot just above the kneecaps. "Patience," he thought, wincing, "Not much longer. It will all be over soon."

In the distance, the old man could see the lights of Saint Louis Cathedral; the sight gave him strength to push onward. For the next few blocks, his will fought a grueling battle: his mind craved desperately to remain lost in memories of the past fueled by the very air of New Orleans, but his aching body demanded attention over and over again. His sense of smell was his mind's strongest ally. "I guess it's true what they say," he thought, as a sex worker crossed his path and the pursuing scent of her cheap perfume lofted onto the breeze. "Odors always trigger the strongest memories." The prostitute walked arm in arm with her liberally intoxicated new friend, her forced laughter echoing off the brick buildings as they made their way from Bourbon to who knows where. Business was escalating, the old man surmised. With Mardi Gras approaching, the energy of the Quarter was beginning to quicken – like the first wave of ants from an upset mound. In a few short weeks, the colony would be swarming at full tilt and the resulting chaos would provide a fantastic veil. Streetwalkers would be a dime a dozen, he thought, easily overlooked and hardly missed. The thought brought him to Saint Ann Street with no further consideration of his pain.

As the old man crossed St. Ann, his view opened into the square. The cathedral's powerful floodlights illuminated its face like the mid-day sun. Its three tall spires stretched for what seemed like miles into the night sky, their sharp peaks lost to the darkness.

Thunder rumbled low as the lightning persisted, and the old man took in the static-charged air like his first breath on earth. Though his body was crippled by age, his hearing was remarkably intact. Listening closely, he could make out raindrops falling on the foliage of Jackson Square, though he could not yet feel the drizzle.

The mall area in front of the cathedral was alive with people huddling together and bundling their coats in preparation for the coming rain. The benches near the streetlamps cleared as visitors sought shelter. Several fortune tellers had already blown out their candles and taken up their card tables and make-shift altars. One, however, remained. She sat directly across from the cathedral's entrance and stared up at the clock, as if it were not yet time to leave – as if waiting for someone.

The old man tightened his grip on the polished silver handle of his cane. His palms began to sweat in tethered anticipation as he clutched its contoured surface. Driving the cane hard against the brick street with each step, he approached the motionless gypsy. The woman's face was worn with unkind years and the flickering glow from her array of candles did little to hide her lines. She wore a lavender, silk scarf around her head adorned with thin, gold chains and tiny coins. The cheap decoration was intended to elicit the confidence of naïve tourists who considered her service novelty. Other card readers who frequented the square nightly saw no need for such trite, costumed attire, preferring to work in street clothes while rolling their eyes in contempt. Madame Zoe, however, confident in her craft, having honed it over years of study and practice, was business-savvy enough not to cast aside a simple ruse that more than doubled her revenue. An outfit of silk scarves, heavy eyeliner, and copious hoop bracelets was a small price to pay for a competitive edge and additional income. Tourists were delighted by Madame Zoe's appearance, and her regular clientele didn't object to the charade; they were convinced of her talent and foresight, having witnessed many years of accurate predictions. Tonight, her heavily painted eyes turned slowly toward the approaching stranger.

The old man kept his face hidden beneath the brim of his top hat as he silently slipped his hand into the pocket of his coat. Without a word, he dropped a fifty dollar bill onto the weathered card table and waited patiently.

Madame Zoe was uncomfortable. The growing anxiety plaguing her since early in the evening now culminated in a near-crippling state of paranoia. With trepidation, she took the bill and folded it twice before slipping it into the small, beaded coin purse she kept on a chain around her neck. Surprised by the slight tremor in her hands, she moved a tall candle from the edge of the table to better illuminate the center, then slid a well-worn tarot deck to the other side. As she motioned for the stranger to cut the cards, Madame Zoe bent low trying to see the man's eyes. Her effort was unsuccessful. The stranger pulled his hat down a bit more while he silently split the deck. Setting his feet, he relaxed into a more comfortable stance, resting both hands on his cane to take the weight from his aching knees.

Madame Zoe retrieved the cut cards and held them between her outstretched palms. A disturbance deep in her spirit told her to drop them and run, but the same feeling that held her in the cathedral square drew her to the mysterious stranger: an unnerving assurance that she was exactly where she was supposed to be. Closing her eyes, Madame Zoe placed her thumb firmly on top of the deck and began to deal her signature pattern – an eight card variation of the familiar Celtic cross. One by one, she placed the cards face down on the table.

When the pattern was complete, Madame Zoe put the deck aside and with her thin, heavily-ringed fingers, turned over the first grouping. A deep breath later, she opened her eyes. The sun card, the ten of pentacles, and the nine of swords reflected the man's past. "You've lived a long life," she said, lifting her eyes.

The old man sighed. He did not need a mystic to tell him when he was born. He was, in general, quite disinterested in his past, but like the necessary evil of the tourists in the quarter, it was a critical part of the reading. He knew without an accurate interpretation of his past, Madame Zoe was powerless to reveal his future. He harnessed what was left of his patience and waited.

Sensing his tension, Madame Zoe turned her eyes back to the cards. "You've known great wealth in your lifetime," she relayed as her mouth grew unusually dry. Clearing her throat she continued, "But you've also seen intense suffering and heartache. Your life is scarred by it, more than I've ever seen – like a great shadow of sadness choking everything you... once loved."

The old man swallowed hard as hatred swelled in his throat. The truth was painful. He wanted to take the cane, wield it like a bat and strike the woman in the temple until her blood flowed like a tiny river between the bricks, but he resisted the urge. He was now confident the old gypsy's talent was still dead-on.

Satisfied, he raised his head slightly as Madame Zoe closed her eyes and turned over the pattern's next group of three.

Thick clouds rolled in over the river, bringing a fantastic display of lightning. The square was still alight when the gypsy opened her eyes to read the cards. The three of wands, the fool, and the devil card revealed the old man's present. Madame Zoe was taken aback. Never before had a reading stirred her spirit to fear, but it gripped her now like a tightening vice. Years of reassuring clients the devil card simply indicated a concern for the subject's own inner fears suddenly all felt wrong. Now visibly shaking, Madame Zoe knew, without a doubt, this card represented an outward terror. Nearly afraid to speak, she chose her words carefully, focusing instead on the other cards. "I see business," she stammered, "A new beginning. Travel. You've traveled here recently, but you are no stranger to the area. You've been to New Orleans before, lived here, many years ago." The man's awkward silence persuaded Madame Zoe to continue, concerned. "There's something else here," she said, shifting in her seat. "I don't know what it is you're running from mister, but it stalks you like a wolf."

Madame Zoe stopped there. Whatever hunted the man was nothing compared to his passion for that which he hunted; she saw it in the cards and she felt it in her bones.

For the final time she closed her eyes and flipped over the remaining two cards. As they fell onto the table, time stood still. A sinking sensation overcame Madame Zoe, like dropping too fast in an elevator. A bright flash of light blinded her inner eye as a vision of her dear friend Mama Lu danced across the stark-white canvas. The figure spun slowly, her face stretched in a wide smile, her garments swaying grandly. With a whip of her neck, Mama Lu stopped spinning and slowly approached the waiting gypsy. As her face grew larger against the bright canvas, her smile began to fade. By the time her image filled Madame Zoe's field of vision, Mama Lu's expression was pained. With an abrupt jerking motion, she launched into a hollow scream just before her face burst into flames. Madame Zoe watched in horror as Mama Lu was consumed by fire, leaving only the remnants of a smoldering, tortured skull.

Searing pain shot through the gypsy's temple, traveling along the nerves to the base of her neck while the vision went dark. Weakened to a vulnerable state, Madame Zoe gathered her strength and dared to open her eyes. Her frightened gasp was audible. In the center of the spread lay the high priestess crossed by the death card. With her mouth fixed open, Madame Zoe gazed up at the mysterious stranger. She watched his eyes emerge from beneath his hat as he studied the final grouping. For the first time in her life, the old gypsy was petrified, unable to move. In his eyes she saw something she never thought possible: a visible manifestation of unbridled evil – pure hatred. Anxiety closed her throat like setting concrete. She tried to speak but could not form words. She tried to move, but her muscles were bound by unseen restraints. Slowly, her eyes drifted upward to the clock at the top of the cathedral, and she stared while its great hands came to a dead stop. Catatonic, she sat helplessly as the rain began to fall.

A bold wind whipped icily through Jackson Square as the crippled man hobbled around the table. Positioning himself behind the stoic gypsy, he slipped his hand around her neck. She felt his warm breath on her cheek as he whispered in a language she did not understand. As the old man's chant-like phrases cascaded across her ear, Madame Zoe felt a presence wash over her, consuming her consciousness. Though she could not identify it, she knew it was not of this world.

A thin smile crept across the old man's face as heavy raindrops rolled off the brim of his top hat. He did not need to hear the gypsy's interpretation of the final cards; he saw what he came to see. Producing an antique, gold pocket watch from beneath his coat, the old man flipped the cover open and stared at the hands as if expecting them to move. They did not. Furious, he snapped the watch shut and shoved it deep into his pocket. With his cane tapping loudly across the bricks, he limped off in the direction of Decatur Street, leaving the crowd's few remaining stragglers scurrying for shelter in his wake – all but the one gypsy, who sat at her table staring at the motionless clock high atop the face of St. Louis Cathedral while the pouring rain extinguished her candles and dampened her cards. In defiance of her tightening muscles, the old woman harnessed every ounce of energy she could muster, extended a single finger, and drew lines on the wet table. As the drops fused together in the trail of her fingertip, Madame Zoe scrawled a single word of warning in the gathering rain. By the time she formed the last letter, the first was already gone. Soon, the message was entirely washed away, along with the remains of her consciousness.

Hours later, the shrill scream of a fair-skinned young girl echoed off the flat, metal side of a dumpster in an alley just off Bourbon Street. It scarcely drew attention; not a single head turned.

Chapter Two

The clacking of the streetcar's electric motor was mind-numbing. Still, for Nalia it was a welcomed distraction from the prying eyes of early morning riders on the Saint Charles line. Most were regulars Nalia saw every Monday – the same passengers with the same newspapers, the same blank expressions, and the same trite conversations. There was the older gentleman who sat up front, always wearing the same short-sleeved, pale blue shirt, and the girl with the wet hair and funky glasses who boarded at Dufossat Street, always late and running for her ride. Nalia didn't mind the locals. They generally kept to themselves, lost in their devices or their coffee cups, still trying to wake up before reaching their jobs. The tourists, however, were different. Though there were never many out at this hour, the few early risers were always loud, never had the correct change, and possessed an uncanny knack for choosing the seat next to Nalia. The sound of the electric motor was often her only escape.

Unfortunately, the seat near the motor was also directly behind the seat with the window stuck halfway down. The high humidity and chilly breeze made for a biting, wet kind of cold. Nalia was glad she turned back to retrieve her jacket before leaving the house. Warming her hands on her plastic coffee cup, she stared out into the remnants of last night's storm. Though the weather was still cool, the grass and trees were already showing signs of what would soon become a rich, green hue. Warm weather was never far away in the Crescent City. Such was life along the Gulf Coast.

Nalia watched as the streets slowly filled with pedestrian traffic. Morning joggers began to populate the grassy median. Nalia recognized several of the regular, devout male runners determined to go shirtless despite the cooler temperatures, earbuds drowning out their surroundings. Perhaps they were listening to their own electric motor, Nalia thought. She couldn't help allowing her eyes to linger on a few of the fit physiques jogging past. Though she was far from being ready to entertain the thought of dating again, she did enjoy the eye candy. Nalia had a new appreciation for visual stimuli since her eyesight fully returned last fall. The doctor said her vision was even slightly better than before. This morning, everything just seemed slightly brighter.

Nalia breathed in the cool morning air of the garden district as the streetcar made another stop. She took the opportunity to savor a long sip of her chicory coffee, enjoying the blend of hazelnut creamer and wildflower honey. She found it interesting how one's taste could change based on geography. While away at college, Nalia grew accustomed to taking her coffee black. Now home, she enjoyed it a little less bitter. Maybe it wasn't so much location as the idea all things were sweeter at home.

The decision to make New Orleans home again was not an easy one. A rollercoaster of emotions directed where she should go and what she should do, leaving her dizzy and confused. In the end, Nalia elected to stay with Mama Lu, finish her courses online, and try her hand at managing The Doll Maker. Mama Lu always said she hoped to turn her business over to Nalia eventually; for now a partnership seemed a good fit.

Mr. John was overjoyed when Nalia announced her decision to stay. Having been the only father figure Nalia ever really knew, Mama Lu's neighbor and friend always considered her family and took to calling her "baby girl" instead of her given name. Over the last several months, Mr. John spent as much time with Nalia as he could, as if trying to catch up from her years away at college. Each morning he would walk across the narrow, gravel drive separating the back of his house from Mama Lu's, let himself into the kitchen, and put on a pot of coffee before his ladies made their way downstairs. The trio would sit and visit over hot java and breakfast, a time for solidifying the importance of family. Nalia found herself missing that time today as the streetcar made the curve around Lee Circle, but Monday was her day to get an early start at the shop while Mama Lu and Mr. John slept in.

Lee Circle was the spot on the St. Charles line where the scenery changed, the point at which riders first began to feel the city. Leaving behind the peaceful, oak-lined streets of the garden district, the wide curve offered the first sites and sounds of the bustling underbelly of metropolitan New Orleans. As the car made its way up Carondelet, Nalia observed the first wave of zombies hitting the pavement. Early morning commuters and out of town businessmen emerged from their hotels, red-eyed and miserable from the previous night's binge. It was common practice, a requirement it seemed, for businessmen to fly in over the weekend and hit Bourbon Street running, only to regret it Monday morning as they stumbled to their meetings and conventions.

When the towering palms of Canal Street came into view, Nalia collected her belongings and headed for the rear door eager for a walk, having had her fill of the clacking motor and wet-hair's popping gum. As she made her way down Canal toward Decatur Street, she brushed past another group of zombie businessmen exiting the J. W. Marriott. Nalia found it amusing their pounding heads did little to deter the gawking. She could feel them staring as she passed.

Nalia was an attractive, young woman. Her silky, dark hair and creamy, light almond skin were compliments of a white father and mixed-race mother, both of whom abandoned her as a child. Though she'd heard the older Creole women say she could "pass for white", Nalia felt right at home among the black population of New Orleans, having been raised by Mama Lu and Mr. John. Her figure was trim and fit, and she enjoyed clothing that accented her curves. To keep in shape since returning home, she joined the ranks of evening joggers, an

activity which took the place of her preferred swimming.
Finding a pool she enjoyed as much as the campus' was still on
her growing to-do list.

This morning, Nalia's hair was pushed back by sunglasses
resting atop her head. The sky was still overcast from last
night's storm, and aside from the occasional offensive whiff of a
ripening trash bin, the air still smelled of rain – at least until
Nalia approached Jackson Square where it was overpowered by
the strong scent of soap. The street sweepers were out in force,
blanketing Decatur in a sudsy layer of white foam.

Nalia crossed the intersection carefully near a pair of orange
construction barricades, sipping the last drops of coffee from her
cup just as a brisk wind blew in from the river. Motorist's
headlights met the wet pavement sending a ballet of long
reflections dancing between her steps as Nalia made her way to
Café Du Monde.

Even before she was shadowed in the patio's canopy, Nalia
was greeted by the clanking sound of cups on saucers and the
sweet aroma of hot beignets. There was nothing greater in all of
New Orleans, she thought, than the smell of Café Du Monde in
the morning. Tourist trap or not, it was still her favorite. After
refilling her cup with their signature café au lait and collecting
her beignets to go, Nalia continued on to the shop with a fine
dusting of powdered sugar coating her hair and blouse.

Occupying the center space of a large, two-story, red-brick
structure trimmed in decorative wrought iron and lush hanging
ferns, The Doll Maker was unlike any other shop in the Quarter.
Its two large display windows held the finest collection of
porcelain dolls ever assembled, arranged in small scenes like
moments frozen in time. Passersby often stopped and marveled
at their astoundingly realistic poses and expressions as if waiting
for them to spring to life.

The other two spaces in the shared building held an antique
shop and a recently vacated storefront, its most recent occupant
having gone out of business just before Halloween last year.

While the antique shop, Glorious Finds, had been in business almost as long as Mama Lu, the location on the other side of The Doll Maker struggled to keep a tenant throughout the years.

Mama Lu and Mr. John joked about the vacant space being cursed, but locals had another theory for why businesses didn't last there. Fixed in between The Doll Maker and Glorious Finds was a little shoeshine stand belonging to Mr. John, or as the residents called him, "The Doctor". While Mr. John didn't much care for it, his powerful remedies, potions, and gris-gris earned him the nickname. In the thriving underworld of New Orleans, the roots of Voodoo were alive and well, creeping into more prominent circles than society cared to admit. To many, it was not surprising the two thriving businesses in the building were located on either side of "Doctor" John.

Nalia put her coffee cup down on the concrete corner of Mr. John's stand and her bag of beignets in one of the chairs while she unzipped the shoulder bag containing her laptop and her keys. Determined to carry everything at once, she held the Café Du Monde sack between her teeth, retrieved her coffee and stepped to the richly-stained, cherry wood door with keys in hand. She was just about to turn the lock when she realized something was wrong.

Leaving her keys in the door and setting her belongings beside the step, Nalia walked along the sidewalk in the direction of the vacant storefront. Sure enough, the "For lease" sign was gone, apparently taken down over the weekend.

"Looks like we are going to have new neighbors," she thought. As the words scrolled across her mind, Nalia felt a familiar, yet unwelcome emptiness in the pit of her stomach. Her head began to spin and her vision grew dark. Feeling as if she would vomit, Nalia tried to lean against the side of the building for support, but vertigo had already taken over. She didn't have time to brace herself before her head hit the bricks.

Chapter Three

Nalia's world went black as time stood still. She could feel her body, but only just. Her mind floated somewhere between reality and dream. Unsure of her surroundings, anxiety gnawed at a part of her spirit desperately clinging to the real world. What amounted to only a few moments seemed like a lifetime.

Without warning, the darkness was shattered by blinding white light slapping Nalia violently in the face, bringing her to what she thought was consciousness. Over and over the light berated her senses. She could feel it physically jarring her body as each assault increased in intensity, bringing a series of frightening visions. In the first, Nalia saw an antique gold pocket watch. The cover of the aged time piece slammed shut quickly as the vision faded to black. Almost instantly, a second image flashed like lightning, shaking Nalia's body so violently she could feel the pavement scraping her side – the ghostly image of a pale horse with a skeletal rider. The rider turned its head to stare, sensing her presence, but the world went dark again. Pain surged through Nalia's limp form as a third flash of light rocked her with such force she flipped onto her back – a darkened alley and a screaming woman. Suddenly, blood spattered across the woman's face. Her scream fell silent as a looming shadow covered her eyes.

Nalia's mind drifted, as a shuddering chill of fear ran the length of her paralyzed spine. Over the next few moments, the relentless pounding in her skull became Nalia's first sign that her spirit was returning to reality. Her vision slowly cleared, and soon she was able to make out the thick wooden sign hanging above the door. Reading the old-English letters brought her bearings around until Nalia remembered she was outside The Doll Maker. Her head hurt, her side hurt, and the pavement was hard, cold, and unmistakably tangible. With focused effort, she brought her body gingerly to a sitting position. As Nalia leaned against the brick building, passersby moved to the far edge of the sidewalk, conveniently ignoring her struggle. No one bothered to help. They simply assumed she was another one of the zombies losing her own Monday morning battle.

Anxiety setting her nerves on end, Nalia moved as quickly as she felt able. Still trying to regain her bearings, she turned her key in the lock. In the periphery of her vision she sensed movement in the window next door. An intrusive feeling she could only describe as sinister shot a wave of fear through her body. A quick glance at the empty window was enough to convince Nalia she was mistaken and quite possibly crazy.

As she pushed open the door of The Doll Maker, a loud, high-pitched tone startled Nalia fully to her senses; perhaps it was the lingering anxiety or simply the fact she was not yet used to the alarm. She quickly gathered her things from the step and went inside, silently counting the seconds in her head. Moving past the tall displays, she set her belongings down on the glass-topped counter and punched the deactivation code into the glowing keypad on the nearby wall. The silence was comforting.

The alarm system was a recent addition, following the store's first break-in last summer. After much debate, Mama Lu grudgingly agreed to install motion sensors in the storefront as well as the workroom. Breach alarms were placed on the front and rear doors, and glass-break sensors on the two large display windows. Mama Lu viewed its installation as the end of an era. For years, the reputation of its owner served as the shop's only means of security. Mama Lu held the title of Mambo, a high-priestess of her traditional Haitian line – well-respected Voodoo royalty. Before taking Nalia to raise, Mama Lu was known far and wide for unrestrained and questionable practices. Rumors of dark magic, powerful gris-gris, spells, and even individual's disappearances made sure The Doll Maker stayed well protected. No one dared cross the great Mambo.

Over time, guidance and discipline nurtured Mama Lu's practice to more religion than wrath, but stories of her unbridled past still surfaced from time to time, fueling exaggerated legends and providing ample security for the store. Last summer changed all that, and while the alarm's installation was supposed to promote a sense of safety, it did little more than serve as a reminder of vulnerability.

Nalia flipped the switch for the overhead lights and a thousand tiny eyes sparkled to life. Mama Lu's beautiful, life-like creations of porcelain and silk were displayed lavishly around the shop in posed interaction, like a snapshot of the Quarter's crowded streets. Most of them religious in nature, the dolls lined walls, cases, and display trees in a surreal arrangement of delicate craftsmanship.

Mama Lu was a world-renowned porcelain crafter. Her attention to detail was unmatched and her castings were so sought-after they had drawn the attention of two Popes. Her dolls were on display in cathedrals and basilicas throughout the world. She had developed techniques that re-defined the beauty and strength of the medium, casting porcelain feather-thin yet hard as granite. Her work was nothing short of captivating.

While Nalia was not at all prepared to take over Mama Lu's craft, she was determined to help bring the store properly into the information age, applying her education to develop an attainable business plan and marketing strategy. She was currently building a website with a detailed real-time inventory and pricing guide.

Retrieving her keys from the counter, Nalia returned to the door and locked herself in. The store did not open until eleven on Mondays, leaving her several hours to work alone. Before Nalia could get started today, however, her head needed attention.

Nalia shoved open the swinging door behind the counter and made her way through the workroom past a large table filled with porcelain doll parts. Beside a storage closet under the stairs was a tiny restroom where Nalia was certain she had seen a first aid kit. She located the dusty tin under the sink behind an empty bottle of bleach. Inside she found Band-Aids, alcohol swabs, triple-antibiotic ointment, and to her surprise and delight, a package of aspirin which she took immediately. While assessing the wound on her temple as best she could, Nalia made a mental note to put "buy the shop a larger mirror" on her to-do list next to finding a suitable swimming pool. Struggling to see herself in the small, time-worn, glass pane, she wiped the blood from the side of her face with an alcohol swab and began the stinging process of cleaning the wound. From what she could tell, the cut was not severe, but the skin was well-scraped and swelling. The injury would not be easy to hide. *Had that thought really crossed her mind?*

The contents of the first-aid kit were individually wrapped and Nalia fumbled clumsily with the packaging; her hands were still trembling. Finally opening the ointment, she tried to make sense of exactly what happened. Her initial instinct was to simply explain it away, like before, but this time the vision could not be denied. This time was different.

Since the passing of her grandmother, Nalia experienced several episodes of what she was reluctant to identify as clairvoyant vision – *the sight* as the old Creoles called it. Madame Toulouse, the woman Nalia called grandmother, was exceptionally gifted with it. Nalia once witnessed her accurately predict the finishing order of every horse on the schedule at Fairgrounds Raceway, a keen talent that kept her purse well-lined. Madame Toulouse's gift, however, was much more than a simple parlor trick, or the ability to guess winning horses; it was part of who she was. She didn't just look into a person's past and future, she saw their very soul. *The sight* defined Madame Toulouse and touched every part of her life. It frightened Nalia.

While not afraid of *the sight* itself, Nalia was uncomfortable with the way it seemed to seek her out, to force its will on her uncontrollably. She was definitely not a fan of the violence with which it just occurred. This was a new and unwelcome development.

Before today, the visions were somewhat benign, pleasant even. Her first, on St. John's Eve last year, was a vision of her grandmother dancing through the spirit world, more of a view beyond the veil than a glimpse of the future. Nalia was delighted with the ability, especially in the absence of her physical sight, but as time progressed, she grew uneasy. *The sight* seemed determined to settle on her, a gift Nalia wasn't sure she wanted. She heard the trite expression in the back of her mind about great power and great responsibility. To Nalia, *the sight* was an open door to a world of which she wanted no part. Though she was raised around the traditions of Voodoo, certain aspects frightened her like the demons from her past she couldn't seem to conquer. For this reason, she kept her gift hidden from Mama Lu. Now, her head wound mocked her secrecy.

"She doesn't need to know about this," she thought, "I slipped and fell." Even while the thought was still forming, a voice in the back of her mind reassured Nalia that Mama Lu would never buy the excuse. What's more, considering the forceful nature of the episode, she couldn't believe she was actually entertaining the thought of hiding it. No revelation was ever so violent before, so disturbing; she never blacked out, and she never felt helpless. For some reason, this time was different – like the vision was screaming for attention.

No previous manifestation of *the sight* even came close to affecting her so radically. On the night of St. John's Eve, Nalia's vision of Madame Toulouse was comforting and the message unmistakable. Nalia saw her grandmother plainly, as if she were actually standing in front of her, dancing among a collection of lamp stands. Madame Toulouse spoke to her – not audibly, but in her mind, reassuring her everything was alright. She asked Nalia to be her voice, to tell others not to weep for her, but rejoice in the assurance of lasting peace. It was the last time

Nalia saw her grandmother's spirit, though she felt her presence often.

There was also Nalia's vision of Marcus. While unpleasant, the image was far from violent, more like a dream than a nightmare. After a long night of restlessness in early October, Nalia awakened at precisely two in the morning to a sudden and strange memory of her old boyfriend. The memory was followed by short series of visions flashing through her mind: images of police lights, handcuffs, and cold metal bars. Being only just awake, Nalia convinced herself the episode was a dream. Two days later, a news story trending on YouTube changed her mind. Allegedly, Marcus forced himself on a young lady he was seeing, while visiting her campus dorm room. Fortunately, the girl's roommate heard the struggle and ran for help. Four members of Delta Tau Delta fraternity, three of whom Nalia knew to be on the university's powerlifting team, came to the rescue. Marcus received substantial injuries before being turned over to the police. He was now behind bars awaiting trial. Nalia wondered if Mama Lu or Mr. John had anything to do with the situation. They would never tell and she would never know, but one thing was certain – her vision was no mere dream.

The only other occasion when *the sight* came upon Nalia was in late December at St. Louis Cathedral while attending the midnight mass. Mama Lu introduced Nalia to an old friend, a woman she called Madame Zoe. Nalia could not explain the phenomenon, but when she took Madame Zoe's hand a strange sensation overtook her. There was no flash of light, no vision in the traditional sense, just a very solid assurance of a single image. It lasted no more than a second, but Nalia saw Madame Zoe sitting in the rain outside the cathedral, staring at the clock. She had no idea what it meant and would not even consider it a work of *the sight*, were it not for the same sense of certainty that accompanied the vision of Marcus. Whatever happened, the look in Madame Zoe's eyes told Nalia she felt it too.

It was uncomfortable, but by no means threatening – not like today. Now with the sudden change in their manifestation, the visions made Nalia more than uneasy, they scared her. She tried to make sense of the images she remembered, hoping it would help, but nothing seemed logical. The only person she'd ever seen carry a pocket watch was Mr. John, but his was antiqued silver; the one in the vision was definitely made of gold. The pale horse with the grisly rider struck Nalia as a familiar scene, but she didn't know why. Her mind would not cooperate. The final image of the bloody young woman was most disturbing. Nalia didn't recognize the girl or her surroundings, but she felt a screaming sense of urgency surrounding the image. Nothing made sense, least of all the forceful attack.

Nalia finished up by placing a Band-Aid over her wound and washing her hands and face. With any luck, she could put this mess out of her mind and salvage what was left of the morning for inventory. Her sore back and side suggested otherwise.

Walking back to the storefront, Nalia retrieved her coffee cup and took a long sip of café au lait. Time left it lukewarm but Nalia didn't mind. The flavor helped bring a brief sense of normality. With cup in hand, she walked around the counter and through the displays. As she stepped to the door, all the dolls seemed to follow her with their eyes, watching for her reaction as a large white moving van pulled to the curb outside. It stopped just shy of the corner, right in front of the vacant shop next door.

Nalia's coffee splashed across her shoes as her cup made impact with the floor. She had just enough time to brace herself against the door frame before the world went dark again.

Chapter Four

By the time Mama Lu and Mr. John arrived at the shop, Nalia was resting her head against the cool side of the porcelain bowl in the small restroom near the back door. Having already emptied the contents of her stomach, she was still dry-heaving when Mama Lu found her on the concrete floor.

Mr. John retrieved a clean rag from the workroom and soaked it with cold water. After wringing it out, he handed the damp cloth to Mama Lu who lovingly wiped Nalia's face, neck, and forehead in an attempt to keep her cool and clean her up. Nalia felt warm. Sweat was forming at her hairline and dripping down her ashen face. Her eyes were glassy, her body exhausted and lethargic.

Images of Nalia's childhood surfaced in Mama Lu's mind. Plagued by frightening nightmares after her parent's departure, Nalia often awakened in a similar, sallow state several times a night. Mama Lu and Mr. John tended to the child, and eventually saw her through the tumultuous episodes. While those incidents were triggered by fear, Mama Lu hoped the present situation was simply the lingering effect of a nasty stomach bug.

Despite her sickly appearance and labored breathing, Nalia was still in full command of her senses. Her face did not express the slightest hint of disorientation. In fact, she looked disgusted. Nalia was a strong-willed woman like her Mama Lu; she did not deal well with feelings of weakness and vulnerability. Mama Lu knew she would be particularly angry later when she saw the petechiae around her eyes.

"Well if I didn't know better," Mama Lu said with a grin, "I'd think you tied on a good one las' night." Nalia rolled her eyes and shook her head. Her fragile hint of a grin comforted Mama Lu.

From the doorway behind her, Mr. John exhaled in relief, like he'd been holding his breath for hours. Mama Lu wasn't the only one having flashbacks to Nalia's childhood. Mr. John was not the type to worry about a great many things, but when it came to his baby girl, all bets were off.

Nalia's brain was scrambling, trying to fabricate a believable explanation of what transpired. She and Mama Lu had already discussed *the sight* on many occasions and she did not want the subject revisited today. Though frightened by the manifestation of the vision, she preferred to work things out on her own rather than be urged down a path she had no intention of walking.

"What you think soured yo' stomach, chil'?" asked Mama Lu, still daubing Nalia's forehead with the damp cloth.

Nalia caught herself avoiding eye contact and immediately corrected the damning error. Keeping a secret from Mama Lu would be no simple task. "Don't know," she replied without hesitation. "Just got really sick all of a sudden. It might have been the smell of that street soap. It seemed pretty powerful this morning." *Weak.*

"I smelled it when we got out o' the truck," Mr. John said, cracking the back door and sniffing the air.

Mama Lu was not convinced. Her eyes had been scanning the area ever since she noticed the Band-Aid wrapper clinging to the side of the wastebasket, and the fact that Nalia was skillfully hiding the right side of her forehead indicated there was still more to learn. Nalia read Mama Lu's expression as doubtful, and when the woman purposefully leaned over to see the wound on her head, she knew for sure.

"Dat soap hit you in the head too?" she asked.

Nalia managed to pull off a confused expression, then smiled with reassurance. "No Mama, I was saying the soap seemed pretty strong this morning, and I think that's why I got dizzy. I fell outside and hit my head on the brick." *Better.* "When I was patching it up I got really sick all of a sudden and started throwing up." *Much better.*

Mr. John looked alarmed. "Check her eyes Lu, she might have a concussion."

Mama Lu grabbed Nalia by the chin and turned her head to face her directly. She studied her eyes, first one then the other. *I'll never be able to hide it now.*

"They don' look dilated. If she had a con..."

"I think it was the blood," Nalia interrupted. "I haven't mentioned it 'cause I thought it was stupid, but the sight of blood has nauseated me ever since I got my sight back, ever since... the memories."

Mama Lu felt a sting of guilt. Nalia hadn't intended to go there but the subject provided a welcomed diversion. When Mama Lu looked away, Nalia could feel her pain. "I think I'll be fine," she said quickly. "Help me up, let's see if I can manage to stay on my feet." Nalia was still weak, but she fought through it, more for Mama Lu's sake than her own. Once the initial dizziness from standing subsided, Nalia convinced Mama Lu and Mr. John she would be fine to walk. She pulled off steady steps surprisingly well considering her mind was still trying to tell her legs not to collapse. Mama Lu and Mr. John followed her closely into the workroom where Nalia decided she'd had enough attention. "Looks like we are going to have new neighbors," she said like it was a daily occurrence. Mama Lu stopped in her tracks.

"New neighbors?"

"Yeah, looks like somebody's moving in next door," Nalia continued, "Where Toujours used to be."

Mama Lu cut a look to Mr. John so quick he jumped in surprise. "What you know 'bout dis?" she asked, narrowing her eyelids.

"If I knew 'bout dis, don't you think I woulda said somethin'?" he answered. "I ain't heard nothin' 'bout no new neighbors." Mr. John's frustration was apparent. He did not like being surprised with events in the Quarter. Mr. John prided himself on being privy to all the latest "goings on" in the neighborhood. In addition to being a distribution outlet for the "doctor's" remedies, his shoeshine stand served as a bustling hub of information. On more than one occasion, Mama Lu had accused Mr. John and his clientele of sharing more gossip than a sewing circle, and to a great degree she was right. If something was happening in the French Quarter, Mr. John knew about it well in advance. Lack of news about this new tenant on his street, in the very building where he set up shop, caught him off-guard to say the least.

"How'd dat lil' tidbit slip by you and yo' buddies?" asked Mama Lu, adding insult to injury.

Mr. John raised a finger in response, but before he could speak, a hurt look veiled his eyes. Without a word he walked past Mama Lu and through the swinging door to investigate. Mama Lu followed.

By the time Nalia made it through the door and slipped behind the counter, Mr. John was already outside surveying the sidewalk, and Mama Lu was examining the sticky substance holding her shoe to the floor.

"Sorry about that," said Nalia, "Forgot to mention, between face-planting on the sidewalk and vomiting my toes up, I also spilled my coffee. True grace and coordination triumph again."

Mama Lu did not say a word. She was busy watching Mr. John peek into the open back of the moving van parked curbside in front of her store. A long ramp extended from the van's rear to the street and a team of movers took turns unloading crates, wheeling them onto the sidewalk and past The Doll Maker's windows.

Mr. John stepped out of the way as one of the workers dollied past with a large display case. Before he could ask about the crates, he heard the slamming of a truck door across the street, followed by a loud voice.

"Hey, hey, hey! What are you guys doin'?" shouted a portly man hurrying up to one of the movers. "I got a crew comin' to paint the walls. Dis place is supposed to be empty." The mover who appeared to be in charge stepped up to confront the man, removing a folded stack of papers from his back pocket. Taking the pencil from behind his ear, the mover traced several lines of text on the page as he read.

"I got instructions here says this stuff is supposed to be moved in today," the man argued. "Says to stack everything in the middle of the showroom. Black and white, right here." The man seemed to take pleasure in showing the orders to the painter, tapping his pencil adamantly on the pages while he spoke. "Guess you're just going to have to work around it."

"Christ!" said the painter, motioning to a crew already crossing the street with heavy drop cloths. "Stack it up outside, guys. We got to wait for these clowns to finish up."

"Sounds like he ain't too happy," said Mr. John, startling the mover who was shoving the wad of papers back into his pocket.

"Can I help you?" the man asked, sidestepping another mover with a dolly of small boxes.

"John Barrett, pleased to meet you," said Mr. John, tipping his Fedora and displaying a wide smile. "I run the shoeshine stand over there. I was jus' wonderin' how much longer you boys gon' be blocking up the front o' the building."

"Hard to say," said the man, scratching his head and motioning to the painters. "Depends on how much opposition I get. My guys are pretty fast, but we still got a ways to go and most of these crates are fragile."

"Oh, don't mind me, I ain't rushin' y'all," Mr. John continued, apologetically. "I understand y'all gots a job to do. I's jus' curious, dat's all. Wha's so fragile 'bout dem crates? What you got in there? What you gon' be sellin'?"

"Oh this ain't my place," replied the mover, tucking his pencil back behind his ear. "I'm just moving this stuff in."

Mr. John had already gathered as much, but knew sometimes playing dumb garnered more information. Folks were trusting and forthcoming when they took Mr. John for simpleminded. He played the role well when necessary. "Mus' be some fine items all crated up like dat. What you got, crystal? Stained glass?"

"Clocks," replied the mover, fielding Mr. John's questions with a growing annoyance.

"Clocks, huh?"

"Yeah, clocks. All kinds of clocks, according to the paperwork. Guy sells clocks, what can I tell ya?" The mover repositioned his dolly, attempting to wheel around Mr. John. Sidestepping quickly, Mr. John blocked his escape and continued to fire off questions.

"What guy sells clocks? Who leased the place?"

The muscular mover's brow furrowed as he sighed heavily. His exhausted expression reflected a growing suspicion of Mr. John's inquisition. Mr. John simply smiled, allowing the uncomfortable silence to do its job. Finally, with a heavy sigh, the mover reached into his back pocket and retrieved the folded invoice. He opened it just enough to read the information at the top of the page.

"Haufmann," he said, raising his eyebrows and looking up to see if Mr. John was satisfied. "Guy's name is Haufmann. That's all I got. Happy?"

Thwarting another attempt to pass, Mr. John continued his interrogation. "Well, where is dis Mr. Haufmann? He comin' by today?"

With all the restraint he could manage, the mover tightened his grip on the dolly and summoned his last ounce of patience. "Look mister, I don't know. I'm just doin' my job here. All I can say is I got instructions to leave the keys in the drop box at the real-estate firm, if that tells you anything. Now please, if you'll let me get back to work, I can finish this job before Mardi Gras."

"Oh, don't let me keep you," said Mr. John as the mover rolled his eyes. "I don't want to get in the way of men doin' they job. Old man like me jus' wants to get a feel for who his neighbor's gon' be, y'understand?" Stepping aside, Mr. John allowed the bulky man to pass, then quietly walked to the door where other men were busy handling crates and boxes with their dollies. Peering around the corner of the door, Mr. John began inching his way inside.

"Hey, where you going'?" the pencil-eared mover called from the rear of the truck.

Turning around, Mr. John looked annoyed. "What?" he asked, "We gon' be neighbors. It ain't like I'm a stranger. I'm jus' gon' have a quick look around, dat's all."

The mover no longer cared. Shaking his head, he continued up the ramp and into his truck as Mr. John slipped inside the building.

The shop smelled dusty and stale. A distinct echo lingered in the air as the sound of dropped boxes cut through the emptiness. The morning sun filled the room with its only light through the large window and open doorway. Mr. John cast a long shadow down the center of the room, where stood two long, glass cases, the kind used to display jewelry. Next to them sat the growing assortment of boxes and crates of various shapes and sizes. Several tall, pine boxes were marked with stenciled red lettering: THIS END UP, FRAGILE, HANDLE WITH CARE, and CAUTION. Someone was adamant about their pieces arriving without incident. Mr. John's mind raced with excitement wondering what delicate works waited inside. As a master woodworker, he envisioned exquisitely detailed grandfather clocks adorned with intricate carvings. He salivated at the possibilities.

Curiosity getting the better of him, Mr. John decided to see just how securely the crates were sealed. Retrieving a pocket knife from his trousers and waiting for a break in the dolly traffic, Mr. John shifted his body to conceal his actions. When he felt he could proceed unnoticed, Mr. John slipped his blade into the seal of a large, pine crate and began to pry off the facing. The wood creaked loudly under tension as the nails were pulled from their secure home. Mr. John jumped at the sound, turning to make sure he was not discovered. Determining the coast was still clear, he resumed snooping and soon managed a crack wide enough to slip his fingers inside. Prying as best he could without risk of removing the panel, Mr. John peeked in, but before he could see anything, a wide shadow climbed slowly up the edge of the crate.

Before he even heard heels hit the floor Mr. John recognized the distinct shape of the shadow cast by a wide-brimmed hat. When the shrill voice echoed behind him, Mr. John didn't need to turn to know it belonged to "Madame" Vivian Luciénne.

"Well hello there, John," came a silky Creole accent laced with sassy, southern drawl, "Pryin' into things that don't concern you, I see."

Chapter Five

Mr. John froze. The icy voice of Madame Vivian Luciénne sent a chill up his spine, piercing his brain and triggering a twitch in a particular vein on his forehead. If there was one person alive in the world Mr. John wished he could strangle – literally wrap his calloused fingers around her throat and squeeze slowly until the last breath of life expelled from her body like a withering balloon – it was Madame Luciénne. Presently however, his fierce loathing took a brief back seat to the anxiety clinching his muscles. Caught with his hand in the proverbial cookie jar, Mr. John's breath caught somewhere between his throat and his chest as his eyes bulged with surprise. His back stiffened quickly as his heart raced. The sensation lasted only a moment before Mr. John resigned himself to the fact he was busted. With tongue in cheek, he removed his knife from the seam of the wood. Flipping the blade over in his hand, Mr. John briefly entertained the thought of slitting the vile woman's throat, but knew Mama Lu would not approve.

While Mama Lu's history was seldom a shining example of grace and mercy, the passing of her mentor opened her eyes to the higher calling sought by so many in her religion – a level of enlightenment where even the most serious offenders were offered forgiveness. Mama Lu didn't view herself as having attained this level, but the goal stayed in the forefront of her mind. While she still believed there was a time for justice and punishment, Mama Lu now realized she was not to serve as judge and jury. The mantra of her mentor, Madame Toulouse, frequently echoed in her mind, "Like a spinning wheel, everything you do gon' come back 'round to you." Mama Lu was taught this truth many years ago, but only recently realized that learning it and living it were two different things entirely.

She committed herself to honoring the words of her mentor, even though it meant withholding judgment from Madame Luciénne.

Mr. John thought of Mama Lu and recalled the words of Madame Toulouse as he slowly folded the knife against his thigh and returned it to his pocket. Turning toward the doorway, he struggled to force a smile through clenched teeth, an effort that would make Mama Lu proud.

Madame Vivian Luciénne's slim figure stood silhouetted against the open doorway, the sun creating a dazzling backlight. Her head was held high and cocked to one side in self-assurance. The dress hugging her hips was the same deep shade of plum as her oversized hat. A silk, ivory band encircled the crown, tied in the rear, and dropped off the back of the wide brim. A matching ivory wrap was draped heavily around her shoulders and gathered in front with a large gold hoop.

Madame Luciénne had already donned her charming smile, and despite the well-hidden scar on her chin, Mr. John had to admit the woman was working what she had. Her jewelry was fake, high-dollar imitations – not at all garden-variety costume grade – but fake nonetheless. It adorned her neck, ears, and fingers like an unwelcome resume.

She was dressed to impress, thought Mr. John, but certainly not him. She was here for business. He could see the intensity in her sparkling eyes.

"I have to say, John," she said in a dripping sweet voice oozing with accusation, "I suspected I might run into you today, but I didn't expect to find you over here pokin' around yo' new neighbor's inventory, tamperin' with the merchandise, so to speak."

"Lil' curious, dat's all," he explained. "Can't blame a man fo' bein' curious, 'specially when all dis came as such a surprise. Seem like I ain't the only one doin' a little spyin' 'round here. What brings you down here to the Quarter, anyway? What you know 'bout all dis?"

Madame Luciénne tucked her clutch underneath her arm and entered the store, allowing the movers to continue their path in and out of the building. She sauntered to the center of the room where Mr. John stood among the boxes. Tossing her clutch atop one of the shorter, up-ended pine crates, Madame Luciénne moved uncomfortably close and looked Mr. John in the eye with an amused grin. "Guilty," she said, dropping her gaze and shaking her head. "Got a lil' curiosity goin' on myself. I stopped by to meet the new tenant in person."

Mr. John was visibly bothered. *She knew. How did she know about dis and I didn't?* Mr. John's network of chattering informants always kept him at least one step ahead of nearly everyone else on the latest news and "gossip". Always.

"In person?" Mr. John pried. "What you mean you wants to meet him in person? Dis somebody I ought to know or somethin'? Some kinda celebrity?"

Amused at his frustration, Madame Luciénne decided to chide Mr. John a bit, just for a rise. "You didn't know 'bout dis, did you?" she said, leaning on the crate and slipping her tongue tauntingly into her cheek. "My, oh my! Somebody settin' up shop right next door to John Barrett, and he don't have a clue. John, that's like NORAD missin' a mile-wide meteor. How'd you let that slip by you?"

Mr. John's brow furrowed. The crinkled smile on Madame Luciénne's face said she was having a fantastic time toying with him, and the lingering quiet she coddled climbed his spine like a spider. He was uncomfortable, slightly embarrassed, and loathing the heavy blow to his pride. Just as he was about to allow frustration to best him, Madame Luciénne broke the silence.

"Mr. Haufmann and I have done a bit of correspondin'," she said. "That's yo new neighbor's name, by the way, Haufmann."

"Yeah, I got dat much out of the friendly fella over there," Mr. John responded, feeling a new sting of inadequacy. "What you mean, correspondin'?"

"Oh, we've been chatting a bit through email," said Madame Luciénne, with a confident hand on her hip. "He's a jeweler, of sorts – makes watches. Fine watches, from what I understand. Deals in antique clocks too, timepieces of all sorts. Of course you probably already figured that out too, what with all yo' pokin' around his crates. Find anythin' in there you like?"

Mr. John's stare was cold. He began to play various scenarios in his mind, all of which had an incredibly painful outcome for the smirking woman before him. Then it hit him, and a satisfied glaze slowly graced his eyes. "You got a deal workin', don't ya?" he said, straightening his back. "He got somethin' you want. Dat's why you done come by here. You turnin' on the charm 'cause you got somethin' up yo' sleeve. What you after? What kind of connections our Mr. Haufmann got dat you tryin' to exploit?"

Madame Luciénne's smile turned like fake gold. She didn't like being called out any more than Mr. John. People were mere pawns in her grand chess match, and Madame Luciénne played for money. She did not take it well when folks like John Barrett called her game for what it was.

Realizing he touched a nerve, Mr. John smiled wide. "So, why you interested in dis watch maker?"

Madame Luciénne scanned the room. The rear of the store offered no indication of movement. The smell of dust and pine lingered in the air with a prominent sense of solitude. Aside from the movers, trucking their dollies in and out the open front door, there was little doubt she and Mr. John were very much alone. Resigning herself to the conclusion she would not be meeting Mr. Haufmann just yet, Madame Luciénne dropped her veneer. Her smile faded, revealing her natural disinterest in anyone or anything but herself, and her eyes expressed a rare candidness as she answered the question. "I have no interest at all in the watch maker. It's the grandson I want to talk to."

Mr. John's face twisted in confusion. For a moment, he could not find his voice. He stood still, staring with his lips slightly parted. Madame Luciénne continued in the exhausted tone of a comic having to explain a joke. "Two men, John. The old man is the watch maker, but apparently doesn't get around so well anymore. His grandson helps him out with the business. He's the one I want to meet. He's a writer, a historian, of sorts. He's gon' be doing some research here that has piqued my interest... a little publication that stands to be very lucrative for my newest venture." Madame Luciénne popped the clasp on her clutch and produced a shiny, black business card with metallic gold lettering, a high-dollar job designed to make a stately impression. Flipping it over her index finger with her thumb, she extended the card to Mr. John who read it aloud with amused disdain.

"Laveau's Business League of New Orleans – Network your way to the top! – Madame Vivian Luciénne: Executive Director." Mr. John's expression resembled that of a lost motorist forced to ask directions. With a raised brow he looked over the card at Vivian's cat-like grin. "Dis is you? Wha's all dis about? How come you usin' the name Laveau?"

"It's all about numbers John," she replied as if speaking to a child. "Coupling 'Laveau' with 'New Orleans' in the domain name gets the website a hundred times the hits from search engines."

Mr. John's eyes moved back to the glossy card. Moving his thumb, he saw the web address printed across the bottom. "Wha's it for? Wha's dis business league?"

Madame Luciénne began to answer but hesitated, allowing the mover with the last crate to deposit it beside them and depart before continuing. "It's what you might call an exclusive club," she said. "It's a networking society designed to increase the profits of small businesses in the Quarter. Small businesses like yours."

Mr. John bristled. He was familiar with Madame Luciénne's numerous schemes which were supposed to benefit businesses in the Quarter. Some were ill-founded, others were simply a ruse, but all had the same result – they benefited Madame Luciénne, not the Quarter. "So how does it work?" he almost didn't even bother to ask.

"Well, the network is organized online, through an invitation-only social media site, then once a month we get together for a party, a social gatherin' where everyone can get to know one another and mingle."

"Charmin'," replied Mr. John, still waiting for the catch. "Sounds like a grand time." As he spoke, they heard the movers outside loading their dollies into the truck and taking up the ramp. The muscular man with the pencil behind his ear was motioning and yelling instructions to the painters who once again darkened the doorway, gear in hand. One of them interrupted the conversation.

"Excuse me Miss," he said to Madame Luciénne, "We're going to need to cover dis area, if you wouldn't mind stepping outside we can get started."

Madame Luciénne looked the man up and down. The fake smile plastering her face threatened to crack. The man, who bore a mild resemblance to the Pillsbury doughboy dressed in customary white pants and tee-shirt, only stared back with his own bothered expression.

"Certainly," she said sarcastically, gripping her clutch and motioning for Mr. John to follow her outside. The painters began to unfurl drop cloths as the two made their way to the door in silence.

"So how are these parties of yo's gon' help businesses?" Mr. John asked, still fishing for the catch as they emerged on the sidewalk.

Luciénne thought for a moment, wondering whether or not to continue divulging information she might deem private. Mr. John's social circle could certainly deal damage to her cause if the particulars were not handled properly. Conversely, if she were to offer him a reasonable deal, it could work to her advantage. In the end, greed and pride prevailed.

"It works like dis," Madame Luciénne went on as they watched the rest of the painters stalling with their gear in front of the moving van, blocking its exit. The pencil-eared driver blasted the horn as the painters leisurely cleared the area and offered obscene gestures. "Let's say I'm a painter," she continued, "Now obviously these painters and these movers do not get along, but let's say there was a movin' company I knew and respected – one in the network. As a painter I'm bound to run across clients who need movers, or construction contractors, landscapers, or any number of other service providers. When I do, I recommend someone in the network. Then I contact the network and pass along the client's information. The movers do the same for me and everyone's back gets scratched. Same goes for shops in the Quarter. If I'm an antique dealer whose customers are consistently askin' about a nice place for Sunday brunch, I recommend a café in the network."

"How you decide which one? Suppose you got seven diff'rent cafés in the network, what then?"

"You're missin' the point John. I told you, dis is a *very* exclusive club. There will be only one café, only one antique dealer, only one painter. Understand?"

"Now I see," said Mr. John, clarity filling his eyes. "Yo' lil' network supports itself while drivin' out anybody who don't belong to the club. It's like yo' own private chamber o' commerce."

Madame Luciénne smiled.

"And I suppose membership into yo' exclusive society costs a pretty penny, don't it?" Mr. John went on. "And the more successful it becomes, the more dat cost'll go up, I'm sure."

"Well of course every good business league has its dues for membership, John. Dis one is no different from any other."

"And folks who refuse to join, or refuse to pay yo' 'dues' get run out of business, dat right?"

"Let's just say those companies under the protection of the partnership will find it much easier to do business in the

Quarter. Hell, with the city councilmen I've got backin' me on dis, they may even avoid some unpleasant taxation, permit requirements, inspections, fines, you name it. Do you have a street vendor's permit for your… wares, apart from yo' shoe shinin' business, John?"

Mr. John reddened with anger. "Protection money! Dat's extortion, dat's what dat is."

Madame Luciénne raised a hand to her bosom in offense but donned a smile that revealed her delight.

Inside The Doll Maker, Mama Lu watched through the window as Mr. John raised his voice.

"Dat wha's goin' on? Dis guy Haufmann yo' newest club member?" As his blood began to boil, Mr. John caught a glimpse of Mama Lu in the window, and a calming voice inside his head spoke. *She ain't worth it. Get yo'self together.* Mama Lu gave a reassuring nod.

"Mr. Haufmann is considerin' membership, yes. Although I'm still not sure how to categorize his business: antique dealer, jeweler... clock maker seems a bit obscure but might carve out a nice niche."

"I thought you was here fo' business wit' the grandson, the writer. Wha's he got dat you want?"

"He's the one who contacted me through the website," Madame Luciénne explained. "He's been doin' research on Marie Laveau for years now, tracin' family lineage. He's gon' look into my family history and see how close the lines run. If he can authenticate my family lineage to Marie Laveau, I'm gon' be worth a fortune, and so is my business."

"I'm guessin' your lil' club is gon' be promoting his grandfather's shop so as to help influence dat research, huh?"

Madame Luciénne swallowed hard. "Well it's certainly not gon' hurt, now is it?"

"You a real piece o' work, Vivian," said Mr. John, shaking his head, "A real piece o' work. Looks like you got all gussied up fo' not'in' today, though. I ain't seen hide nor hair of your

Mr. Haufmann, jus' a bunch o' contractors. You welcome to go put the moves on dem. I'm sure they won't mind." Mr. John smiled in amusement as he pulled a hand-carved pipe from the pocket of his shirt and clenched it between his teeth.

Madame Luciénne's lip curled, and her fingers whitened around the knuckles as she tightened her grip on the clutch. A venomous retort was nearly off her tongue when she caught a glimpse of Mama Lu standing in the window of The Doll Maker. Cold eyes stared through the glass, full of contempt and of pity. Mama Lu might just as well have been one of her porcelain dolls, her static expression a reflection of her resolve.

Madame Luciénne stiffened her back in defiance, her spirit shrinking within her. She had been successful in avoiding Mama Lu since last summer, guilt and fear lending to a wide berth. She hoped to continue her streak today, but was now exceedingly uncomfortable – a situation she loathed. Cutting her eyes back to Mr. John, Vivian tried to regain her composure and some sense of control. "No bother," she said in the midst of a deep breath. "I'll simply drop back by tomorrow. 'Til then, please try to keep yo' hands off the man's inventory, John. I'd hate havin' to tell him about his new neighbor's criminal tendencies."

Mr. John laughed. "If being nosy was a crime they'd have locked us both up a long time ago."

Madame Luciénne's smirk melted in the wake of Mr. John's humility, and she almost managed a smile before replying, "Fair enough. Keep my card, John Barrett. I'm willin' to offer you a sweet deal on inclusion."

Turning on her heel, Madame Luciénne hurried past The Doll Maker to the open door of her black Lincoln. She kept her eyes on the sidewalk as she passed, partly out of fear, and partly out of respect for the woman she knew was still staring through the window. Madame Luciénne knew their paths would cross again soon, but thankfully it would not be today. As her driver shut the door behind her, Madame Luciénne stole a quick peek at The

Doll Maker's display window. To her surprise, Mama Lu was gone. A sting of guilt pricked her spine once more.

Chapter Six

Daylight was only a recent memory when Mr. John crossed
the narrow, gravel alleyway that served as a road dividing his
property and Mama Lu's. The road was unlike anything else in
the neighborhood, a geographical anomaly resulting from
decades of land disputes, butting the back yards of the two
properties together. Loose gravel crunched under Mr. John's
feet as he turned his eyes toward the night sky. The clouds once
again held a threat of rain, and rising humidity dampened the
air. Though spring was still many weeks away, Mr. John was
sure he heard the faint chirping of crickets in the underbrush
around the crepe myrtles.

Mr. John loved the rain, despite the fact his knees tended to
protest the weather change – another reminder he was not
getting any younger. As of late, Mr. John pondered his mortality
more frequently. He mulled over his accomplishments and
lamented the unfinished. The latter dominated much of his time
over the winter, and even now it was the reason for the
distracting weight in his left front pants-pocket.

Normally a place reserved for the loose change aging men
tend to keep on their person, the pocket housed a new tenant
over the past several weeks: a small, black, velvet-covered box
in the shape of a cube. Mr. John carried the same box once
before, many years ago. It took three weeks of palming the box
in his pocket to finally work up the nerve, but before he could
ask the question, Mama Lu reaffirmed her position of
independence. She was never dependent on a man for anything
in her life and she was not about to start. Mr. John had hoped to
surprise her with the ring, but the chance never came. There was
no surprising Mama Lu. *The sight* was a powerful ally, but a
cunning adversary.

For years afterward, the box remained in a dresser drawer in Mr. John's bedroom waiting for an appropriate time when he might choose to brave the waters of uncertainty once more. This time, if he could work up the nerve again, he hoped Mama Lu might reconsider her position on the matter. Until then, the box would remain in his pocket, a reminder of unfinished business and the one true desire of his heart.

Mama Lu's back yard was bordered by a high wrought-iron fence. Mr. John lifted the latch and listened to the old hinges whine as the gate swung open. As he ambled up the walk, Mr. John smelled the sweet aroma of creole mustard wafting from the cracked, kitchen window. Mama Lu typically cooked red beans and rice in her crock-pot on Monday, a New Orleans tradition dating back to its founding when Monday was wash day and the dish could easily simmer all afternoon while laundry was tended. For the last two months, however, Mama Lu grew fond of a chicken dish with a sweet creole mustard sauce. It quickly became a favorite of Mr. John's, who held a standing invitation to dinner anytime Mama Lu was cooking.

The old steps creaked as Mr. John made his way up and across the back porch. The door was open, and the smell of spices mingled with citrus pervaded the air. Mr. John's mouth began to water. "Everythin' dat woman touches is golden," he thought, letting himself in and breathing deeply to savor the aroma.

"Mmmmm, mmmmm," he said loudly, announcing his arrival. Nalia was setting the table while Mama Lu put the finishing touches on the meal. "Dat smells like heaven. Got me so hungry my belly's tryin' to eat itself."

"Well help yo'self to wha's on the table," said Mama Lu without turning from the stove. "Dinner'll be ready in few minutes."

Mr. John turned his attention to a tall white ceramic bowl in the center of the kitchen table and peered over the edge.

Absentmindedly, he folded his hands delicately to his chest as if in reverence. His mouth hung slightly agape.

In the bowl was a rare treat, Mr. John's unrivaled favorite dish. Nalia smiled when she saw the awestruck look on Mr. John's face as he stared at Mama Lu's Creole ceviche. The dish was a blend of redfish, shrimp, and fresh crab meat cooked by marinating overnight in the acidic juice of several oranges and limes. Mama Lu modified her traditional marinade over the years to include minced red onion, garlic, and red pepper. The following morning she would add fresh diced tomato, avocado, and mango, then refrigerate the mixture again all afternoon. Finally, just before serving, she would toss in a few Serrano peppers and a healthy dash of Tabasco. Mr. John considered the dish a delicacy.

Eyeing the plate of crackers next to the bowl he retrieved a scalloped spreading knife and helped himself. The ceviche was thick, and Mr. John scooped a generous portion onto a saltine. He hummed to himself in satiated bliss as the blend of flavors toyed with his palette.

Mama Lu did not turn around but smiled to herself, knowing Mr. John was enjoying the dish she prepared especially for him. So as not to let him know, she steeled her tone before she spoke. "Don't go fillin' up on dat now, you better save some room fo' dis chicken I got bakin'."

Mr. John mumbled a response, but his mouth was full and his message unintelligible. Mama Lu smiled once again and retrieved her rooster-print oven mitts from the drawer beside the stove. When she opened the oven door, the kitchen filled with the thick, hearty aroma of mustard and spices. Nalia finished setting the table and poured three glasses of southern sweet tea while Mama Lu removed the ceramic baking dish and placed it in a wicker holder in the center of the table.

Plating three servings of rice, Mama Lu topped them with okra and tomatoes from a simmering pot on the stove-top and sat down with Nalia and Mr. John. After appropriate recognition

was offered to the saints, they raised their glasses in
remembrance of Madame Toulouse. The practice became
standard shortly after her passing.

Mama Lu removed the lid of the baking dish and a rush of
sweet smelling steam billowed from beneath its edges. Inside
were three large chicken breasts simmering in a mixture of
garlic and creole mustard under a layer of onion and orange
slices. Mama Lu served them up, drizzling the mustard sauce
liberally over the pieces while Mr. John doted on her cooking.

Wasting no time cutting into his entree, Mr. John savored the
first bite. "How you get so much flavor in dis bird?"

"Now you know I ain't gon' give away all my secrets,"
Mama Lu replied with a wink.

"Well, long as you keep cookin' like dis, you can keep all the
secrets you want."

Nalia listened quietly to the banter between Mama Lu and
Mr. John as they ate. Outwardly, she kept a formal posture, her
back straight against the chair, one hand in her lap on her
napkin. Inwardly, she reclined in relief. The simplicity of benign
routine was like a cool glass of water after a run. Here at this
small table, in this familiar kitchen, Nalia felt safe. She breathed
a long-awaited, silent sigh of relief, grateful to be removed from
the world where violent visions freely attacked her mind.

The conversation was pleasantly mundane as well, with no
uncomfortable discussion of destiny, fate, or what course her
life would follow. Nalia felt the weight of the day lifting as
Mama Lu and Mr. John continued chatting about topics of little
consequence to her. She was just over halfway finished with her
meal when the room grew quiet and Mama Lu turned to face
her.

"So, we gon' talk 'bout these visions you havin' or what?"
she asked, with all the tact of a party crasher.

Damn it!

Noticing a sharp pain in her jaw, Nalia realized she was
clenching her teeth. In a split second she had to decide whether

to continue bluffing or show her hand. She settled for what she considered neutral ground. Swallowing hard, she replied, "They're really not a big deal."

Somewhere in the middle of the sentence Nalia realized her fork was halfway to her mouth and had been for some time, not at all a reaction one would associate with a discussion that was "no big deal". She released the tension in her muscles and allowed the fork to follow the intended path to her mouth, trying her best to chew as if nothing was the matter. When she allowed her eyes to cut back to Mama Lu, the woman was staring intently at her scraped forehead.

"How long was you gone when you blacked out?" asked Mama Lu in a stern tone. "And what did you see while you was lyin' there?"

Nalia was silent. She wondered how she could have ever thought it possible to hide something like this from Mama Lu. *That's what the sight does. It intrudes, it breeds resentment. That's why I don't want it.*

"You think I don't see wha's goin' on?" Mama Lu continued. "You think I ain't ever had a vision dat caused me to vomit my guts up? You think I don't know what kind of power comes wit' visions dat strong?"

Mr. John looked up like a bomb went off. He had no idea what Mama Lu was talking about or why she was so insistent. He couldn't imagine Nalia hiding the truth, but one look into her eyes told him Mama Lu was right.

Memories of the visions raced through Nalia's mind: the pocket watch, the pale horse, the screaming girl. She couldn't make sense of them, but she wasn't keen on revealing them either.

"Why is this happening to me?" she exclaimed, breaking the stone silence. She pushed back her chair and slammed her fork down beside her plate. "I don't want this! I just want a normal life... just a simple normal life. I don't want the sight, or the power, or any..."

"Responsibility?" Mama Lu interrupted. "No sense of gratitude for the blessin' dat's been given to you? Dat's like sayin' you don' want dem legs, so you gon' quit walkin', or you don' want yo' mind so you gon' quit thinkin'.""

Nalia stared at her plate as her face continued to redden with anger.

"It's a gift, chil'. When you gon' realize dis is who you are and there ain't no hidin' from it?"

"It's not who I am," Nalia retorted. "I choose who I am, not some mystical energy. I will not let this control me!"

Mama Lu stared again at the wound on Nalia's head. "Looks like you doin' a bang-up job."

Nalia was furious. With her napkin wadded tightly in her fist, she rose from the table, threw it into her unfinished meal, and tried not to cry as she stormed off toward the stairs.

"What you afraid of?" Mama Lu called after her, immediately regretting it. Her words echoed in the uncomfortable silence. Mama Lu took a deep breath and exhaled slowly. She placed her elbows or the table and linked her fingers in front of her lips, allowing her chin to rest on her thumbs. Her heart was pounding and her nerves were standing on end.

Mr. John shook his head, trying to make sense of what had transpired. "You want to explain what dat was all about, or you jus' gon' leave me sittin' here in the dark?"

"Same thing dat's been goin' on ever since Madame Toulouse passed," explained Mama Lu in pained reflection. "The sight has settled on her and she's resistin' it. She must be puttin' up one hell of a fight too, 'cause I ain't never seen it latch on to somebody so strong." She sat back, wringing her hands as her eyes shifted nervously from side to side. "Jus' lately, somethin' ain't right. There's somethin' dark on the horizon, John. I can feel it clear as I can smell the rain dat's about to roll in. She can see it, I know she can. She been seein' visions, powerful ones. Dat's what tore her up so bad dis mornin'. The sight ain't gon' quit knockin' 'til she lets it in, and if she got a mind to resist, she's in fo' one rough ride."

"Maybe she jus' needs some time, Lu," said Mr. John, sympathetically. "Maybe we can jus'..."

"It ain't up to us," interrupted Mama Lu. "The sight is tryin' to show dat girl somethin', and by the look of what happened today, it's somethin' urgent."

Mr. John's tea glass was almost to his lips when concern washed across his face. "How you know all dis?" he asked.

"You think she's the only one seein' visions?"

Chapter Seven

By the time Nalia reached the bathroom at the top of the stairs, her tears were overpowering the will to hold them back. Rushing quickly inside, she shut the door hard behind her and collapsed against it, locking the world away. Nalia tried to catch her breath, but her racing heart and swelling sinuses made it difficult. She wasn't sure exactly why she was crying, but she hated it. Nalia despised weakness, and to her, crying was nothing more than its physical manifestation. Whether due to anger, distress, or fear, the result was the same, a lack of self-control.

Wiping her eyes dry with her fingers, she attempted to slow her heart rate with a meditation exercise. She closed her eyes and concentrated on slowing her breathing, but the questions racing through her mind proved difficult to overcome. Why her? Why had *the sight* chosen her and why couldn't she shake it? Why could she not have a normal life, with normal issues like when to start dating again, who to vote for, or how to fix the slow-draining sink? Why did her life revolve around questions like 'should I embrace the call of the spirit world' and 'why are my thoughts injuring me'?

"Normal?" she thought, "Who am I kidding?" Since birth, Nalia had never been normal, her parents made sure of it. She was neglected, abused, and abandoned. Even in her deliverance, she was taken in by a Voodoo high-priestess. Her childhood was a lie. Her identity was a mystery. She communicated with the spirit world, and even spent time there once. Sliding down the bathroom door, Nalia sat down on the cold tile floor with the realization she had no idea what normal was.

Her instinct was to run. She wanted to get up, pack a bag and run, but she knew it would avail her nothing. She was already running in her mind and had been for a long time. Deep down, in a part of her soul she didn't like to acknowledge, Nalia knew there was one thing buried she had yet to uncover and conquer. It was the ugly truth she knew controlled her. At the very core of her existence was a dark and persistent fear of becoming just like her mother.

Last summer, fourteen years after her departure, Margaret Barronne walked back into Nalia's life in a way she could never shake. It was then Nalia saw the true face of evil, and her fear was unearthed. Forever in the back of her mind loomed the terrifying potential of heredity – the chance she could become as cold, callused, and calculating as her mother. The thought was crippling.

Pulling herself together, she rose and turned on the shower. While she waited for the water to warm, Nalia washed her tears away in the sink with a cool washcloth. Looking in the mirror she noticed redness around her puffy eyes, brought on by the crying. It seemed to accentuate the petechiae from her earlier vomiting. Her head was throbbing. Hoping for aspirin she searched the medicine cabinet, but found only antacid and ointment.

Closing the mirror in disappointment, Nalia's heart leapt from her chest. Behind her in the reflection was the darkened image of an old man wearing a top hat. The vision lasted only a moment, long enough for Nalia to jump and close her eyes. When she opened them again, he was gone, but her nausea returned.

Chapter Eight

"The visions been comin' mos'ly at night," explained Mama Lu. "Some are clear as water, others are jus' feelings, but they all diff'rent... diff'rent than normal, I mean."

"Diff'rent how?" asked Mr. John.

"I can tell she's seein' things dat mean somethin' but I don't know what. I know 'cause I keep seein' visions of her. I see her strugglin'."

Mr. John began clearing the table while he listened. The thought of Nalia suffering any kind of hardship always put him on edge. He knew she was a grown woman. No doubt unpleasant situations would always arise, and while he was confident Nalia was equipped to handle them, she would always be his baby. Somewhere inside, Mr. John would always see the wounded child, broken and vulnerable – the child he spent his life protecting. Realizing he could no longer run to her rescue was difficult. It made him nervous, prompting the need to do something with his hands. He rinsed the cutlery and plates in the sink while Mama Lu continued.

"I can see her fightin' and I want to fix it..."

"But it's her fight Lu. You can't fix it fo' her, she got to do dis on her own. Trust me, I want to jump up and fix it too, but dis is her decision."

"Is it?" Mama Lu asked, as a weight fell over the discussion. "Is it really? There's forces at work here dat's bigger than her. Bigger than all of us, John. You know dat."

"It's still her choice. If she rejects the sight, it's gon' be a battle, but it's her battle to choose."

"It's not about the sight, it's about *her*. The sight has already chosen her, it's done. The question is, will she accept who she is, or run from it? She thinks she's strugglin' against the sight, but she's strugglin' against herself."

Mama Lu went to the cupboard and retrieved a small glass jar where she kept a mixture of black tea, chamomile, and spearmint. Mr. John filled the stainless steel kettle with water and placed it on the burner.

"When the visions come to me," Mama Lu went on, "I see Nalia, and she's always blindfolded."

"Well maybe she ain't really seein' nothin' then," argued Mr. John. "Maybe she can't see what the sight is tryin' to show her."

"No, John" Mama Lu said sternly. "In the vision, she's tyin' the blindfold on herself. I try to look at what she's hidin' from but I can't, like it's not meant fo' me. Then I back away and see dat she's bound up tight with ropes. The knots are right in front but she can't see 'em. She could untie herself if she'd just take the blindfold off. Dat's what's so hard to watch, John," she said as tears pooled in the corner of her eyes. "She ain't strugglin' to get free; she's fightin' to keep the blindfold on."

Mr. John stared at the floor while Mama Lu put a healthy portion of tea in her ceramic steeping-pot. By the time the next word was spoken, the kettle had whistled and the tea was nearly ready.

"You gon' run dis up to her?" Mama Lu asked. "She probably don't want to talk to me jus' now. Can't say as I blame her."

Mr. John nodded.

Mama Lu poured the tea into a thin, china cup and added a teaspoon of wildflower honey before placing it on a tray next to a small glass of water and two aspirin. "She's gon' have a headache. She always gets a headache when she's been cryin'."

Mr. John placed a hand on her shoulder and squeezed. It was just enough to draw a bit of tension from the muscle, allowing Mama Lu to relax a little more.

As she sat back down at the table, Mr. John saw her hand slip into her pocket. He knew she was reaching for the small, twisted bit of High John root she kept there. Johnny the Conqueror was Mama Lu's old standby whenever she was nervous or upset. Rubbing the root always helped bring her peace.

With a deep breath and a heavy heart, Mr. John lifted the tea-tray and carried it up the stairs. When he reached the landing, a distinct memory came to mind. It was an occasion Mr. John hadn't thought of in a long while. Perhaps the spearmint-laced aroma triggered the memory of climbing the same stairs with the same tea many years earlier. On that evening, Mr. John made the tea himself, a cup for Mama Lu who was downstairs nursing a cold, and a cup for Nalia, upstairs with the same ailment and a tummy ache. The child was no more than eight. Mr. John remembered the smile on the sick child's face when he entered the room. He sat at her bedside while she sipped the tea, and told her stories until her eyelids grew heavy and she finally drifted off. He caught the cup just before it slipped from her tiny fingers and placed it on the bedside table. Mr. John thought she looked like a little angel as she lay sleeping peacefully in her big bed. He fluffed her pillow tucked her in and switched off the lamp. As the switch clicked and the room went dark, Nalia stirred slightly and whispered, "G'night, Papa." It was the first time she ever called him that. Tears filled his eyes as he turned toward the door to find the silhouette of Mama Lu leaning against the jamb.

"You done good, you big sap," she said, gently wiping the tears from his eyes. "You done good."

As Mr. John reached the second floor, the aroma of the tea was overpowered by the lingering scent of rainforest body wash trailing from the open bathroom door where the air was still heavy with steam. Noticing Nalia's bedroom door was slightly ajar, Mr. John turned his eyes toward the floor and balanced the tray on one arm while tapping a knuckle on the jamb.

"You dressed, baby girl?" he called out.

"Yep, c'mon in," came the reply.

When Mr. John pushed open the door, he found Nalia sitting in the high-backed chair in front of her vanity, wearing an oversized tee-shirt and brushing out her wet hair with her polished silver brush.

The brush held great sentimental value for Nalia. Madame Toulouse gifted her with the polished silver antique on her twelfth birthday. She wanted Nalia to have a gift that would help her feel more like the young woman she was becoming than the child she was leaving behind.

The nightly ritual of brushing out her hair held a bit more meaning for Nalia now that Madame Toulouse was gone. During this time, Nalia felt her grandmother's spirit most often. Foreseeing the routine's importance, Mr. John made sure to replace the vanity's broken mirror quickly, after it was shattered last summer.

"I got some chamomile tea and some aspirin fo' you, baby. I'm jus' gon' set it down here on the night stand," said Mr. John, crossing the room with the tray. Though he'd seen Nalia's bedroom several times since the incident, Mr. John was still taken aback by its appearance. Before last summer, the room always retained a certain child-like charm, filled with dolls placed lovingly here and there. He could still see the marks on the wall near the ceiling where high shelves containing a fine collection of Mama Lu's handiwork used to hang.

The room had an older feel now, the personal space of a young woman, not a little girl. The dolls were gone, destroyed. Most notably absent was the large likeness of Nalia's mother, Margaret Barronne that once topped the dresser. In its place was an antique, brass picture frame holding a smiling photo of Madame Toulouse. At the frame's base lay a tortoise-shell cigarette holder, an elegant woman's sophisticated heirloom.

Beside the picture sat the room's only remaining doll, a worn, porcelain-faced figure named Queen Marie. A small scale replica of a grand likeness of Marie Laveau that was once the pride of Mama Lu's shop, Queen Marie was the first doll Mama

Lu ever made for Nalia. The doll held many special memories, not all of them pleasant. Nalia kept Queen Marie as a reminder to always trust her family above all others – a concept she wrestled with presently.

Though the room lacked its once-abundant, child-like distinction, Mr. John stopped momentarily to admire one surviving feature. On the headboard of Nalia's four-post bed, just above where the pillows lay, was the raised carving of a circus train. Its paint chipped and faded, the relief was a mere shadow of the brightly colored focal point it once was, but its history was rich. Mr. John did the carving when he crafted the bed and the rest of Nalia's furniture.

"I stare at that train every night," Nalia said, sideling up to Mr. John. "It calms my spirit."

Mr. John smiled as he put his arm around her shoulder and gave her a gentle squeeze. "Dat's what it's there fo'."

"Why the train, Papa? Why not flowers or butterflies, something easier to carve? I've studied this thing, and I know it couldn't have been a simple task, even for a master like you."

Mr. John stammered slightly, "You jus' loved animals when you was lil'. Me and yo' Mama Lu used to take you down to Audubon Zoo all the time and..."

Nalia looked up at Mr. John with a tilted head and a raised brow, "Don't feed me that line. Anything you put that much work into is more than a simple reflection of my affinity for animals."

Mr. John kept silent. His gaze dropped to the floor and he seemed to have some difficulty figuring out what to do with his hands.

"You carved the same thing on my dresser, so don't even try to deny it," Nalia said. Her eyes and her voice were both smiling now, and Mr. John's mouth began to match them with a thin smile of his own.

"You too smart fo' yo' own good. You know dat?"

"I'm waiting."

Mr. John took a deep breath. "It's a totem, baby girl," he finally replied. His voice was hushed and solemn. "It's meant to channel energy, help watch over you... protect you. See, when you came to live wit' yo' Mama Lu, you was jus' a broken shell of a lil' girl. Yo' whole life jus' been shattered to pieces. You was terrorized by the demons in dem awful nightmares, and we was doin' everythin' we could to help."

Nalia leaned in a bit closer to Mr. John, the little girl inside her wanting to be held. Mr. John felt his voice catch in his throat as memories of the frightened, tiny child flooded his mind. He fought back tears as he continued. "Dat's why the lion is there. He represents strength, courage, and dignity – all things you needed to rebuild. The zebra is there fo' yo' self-esteem. Comin' from a mixed-race family always bothered you 'cause befo' you came to live wit' Mama Lu, dem kids at yo' school would tease you and pick on you. He's there to remind you it's okay to be diff'rent, to be proud of who you are." Tears pooled in Nalia's eyes now, too.

"The monkey is there 'cause he's playful. So much of yo' innocence was taken away from you as a child, I wanted you to know it's okay to jus' be a kid and have fun, to take yo' time growin' up, and to keep dat child-like playfulness in yo' heart as long as you can." Mr. John paused for a deep breath. The lump in his throat was growing. He coughed lightly to clear it and pointed to the giraffe. "Now, dat fella there is special. He's there for two reasons. You see, the giraffe is a very large animal, but he's a leaf eater wit' a calm demeanor. He's there to help you stand tall and proud, but also so you'll remember to be gentle, meek, and merciful."

As Nalia listened to Mr. John, she began to realize how much of his and Mama Lu's lives had been devoted to her protection, her growth, and her spiritual health. In a sense, they gave the better part of their lives in sacrifice for a little girl they barely knew. She was not sure she ever felt more loved.

Before moving on to the train's engine, Mr. John thought about the heated dinner conversation between Nalia and Mama Lu. Not wishing to rekindle any spark of animosity, he chose his words carefully. "Now, the snake is the conductor, and he represents the spirits and the ancestors. He's in the driver's seat, leading all the others. He's smiling so you know not to be 'fraid of him, like some folks. The track is already laid out before you, he's just helping guide the train. Dat's all I'm gon' say 'bout dat. You got yo' own mind to make up, far as dat goes."

Mr. John gave Nalia one last squeeze, kissed her forehead and turned for door.

"No. I want to know what you think," said Nalia, to Mr. John's surprise. The man stopped in his tracks. "You are always so quiet, so patient. I know you won't try to influence me one way or the other. I just want to hear what you have to say."

Silence hung thick as Mr. John stared at his shoes. He couldn't call to mind a time when anyone wanted his opinion on such a heavy issue. Many were inclined to hear his advice on remedies and gris-gris, of course. Those were his specialties. Others enjoyed hearing him expound on rumors and gossip around town, but when it came to serious matters, the folks he knew traditionally consulted Mama Lu or Madame Toulouse. Mr. John never flattered himself a wise man or an eloquent speaker, and his vernacular was certainly less than impressive. Yet, in this moment a fragile young lady on the edge of her destiny looked to him for guidance. He was stunned.

Mr. John turned slowly and looked into Nalia's soft eyes. "You're right, sweet girl," he said, "I won't try and sway you 'cause I ain't got the answers you lookin' fo'. But I can tell you one thing I know fo' certain. When you find yo' callin' in dis world and you know without a doubt it's yo' destiny, you only got two choices. You can run from it and spend yo' whole life tryin' to be somebody you not, or you can accept it and embrace it."

The look on Mr. John's face was gentle but stern. His chin was dropped in humility, but his brow was raised in absolution. His words held more weight than any Nalia ever heard him utter. "But here's what I want you to understan'," he went on. "It's alright to walk into the water, 'stead of jumpin' off the pier. When you choose to embrace yo' fate, you ain't got to tackle it all at once. Sometimes it's best to jus'... lean into it."

Nalia had no words. Even if her mind could form them, her closing throat would not allow her mouth to speak. She simply looked Mr. John in his twinkling eyes and nodded affirmation.

The aging man turned on his heel and shuffled out of the room closing the door behind him. He did not see the tears of admiration steaming down Nalia's cheeks.

Downstairs, at the kitchen table, Mama Lu rubbed her thumb against Johnny the conqueror and listened to the rain as it began to fall on the back porch. She didn't hear the words spoken by Mr. John upstairs, but she felt the energy of the house change, as if peace was falling with the rain, cleansing the mind and spirit. "You done good, you big sap," she whispered. "You done good."

After climbing into bed, Nalia finished her tea. She was grateful for the warm beverage's soothing effect on her mind and stomach. She had thrown up her dinner after seeing the spectral image alongside her reflection. In fact, her inability to keep anything down all day was becoming a concern, but for now her stomach was settled. Nalia saw the old man again each time she closed her eyes, and when she turned off the lamp, images of the pocket watch, the horseman, and the screaming girl joined in. Fortunately, Mama Lu's chamomile tea was powerful. Nalia grew weary quickly, and the visions slipped from her consciousness. Snuggling deep into the warm covers of her four-post bed, Nalia succumbed to sleep. She had been dreaming less than half an hour when a disturbingly familiar, icy chill grabbed the base of her spine.

Chapter Nine

Decatur's street lights blazed like beacons off the freshly waxed finish of Madame Vivian Luciénne's long, black Lincoln. With her business booming, Luciénne once again enjoyed the luxury of being chauffeured around town like a visiting dignitary. Checking her makeup in a sleek, illuminated compact, she hoped the scar on her chin was sufficiently covered to make an acceptable first impression. The blemish proved a nagging source of frustration, shaking Madame Luciénne's self-confidence to a shadow of its former glory. She struggled to present herself a polished professional, despite constant scrutiny of her flawed appearance. She found it difficult to pass a mirror without instantly noticing her chin. Each time she saw the nearly vertical scar, Madame Luciénne recalled the sharp, stinging pain of the blade that sliced her flesh to the bone; the memory fueled a rage for which there seemed no release. Questions, doubts, and self-loathing roiled her to a state of nausea whenever she thought of how she'd been manipulated and ultimately conquered, but the most bothersome notion was her reaction to Mama Lu's favor. Somewhere in the corner of her mind, and dare she say it, her heart, sparked a pesky flame that would not die, a foreign emotion known as gratitude.

Closing the compact, Madame Luciénne pushed the memories from her mind as her vehicle slowed to a stop outside The Doll Maker. Her gaze instinctively drifted to the second floor gallery. Making a conscious effort to divert her eyes, she focused her attention on the shop next door where an inviting glow spilled gently through the window and onto the walk.

By the time her driver opened the Lincoln's rear door, Vivian Luciénne was nervously adjusting every article of jewelry her fingers could find. Retrieving her beaded clutch, she stepped from the vehicle and paused briefly on the sidewalk, pulling a wrap tightly around her shoulders to battle the brisk night air. A final pat of her meticulously styled, short coif assured it was in place and agreeable in the absence of her familiar, wide-brimmed hat. Finally, with a deep breath and a confident stride, she set off toward the door of the new tenant's shop.

The recently installed blinds covering the window were parted just enough to allow a hint of visibility. Madame Luciénne stopped briefly for a peek, watching for movement inside the shop before rapping on the door's glass panel. The loose pane rattled with more noise than she expected, shaking the manila shade on the other side. Madame Luciénne's heartbeat quickened slightly as she waited for a response.

In a short telephone conversation earlier in the afternoon, she finally heard the voice of the man with whom she previously corresponded only through email. Prepared to leave a message, Vivian was startled when a voice like melted caramel answered the line and invited her to a late meeting.

The shade jolted then drew up revealing an attractive, rugged face inches from the glass. The man's azure-blue eyes gave pause, then sparked with recognition as a warm smile brightened his expression. With a quick turn of the bolt, the door opened, and the smell of fresh paint mixed with an inviting, earthy cologne wafted out onto the chilly, night breeze.

"Vivian," acknowledged the caramel voice, "Please, come in."

The glow from the overhead lanterns cast a bold shadow on the man's square jaw accentuating a perfect crop of day-old stubble. Madame Luciénne stammered, caught off-guard by his stunning features. She felt her cheeks go flush and a slight tingling sensation on the soft flesh behind her ears. Seconds ticked by like hours as she studied the way his thick, dark hair parted flawlessly on one side, then curled to a point toward his piercing eyes. The man was gorgeous. Madame Luciénne was still staring when he stepped back and gestured her inside. Swallowing hard, she finally dropped her gaze and obliged.

"Jack Haufmann," the man said, closing the door and extending a firm hand as Madame Luciénne swung around to take it. "So good to meet you," he continued. "In person, I mean. It's always a bit awkward when you finally meet someone you already know from the internet." Madame Luciénne could only offer a dumbstruck expression as she continued to shake the man's hand until uncomfortable silence filled the room. With a waning smile, Jack managed to slip his hand from Madame Luciénne's lingering grasp, calling her drifting mind back to the moment.

"Right," she responded, "I suppose we have already met, haven't we?" Realizing her distraction was obvious, Madame Luciénne struggled to regain her composure. With her cheeks still warm, she decided brutal honesty was unavoidable. "Allow me to apologize for my lack of manners Mr. Haufmann, I feel like a silly school girl. I'm embarrassed to admit I was not expectin' someone of such strikin' good looks."

Jack's cheeks reddened at the compliment. While he was not unaccustomed to flattery, such an awkward introduction was anything but typical. He offered a half-grin in response, hoping to mask his guarded disposition.

"Curiosity got the best of me after our correspondence," explained Madame Luciénne with a nervous chuckle. "I did a lil' innocent diggin' online and found a profile for you with some basic information but not a single picture."

Still battling a surprised silence, Jack's expression faded to a mixture of confusion and curiosity.

"Usually when folks are reluctant to post pictures, there's a reason," Madame Luciénne continued with a raised brow.

"You were expecting an ugly guy," Jack finally repsonded, with a lighthearted laugh of understanding. "Well, in that case I'm happy to disappoint you." The warm smile returned to his face. Tucking his hands into his pockets, he relaxed his stance. "I guess I've just never been much for pictures."

"I'll say," Madame Luciénne went on, "Not even on yo' book jacket."

Uneasy, Jack turned to draw the shade back over the door's glass panel. "You've done your homework, haven't you?"

"Public Executions of the Late 1800's, a surprisin'ly good read considerin' its gruesome content but not a photo of you anywhere."

"Well, historians rarely write best sellers," said Jack, his back still turned. "I didn't see the need to clutter the jacket with some pompous picture of myself."

"Pity," said Madame Luciénne, clearing her throat as the awkward silence returned.

Swiveling pointedly, Jack attempted to get back on task. "What can I do for you, Ms. Luciénne?"

"Madame," corrected Vivian. Her host's oblivious misstep caused just enough bristling to reset her mind to more important matters. Tucking the clutch under her arm she turned with dismissive confidence and made her way across the room. Haufmann followed, arms folded across his chest.

"Yo' shop is comin' along nicely," said Madame Luciénne, noting its remarkable difference. The large boxes and crates were relocated to the rear, and the walls were painted a rich burgundy with taupe trim. Hunter green carpeting was roughed in but not finished, and the show cases were in place albeit minimally stocked. The shop was by no means ready to open, but an impressive amount of construction had taken place for one day. Exposed wires hanging from the overhead track lighting indicated it was yet to be connected, but the showcase countertops were lit.

"I would hope it's coming along nicely," said Jack. "You wouldn't believe what I had to go through with the commission just to get paint and carpet in here. They won't allow you to do much of anything to these old buildings in the way of renovation. The permits are ridiculous."

Depositing her beaded clutch on the display case, Madame Luciénne couldn't stop the sly smile from creeping across her face. Perhaps, her plan would be easier than anticipated. Peering into the lit cabinet, she looked over the inventory under the glass.

"Such beautiful pieces," she declared with a hand on her bosom and a gleam in her eye as she scanned the case up and down. A bed of tan velvet cradled roughly a dozen intricately crafted timepieces of various shapes and sizes, finely detailed works of silver, gold, and platinum with bright white faces and bold numbers. Some were open, with a delicate assembly of tiny, precision gears on display. One featured a small dial inside the main face where a separate clockwork swept a second hand over its own set of tiny numbers. Another was a classic pocket watch, closed to present the cover's ornate design, the work of a master craftsman. Madame Luciénne had no working knowledge of such watches, but she knew they looked expensive, a notion which made her smile. "Are these all hand crafted?"

"Some of them are," Haufmann answered as Madame Luciénne continued to marvel. "That's my grandfather's passion, not mine. I'm just here to help him out. Forgive me for being forward Vivian, but you seemed eager to meet with me and I'm quite sure it had nothing to do with the remodeling of our store or the quality of our inventory."

Madame Luciénne's smile faded to a thin grin, veiling offense. She clicked her tongue against her cheek and turned to face Mr. Haufmann.

"I can only assume," Jack went on, "You want to discuss my reluctance to join the business league you emailed me about." His brow creased, and his tone thickened. "When I first contacted you, Vivian, I was simply doing research. I was sorting through a very long list of search results claiming ties to

Marie Laveau for my upcoming book. I really had no interest in joining a business league. At the time, the move to New Orleans was still up in the air. I wasn't sure my grandfather would be willing to relocate, even though he still calls this city home."

"But you did relocate and you are in business here now, which means my services could prove very beneficial." Madame Luciénne stretched her long neck to one side in a playful, flirty gesture, but Mr. Haufmann showed little interest. His folded arms tightened against his chest.

"I read through the literature you sent me and I have to say, it alludes to some questionable ethics. I'm really not sure..."

"Mr. Haufmann," Madame Luciénne interrupted with a biting tone, "I assure you my practices are entirely legitimate. I simply help create competition among merchants. Competition fuels commerce in dis town, Mr. Haufmann. You and yo' grandfather will find that out soon enough, and when you do, you'll want the edge my business league can help provide." She stared with unwavering resolve while Jack's neck began to redden.

"Sounds a lot like you plan to drive out those who don't join."

"I'm merely sayin' yo' business will stand a much better chance of thrivin' if you're a member, especially with the deal I'm prepared to offer."

Jack Haufmann was at a loss for words. Try as he might to remain calm, his composure was slipping. He did not like being threatened, but there was little room to bargain. His grandfather needed the store to thrive; it was all the old man had. The business did well in Atlanta, but the move meant a significant shift in reliable earnings. Bouncing back would take time. The meager revenue Jack's writing career contributed did little to assist, and provided no guarantee of sustainable income. To top it off, the old man's health was declining and Jack knew his days were numbered. When his grandfather was gone, the business would likely be Jack's sole means of survival. Without a major publishing deal, historians fared financially on par with starving artists. As much as Jack hated to admit it, Madame Luciénne seemed to hold the ticket to fast-tracking commercial establishment. Skepticism and pride were the only things holding him back.

Unwilling to abandon his dismissive demeanor, Jack leaned against the counter. "I'm not sure there's any deal you could offer that would change my mind."

Madame Luciénne smiled and slid closer. This was the kind of challenge she lived for. "We'll get to that in a moment," she said, reaching into her purse for a cigarette. Despite the disapproving glare from her host, she lit it with a miniature, dime-store disposable. "First I want to discuss the real reason I came by." Taking a long drag for effective pause, Luciénne followed with a dramatic exhale. "Yo' book."

Mr. Haufmann looked surprised.

"I'm very interested in the research you're doin' on Marie Laveau. I know you're tracin' her lineage and interviewin' descendants. As I'm sure you're already aware, my family history draws a fairly convincin' line straight back to her era in dis city. So..."

"Let me stop you there," Jack interrupted. "As I mentioned in my last correspondence, my book is going to contrast the legend of Marie Laveau with accurate historical accounts of her life. I'm only interested in interviewing those persons who can prove a legitimate lineage. As far as I can tell, your claim doesn't quite hold up."

Madame Luciénne managed an affronted expression, for show. "While I understand a few gaps may raise a bit of uncertainty, I'm sure some further research will no doubt authenticate my claim." She produced one of the flashy "Laveau" business cards from her clutch and pushed it across the glass countertop. "You see, dis business league is sort of a secondary venture for me Mr. Haufmann. My primary vocation is that of what you might call... an advisor." Her host tensed as she explained. "While dis city may present the face of any other in the country, with its tourism, its industry, and its NFL team, the pulse drivin' it is altogether different." She gestured widely with her cigarette, then cut a pointed look back at Haufmann. "You'll never see it in the daylight, in the faces of yo' politicians, celebrities, and entrepreneurs. But pull back the curtain and you'll find it hidin' in the corner of the closet with the rest of the secrets folks don't want to talk about. There's a rich history here, I don't have to tell you that, and despite all the glitz and glamour it's just as dirty as it ever was. So when you know who is sleepin' with whom and whose money is slidin' into whose pocket behind closed doors, dis city is a hotbed of opportunity. Fortunately my... network keeps me abreast of a wealth of information on many of its influential players."

"Much like Marie Laveau," added Jack.

"So some would say. Of course, as an advisor, prophetess, priestess, whichever you prefer; my reputation is my business. Just imagine how lucrative a venture run by a legitimate descendant of the Voodoo Queen of New Orleans could be."

Recognition hit Jack Haufmann between the eyes. "So you want to offer me some type of membership in your business league in return for claiming you're the real deal."

"I told you we'd get to that," Madame Luciénne said, her satisfaction showing in her smile. "I've explained how it works: one exclusive recommendation per business class creatin'..."

"Strength in numbers, the strong survive. I get it. Go on."

"Here's what I'm willin' to offer: a waiver of all initial fees and dues, plus exclusive promotion in the categories of jewelry, clocks, and antiques, for the first year. Nobody is getting' that kind of a deal, Mr. Haufmann, and I can assure you with my support and the support of my colleagues, it will prove insanely profitable. No one else in dis city will be able to touch you. And of course, since I'm intimately acquainted with most of the commissioner's board, I'll do what I can to influence their decision on any subsequent permits you have yet to acquire."

Jack felt like he'd been slapped in the face, but refused to let it show. He could not afford to back down from his position easily. "And if I refuse?" he asked.

"Strength in numbers, Mr. Haufmann," replied Madame Luciénne, bouncing her eyebrows. She allowed the ashes from her cigarette to fall carelessly onto the new carpet as she stared Jack down with an arrogant glare. "The strong survive. You do want yo' grandfather's store to survive, don't you?"

Anger swelled in Jack's eyes, but he managed to keep his mannerisms in check. He couldn't believe the brass of the woman smirking before him. Extorting a business before it even opened was a mob tactic he'd only seen in movies. On the silver screen, it was glamorized: in person, it was demoralizing. His knuckles were just beginning to turn white when a loud crash from the back room drew his attention. "Pops, you alright?" he called.

A grumbling, raspy voice answered back, "Fine."

Madame Luciénne was startled. Having presumed she and her host were alone, she believed their negotiation was private. The possibility of a third party listening in threw her slightly off her game. Not once during their conversation had Jack Haufmann let on his grandfather was present – no indication nor introduction, not so much as a casual nod to the back room when the old man was mentioned. Madame Luciénne bristled, suspecting Jack of purposeful deception. The old man continued from the back room in a low mumble. "How am I supposed to get around with these boxes stacked right in the doorway?" The shuffling of feet became more audible as he came around the door frame carrying a small box. His brooding demeanor was heavy, as if a presence entered the room with him. With his head down, he approached the case and set the box down next to Madame Luciénne's clutch on the glass. Inside was a ladies wristwatch, white gold with petite gems lining its dark face. It sparkled in the tiny lights of the cabinet when the old man placed it next to the others. Lovingly, he positioned the piece at what he determined was the perfect angle sending a full spectrum of refracted light dancing across Madame Luciénne's face. When he was finished the old man slipped a hand into his vest and produced an antique gold pocket watch. He opened its ornate cover and stared at the face. When he finally raised his eyes, Madame Luciénne nearly gasped. His gaze was menacing, filled with animosity. The old man glared at Jack, then at her, then back at Jack. His expression showed displeasure. With a swift motion he slammed the cover of the pocket watch and slipped it back inside his vest. "The watch tells me it's late," he coughed, eyeing Jack. "We still have business that needs attention."

Turning around, he shuffled back through the doorway, his footsteps trailing until silence once again filled the shop. Both Jack and Madame Luciénne exhaled the captive breath neither realized they were holding.

"Think about my offer," Luciénne said finally, gathering her composure and collecting her clutch. "It'll be good for both of us." Turning to leave she brushed close to Jack. "Keep researchin' my lineage, Mr. Haufmann. I'm sure you'll find just what you're lookin' for," she purred. At the door Madame Luciénne drew a final, sultry drag from her cigarette before flicking it into the street and casting an over-the-shoulder wink in Jack's direction. "When you do, you've got my card."

Jack slid the card to the edge of the counter and picked it up as he watched her leave. She was a beautiful woman, no doubt, but her threatening demeanor left a bad taste in his mouth, like the waxy after-taste of cheap chocolate. Jack shook his head in disbelief as he turned the card between his fingers. "Laveau's Business League," he thought with a grin, "What a sham." Madame Luciénne was not the only one who had done her homework. Jack already knew "Madame" Vivian Luciénne had absolutely no blood relation to Marie Laveau. What she did have, however, were connections and information. The woman's social ties and secrets practically put the city of New Orleans in her pocket. While he had no interest in researching her any further, Jack was confident Madame Luciénne could help him track down the person he was looking for, the reason he left Atlanta for The Big Easy in the first place. All his research on Marie Laveau's lineage pointed to a woman who disappeared from New Orleans after her husband's murder roughly fifteen years ago and had not been seen or heard from since – an elusive debutante named Margaret Barronne.

Chapter Ten

The chilling sensation startled Nalia to what she believed was an awakened state. A toxic swelling in her stomach bubbled acid into her esophagus leaving a bitter, rancid taste in the back of her throat. Memories of the green-eyed beast from her past instantaneously triggered a cold sweat and an escalated heart rate. Her eyes quickly scanned every corner of the room for any trace of the monstrous creature. Nalia found herself backed into the headboard assuming a defensive posture, her muscles tense and rigid. By the time she realized she was holding her breath, her brain was already deprived of oxygen. She needed air.

With no sign of the beast, and with the cold sensation in her spine dissipating, Nalia released the captive breath and allowed her shoulders to relax. One by one, she released her fingers from their death-grip on the duvet, but found it difficult to keep her eyes from surveying the room. They continued to wander until acute pain in her legs captured Nalia's attention. Stinging cramps revealed just how much rigor was locked in her muscles. She stretched them out as far as she could, breathing deeply until the pain subsided. When the cramps finally released, Nalia closed her eyes, leaned against the headboard, and attempted the circular breathing technique she practiced often but never quite mastered. The smell of rain was comforting... until she questioned its presence.

Startled, Nalia noticed her sheer curtains blowing into the room on the breeze from her open window. The icy chill attacked again, not just her spine but her entire body. Her dark hair blew across her face as the wind intensified. Nalia was certain her window was closed and locked when she went to bed, and she had spent enough time walking through dreams to wonder whether she was truly awake. Other odd discrepancies fueled her suspicion: the lamp was on, the teacup was missing, and her door was slightly ajar. Instinctively, she looked for Queen Marie. The doll that shared her first astral voyage sat atop the dresser right where she belonged. The photo in the brass frame however, was missing, as was the tortoise-shell quellazaire.

The wind blew strong again and Nalia shivered from the chill. The lightbulb in her bedside lamp went dark, like a candle blown out by the breeze, leaving only a bold moonbeam to light the room. Darkness heightening her senses, Nalia noticed the wind's faint howl, like a voice in the distance.

Come.

Drawn, she stood and approached the open window. As the terrain below came into view, Nalia's spirit stirred with trepidation. Heavy fog covered the ground, bathed in the bluish luminescence of the moon. The air was hazy, and the scene's lack of clarity gave the illusion of emptiness, but Nalia sensed something lurking in the void.

She could just make out a slight drizzle falling through the glow of the street lamps. Raindrops tapped against the ground beneath the fog as leaves continued to fall from the trees, spinning and flipping like parade confetti. Spring should be just around the corner, Nalia thought, yet everything here was dying. It was barren and somehow sinister. A chill gripped Nalia again, on the inside this time, like a tug at her soul.

As she tried to shake the wicked sensation, Nalia's bedroom door creaked with the labored moan of neglected hinges. Turning, she found it open wide to a brightly illuminated hallway. For a moment she was motionless while the wind howled again throwing the sheer curtains up and over her shoulders like a threatening embrace.

In the void of the doorway was a shadow. It did not fall against the wall, as if cast by an object opposing the light. It stood as its own entity in the middle of the hall, a phantom apparition the shape of a human. It was small in stature but carried a grand presence. On the shadow's head was a large, floppy hat, in its hand an elegant quellazaire. Nalia had no doubt if the shadow were tangible the cigarette holder would be made of tortoise shell.

Instantly, her stomach settled, and her fear released its grip. A warm sensation moved throughout Nalia's body, as if she could feel her blood flowing. A relieved smile fell across her face. "Out on the town, Madame T?" she whispered as another brisk breeze hit her square in the back.

The figure turned and slowly moved down the hall gliding over the floor like a feather on the air. The wind howled again

Come.

This time, the voice was in Nalia's head, the voice of Madame Toulouse.

"I think I'll get my coat," Nalia thought, walking quickly to the closet. She was disheartened to find it empty.

Come.

Nalia looked around in desperation for anything to keep her warm. On the foot of her bed, a small throw sat folded into a neat rectangle, as if it materialized out of necessity. Wrapping it around her shoulders, she headed for the door but stopped short. Journeying to a different plane of the spiritual realm often brought more questions than answers. Nalia was quite sure she had enough riddles to solve already. Reluctant to cross the threshold, she held her breath while her eyes danced between the hallway and the bedroom in hesitation.

Come.

Nalia's shadowy guest floated effortlessly toward the stairs, lingering beside the rail, waiting for a decision. The moment Nalia committed, her guide disappeared smoothly down the stairs. As Nalia followed, she heard the bedroom door creak to a close behind her. She did not look back.

With the light in the hall fading, Nalia came to a puzzling realization – the light was following the shadow. Though the figure was visually just a coal-black relief, light emanated from it; the world was lit by it. Nalia had only moments to follow before she would be left in a completely darkened hallway. Pulling the throw tightly around her neck, she pressed on.

In the waning light, the hallway took on a peculiar appearance. It was dusty and un-kept, like the house was abandoned. Wallpaper peeled above the chair rail. Worn paint riddled the door facings, and cobwebs gathered in thick clumps along the molding. When Nalia reached the banister, it was ice-cold to the touch. The aged wood cried out in starvation, like it hadn't been polished for years.

Nalia descended the stairs carefully, her apprehension swelling with each step. A storm of images swirled through her mind: the gold pocket watch, the pale horse with its skeletal rider, the screaming woman's spattered blood, and the old man in the top hat. Reaching the bottom step, Nalia placed a bare foot on the hallway's carpet runner and peered into the kitchen. She watched the moonlight spill across the linoleum through the open back door.

"Come," said the reassuring voice inside Nalia's head. "Don' be afraid, chil'."

The kitchen floor was cold under Nalia's feet, or so she thought until she stepped through the doorway onto the icy porch. Nalia wished for the time to search for shoes, but feared she would find them as elusive as her coat.

A cutting wind blew a mist of frigid, drizzling rain into Nalia's face. Turning to shield herself, she flipped the throw over her head and gathered it securely under her chin. Thunder rumbled gently in the distance as lightning illuminated the terrain for seconds at a time. Flashing through the dead trees, the light cast heavy, claw-like shadows over the fog, but none dared approach Madame Toulouse.

Outside in the open air, the image of Madame Toulouse took on a lifelike appearance. Backlit buy the moon's glow, the shadow looked natural, as if Nalia's grandmother was actually standing there in the yard. For a moment, Nalia believed she was. "Odd how easily the mind can be fooled," she thought.

Slowly, Madame Toulouse began to move, gliding through the fog, parting it like a plow through a cane field. Holding the quellazaire aloft gracefully, she floated silently through the gate and turned on the gravel road beyond, beckoning Nalia to follow in her wake. Darkness swelled as Nalia heard the voice again.

"Stay close, chil'."

Lightning flashed across the sky once more as Nalia braved the rain, stepping from the porch onto the walk. The farther the shadow of Madame Toulouse strayed, the more Nalia felt the deadly, sinister presence growing again. The cold wind surrounded her angrily, flipping up the edges of her throw and tugging at the hem of her oversized tee.

"Stay close, chil'," the voice called once more. This time, Nalia took heed. She followed for what felt like days. Time seemed to have no meaning in this place, nor did geography; Nalia had no idea where she was. Nothing looked familiar. Massive trees lined her path, their long, dead branches weaving a canopy of decay overhead like boney hands reaching to snatch her from above. They scraped against one another with a racket like disembodied screams. Cowering beneath her wrap, Nalia quickened her pace as the last few leaves succumbed to gravity and spiraled down around her.

"Jus' a little further now."

Soldiering over the coarse, sharp gravel, Nalia fought to catch up. She could feel the sinister presence following her in the darkness, watching. Fear was a tremendous motivator, but as she approached Madame Toulouse, Nalia felt the flood of peace and tranquility wash over her again. Even the pain from the gravel on her bare feet began to fade. Clouds in the night sky peeled back like a curtain, allowing the moon to bathe the ground in a patchwork of light and shadow through the canopy, as the rain finally relaxed.

"No need to be afraid, chil'. Jus' follow me."

Nalia focused her entire existence on Madame Toulouse until even the bitter cold was no longer a concern, and the thick grove of trees opened at the foot of a high, iron fence. The massive structure stretched out either direction into the dense fog. Nalia suddenly felt small. Just beyond the fence line she could see a well-manicured lawn extending into a thick haze. Glowing orbs appeared to hover twelve feet in the air over the dewy courtyard.

The shadow of Madame Toulouse stood near a thick stone archway with wrought-iron gates, like prison bars, reaching to the top. Light from the orbs sent the gates' long straight shadows crawling across the ground beyond Nalia's feet. In the top of the arch was a large opening like a porthole and in its center, a web of decorative iron, intricately woven into a complex symbol.

Madame Toulouse did not move, but gestured toward the archway with her shadowy quellazaire. As the whine of rusty hinges filled the air, the gates creaked open and Nalia felt the sinister presence growing strong once again. Fear climbed her spine.

"Is that where I'm supposed to go?" Nalia asked, with hesitation.

The spectral voice in her head answered, "Dat's why we are here. What you need to see is beyond dis gate."

"You're coming with me, right?" Nalia asked, fearing she already knew the answer.

"I cannot enter the courtyard, chil'," replied Madame Toulouse, pointing to the symbol above the arch. "Where we stand is the land of the dead. Beyond the gate lies the world of the living. You must enter alone."

Nalia felt her throat closing like a vice. She wanted to speak but found it difficult to form words. Sensing Nalia's fear, her grandmother spoke again. "Do not be afraid, chil'. Can't nothin' hurt you in there, try as it might. You carry me with you in your heart, you'll be safe y'hear?"

Nalia took a deep breath but did not feel better. She stared at the open gate as a wolf-like howl echoed in the wind. A wave of uncertainty raced through Nalia's blood, but if there was anyone at all she could trust, it was her Madame T. Looking back to her grandmother for reassurance, Nalia made up her mind. Madame Toulouse did not speak again, but continued pointing at the massive stone arch.

Straightening her back, Nalia stepped toward the gate. The warmth that filled her body while in her grandmother's presence faded, and the icy chill once again bit her flesh. She tightened her grip on the throw, but it was cold, wet, and useless. Casting it aside, she crossed into the courtyard, shuddering like flame in the raging wind.

Chapter Eleven

As Nalia passed beneath the archway, a tingling sensation rushed from her scalp to the base of her spine, like a thousand tiny spiders scrambling to reach the ground. Every nerve in her body was on high alert. Nalia was sure someone or something was watching her every step. The sinister presence swelled again, but this time the stakes were higher – Nalia was on its turf.

Despite its unnerving air, the courtyard was a breathtaking sight. Its high fence curved toward the center, suggesting a round perimeter, with tall stone structures staggered equally along the length. Nalia could now see the glowing orbs were lampposts, rising high into the haze and stretching out into the distance. Her visibility was limited, and the fog seemed to thicken and close in around her as she walked. A faint, metered clanging, like the harsh noise of a foundry heightened her paranoia. She tried breathing deeply to calm her nerves, but the chilly air formed jagged ice crystals in her throat.

Her way unclear, Nalia chose to follow the sidewalk stretching into the mist. Residual drops of rain materialized out of the darkness as they fell through the glow of the lampposts. On either side of the walk, large marble benches stood in the lush grass. On her left, two long slabs ran parallel like a giant roman numeral. On her right, another formed a large "X". Nalia tried to remember what the numeral "IIX" represented but could not recall.

As she continued down the frozen walkway, Nalia noticed other sidewalks to her left and right. The longer she walked the closer they drew, converging on a central point. The energy of the grand, courtyard was drawing her in, its infernal noise growing steadily louder.

Nalia's breathing quickened, and her extremities grew numb. She could barely feel her feet at all. As she approached the point where the sidewalks met, the clamoring sound became a cacophony of industrial noise. Metal groaned in pain, whining and clacking like the inner-workings of a giant machine. Nalia clearly identified the ratcheting of gears and the grinding of iron on iron. The rhythm was strangely intoxicating, softening her mind like a drug. Before she realized, the pace of her feet matched the rhythm of the gears, and Nalia quickly found herself at the center of the courtyard.

The haze slowly rose, as if summoned away, lifting the curtain of obscurity. The sidewalks, at least a dozen, met at a central hub, a large, circular slab of granite. A foot tall and wider than a city block, the platform gleamed like a polished gravestone. Its face was a maze of deeply grooved lines and symbols. At the heart of the massive slab, a tall spire of iron and stone stretched into the sky like a tower, its apex obscured by the rising mist.

With the sensation of taking the stage for an unseen audience, Nalia stepped onto the grooved platform. When her bare feet touched the cold stone, the surface trembled with the force of an earthquake. The noise of the machine swelled to a deafening rumble and the stone spire began to move, revolving on a giant vertical axis. Nalia's head and eardrums erupted with pain from the grating noise. Her teeth chattered from the cold, the vibration, and the fear welling inside her.

Slowly the tower turned, grinding like a millstone against the granite slab. As it approached a full revolution, anxiety gripped Nalia's soul. Her unseen watcher appeared, no longer hidden in the shadow of the spire. Thirty feet in the air, clinging to the side of the tower with one hand, hung a well-dressed figure with stark-white hair sprouting from beneath his top hat. His tailcoat was stylish, but dingy, and while his shoes were shined to a high gloss, their leather was cracked and ripped along the sides. His feet were planted one in front of the other, in a deep groove encircling the spire. The figure stretched out his other arm in a grand gesture, cane in hand. He owned the tower with the commanding presence of a seasoned carnie on a slow-rolling carousel. Nalia almost expected calliope music.

Compelled to watch as the figure rotated into full view, Nalia finally saw his face. The man was old with leathery skin so worn each wrinkle was etched with tremendous clarity. His expression was stern, but guarded; his sinister smile showed a hint of surprise. When their eyes finally locked, a high-pitched tone pierced Nalia's brain, like a tuning fork vibrating in her skull. The old man's eyes began to glow a deep bloodshot red, and Nalia grew dizzy. She felt her consciousness slipping away from her body, away from the courtyard. Soon the world around her turned with the speed of a high-powered blender and her vision faded to darkness.

When the vertigo eventually released its grip, Nalia felt nothing. She sank into a barren chasm devoid of matter and energy. There were no sights, no sounds, no emotions - most notably, no fear.

Gradually, a faint flash of light broke through the void, soon followed by the dank smell of dust mingled with spices and incense. The tiny light flickered as it grew and soon became a candle illuminating a large, round table draped in red velvet. One by one, other candles sprang to life around her, filling the small room with a warm, amber glow. Nalia heard distant thunder and the soft sound of rain on the roof overhead.

Light from the candles in the center of the table lit the faces of three figures. On one side, a young couple huddled together, wet from head to toe and shaking, though Nalia could tell it was not from the cold.

The young couple didn't seem to notice Nalia's presence. In fact, Nalia wasn't sure she was present at all. She was in the room, but there seemed to be a transparent membrane stretched tightly between her and the others. Nalia sensed she was quite invisible.

The fair-skinned man removed his rain-soaked hat and ran his fingers through his thick, dark hair. He clutched the hat nervously at the edge of the table, wringing his fingers along the brim. The young woman was equally skittish, her mannerisms quick and guarded. Her wet hair clung tightly to the sides of her thin, pale face as she tried desperately to avoid eye contact. Conversely, the young man's eyes were pleading and desperate. With a trembling hand he removed a gold pocket watch from his vest pocket and slid it across the table.

The hand that took it belonged to the third figure, a light-skinned black woman whose face held a reddish hue. Her hand was rough but feminine, with various rings adorning her fingers and large, gold bracelets dangling from her wrist. Her slightly bulging eyes stared with intent, not at the watch but at the man, gauging his reaction as she picked up the timepiece. She studied him for a long moment, looking for something… looking for truth. When she was satisfied, she turned her attention to the gold watch. The piece was costly, and intricately detailed, but the woman's brow furrowed when she noticed the engraving.

Nalia's lips slowly parted – a precursor to her mouth falling wide open. The woman she watched wore a blue tignon tied in seven knots around her head. Gold hoop earrings fell gently against her cheeks, and her fierce eyes were full of mystery. As sure as Nalia knew her own heartbeat, she knew she was staring at Marie Laveau. Stunned, she could not look away. The world around her became inconsequential. It took several moments to realize Marie's bulging, caramel eyes were staring back.

Slowly darkness faded in again, and Nalia was paralyzed by the high-pitched tuning fork in her brain. Trying to quiet the piercing tone, she brought both hands to her ears only to realize she could not feel her head. She could not feel anything.

Fright was the first sensation to return as the grinding sound of the giant machine once again filled the air. Nalia gasped, seeing the old man's bloodshot-red eyes cut through the haze. He was close, and this time Nalia noticed something in his gaze she did not see before – fear. Before she could speak, the old man vanished, disappearing into the returning fog.

Feeling rapidly returned to Nalia's body. Cold and wet, she shivered as the rain commenced once more. Before she could regain her bearings, terror pierced her soul like a thousand silver daggers. Nalia felt the old man's hot breath on the back of her neck. With no warning, pain shot across her throat and a warm sensation flowed heavily down her chest. In a panic, Nalia quickly brought both hands to her neck. When she pulled them away, blood covered her palms and ran the length of her arms. Frantically she grabbed her throat and tried to apply pressure, hoping to close the wound, but the cut was deep and the loss of blood made her weak. She tried to scream but her vocal chords, severed in the attack, were useless. In shock, Nalia's head grew light and dizzy while her body dropped like lead. The last thing she saw before hitting the ground was the tall spire stretching high into the sky, raindrops racing down its length.

In the quiet comfort of her darkened bedroom, Nalia awoke with a start, cold sweat covering her shaking form. Instinctively, her hands cupped her quivering throat, examining it anxiously. Thankfully, she found only soft, smooth flesh. After catching her breath and calming her heart rate, Nalia climbed out of bed and fetched Queen Marie from the top of the dresser beside the picture of Madame Toulouse. She held the doll tightly and climbed back under the duvet.

Chapter Twelve

Three a.m. was not an hour Mr. John was generally awake. This morning however, he was standing in the open bay door of his shop, staring across the gravel road, attempting to ascertain why he startled awake in a panic. A heavy sense of dread sat upon his chest and tightened like a noose around his throat. The sensation lasted only a moment, but long enough to convince Mr. John something was dreadfully wrong.

Having made a quick sweep of his premises and finding nothing out of the ordinary, Mr. John surmised the omen originated across the street. Staring at the back of Mama Lu's house, he could see Nalia's bedroom window clearly. The house looked calm, but its benign appearance did little to quell the tightening knot in Mr. John's gut. He had seen quiet nights turn treacherous too many times to be comforted by the present silence. It was too tranquil, he thought, like the barometric pressure drop before a hurricane.

Too many nights of his life were spent in the bay door of his workshop watching Mama Lu's house, studying its shadows. Through the years, Mr. John grew quite adept at correctly interpreting patterns of light and shadow in the windows of the old house across the street, determining and predicting the activity going on inside. The lack of movement tonight should be comforting, thought Mr. John, but the uneasy feeling continued to gnaw at his soul.

Anxious, he scanned the neighborhood up and down the narrow road. The glow of the street lamps revealed nothing, but a lack of physical activity was not an accurate indicator of spiritual energy, and Mr. John felt something in the air.

The breeze was cold, chilling Mr. John's shirtless, tattooed torso to the point of goose bumps. His mind, however, remained undeterred. He focused his spirit and all his energy on the ladies across the way.

Convinced something was amiss and unable to shake the feeling, Mr. John retrieved his maple pipe and a fresh plug of his signature tobacco blend from the workshop table and lit it with a wooden match. The glow from the flame illuminated his purposeful eyes as he turned them back toward the window. Tossing the spent match into the drive, just beyond the bay door, Mr. John absentmindedly puffed his pipe allowing the blend of perique tobacco, cloves, and mint leaves to dance across his palette. Still unnerved, he sat down on the edge of his hand-crafted rocking chair, slowly slid to the back, and tried to clear his mind. Mr. John did not have *the sight* like Mama Lu, but the hairs prickling on the back of his neck were a decent enough indicator when something was wrong. Tonight, they stood on end.

He knew if he was needed, Mama Lu would call out for him. They shared a unique, near-psychic bond, not of the mind but the spirit. She'd called for him countless times before, and he always heard; the bond was strong between their souls. Until then, he sat vigil in the darkness, his face bathed in the soft glow of his pipe, smoke circling his head. In his mind and on his lips were old Creole songs and chants of peace, serenity, and protection.

———————

Just before three a.m., Mama Lu's slumber grew restless. Though unaware of their movement, her muscles twitched and jerked sporadically in discomfort. Her palms began to sweat, and her fingers flinched open and closed as if trying to catch an unseen insect. Her breathing, normally heavy and steady during sleep, was now quick and halting. She cycled through a ragged pattern of inhaling, holding her breath for an unusually long period of time, and releasing it with a long, slow whistle. Her heartbeat raced well above normal, and though she was deeply asleep, her eyes were wide open.

Fueled by an all-too-recent memory, Mama Lu's mind slipped into a familiar, recurring dream. The afternoon sun warmed a carpet of lush green grass while a lone trumpet blew a somber rendition of "When the Saints Go Marching In". The horn's tone was hypnotic, smooth and mellow like warm pudding just starting to thicken. Its song was sobering and Mama Lu fought back tears as sorrow swelled her eyes and throat.

Across the well-trimmed lawn, on a small, velvet-covered platform sat an emerald green casket topped with a spray of peace lilies. It rested in the shadow of a large tomb bearing the name Toulouse. The vision thickened the lump in Mama Lu's throat.

Standing before the casket was a trim, young lady in a knee-length white dress. She wore a large, white hat with a thin, black veil and white, theatre-length opera gloves. Though the girl's back was turned, Mama Lu recognized her. It was Nalia, standing at the gravesite of her grandmother.

Her posture was perfect, lacking the sorrowful slump often exhibited by those in mourning. Her head was high and fixed, almost proud. Mama Lu watched as Nalia peeled off the opera gloves and laid them across the floral spray. She lifted her veil, resting it delicately on the brim of her hat. With a hand on either side, she removed the hat and placed it near the head of the casket.

Pivoting on her heel, Nalia turned her back on the gleaming emerald box, stretched out her hands, and took a deep breath. From thin air, a long, black strip of cloth materialized across her palms, its ends blowing in the subtle breeze. Raising it to her eyes, Nalia wrapped the blindfold around her head and secured it tightly.

Mama Lu watched anxiously as thin vines of ivy sprouted from the ground at Nalia's feet climbing slowly until they encircled her ankles. They embraced her softly at first, lovingly, but in time their movement became hostile, angry. Stronger and thicker they grew, winding their way up Nalia's body until they wrapped securely around her torso. Binding her waist, the vines took on the appearance of heavy rope. They stretched tightly around Nalia's body, winding their way to her neck. Squeezing like boa constrictors, the ropes stole the breath from Nalia's lungs and tied themselves in knots around her breasts. Nalia's arms were the only part of her body free from restraint. They were raised to her head, securely holding the blindfold in place.

Mama Lu began to weep. Desperate to release her daughter's bindings, she tried to run across the lawn only to find herself slipping in the grass. Her struggle was futile, like walking against the flow of a tidal wave. Helpless, she could only watch as the snake-like cords choked the life from her daughter.

"Fight it, chil'!" yelled Mama Lu. "Throw off dat blindfold an' free yo'self!" Through the frightened tears she screamed until her throat was raw and her voice was ragged, but Nalia refused to listen. Her hands remained gripped around the strip of black fabric, holding it firmly over her eyes with increased vigor.

Unable to watch the horror of her daughter dying, Mama Lu muttered swears of denial and shut her eyes tight, but the image would not disappear. In her mind, she could still see the ropes tightening and Nalia gasping for air like a beached fish. The agony was crippling. Mama Lu longed to free Nalia, even take her place, but knew she could do nothing. She tried shutting her eyes again, but the scene remained. Desperate, Mama Lu attempted to regain control, to pull herself from the dream, to wake up.

At the height of her despair she felt a new sensation, like a cold hand on her shoulder. Leaping with surprise, her heart skipped a beat and her stomach turned upside-down. On impulse she turned, assuming a defensive posture but found no one there, only the whisper of the wind. As Mama Lu listened closely, the whisper swelled to a low rumble. Leaves began to quiver and then to shake violently as a tremor swept through the lush terrain. The earth beneath her shifted and lurched. Her legs grew weak in a dizzying wave of vertigo as the horizon began to rise on one side. Like a ship tossed by a wave, her surroundings began to slide.

Mama Lu's vision blurred and the colors of her world began to bleed. The rich blue of the sky above dripped into the green of the foliage like too much paint running down a canvas. Songbirds ceased their serenades as they melted into the viscous display. Mama Lu braced herself, reaching for the branches of a nearby shrub only to have them liquefy in her hands as the ground continued to tip, one astral plane pouring into another.

Greens became gold and blues became sporadic patches of vibrant color against a great ivory canopy of clouds turned hard and smooth like stone. Billowing swirls became hard lines and earthy, organic textures glossed over to slick, shiny surfaces. The afternoon's warm air grew cold and stagnant as the grass beneath Mama Lu's feet softened into velvet. The whisper of the wind in the wide-open cemetery echoed back as if suddenly walled off. In the distance Mama Lu heard the bells of St. Louis Cathedral.

As the world fell back into focus, Mama Lu found herself standing on a soft field of crimson carpet near the gilded altar of the cavernous Catholic hall. A new chill swept through her body. Her recurring dream of Nalia bound with the rope-like vines always ended when she closed her eyes. This fresh development was unnerving.

The chill lasted only a moment before Mama Lu found herself oddly captivated by the beauty of the cathedral. Though she visited often, she could not recall ever being this close to the altar. The pillars on either side rose high into the ceiling, mimicking the spires on the building's exterior. From her unique vantage point, Mama Lu could look straight up the columns to the statues gracing their crowns. On the left rose the statue of hope and on the right charity. The trinity was completed by the statue of faith, seated just below Humbrecht's massive depiction of King Louis IX commencing the seventh crusade. Not far below, looking over the altar and over Mama Lu, were statues of St. Peter and St. Paul. Mama Lu stocked her own renderings of the saints in her shop, ones much more life-like than the two placed here. Only now, these seemed to follow her with eyes of fire. Looking around the great cathedral, Mama Lu felt all the statuary watching her, turning their heads to fix her with curious stares.

Fascinated, Mama Lu stepped down from the altar onto the cold, black and white checkered, tile floor. She watched the stained-glass windows as she walked the aisle between the rich wooden pews. Each window depicted a scene from the life of St. Louis, but the figures in the glass were not focused on each other; they stared back at Mama Lu. Even the flags overhead seemed drawn to her as she passed beneath the watchful paintings of the apostles gracing the arched ceiling. The attention weighed balefully on Mama Lu as if the building would collapse and devour her at any moment, but the saints seemed to guard her, protecting her path.

Quietly, she walked across the icy tile, a tiny player in a grand arena of unnatural spectators. As she approached the great wooden doors, the statues of Joan of Arc and King Louis himself nodded their approval. The doors swung open.

The cathedral foyer felt altogether different: small, dark, and cold. A frigid gale beat against the exterior doors, licking around them like a hungry flame. Something dreadful waited beyond the threshold; Mama Lu could feel it. Unwilling to retreat, she steeled her mind for whatever waited on the other side. At her command, the doors burst open.

Carrying the thick smell of decay, a freezing gust of wind hit Mama Lu square in the chest, pushing her back and nearly knocking her down. Staggering, she gripped the doorpost for stability and peered out into the night. The courtyard was cold and dark, but the full moon hung over the river like a beacon. Staring across Jackson Square, Mama Lu found only emptiness. A fresh chill filled her bones that was not the wind. The landscape was distressed, unlike anything she ever saw in the French Quarter. The normally green foliage was withered and hollow. Only the scattered sprouting of barren twigs escaped the naked underbrush. Stumps littered the ground where lush trees used to thrive. The high, iron fence was rusted and frail.

Motion ceased to exist. The spindly branches of rooted twigs were unaffected by the gusting wind. Dead leaves and sticks lay flat against the dark soil like stones. No pedestrians trafficked the courtyard, not even on the far side, near the river. Mama Lu felt as if she were staring into a painting, a moment frozen in time.

Letting the door close behind her, she walked out onto the steps of the cathedral into the peculiar scene. Aside from the glow of the moon, the courtyard's only light spilled over from the building's face, a reflection of the powerful flood bulbs. Mama Lu turned, looking skyward, up the cathedral's magnificent spires. Their sharp relief against the night sky was nearly blinding, but she could still make out the face of the clock. It was as motionless as the street.

Turning back toward the square, Mama Lu found it not quite as empty as before. Mere inches away stood a dark, shadowy figure. Startled, Mama Lu stepped back quickly. When she moved, the reflected light from the white, stone of the cathedral spilled around her, revealing the figure's face. Wide-eyed with pain and fear, Madame Zoe stood before her.

Mama Lu's stomach lurched in response. The figure was nearly unrecognizable. Madame Zoe's face was ashen and rotting. String-like remnants of hair fell from beneath her faded head-wrap. Her eyes bulged with bloating pressure in a static glaze, staring intently at the cathedral's center spire. Her clothing was dirty and torn as if from a struggle, and she reeked of earthy mold.

Mama Lu's eyes were immediately drawn to Madame Zoe's mouth. Tightly closed, her lips were sewn shut with heavy, leather cord. Large stitches stretched from top to bottom preventing her mouth from moving at all. In some places, the skin was ripped and torn, rent by failed attempts to scream. In the resulting fissures, Mama Lu saw the cord was stitched not only through the lips, but through the gum line and in some places, even through the bone.

Mama Lu covered her own mouth in disbelief. "Who done dis?" she thought, just as Madame Zoe attempted to speak. Violently, she struggled against the rough, leather cord. Choking on her own fluids, she managed only the gurgling moan of a drowning victim. Blood seeped from the stitches, flowing down her chin in dark trials as tears filled her swollen eyes.

Shocked, Mama Lu slowly stepped backward onto the steps of the cathedral. Unable to divert her eyes from the leather cords, it took her several moments to notice other figures materializing in the darkness. One by one, thin, ashen faces with sunken, haunted eyes faded into view. Each frail figure was young, female, and mortally wounded in precisely the same way: throat slashed clean through from one side to the other. Mama Lu gasped in disbelief as she watched the crowd of dead girls grow in number behind Madame Zoe – forty, fifty, too many to count. Finally, Madame Zoe lifted her arms, stretching them out to either side in a grand display, as if taking a bow before the host of lifeless bodies.

Before she could curtsy, winds whipped around the square again and motion returned to the backdrop. Sheets of discarded newspaper blew in from the peripheral darkness, racing across the square, flattening against the corpses. As Mama Lu watched, more and more trash trailed in, stopping and stacking against the young girls until a great wall of newsprint and garbage separated her from the macabre scene. Soon, only Madame Zoe's eyes remained, fixed on the clock in the cathedral's center spire.

Angry with unexplainably guilt, Mama Lu was unable to watch any longer. Turning to re-enter the church she found the heavy doors missing. In their place, stood her refrigerator.

When Mama Lu snapped back to wakefulness, she was wearing her night dress and standing in the middle of her kitchen, shaking and sweating.

Chapter Thirteen

Doctor Prejean clicked his stainless steel, ball-point pen with nervous abandon as he looked over the patient's chart. Jane Doe 486 had been in his care since her arrival two days earlier, and he was still at his wit's end regarding her identity. She was found with no form of identification and no belongings but the rain-soaked clothes on her back. In two days' time, no one had phoned or been in to check on her, and an inquiry to the police department's missing persons division turned up a dead-end.

Her condition was equally baffling. A case unlike any Dr. Prejean ever saw, 486 was brought in by paramedics early in the morning, just before sun-up, on the stale end of a long and busy night shift. According to the report, she was found in the courtyard at Jackson Square by a passerby, certain she was dead. She was lying on her side in the pouring rain, stretched out on the stone pavement, completely non-responsive, eyes wide open.

Upon her arrival, the paramedics updated Doctor Prejean on the patient's condition. It was their conclusion she had been lying in the rain for quite some time. Her body temperature was dangerously low, and her breathing was shallow and labored. She had no apparent airway obstruction and circulation was normal. Aside from the obvious catatonic state, the only significant sign of distress exhibited by Jane Doe 486 was an elevated pulse, a condition which prompted Doctor Prejean to order a series of tests. So far, the results offered as much of a mystery as her identity.

Jane Doe 486's EKG confirmed an elevated heart rate, which, despite the administration of antihypertensives and beta blockers, continued to be a concern. An EEG ruled out head trauma and abnormalities in the brain, and x-rays showed no fractures in the skull or neck.

Doctor Prejean ordered a catheter and IV feeding with D5W fluids for the simple fact that 486's excessive heart rate was causing her to burn through calories like crazy. Despite her IV fluid intake and her static appearance, the patient's muscles were tense and rigid. She was beginning to show signs of contracture; her extremities were drawing up and turning in on themselves.

Doctor Prejean was baffled as to why 486's heart rate refused to stabilize. "It's like she's running a marathon in her mind," he thought. Closing the chart, he determined to leave her on the cardiac floor and on the heart monitor for one more day to see if her condition improved. If it did not, his only option would be the psych ward.

As the chart's cover fell closed, Doctor Prejean noticed a new scribbling near the printed name-label. If he was deciphering the script correctly, someone had written the name "Zoe" followed by a question mark. The pen stopped clicking.

"Kimmie?" called the doctor across the nurses' station without looking up. A dark-haired RN peeked out from behind the filing carousel. She was freshly awake, the caffeine from her second cup of the hospital's mediocre prepackaged brew just hitting its stride.

"It's Tammy," she answered.

Without apology, Doctor Prejean looked up from the chart to address her. "Did you write this?"

Having written countless bits of information on an equally countless number of charts since her shift began an hour ago, Tammy tried to conceal her disbelief the doctor had actually asked the question from across the room, expecting her to have any knowledge of what in blazes he was talking about. With a wide smile, she walked around the circular desk in the center of the station and took the folder from the doctor's hand.

"Nope, not my writing. It might have been Edith. She was on shift last night. She's still here if you want me to check."

The doctor's response was polite, though his expression read impatience, "If you don't mind?"

"Because I wasn't busy at all," thought Tammy, smiling and dropping the chart on the desk beside the doctor. Turning, she hurried off to the break room as he resumed clicking his pen behind her.

Over the next ten minutes, Doctor Prejean confirmed Edith had, indeed, written the name "Zoe" across the front of Jane Doe 486's chart.

"At least I think that's her name," she allowed. "I remember her from the Quarter. She's one of those Gypsy fortune tellers who do tarot readings down in the square at night. I've seen her there a couple of times, never got a reading though. I remember somebody calling her 'Madame Zoe.' I jotted it down on the front because I wasn't a hundred percent. Besides, even if she is 'Madame Zoe', who knows if that's her real name or just some persona?" Though Edith's recitation was delivered through a series of pauses, "ums", and smacking gum, the information was eventually relayed, resulting in the doctor's curious expression.

"It's a start," said Doctor Prejean. "Kimmie, can you follow up on this?"

Chapter Fourteen

Nalia could not recall ever feeling so relieved to see the sun rise. Little by little, the dawn's amber glow filtered through the sheer curtains until her bedroom was alive with morning light. Stiff and sore from muscle strain, Nalia slid to the bed's edge, her mind still reeling with thoughts of the old man and the spire. In the dark hours after the vision, Nalia was unable to return to a restful state of sleep. Hyper-aware of every noise, including her own heartbeat, she drifted in and out of consciousness, riding the fence between reality and dream. Each time she slipped across the line into shallow slumber, she awakened immediately, reaching for her throat to verify its integrity.

The sunlight was comforting. Demons of the darkness hid from the light of day, and Nalia breathed a deep sigh of relief at the notion. She left Queen Marie resting against the pillow while she dressed, still trying to shake the memories from her mind. The doll was a comfort in the long hours waiting for daylight; she always had been. Holding Queen Marie gave Nalia a tangible point of reference when the line between lucidity and sleep began to blur. It also kept her from pulling her hair out by the roots.

Nalia dressed as quickly as her sore muscles would allow, intentionally avoiding the mirror for fear she might glimpse the old man again. A few quick yoga poses helped release the tension in her body, but her mind was less willing to cooperate, and her eyes refused to fully open. The long night seemed sure to yield an even longer day, and Nalia couldn't bear to face it without caffeine. Gathering all the faculties she could manage, she took to the stairs where the smell of chicory coffee was already thick on the air.

Nalia was up prematurely, but from what she could ascertain, Mama Lu and Mr. John were already a step ahead of her. Their presence downstairs at this hour was unexpected, to say the least. Even if there were any merit to Nalia's fear Mama Lu wished to continue their uncomfortable conversation from last night, this was extraordinarily early.

When Nalia reached the foot of the stairs, she stopped dead in her tracks. The atmosphere in the kitchen was insanely heavy. Mr. John's brow was twisted with concern the likes of which Nalia had not seen since she was a girl, and though Mama Lu's back was turned, her posture was tense and rigid. Stepping just inside the doorway, Nalia could see the telephone's handset pressed firmly to the side of Mama Lu's face. There was a noticeable lack of conversation.

Quietly, Nalia stepped into the kitchen and up to the table, making eye contact as Mama Lu waited for a response on the line. Her coffee was cold and untouched. If nothing else was out of the ordinary, Nalia would still know the gravity of the situation by one simple fact - Mr. John had yet to smile. The man who was always overjoyed at the sight of his baby girl, no matter the circumstances, held the same stern face Nalia first saw from the foot of the stairs.

"Still no answer," Mama Lu said, finally breaking the silence as Nalia looked back and forth between them like a spectator at a tennis match. "All morning, no answer."

"Well, it's early yet," allowed Mr. John, attempting a reasonable explanation, knowing it amounted to little more than wishful thinking. When *the sight* told Mama Lu something was wrong, it was exactly that. If his gut hadn't told him his attempt to rationalize the situation was misguided, the look on Mama Lu's face certainly did.

"Somethin' is wrong, John, don't matter what time it is. I know it. I can feel it. Zoe's in some kind o' trouble, sure as I'm sittin' here."

Nalia recognized the name. "Madame Zoe, your Gypsy friend?" Mama Lu only nodded in response as she dialed the number again with trembling hands.

Mama Lu's eyes drifted toward the ceiling in an unfocused glaze as she waited once again for an answer on the other end of the line. Nalia looked at Mr. John who offered only a dismissive shake of his head. Slowly, he lifted his coffee cup to his lips and took a small sip. His cup, like Mama Lu's, was still full.

Feeling slightly more awake and decidedly more concerned, Nalia moved for the coffee pot and filled a travel mug with the time-seasoned brew. The slightly burned aroma made her wonder how long Mama Lu and Mr. John had been up.

"You want me to make up a fresh pot, baby girl?" asked Mr. John, seeming to snap from his trance. "Dat's been sittin' a while."

"I'm sure it's fine," replied Nalia before noticing the coffee's color was quite a bit darker than normal.

"Nothin'," interrupted Mama Lu, distressed. "Still no answer. Somethin' has happened."

"Or she ain't at home," John said, still wishing.

"Did you try her cell?" asked Nalia, trying to help him out.

"I don't have a cell numbed fo' her," Mama Lu said, "Only the house."

Mr. John pursed his lips in disbelief. "Why didn't you say so befo', woman?" he asked, pulling an outdated cellular device from his pocket. The man went to work activating a network of contacts the breadth of which Mama Lu and Nalia could only imagine. He was confident, with time, he could produce the information Mama Lu needed.

Nalia added a bit more creamer than usual to counter the strong flavor of the stale coffee. She was concerned for Madame Zoe but more so for Mama Lu. It was rare to see her rattled.

"So Madame Zoe is not at home? I don't understand why that's so important at this hour," Nalia offered in a hushed tone, as Mr. John and Mama Lu both had phones to their ears. Mr.

John sat back in his chair, crossed one knee over the other and held the flip-phone to his ear but away from his mouth as he replied.

"Yo' Mama Lu had a vision last night. Pretty vivid one."

"I was sleepwalking, John," Mama Lu interrupted distancing the phone from her lips in like manner. "You know how many times dat's happened befo'? Zero! Never. I'd say it was a lil' mo' than vivid. I'd say it was pretty serious, so stop tryin' to dismiss it. Shit! Still no answer. Excuse my language." She hung up the phone and rose to put the handset back on its base in the parlor.

Mr. John made eyes at Nalia but quickly cut away as his party picked up the phone. "Freddy, what you say dis mornin'? Yeah, I know what time it is. Listen, dis is important, I need a favor..." His voice trailed in Nalia's mind as she sat down at the table and waited for Mama Lu. Somewhere, a tiny piece of her mind was grateful for the morning's distraction. She certainly did not wish any ill will on Madame Zoe, or anyone else for that matter, but she was thankful Mama Lu's attention was shifted from berating her about her destiny.

When Mama Lu returned to the kitchen, her hand was tucked deep into her pocket, rubbing the twisted bit of High John root with reckless abandon. "We all have our Queen Marie," thought Nalia. The look in Mama Lu's eyes, however, told her the charm was providing very little comfort.

"Talk to me, Mama. Tell me what's happened," said Nalia as Mama Lu sat back down in front of her coffee.

"I don't know wha's happened, but Zoe's in trouble," she replied. "I saw her plain as day, but she couldn't tell me what was wrong. She couldn't tell me nothin'." She sipped the coffee and grimaced as she continued. "Somebody done hurt her somethin' serious. There's a lot of young girls been hurt too, or gon' be." Mama Lu pulled the hand from her pocket and tapped a stern finger repeatedly on the folded newspaper in the center of the table.

Nalia turned the Times-Picayune around until she could read the print. The paper was open to a page in the back where there was a small article underneath the heading "Body Found Off Bourbon". Nalia quickly skimmed the print. The story, which would have been front page news in other parts of the country, told of a young woman found dead behind a dumpster just off Bourbon Street. The article was vague on the particulars but mentioned a wound to the throat, and the phrase "obvious foul play". Nalia's hand instinctively went to her neck as memories of her own vision rushed to mind. She could almost feel the old man's breath behind her ear. She rubbed her throat back and forth absentmindedly, her fingertips finding solace in the unharmed flesh.

"Dat girl ain't the only one," said Mama Lu, producing Johnny the Conqueror from the pocket of her house-dress. "There's more, lots more. Or there's gon' be lots more. I seen 'em. Zoe showed 'em to me, but she couldn't speak. She couldn't tell me nothin' ' bout 'em, try as she might." Her voice cracked and trailed off as her eyes resumed their unfocused scanning of the ceiling.

The newspaper article did not reveal the victim's name. "Surely you don't think this is Madame Zoe," Nalia asked.

"No. No, dat ain't Zoe, but her fate may not be far from the same." Reluctant to share the grisly details of her vision, Mama Lu could not shake the image of the leather cord through Zoe's lips. She was no stranger to gruesome spectacles and was, in fact, adept in several forms of uniquely nasty torture – a product of the unbridled practices of her youth. But for a reason she could not explain, seeing her friend in such agony was hard to stomach. Madame Zoe was a kind, benevolent soul, sincere and trusting but far from naïve. Whoever harmed her was cunning and formidable. With a nervous twitch, Mama Lu rose to retrieve the phone again.

"Alright, get back to me," Mr. John said, finishing his conversation, flipping his phone closed and slipping it back in his pocket. His expression was grave as he glanced at the paper, then back at Nalia.

With Mama Lu out of the room, Nalia whispered her concern, "This is bad, isn't it?"

"Yo' Mama Lu's had the sight ever since I can remember," he said in a hushed tone. "She done seen so many visions, couldn't nobody begin to count. But I ain't never known one to have her up walkin' round the house in the middle o' the night wit'out knowin' what she doin'. She always got control o' the vision. Dis time the vision took control o' her. I'd say it's pretty serious."

"Yeah, it's not much fun when that happens," said Nalia, with shying eyes. "She's never had it affect her like this before, not even in ritual?"

"You heard her," Mr. John shrugged, "Never. She been rattled lately tho', says everthin' is diff'rent."

"What do you mean?"

Mr. John hesitated, shifting his gaze from Nalia to his coffee cup and back. When he spoke, his tone was more hushed than before, and his eyes watched the door for Mama Lu's return. "She says ever since the sight started settlin' on you, her abilities are diff'rent. She can't see things as clear as she used to... sometimes not at all. It's like the sight's pullin' away from her."

An uncomfortable wave of guilt hit Nalia square in the gut. She would rather have continued her argument with Mama Lu, defending her right to choose her destiny, than hear *the sight* might be leaving Mama Lu for her.

"You see, baby girl, the sight is not a possession you can hold. It has its own energy, its own will. It'll grow to know you jus' like you grow to know it... like a close friend. It becomes part of you."

Nalia was confused. "If it's part of Mama Lu, then why is it leaving?"

"Oh it won't leave altogether. When the sight moves from one person to the next, it never truly leaves the first. Just like a father givin' his daughter away on her weddin' day, he'll always hold a part o' her in his heart, even tho' she belongs to another. But jus' like dat daughter, the sight generally waits to be given away, to be released. Dat's why the rite of transference is so sacred, and dat's why yo' Mama Lu is concerned. The sight is drawn to you so strong it's startin' to exercise its own will. It's leavin' her wit'out bein' released. She's okay wit' dat... long as you the one it leaves her fo'. But if you gon' reject it..." His sentence was cut short by a jazzy ringtone that made him jump. Reaching into his pocket, he flipped open his phone and quickly checked the number before accepting the call. "Whacha got fo' me?" was his greeting as he sat forward in the chair and motioned for Nalia to fetch him a pen.

Before she could reach the drawer beside the refrigerator, Mama Lu returned with a pencil and a near-spent pad of Post-it notes. She dropped them on the table in front of Mr. John and waited impatiently.

"Uh huh," affirmed Mr. John. "Yup, got it," he said, scribbling a number across the small pad and sliding it across the table. "Thanks Freddy. Owe you one? Why don't we jus' say you owe me one less?"

Mama Lu was already dialing when Mr. John re-pocketed his phone and winked at Nalia. Both watched Mama Lu with anticipation. Almost instantly they overheard a muffled electronic voice through the handset as Mama Lu held it away from her face in frustration. The automated announcement verified the number and offered the option of leaving a voicemail. Wiping her brow heavily, Mama Lu paced back into the hallway leaving a concerned message for a friend she feared would never hear it.

Nalia and Mr. John exchanged looks of desperation in silence. Mr. John saw no need to continue their discussion of *the sight*. He sensed her discomfort and desire to avoid the subject.

Validating his hunch, Nalia used the opportunity to make an escape.

"I'll see you guys at the shop," she said, collecting her belongings. She offered Mr. John an awkward, crooked smile before heading for the door. "I'll take the St. Charles in again, sounds like you guys might be here a while." Mr. John fingered the rim of his cup and nodded without looking up. In a moment Nalia was gone and Mama Lu stood in frightened silence at the kitchen doorway.

"Straight to voicemail," she said when she could speak without choking. "Didn't even ring. You sure dis is the right number?"

Mr. John opened his palms and shrugged. "Not a hun'red percent, I guess, but it's all I got. Freddy seemed pretty sure."

"We gon' have to go find her, John."

"She still live in dat ol' house in Gentilly?"

"Far as I know," said Mama Lu with a deep sigh. "Get yo' keys, I'll go get dressed."

Chapter Fifteen

Nalia barely noticed the clacking of the street car's electric motor. She was still pondering Mr. John's marriage analogy. "So the sight wants to skip the wedding ceremony and run off to Vegas with me... fabulous," she thought. Try as she might to lessen the burden on her mind, she could not dismiss the situation's gravity. No matter how she resisted, *the sight* seemed determined to manifest itself within her, and considering Mr. John's explanation, she felt even more trapped. Nalia simply couldn't bear the thought of Mama Lu losing her power. The notion was like New Orleans without jazz; she couldn't imagine one without the other. "The sight is part of who she is," thought Nalia. "If it leaves her for me..."

Passengers stirred as the street car made its stop at Carondelet and Canal, pulling Nalia from her daze. She gathered her belongings with hope the walk would clear her mind. Before Nalia could rise from her seat, a skinny girl with short dark hair and metal music screaming from her Skull Candy earbuds strode past, heading for the rear exit. Nalia did not recall seeing the girl board and was sure she'd never noticed her on the morning commute before. The girl walked with a quick, determined pace. She wore all black and carried an olive green, military style shoulder bag. Her hair was spiked with hot pink highlights and buzzed short over one ear, revealing an all-too-realistic tattoo of a black widow spider climbing her neck. She wore three silver rings in her bottom lip, heavy eyeliner, and a brooding demeanor, but it was her tee-shirt that caught Nalia's attention. It was cut to rough edges at the neck, sleeves, and hem, and featured an all-over print of white lettering advertising Marie Laveau's Voodoo House, a novelty and occult shop a few blocks over on Conti Street. In the center of the tee, between the lettering, was a pair of eyes that seemed to watch Nalia as they passed.

A shiver ran up her spine, shooting goose bumps down both arms as the dream pierced Nalia's consciousness again. Distracted by her conversation with Mr. John, she had all but forgotten about the vision. The image of Marie Laveau's haunting eyes stunned Nalia to the point of nearly missing the stop. Unlike any vision before, Marie Laveau seemed to stand out, separated from the unfolding scene. Nalia was sure the spirit of Marie Laveau saw her. Somehow, through time and space, through the veil of the spirit world, Marie Laveau looked right at her. The image birthed a crippling sense of vulnerability, like standing naked in the middle of a busy street, exposed and unprotected.

With the tee-shirt and the memory triggering a state of desperation she couldn't shake, Nalia scrambled to her feet and exited the street car quickly, bound for Decatur. As she walked, Nalia tried to occupy her mind with the sights, sounds, and smells she loved so much about the city's early morning bustle, anything to assuage the jitters. Despite her efforts, the lingering paranoia proved spitefully persistent. She could feel a nearly tangible shadow clinging to her, watching her.

People on the street stared as she passed. Eager to avoid their lengthy gazes, Nalia kept her head down but couldn't resist occasionally lifting her eyes to see if passersby were still leering – they were. As if their eyes were strangely drawn to her, their heads turned revealing scowls of judgment and condemnation. Agitation besting her, Nalia quickened her pace.

Approaching Jackson Square, she caught a glimpse of the cathedral on the far side, its tall, stone spires stretching high into the morning mist. Though the clock was not moving, Nalia heard it steadily ticking in her head, and a distinct memory of Madame Zoe swept briefly through her mind.

It was near Christmas and just after mass when Mama Lu introduced them. They were standing in the rear of the sanctuary, near the statue of Joan of Arc when Zoe made a comment Nalia had forgotten until now. When Madame Zoe extended her hand, Nalia felt the same paranoia, as if the entire cathedral suddenly turned to look at her. The sensation lasted only a moment before their hands met and the vision hit: Madame Zoe sitting alone in the rain, staring at the clock on the face of the cathedral's center spire. At the time, Nalia wasn't exactly sure what happened, but it was obvious Zoe knew. Pulling her hand away, Madame Zoe turned to Mama Lu with wide eyes and a slightly-crooked, Cheshire grin. She gazed down at her open palm like she'd been burned, then back to Mama Lu with parted lips.

"She drew energy from me," Madame Zoe said, before pulling Mama Lu aside for a brief, private chat.

Later that evening, Mama Lu explained only the gifted could draw a seer's energy and asked if Nalia saw or felt anything when they touched.

"Nothing," Nalia lied. She knew what it meant to draw energy, but she did not comprehend what it meant for her future. Nor did she want to.

As Nalia approached The Doll Maker, her heart rate accelerated to match her pace. Paranoia became anxiety, and passing the newly-leased shop next door, anxiety became maddening fear. She could not find her keys fast enough. Her breathing quickened and her throat closed as if an unseen hand was tightening its grip around her neck. The eyes of the city stared her down with vigor. Pedestrians, merchants, birds, squirrels, and insects – even the leaves on the trees and bricks on the buildings seemed to sprout eyes and glare at her. Nalia's hand shuffled the contents of her bag in a desperate race against the capacity of her lungs. She would be able to breathe if she could just get inside and close the door. Frantically she searched, her lungs burning for air until finally, she heard the distinctive jingle of her keys. The sound was like sweet salvation.

Nalia had the shop's key nearly in the door when her field of vision blackened along the edges. Dizziness filled her head as the darkness rapidly pursued. The last thing she saw before the world faded away was the taunting plastic sign in the door's glass pane – "CLOSED". Her body was numb before she hit the concrete.

———————————

The air was dank and earthy. The ringing in Nalia's ears gradually faded, trumped by the steady chirping of insects and the distant chattering of heron. As feeling returned to her body, Nalia noticed the rhythmic rise and fall of the world around her, and as her vision grew clear, sunlight stung her eyes, strobing through a canopy of thick, bald cypress foliage. The gentle lapping of water joined the symphony of bugs and birds as Nalia tried, with difficulty, to sit up. The boat she was in nearly tipped twice during the process. Stretching her arms and gripping the sides of the small vessel tightly in surprise, Nalia took in her surroundings. Decatur Street had vanished, and with it, the straggling crowds of leering onlookers occupying its sidewalks. Nalia was alone, stranded in a small craft in the middle of a vast marsh. She found no visible shoreline, only heavy patches of vegetation sprouting from the water through a soupy mist. Though the Quarter's heavy foot-traffic, brick structures, and wrought-iron fixtures were gone, one familiar sensation lingered – the eerie certainty of being watched.

Nalia was curious. The boat moved at a slow and steady pace with no visible means of propulsion. There was no paddle for rowing and no motor. The gentle breeze was hardly strong enough to sustain the vessel's forward motion, yet the boat continued diligently on course, gliding across the surface of the mossy water, guided by an unseen force. Reeds scraped the hull as the boat rocked around the stumps of dead trees where gnats and dragonflies danced on the air. Nalia was surprised she was not being eaten alive by the dense mosquito population. Though she read they could smell flesh over fifty yards away, this swarm seemed unaware of her presence. "Not going to complain about that," Nalia thought as the boat drifted the length of a spider-infested log.

Little by little, the swamp's wildlife made itself known, beginning with several water snakes that seemed eager to accompany the boat along its path. As Nalia rounded a particularly dense patch of reeds and debris, she was greeted by seven turtles sunning their shells in a straight line atop a downed tree. Just beyond, the eyes of an alligator surfaced and sank.

Nalia was just beginning to think land could not be far off when a crooked shoreline appeared in the fog. Suddenly all her questions about where she was going and why were answered; the shadowy silhouette of Madame Toulouse stood on the bank.

As the small craft bumped against solid ground, Nalia struggled to steady herself and stand. With her anxiety finally fading, she stepped out of the boat and toward the darkened figure. Though the silhouette was demure, it carried the air of a queen standing ten feet tall with an army of warriors awaiting her command.

As the scent of lilac and vanilla filled the damp air, Nalia felt the warm sensation of a firm embrace surrounding her body. In life, Madame Toulouse was fond of a perfumed body cream made from essential oils and Shea butter. Lilac and vanilla was her signature fragrance. Nalia closed her eyes and breathed deeply, allowing a sweet memory to carry the world away.

She could not have been more than eight. It was a warm, sunny afternoon, and the soothing scent of her grandmother's perfume cream was pronounced in the midday heat. Madame Toulouse wore a green, ribbon-trimmed bergère hat adorned with tiny, ladybug decorations she'd purchased from a craft booth at St. Anthony's annual bizarre – no doubt made by the children's ministry. She took a very young Nalia by the hand

and led her down the pathways of Audubon Zoo. As the pair
approached the white tiger enclosure, one of the great beasts let
out a sudden, colossal roar. Startled, Nalia began to cry.

Madame Toulouse knelt beside the child and wiped the tears
from her tiny eyes. Taking her firmly by the shoulders, she
smiled reassuringly and said, "You got nothin' to be 'fraid of
chil', long as you wit' me."

Nalia remembered her fear fading in that moment, as if fear
itself was afraid of Madame Toulouse. The elder woman's eyes
twinkled as she took Nalia in a firm embrace, the scent of lilac
and vanilla marking the moment.

Nalia was sure she saw the same reassuring twinkle in the
eyes of the shadow as it turned and slipped along a cleared
pathway in the underbrush. Without hesitation, Nalia followed.

The landscape soon became unusually rocky, not at all what
Nalia expected so close to the marsh. Large, moss-covered
stones rose from the damp soil as the grade grew steep. Though
Nalia experienced some difficulty traversing the path, the figure
in front seemed to glide along with ease, floating just above the
ground.

Higher and higher they climbed until the stones became a
rugged staircase winding along the edge of a vertical slope.
Silently, the figure led Nalia up the stairs until she could look
out over the treetops into a dense, rolling sea of fog. The wind
blustered as they climbed, carrying a chill down from the
summit. A foul stench on the air and an uncomfortable presence
made Nalia shiver.

"You got nothing' to be 'fraid of chil', long as you wit' me."

Soon, the treetops sank into the mist leaving a clear view of a
quilted, mackerel sky against the fiery sunset. The sight was
breathtakingly beautiful, but just as its peace began to calm
Nalia's spirit, another icy blast ripped down the mountain. Nalia
took to reciting her grandmother's reassuring words, and by the
time they reached the wide, flat top of the structure, it was
nearly a mantra.

Gliding between two large stones, the shadow of Madame Toulouse topped the edge and continued on to a small clearing outside a familiar iron fence as night began to fall. She stopped just shy of the stone archway with the high gates.

"Here again," said Nalia, shaking inside. As she approached the shadow hesitantly, a tingling sensation crawled across her throat. "I don't want to go back in there," she said. "Last time..."

"I tol' you befo' chil', can't nothin' in there hurt you."

"I don't understand what you're trying to show me in there."

"I show you nothin'," said Madame Toulouse. "It's him dat's showin' you what you need to see, even though he don't want to."

"Him? The old man? You know about the old man?" Madame Toulouse nodded as Nalia went on with a furrowed brow. "If he doesn't want to, why is he showing me?"

"He ain't willin' it over to you, chil'. You drawin' it from him. The sight is showin' you his soul."

Nalia was stunned. She stood stone-still, unsure of what to say or even feel. She didn't want *the sight*. She didn't want to see other people's souls, least of all the creepy old man with the top hat and the terrifying red eyes, but it seemed now, more than ever, she had no choice in the matter. She would not surrender without a fight. "What if I don't want to see his soul?" she demanded. "What if I don't want the sight at all?"

"The sight is merely a reflection of the truth, chil'," replied her grandmother, calmly. "If you didn't want it, I wouldn't be here. Now it's time fo' you to face yo' fear and do what needs doin', befo' it's too late."

"Too late?" asked Nalia. "Too late for what?"

Madame Toulouse did not respond, but simply pointed to the arch. Nalia was frustrated and afraid, but her only way out was through the gates. Turning toward them, she barely convinced her feet to move. With timid steps, she approached, reciting her mantra in a desperate attempt to convince herself there was nothing to fear. The tingle in her throat screamed otherwise.

When the gate swung open, Nalia stopped cold. Beads of sweat gathered on her brow and palms as the frigid wind nearly turned them to ice.

"G'on, chil'," said Madame Toulouse. "You ain't the only one dat's afraid."

With a deep breath, Nalia stepped under the arch and onto the sidewalk. She cautiously made her way between the stone benches and down the path. One by one, the lampposts flickered to life as a blanket of darkness rolled in on a heavy fog, veiling the distant stone spire. Instantly Nalia noticed the difference. This fog was not like the mist of the swamp, no simple weather phenomenon. It was being controlled, like a giant curtain, drawn to hide the courtyard and the familiar sinister presence accompanying it.

Within moments, Nalia's visibility was near zero, but her heightened inner eye told her she was near the spire. A chilling memory of the old man's blade across her throat gave Nalia pause, but the words of her grandmother were comforting, "Can't nothin' in there hurt you. Face yo' fears and do what needs doing'."

Nalia desperately tried to focus her mind, to be strong and resolute as Madame Toulouse instructed, but the fog hindered her concentration. She recalled the difficult, frustrating months of summer when her vision was, at best, a faded tapestry of blurred color. During that time Nalia often thought it would be better to not see at all, than to have the world displayed before her, tauntingly out of view. The heavy fog veiled her adversary in much the same way, keeping Nalia unnervingly hyper-vigilant.

"I would feel a lot more at ease if I could just see," she thought.

No sooner than the notion entered her mind, Nalia experienced a peculiar sensation. Her skin seemed to tighten against her muscles and every nerve ending in her extremities began to tingle. Warmth radiated from her belly countering the icy breeze, challenging it. Her spirit detected conflict – a contest of wills. She became suddenly aware of her surroundings with a new perspective. She sensed not only the physical realm, but emotions, intentions, and energy.

Like a scared animal, the fog began to retreat, rising into the night sky and dissipating. Nalia was taken aback. She felt her spirit shift, a strange almost otherworldly sensation; she *knew* she was commanding the fog. With a cleansing breath she closed her eyes and centered her mind, focusing solely on the soupy haze. She visualized it vanishing, revealing the old man hiding in its shadow. But the more she concentrated, the more she sensed the struggle growing within. The fog was resisting.

At first, Nalia became angry. Eager to regain control, she increased her effort to will the fog away, but when exercising her own consciousness, her thoughts became scattered and power slipped beyond her grasp. The fog triumphantly settled back to the ground as the courtyard's sinister presence asserted itself in Nalia's mind with arrogance.

Just as she began to entertain the voice of defeat, Nalia heard a different whisper – Mr. John's. "The sight is not a possession you can hold. It has its own energy, its own will." Nalia realized she did not command the fog at all, but simply allowed *the sight* to control it through her. With another cleansing breath, she cleared her mind. Instead of trying to gain control, she focused on letting it go. Soon the warm, tingling sensation returned to her body like a warrior answering the call to battle.

The fog, reluctant to submit, held its ground. Nalia felt the struggle raging in her head, but refused to allow conflict a footing. Instead, she let her conscious mind embrace her spirit in surrender.

Gradually, the fog lost its claim on the ground and on Nalia. Slowly it rose and with it, Nalia's confidence. As she watched the mist grow thinner, her spirit swelled with power. For the first time, Nalia realized *the sight* was working through her, exercising its will over the elements around her, but it was also listening to her desires and granting her requests. She was more than a mere conduit, she was a partner. "It'll grow to know you jus' like you grow to know it... like a close friend. It becomes part of you," the words of Mr. John whispered again.

As the last of the lingering mist faded away, the stone spire came into full view, rising high into the dark sky. Near the top, clinging flat against the face of the tower, was the old man. He was upside down, his neck stretched and twisted unnaturally, staring at Nalia from his lofty perch. His eyes were laser-fixed, filled with anger and something else Nalia read as reservation.

"You ain't the only one dat's afraid." Nalia remembered the voice of Madame Toulouse, but the spark of confidence it inspired lasted only seconds before the unfolding vision gave her pause. Slowly, the old man began to descend the spire, crawling head-down against its face like one of Stoker's creatures. The unnatural sight caught Nalia off-guard, allowing fear to grab her by the throat. She felt the struggle clashing again inside, her advantage slipping away.

Sensing her weakness, the old man quickened his pace. His eyes abandoned their glaze of reservation, growing cold and confident. Nalia felt her power waning as her body succumbed to the terror clawing at the doorway of her mind. Her heart pounded, and her airway closed until breathing was laborious. A sinister smile crept across the old man's face.

In that moment, Nalia felt the spark inside her fizzle and die. Staring at the old man's pompous grin, she became a five-year-old child, weak and powerless against her aggressor. Darkness weighed down on her like a lead coat as the despair of her childhood raped her consciousness. Her spirit dropped like a stone into a vast, black chasm. Escape seemed impossible, salvation hopeless. Petrified, Nalia stood at the base of the spire awaiting her eminent fate as the old man approached the bottom.

Like a reptile, he crawled toward the ground, his long nails gripping the stone like claws. His eyes were steadily fixed on Nalia, all traces of fear gone. Reaching the ground, the old man's body contorted in bizarre fashion as he stepped off the spire and found his footing. The bones of his spine cracked like rifle-fire as he stood erect, stretching his form tall like the tower behind him. With a confident stride he approached Nalia, dropping his chin and staring from beneath his top hat.

By the time the old man reached her, Nalia could not breathe. Though she could not will her limbs to move, her body trembled violently as if overcome by a seizure. The old man was close enough for Nalia to see every white whisker on his scraggly chin. A wintery cold radiated from his body, and his breath smelled of death. He fixated on Nalia's neck, greedily longing for her tender flesh, a ravenous animal ready to feed. With a twisted fascination he lifted his arm, extending a filthy hand from the sleeve of his weathered coat. His long nails found the delicate skin beneath Nalia's earlobe as he drew a heavy breath of anticipation. Slowly, he trailed his dirty fingers down her jawbone and onto her neck where he applied enough pressure for his nails to break the skin.

Nalia's racing heartbeat stopped. Tears streamed down her cheeks as she sensed the muscles in the old man's arm tighten with purpose. She knew with a simple exertion of force he would slash her throat, ending her life. Scenes from her childhood swirled across her mind like a kaleidoscope – horrifying visions of the green-eyed beast and the twin demons who violated her very soul and left her for dead while her mother looked the other way. She was powerless, empty, and alone. Paralyzed with fear, she closed her eyes and waited in her darkened world for the end to come.

Then she felt it. It was not the sharp pain across her throat she expected, but a flame of freedom somewhere deep within her gut accompanied by the voice of Madame Toulouse. "You got nothin' to be 'fraid of chil', long as you wit' me." The words from a long-forgotten trip to the zoo resonated with new meaning, and suddenly heat began coursing through Nalia's veins like a river raging over rocks. Remembering how the fog rose at her command, Nalia felt the child inside her step aside, overshadowed by a strong, confident woman. Fear of death held no power over one who had walked through the veil and returned. She felt her grandmother's energy rise tall within her. Her body tingled once again as she sensed the battle of wills thunder back to action. Truth waged war against lie, and Nalia felt the old man withdraw his hand. Her mind's eye could see his fear swelling like a tidal surge. Darkness began to flee, and Nalia's world brightened with every breath entering her grateful lungs. "I'm a survivor," she thought, opening her eyes and locking them on the old man. "I will never be a victim again."

Fear sparked in the man's eyes as his head jerked back in shock. When Nalia met his gaze, she saw into the very core of his soul. As she stared, the air around them shattered with a deafening sound like the thundering roar of cannon fire. A piercing, high-pitched tone quickly followed as brilliant, white light consumed the courtyard, dizzying Nalia into a state of confusion.

With her surroundings obliterated, vertigo propelled Nalia through the blinding void until the smell of dust, mingled with spices and incense, righted her faculties. The image of a red, velvet tablecloth lit by candles had scarcely emerged from the emptiness when a voice Nalia instinctively knew belonged to Marie Laveau spoke into her mind.

"Don't think I can't see you, chil'."

Chapter Sixteen

Mama Lu was no longer concealing Johnny the Conqueror. She held the twisted root in the palm of her hand, feverishly thumbing it smooth as Mr. John's tired, old truck grumbled its way north to Gentilly. The area recovered well after the flood. Although dealt a lesser blow than the ninth ward, it still required its fair share of rebuilding. Unlike other high-profile areas, Gentilly received no media coverage and very little assistance. No "Habitat for Humanity tee-shirt-sporting rock stars" or A-list celebrities swung hammers for film crews in this community. The residents of Gentilly were left to rebuild on their own, but the neighbors served each other well. Those blessed with more aided the less fortunate. Madame Zoe fell into the latter category. Living alone with better years behind her, Madame Zoe proved no match for the repairs her home required. While her profession made some wary, a few neighbors came to her rescue, helping out when they could. Despite their efforts, the house was still in need of some attention.

Mama Lu sat silently in the passenger's seat of the old truck as it rattled up the street. She had not spoken a word the entire drive. Her mind was focused and sharp, but her spirit was heavy. She searched desperately for a connection to Madame Zoe, anything that would allow *the sight* to flow. Nothing.

She could feel *the sight* leaving her and for a brief moment, Mama Lu's fear shifted from Zoe to herself. She would not be as fortunate as Madame Toulouse, able to realize the full potential of her power even after passing it on. That kind of enlightenment only came when bloodlines were involved. Mama Lu was not a blood descendant of her mentor. Though she could not determine to what degree, Mama Lu knew *the sight* would leave her. It was a certainty. She already felt it slipping away, leaving her vulnerable. The thought made her shudder.

The feeling lasted only long enough for Mama Lu to identify and dismiss it. She could not afford to entertain distraction. Madame Zoe needed her complete attention.

"There it is, John," she said with an anxious breath. "Dat's the house."

Mr. John idled the old Chevrolet to the curb near the end of the walk outside the simple, single story, white structure. The truck's door creaked when Mama Lu opened it and stepped onto the cracked walk. She stood in silence for a moment staring at the house, focusing her energy, desperate to feel something – anything. With drifting eyes and stifled breath she shook her head as a defiant tear escaped captivity.

From the other side of the truck Mr. John slammed the heavy door and looked around. The neighborhood was quiet. Two houses down, an elderly woman sat on her small porch watching her grandchildren play in the yard. The woman bristled at the sight of Mama Lu and sat to the edge of her rocking chair, squinting and staring. Her gaze fixed, she instructed the children to go inside. They argued but the old woman insisted, offering no explanation. With anxious effort, the woman stood and followed them indoors where Mr. John was sure he saw her watching from the window.

"You sure dis is it?" asked Mr. John, walking around the front of his truck, sliding his hand over the warm hood. "I thought it was a lil' further down."

"Dis is it," she whispered, "I remember."

The gravity of the situation hit Mr. John hard when he noticed Mama Lu's arm. It was not shaking with rhythmic motion indicating she was rubbing the twisted root; it was trembling.

"Zoe ain't here," she said as they started up the walk. "I can't feel her. Can't feel nothin'."

As they stepped onto the porch, Mr. John knew she was right. Noticing the full mailbox, he entertained a sobering thought. If Mama Lu couldn't feel Madame Zoe's spirit, the gravest of circumstances was certainly a possibility.

"You think we ought to go inside, jus' to be sure?" he asked. Mama Lu answered with the faintest nod he'd ever seen.

Mr. John was not surprised when a ring of the doorbell and several forceful knocks produced no result. The door was locked and a quick search under the mat and in the concrete planter proved futile. Resigned to his only alternative, Mr. John motioned for Mama Lu to watch his back while he removed a pair of tiny rods from his pocket.

Mama Lu slipped to the edge of the porch and leaned against a post, keeping an eye on the neighborhood while Mr. John went to work on the locks. A glare in the direction of the elderly woman's window resulted in a hurried pull of the drapes. Mama Lu would have smiled with satisfaction if her anxiety allowed. Instead, she turned her attention to several young teens riding bicycles up the street. With a bit of focused energy, she made herself and Mr. John virtually invisible to the group's passing eyes. Her talent was not gone yet, she thought. Moments later, Mr. John bested the locks and turned the knob.

"I want you to wait outside while I check dis out," said Mr. John.

Mama Lu responded with a look he could not discern. It was either defiance or disassociation, he couldn't decide. Nevertheless, he cracked the door and called out for Zoe, expecting no response. When none came, he stepped inside.

The first thing Mr. John noticed was the smell. The front room was mildly perfumed with the lingering scent of patchouli. He breathed a gentle sigh of relief at the home's pleasant aroma. Mama Lu collected the mail and followed him inside.

A lamp was on in the corner, but the house was decidedly quiet. Mama Lu stayed in the parlor while Mr. John moved from room to room calling for Madame Zoe and listening to his own echo. In the kitchen he found the dishes neatly tucked away with the exception of a single, unwashed wine glass left on the countertop next to an ashtray with two crushed butts.

Zoe's bed was neatly made but several scarves and two dresses, still on their hangers, lay across the top quilt. The closet's sliding door was wide open revealing many pairs of shoes and long outfits hanging next to an empty set of stowed luggage. On the bedside table, a half glass of water stood next to a full bottle of prescription medication for high blood pressure. There were no recognizable signs of foul play or struggle. From what Mr. John could tell, Zoe simply stepped out with every intention of returning.

When the bathroom and hall closet produced more of the same mundane clues, Mr. John made his way back to the parlor. He watched from the doorway while Mama Lu brushed her fingers across several of Madame Zoe's personal effects, eyes shut in concentration. She settled on a small, walnut picture frame containing a photograph of Madame Zoe and herself taken several years earlier in the square outside the cathedral. A chilling vision of her friend with taut, leather stitches running through her mouth raced across Mama Lu's mind. The army of young women with open throats stretched out beside her on either side. Mama Lu shuddered but still felt no connection to Zoe's spirit whatsoever. Defeated, she set the photo back down.

Just before the frame made contact with the table, Mama Lu saw the picture fade. A dark shadow fell across the photo forming an ashen skull where Zoe's face had been and for only a moment, a terrified set of eyes appeared deep in the skull's sockets, alive with desperation.

"We in the wrong place," said Mama Lu, whipping her head around, "We need to be checking the hospitals."

Mr. John produced his keys, twirled them around his index finger and slapped them into the palm of his hand. He had already opened the front door when he looked back and found Mama Lu on her knees in the middle of the parlor. All the color was gone from her cheeks and sweat poured like rivers down her face.

"You havin' a vision?" called Mr. John, hurrying to her side. "You know where she at?"

"It's not Zoe," replied Mama Lu, gasping for air, "Somethin's wrong with Nalia."

Chapter Seventeen

"Miss?"

The voice floated through Nalia's brain like white noise, barely recognizable. Darkness still held a death grip on her vision, and Nalia wasn't sure if she was awake or dreaming. Barely conscious, she struggled to grasp any connection to reality. Fragments of thought fell like raindrops on a window, occasionally linking together into random patterns but ultimately blurring the bigger picture.

All at once, she became aware of the ringing – a high-pitched tone like the feedback of overdriven guitars through a wall of amplifiers. It was painful.

"Miss?"

The voice washed through again, distorted and distant. Nalia wasn't quite sure it was really even there. She wasn't sure of anything.

With the softness of a sunrise, light began to pool in the center of her field of vision. It moved like gentle waves lapping at a shoreline, growing brighter with each pass. Soon, the light began to sting, joining the high-pitched ring to create tremendous pressure inside Nalia's head. Intensifying, the light sparkled and spilled around a darkened void moving side to side, forward and back again.

"Miss, can you hear me?"

The voice was definitely there, audible and intelligible if only just, and the darkness between the light began to take human form. Someone was speaking. As the shadow materialized, Nalia identified facial features: moving lips, a nose, eye sockets, and suddenly the eyes of Marie Laveau.

Don't think I can't see you, chil'.

Nalia's entire body jerked like she'd touched live voltage, and instantly, the world was clear. For a moment, she had no idea who she was, where she was, or who was standing over her. Dropped into daylight from darkness with total amnesia, Nalia was terrified. She knew only two things for certain: her head was pounding, and her fear must be evident because the man kneeling before her suddenly moved back and put up his hands in surrender.

"Take it easy, Miss," he said in a reassuring voice, "You're going to be fine. Can you tell me your name?"

It took a moment but her thoughts finally gathered into a useful pattern. "Nalia," she said. The word formed perfectly in her mind but her tongue managed only a labored slur. "Nalia Deminy," she continued, better this time but still not perfect. She felt a gentle hand on her chin and watched anxiously as the man held up a single finger.

"Can you follow my finger with your eyes?"

Nalia tried, but the movement seemed to create more pressure in the back of her head. It was more comfortable to just close her eyes and rest.

"No, stay with me. Keep your eyes open."

As her thoughts became clearer, Nalia was able to discern her location but still could not identify the man speaking or determine why she was so willing to blindly follow his instruction. Perhaps it had something to do with his eyes – the most beautiful blue pools she had ever seen. "Dreamy" was the first word to cross Nalia's mind, a word she had not entertained in a long while.

Cold was the next sensation to return. The chill of hard concrete against her back was sobering. Self-awareness followed, bringing with it a wave of embarrassment. The presence of the attractive young male only made matters worse. Nalia felt her cheeks flush as she tried to sit up.

"Whoa! Wait a minute, Miss," the man protested, "Not sure you should be moving. Let's just wait for the paramedics."

Beautiful, he's called the paramedics.

"I'm fine," said Nalia, leaning over onto one elbow then pulling herself into a sitting position. Immediately, she knew it was a bad idea but wasn't about to let it show, at least not voluntarily. Try as she might to hide it, her unsteadiness betrayed her.

With his hands on her shoulders, the young man examined Nalia's head. "Well, there's not a lot of blood. That's got to be a good sign, but you had a pretty nasty fall."

Good looks aside, Nalia began to feel slightly uncomfortable with the stranger's attention. "Who exactly are you, again?" she asked bluntly.

"Jack Haufmann," he answered, still examining her scalp. "I guess you can call me your new neighbor. I am assuming you work here, given the keys I found on your face."

Oh God, kill me now!

Nalia closed her eyes again, this time in an effort to make the whole world disappear, but the image of Jack's rugged face would not leave her mind. The stubble along his jawline was perfect and his skin was smooth, like a rose petal.

"Nalia is a pretty name," she heard in a voice like flowing honey. When she opened her eyes, she was staring into his – like gazing at the crystal Caribbean Sea. Strangely, Nalia felt her body's tension melting away. The sensation caught her off-guard.

"Thank you," she managed.

"Deminy is the name of the owner, right? Lucia Deminy? I didn't know she had a daughter."

"The one and only," replied Nalia, "Wait, what? You know Mama Lu?"

"We haven't met yet, but I'm looking forward to it. She has quite a reputation," said Jack with a raised eyebrow and an excited smile. "I did a little research when I leased the building, found out who my neighbors were going to be."

A nerve pinged in Nalia's spine as her defense mechanisms sparked to life. With her body stiffening, Nalia felt herself inch backward, involuntarily.

"Well that didn't sound creepy at all, did it?" chuckled Jack, trying to set her at ease. "Sorry, I didn't mean to come off as some kind of stalker. It's just what I do... research, I mean. I'm a writer, I look up everything." Jack presented an awkward smile, affording Nalia a shallow sigh of relief. "I didn't find any mention of you though," he continued, "The strikingly beautiful, yet mysterious daughter."

Nalia's cheeks burned a deeper shade of red. "Yes, the mysterious and clumsy daughter with an affinity for sidewalks."

Jack laughed and Nalia let down her guard a little more.

Even his laugh is adorable.

"To be honest, when I saw you go down I thought you were drunk. I figured it was a bit early to be tying one on, but then again, this is New Orleans. Do you have some sort of freakish medical condition or something?"

Instantly, Nalia's walls went back up, and her limbs grew rigid. Her mind churned up distant memories of grade-school bullies who took twisted pleasure from others' misfortune. Affronted, her voice found a cutting tone, "I get dizzy sometimes. It doesn't happen often."

Jack tried to apologize, but the sound of sirens distracted them both. In a matter of minutes the opportunity was lost and EMT's had Nalia's attention. Jack watched as they helped her into the back of the ambulance and examined her head.

Between the rapid questions and blinding pen-lights, Nalia managed to steal a look at Jack. He was leaning against a post, arms folded with one hand on his chin, a look of genuine concern filling his azure eyes. He was a little rough around the edges, but he meant well. Those eyes didn't lie. With the morning sun shining on his bright white shirt, he almost looked angelic, Nalia thought.

Jack listened intently to the paramedics' assessment, and when the decision was made to take Nalia in for x-rays, he stepped up for a word.

"Would you like for me to go with you?" he asked. "I don't usually leave my grandfather alone for long periods of time, but I'm sure..."

"I'll be fine," Nalia interrupted, still stand-offish.

"Listen," Jack continued, "about earlier, I'm sorry if I crossed a line. I certainly never intended to offend you or be the least bit inappropriate." He was blushing now and looking humbly at the ground. "I spend a lot of time taking care of my grandfather, and even more time in my research. The combination tends to leave me socially... inept. Please accept my sincere apology."

Nalia could not believe what she was hearing. The combination of schoolboy charm and a face that could easily grace the pages of GQ was nothing short of sexy. She found his candid sincerity incredibly attractive, and it showed in the half-grin she tried to hide.

"It's okay, you're forgiven. Go in peace," she replied with a playful wave of dismissal that made Jack smile widely.

"At least let me make it up to you. Lunch?"

Nalia looked at the inside of the ambulance with a raised brow. "I might be a bit tied up today," she said.

Jack shook his head and grinned even wider. Clicking his tongue against his cheek he replied, "I meant tomorrow, perhaps. If you're feeling up to it."

There was a long pause: an exchange of knowing looks, hesitation, and surrender.

"Perhaps," Nalia offered, unable to hold her smile back any longer.

"Perfect," said Jack. "I've been dying to have someone show me around the Quarter anyway."

Jack was still staring when the EMTs pushed him gently out of the way and helped Nalia onto the stretcher in the rear of the ambulance. She could barely see around the busy paramedics, but Jack was there with his hands in his pockets and an awkward grin on his face – a beautiful, awkward grin. Did she just make a date? Was that what just happened? Had a vision of the spirit world and a bump on the head really spawned a date with a handsome stranger? Suddenly, Nalia wasn't entirely comfortable with the notion.

She glanced in Jack's direction one last time as the ambulance doors swung around, hoping to find reassurance, praying she hadn't made a huge mistake. Her eyes however, did not find Jack's face. They were drawn instead to the store window behind him where the blinds were parted by pale fingertips and piercing eyes like those of the old man from her vision. They held her gaze for a moment before the blinds snapped shut.

As the vehicle's door closed and sirens consumed the silence, Nalia's world spun out of control, plunging her into darkness once more.

Chapter Eighteen

Nalia felt her body jerk and sway with the rocky movement of the ambulance, but her spirit was far away from the cramped rear compartment. She could hear the urgent tone of paramedics talking over her, but their voices were muffled and indistinct. The conversation eventually distorted into oblivion leaving only the quickening chirp of electronic, monitoring equipment to linger in the darkness. The accelerating tone quickly became a single steady note, the sound of finality. From the disturbing, high-pitched noise, an unexplainable peace grew, calming Nalia's spirit. Soon she heard the soothing, melodic tinkle of miniature wind chimes tapping on the door of her consciousness, followed by the low growl of distant thunder. The sound rumbled steadily just before a loud clap shook Nalia's awareness like a firm hand rousing her from sleep. Gradually her senses sharpened. A ballet of rain danced gracefully across the rooftop, and the earthy aroma of spiced incense filled the air. Finally, the black veil was pierced by two small embers, glowing red and swelling in size. Nalia watched the coals grow and change color from red to yellow to white. As thunder rolled again, tiny black dots formed in the center of the searing, white embers quickly expanding into pupils – the unmistakable, wide eyes of Marie Laveau.

Nalia felt naked, her soul laid open for examination. The eyes watched with purpose, studying her. Though feeling would not return to Nalia's body, an uneasy sense of entrapment consumed her. She tried to look away from the prying eyes but found it impossible. Her gaze was fixed as if her body and head were bound. Her entire existence was drawn to the eyes.

Sensing displeasure in Marie's stare, Nalia grew nervous and ill. A strong, resolute force began to push against her soul. Nalia still had no feeling in her body, but felt the force acting with bold intention on her presence. It was attempting to banish her. Like breeze through a wind sock, the force penetrated and swirled around her, but Nalia stayed her ground. Though she wanted to turn away, her desire proved powerless against the will of the vision.

Twice more, Nalia felt the forceful push against her presence and again stood strong. The eyes glowed brighter, angrier. Wisps of fragrant smoked began to rise through Nalia's field of vision, allowing the ghostly face of Marie Laveau to take shape in the negative space. Her nostrils flared, and her lip curled in bitter frustration.

Nalia felt Marie's eyes scrutinize her with a newfound, guarded curiosity as the smoke grew thicker, climbing the membrane-like veil between them. She could feel Marie's resentment as the smoke obstructed her view, and the eyes faded into the haze. When Nalia could no longer see, feeling began to return to her body, gravity exerting its heavy force. The next sensation Nalia felt was air filling her lungs. It was warm, damp, and thick with the fragrant incense. Taking in as much as she could, Nalia pursed her lips and exhaled forcefully, dissipating the fog before her. The smoke blew into the candlelit room; the veil was gone.

Still unable to move, Nalia at least had a clear vantage point from which to watch the scene unfold before her. The splatter of raindrops on the roof intensified as the familiar, velvet-covered table came into view. The man on the right removed his rain-soaked hat and ran his fingers through his dark hair. The woman next to him, visibly frightened, darted her eyes around the room, looking at everything except the woman in the blue tignon across the table.

Nalia watched as the dark-haired man once again slid his ornate, gold pocket watch across the table. This time, however, she heard voices. Distorted at first, they slowly became clearer, as if yelled by an approaching stranger.

"It is all I have to offer you," said the dark-haired man, wiping rain from his face and neck. "It belonged to my grandfather. It is a valuable timepiece. The men who pursue me will find us if you do not help. I beg you, please accept this watch as payment."

Marie Laveau palmed the watch while keeping her eyes fixed on the man's face, gauging his reaction. "Who deese men you talkin' 'bout? Dem dat wants you dead?" she asked in a thick creole accent.

"Hired men," the man replied. "Hired by my betrothed's father to track us down." The woman beside him trembled and fixed her eyes firmly on the floor. "Her father is a wealthy man, a rancher from the Republic of Texas. His two sons were killed by the hand of Santa Anna. She is all he has left. This is why he claims he cannot permit us to marry." The man gently took the trembling hand of the woman at his side and rubbed her delicate skin with his thumb. "I am not a wealthy man, Mrs. Laveau, but I am rich in love. My Emily here is with child. I want only to marry her and bring our baby into this world in peace. But if these hired men succeed in finding us, they will kill me and drag my Emily back to Texas where she and the child will likely meet the same fate. Please, you must help us!"

Marie studied the man closely before turning her attention to the watch. His eyes were pleading, desperate and fearful.

Nalia watched the man squeeze the young woman's hand. As the girl looked up into his eyes, her lips parted to speak. The man gently shook his head, cautioning her to keep silent. Her muscles tensed as her eyes continued scanning the room. She looked ready to run. Tightening his grip the man called her attention back to his eyes and gave her a reassuring yet threatening stare. His eyes held a menacing familiarity.

"So what you want me do fo' you?" asked Marie Laveau in a sobering voice, bringing Nalia's focus back to the watch, twirling on its chain above the table.

"Folks around these parts tell me you can cast spells, powerful ones. Can you cast a spell strong enough to protect us from the men who hunt me?"

Marie studied the man's eyes again, as if mentally peeling away layers of flesh until she could see the beating heart of his soul. When she found what she determined was truth, she raised a single eyebrow and reclined in her high-backed chair. She turned the watch over in her hands, examining its markings. "Dis is a costly piece, fine indeed. But it ain't yo's," she said, glaring back into the man's eyes.

His face went flush, and the woman next to him squirmed in her seat. Tears began to form in her eyes. Her lips quivered, and her body shook with angst. The man let go of her hands and gripped his hat nervously.

"Dere's a bad mojo on dis watch. I can smell it like the stink of a cottonmouth, and yo' eyes tellin' a diff'rent story dan yo' tongue. You come to Marie Laveau fo' help, and you gon' try and pay me off wit' a stolen watch?" she said tossing the item back onto the table.

"What I told you is true. It was my grandfather's, I swear," the man nearly interrupted, as Marie's eyes began to burn like fire. Her piercing stare was more convincing than a cattle prod. Breathing deeply, the man humbled his tone and fixed his eyes on the watch with regret. "But it wasn't my birthright." He swallowed hard and looked up into Marie's bulging eyes. "The watch was intended for my brother," he explained. "But long before my grandfather took ill, my brother joined the Rangers in the war against Mexico. He has not been seen or heard from since. When my grandfather passed, I took the watch. My intentions were to keep it safe for my brother should he return, but now I am desperate. I did not intend to offend you, Mrs. Laveau. I simply saw no other alternative." The man gathered his composure and placed an arm around the woman trembling at his side.

"Nor do I," replied Marie. "Takin' dis watch would be robbin' you grandfather's grave. The spirits of Voodoo don' look kindly on such action. I can't accept dis as payment. If you got nothin' else, I'm 'fraid..."

The man was trembling now, as well. He locked eyes with the young woman in silent exchange. Reluctantly, she nodded, and the man turned his gaze back to Marie.

"There is but one other thing we have that is of any value. It is not as costly as the watch, but it is true." As his fiancée continued to cry, the man slipped his hand into a leather satchel beside their feet. When he pulled the shiny object from the bag, it caught the light of the candles, gleaming, almost glowing in Nalia's eyes – a polished silver hairbrush.

Nalia gasped. As her lungs filled with air, she felt a sharp stabbing pain in her arm. The vision quickly faded away as she heard the desperate cry of the one of the EMTs.

"Wait! I've got a pulse! She's breathing."

Chapter Nineteen

By the time Nalia was released from the hospital, a crimson glow washed the western sky. Long shadows stretched across the oak-lined roads as Mr. John tooled his truck home with Nalia and Mama Lu sitting beside him. They were all tired and hungry. Mr. John nursed a slight stomach ache resulting from several cups of bad waiting-room coffee laced with packets of clumpy artificial sweetener.

Mama Lu sat with Nalia most of the afternoon while a team of doctors ordered a series of tests. The bump on her head became a secondary issue; the doctors were more concerned with finding out why Nalia's heart stopped beating during her transport to the hospital. The EMT's report stated her vitals were completely lost for well over a minute. Nalia had no recollection of the drive, only a vivid memory of the vision and a lingering paranoia, like the eyes of Marie Laveau were still watching her.

Even more disturbing was the familiarity of the young man's eyes. They held a blend of fear and anger Nalia knew she'd seen before. It was the same haunting look as the old man from the tower. If her mind was not playing tricks on her, she saw the same eyes in the window, parting the blinds behind Jack. Her stomach turned at the thought.

The trip home was quiet. Mama Lu and Mr. John were silent with worry, Nalia with anxiety. She knew the conflict was coming. She could feel it. Mama Lu had been asking pointed questions all afternoon. Though she was careful and discreet with her choice of words, Nalia knew she was prying for information, trying to find out why she blacked out – what she saw, what she felt. Nalia could tell the charade was over when the doctor revealed she died in the back of the ambulance. She looked to Mama Lu expecting worry and concern. Instead she saw intrigue. Mama Lu's expression reflected a mind racing with questions. The doctors were at a loss for explanation, but Mama Lu was decidedly not. The great mambo was all-too familiar with astral projection and its effects on the body and the central nervous system. She knew mambos and haunguans who traveled into the spirit realm leaving their bodies seemingly lifeless for several minutes at a time, hours in the spirit world. Vital signs often dropped to undetectable or near non-existent levels, while the soul experienced etheric travel to other planes and other times. No, Mama Lu was not at a loss for explanation at all. She was simply lacking answers to a growing lot of burning questions. Nalia knew she would want to know everything.

The confrontation was imminent and unavoidable, but Nalia would not be forced to talk until she was ready. It must happen on her terms. She would love to wait until she sorted the whole mess out for herself before allowing anyone else in, but the look fixed in Mama Lu's eyes all afternoon suggested she would be afforded no such luxury.

Nalia sat quietly between Mama Lu and Mr. John, her skin crawling with anxiety. Thoughts swarmed her mind like bees around a hive: fate, destiny, choices, approval, acceptance, surrender, control, truth. What did Madame Toulouse mean when she said *the sight* was a reflection of truth? *If you didn't want it, I wouldn't be here.*

"But I don't want it," thought Nalia. "Or do I?" The satiety of controlling the fog in the vision was undeniable. When it yielded to her will she felt powerful and complete. For that brief moment she commanded not only the fog, but everything. "No," she thought. "That's exactly the kind of control I don't need or want."

Nalia was terrified of wielding power like Mama Lu, and yet she was intrigued. Embracing *the sight* in the courtyard, she felt a serenity the likes of which she never knew possible: the fulfillment of the universe in harmony with her body and her soul. She was humbled and awed, drawn to a place where every atom of her existence was perfected in its purpose, exactly where it was supposed to be. The streaming sense of nirvana was harder to shake than the call to power.

Nalia's brain vaulted back and forth, trying to sort through a tangled mass of emotions as Mr. John made the turn onto the narrow gravel alleyway separating the back of his house from Mama Lu's. The tension was unbearable. One way or another, Nalia wanted off the rollercoaster.

"C'mon in, John," said Mama Lu when the truck finally stopped. "I'll put something' in yo' stomach."

A hush fell over the cosmos as the trio made their way up the walk. Nalia thought about trying to escape up the stairs but decided the notion was pointless. There was no avoiding the inevitable. She stepped into the kitchen and retrieved three plates from the cupboard while Mama Lu examined the contents of the refrigerator.

Without excess deliberation, Mama Lu removed a Pyrex dish filled with chopped onion, a small package of sliced roast beef, and some pepper jack cheese. Retrieving a well-seasoned iron skillet, she went to work. In no time, Mama Lu had the onions sautéed and the cheese melted over the beef in a steaming pile of sizzling goodness. Using some pistolette rolls, she plated up four small sandwiches, two for Mr. John and one each for herself and Nalia.

Mr. John poured three glasses of sweetened, iced tea from a half-empty pitcher and readied the table. Trying to occupy her hands, Nalia found the Dijon mustard and blended a hearty helping with a few tablespoons of Worcestershire sauce and a dash of Tabasco. When the preparations were complete, the three gathered around the table in awkward silence and began to partake. Mr. John ate heartily while Mama Lu and Nalia picked and nibbled, occasionally catching one another's stare. Finally, Nalia could stand it no longer.

"If you have something to say, let's hear it," she spewed at Mama Lu. Mr. John looked up in surprise. His mouth, full of hot sandwich, gaped open as if he no longer knew how to chew.

Mama Lu's eyes were piercing. She laid her barely-eaten sandwich down on her plate, reclined back in her chair, and raised one eyebrow. "I was not gon' say a word, chil'," she said calmly. "I was content to wait, and let you talk when you was ready. Since you done piped up, I reckon dat's now."

Nalia was dumbfounded. "Sometimes your silence is more persuasive than your words, Mama."

Mama Lu offered a wry smile in reply. "Nalia, I know yo' wrestling' wit' dis, and I hate to see you struggling'. But I can't help when you shuttin' me out, keepin' me in the dark."

Nalia melted. Not at all the reaction she expected, Mama Lu's tender tone caught her off-guard. Where was the stern disposition, the insistent "recommendations", the unsolicited "guidance"? It took only moments for Nalia to recognize her own projection. She was so certain she knew how Mama Lu would react, she had already fought the battle in her mind. Caught up in the frustration of her unresolved expectations, Nalia was at a loss for words. Even more embarrassing, Mama Lu's compassion elicited tears.

"What is it yo' afraid of, chil'?" asked Mama Lu in a voice neither curt or contemptuous, but soothing and concerned. "Tell me wha's goin' on."

Nalia took a breath so deep she thought her lungs would never fill, and quickly inventoried her heart. Part of it wanted to tell Mama Lu everything, part of it still wanted to run.

Mr. John finally remembered how to chew, swallowed resolutely, and tried to be as silent as possible while his eyes darted back and forth between the two ladies.

After a second cleansing breath, Nalia spoke. "I want it," she said candidly. "I want it like I've never wanted anything else. I've seen the kind of power the sight can give and I'm fascinated by the possibilities. I want to see things before they happen, know what shouldn't be known, control the elements of the world around me. I want to feel the peace of knowing I'll never be taken advantage of, or fall victim to someone else's aggression ever again."

Mama Lu's jaw dropped and her eyes widened with shock. It took a moment to realize she was, in fact, awake and hearing what she thought she would never hear. After a minute of stunned reflection, a gentle smile graced her face.

Nalia crossed her arms in frustration. "It's nothing to smile about!" she said, her muscles stiff and rigid. "You asked what I was afraid of, well that's it. I want it. I'm not afraid of the power itself, I'm afraid of how badly I want it – so badly I can taste it! I've tried to convince myself otherwise but it's the truth. What happens when this thirst for power is unquenchable? Who does that sound like?"

Mama Lu's smile faded as her mind filled with memories of Margaret Barronne. Suddenly she understood why Nalia was terrified.

"Where does it go from here?" Nalia went on. "What happens when the fascination turns to obsession and I end up crazed like my mother, with the power of an experienced mambo? Can you imagine how destructive that combination would be? It's a recipe for disaster, and it haunts me every minute of every day." Nalia wept uncontrollably. Streams of pent-up conflict cascaded down her cheeks as she bared her soul in surrender. "If that's where this road leads, Mama, I'd rather turn away now than take the first step."

Mama Lu was speechless. Somewhere in her mind, a logical argument tried to claw its way to the surface, but the sight of Nalia weeping helplessly surpassed her ability to offer solace. Silence was all she could manage.

Frustrated, exhausted, and having lost her appetite, Nalia quietly excused herself and climbed the stairs, wiping her cheeks and desperately trying to swallow the sizable knot in her throat. Mama Lu turned to follow her, but Mr. John covered her

hand with his. Silently he shook his head, indicating Nalia
needed some time and space. Reluctantly, Mama Lu agreed.

The two finished their meal in the quiet kitchen, each focused
on their own set of concerns. Mama Lu did not speak until she
heard the familiar sound of water filling the tub upstairs.

"I worry, John," she said, finally. "I worry fo' her safety."
Mr. John nodded in sympathy. "I know she got her demons to
deal wit', and it's a war she gots to wage on her own. But she
ain't seein' the bigger picture." Mama Lu's tone adopted an
edge, and her gaze trailed off the way it always did when she
was lost in a revelation. "She don't realize dis struggle she's
facin' is secondary. There's something bigger goin' on – bigger
than all of us. There's a darkness so thick it's chokin' me, John.
It's foul and it's fierce and it's makin' my skin crawl like
nothin' I ever felt befo'."

Mr. John fixed his eyes on Mama Lu and listened intently,
the way he used to when Madame Toulouse spoke of such
serious matters. The similarity sent a tingle through his body.
"Tell me what you mean, Lu," he said.

Mama Lu instinctively reached for the twisted root in her
pocket. "The sight ain't leavin' me like I thought," she said,
clearing her throat. She had Mr. John's full attention. "I know
it's trying' to latch itself on to Nalia, so when I couldn't see
Zoe, I felt like it was slippin' away. But today I saw Nalia clear
as a bell. I saw the ambulance. I saw the paramedics workin' on
her, and I felt her slip away. I felt her soul shift, John. The sight
is jus' as strong in me as it ever was."

"What are you sayin', Lu?"

"I'm tellin' you the reason I can't see Zoe ain't got nothin' to
do wit' how strong the sight is workin' in me. I'm bein'
blocked!"

Mr. John jumped like a startled cat. He could not fathom
what he was hearing. He could not recall a time when anything
or anyone blocked Mama Lu's vision, even before she came into
full knowledge of her power. She experienced episodes where

her sight waned due to stress or grief, but she was never blocked. The concept was foreign. His mind searched for other explanations, other solutions, anything making more sense, but he was at a loss. "What makes you so sure, Lu?"

"The vision of Zoe," Mama Lu replied. "All dis time I ain't been able to reach her could be explained if the sight was shifting, but in the vision she's tryin' to reach me. If we both buildin' a bridge and we can't connect, there's only one explanation. We're being blocked. She's knows the answer, and she's tryin' to give it to me. She ain't just tryin' to tell me *she's* in trouble, she's tryin' to warn me we all are. I think I might know how to find her."

Chapter Twenty

Darkness fell thick over the Quarter, but the lights of Bourbon Street glowed like beacons drawing in the revelers. With Mardi Gras just weeks away, the night air stayed charged with energy. Like the tide, it swelled, seen and felt, but never contained. Party-goers of every age, race, and creed flocked to the epicenter of New Orleans' night life in growing numbers. Soon, Bourbon St. would be bursting at the seams, and the party would become a living, breathing entity – the beating heart of the Quarter.

Tonight, Bourbon's crowd was already spilling over into its arteries and veins. Roisterers and intoxicated stragglers filled the streets from Canal all the way to St. Philip and beyond. Dauphine and Royal were nearly as swarmed with foot traffic as Bourbon. Even Chartres saw a fair share of activity, and the old man breathed it in like oxygen. The field lay ripe for picking and the harvest was nigh.

Shouldering his way past entrances to bars and strip clubs, the pulse of the heartbeat assaulted his ears. Jazz, zydeco, and rock music blared past doormen soliciting passersby to come inside. The old man chuckled at the hustler's simplistic trickery, still using the same trite lines he'd heard for ages. Amazed at the number of tourists falling for bets regarding their shoes, the old man focused his attention on the crowd.

He weaved in and out of the gathering throng like a shark through the shallows, casually studying his prey. Clever and masterful as he was, the old man found it increasingly difficult to go unnoticed. The city had grown over the years and the shadows that once served as allies grew scarce, forcing him to rely on his ability to blend rather than disappear. No matter, he thought with a thrill of anticipation. He enjoyed a challenge.

Certain elements worked to his advantage – time, distraction and alcohol topping the list. The more booze flowed, the more enamored with neon bulbs his victims would become as the night went on.

Other conditions stood firmly in the old man's way. While his spirit remained virile, his limitations were unnerving. His body was not as cooperative as it once was. The prying eyes of pedestrians were always a concern, and in the age of mobile devices, everyone carried their own personal alert system.

The pain in his joints was returning. His extensive tour of the streets was just bearable but relief would come soon, completing the vicious cycle once again. One of these young prospects would fulfill his dark purpose.

He inhaled deeply as he passed groups of women, taking in their scent like a bloodhound. He found their aroma intoxicating. He was not opposed to men in a pinch, but his palate was more suited to the feminine gender, the younger the better. Women were generally easier to overpower, and their supple flesh exponentially more tender.

With every waft of sweet perfume, the old man felt the power rising inside him, heightening his sense of superiority; he was a wolf walking in plain sight among so many sheep. In this raucous mass of youths stumbling over one another, distracted by their texts and their selfies, he would find his lifeblood.

Determining the side streets would be a more opportune hunting ground, the old man turned down Dumaine and headed toward Chartres. His nerves tingled with excitement as he watched an amorous female couple, clearly spent by their dizzying dance with Bourbon Street. He listened to their laughter and their trivial conversation. He followed them carefully, their inebriated pace making it easy for his aching bones to keep up. Which one would it be?

Finding her high heels cumbersome, the fairer-haired vixen opted to carry them rather than continue the battle. Even using her partner's shoulder for stability, she nearly fell over twice before successfully removing them, finding the second time as hilarious as the first. With any luck, she would pass out soon, leaving her friend as easy prey.

The old man's pulse quickened as he inched closer, undetected. The smell of sweat from their bodies gave rise to a feral hunger. Slipping his hand into his coat pocket, he gripped the handle of his blade. He furtively studied the faces of the buildings they passed. He needed only a small alcove or short alleyway, even a well-positioned dumpster would suffice. His motion would have to be quick, overtaking one, slicing the other. He rehearsed the motions in his mind, tensing his muscles at the appropriate times, gauging how much force he would need to exert. *Step, grab, shove, cut.* Even if he had to take both of them, he was prepared. Closer and closer he drew, still unobserved as they approached the cross-street. The blonde, nearing exhaustion, put her arm around her partner for balance and laid her head against her shoulder. *All too easy.*

The old man was just about to move on the couple when the blonde stumbled, shifting her weight onto her partner. Falling against the worn bricks on the corner of the building, the couple burst into a round of hysterical giggling. With her back against the wall, the brunette briefly made eye contact. Unable to find the proper angle, the old man slowed his pace and tucked himself into the nearest shadow. He watched as their laughter ceased, their chests heaving from the exertion. The blonde seized the opportunity to press her lips against her partner's neck in a moment of passion. As the brunette's head went back and her eyes closed, the old man saw his chance. Gripping the blade he moved quickly toward them seconds before a shout pierced the night.

"Whoa! Chicks, makin' out! Whoo! Yeah!" rang the obnoxious calls of a drunken group of fraternity brothers approaching from the cross-street. The old man was already doubled back toward Bourbon by the time the girls' middle fingers were in the air and their giggling resumed.

Over the next several hours, similar failed opportunities led the old man to question his timing. Perhaps he began the hunt too early, or perhaps he needed a change of venue. Whatever the cause, the result was unchanged – he was growing tired, and the pain in his knees was escalating. He longed for the assistance of his cane, but his optimism had convinced him to leave it behind. Frustrated, he made his way to a metal chair left at the back door of a bar. Cursing his aged knees, he sat down beside a pile of cigarette butts and a collection of empty beer bottles.

From the corner of his eye, he saw her – a young, doe-eyed prostitute not more than twenty-one, walking alone in the shadow of the buildings. Her face still held the youthful glow of inexperience. Her skin was pale, and her lipstick was fire-engine red. The old man immediately picked her for a novice by the way she laid her trembling arms across her chest. The frequent, uneasy looks over her shoulder were another telltale sign she was not yet hardened by the streets. She dressed the part she thought necessary: leather miniskirt and tight, cotton crop top. She had yet to learn she could attract the same clientele with a quick lip and a brash attitude.

The old man's vigor was instantly renewed. "When the game changes," he thought, "Adapt your strategy."

He had been forced to bring them home before. While the extra precautions were less desirable, the added thrill was rewarding. At home he could take his time, savor every drop, and preserve the spoils. Yes.

His knees groaned in opposition as he rose from the chair, but his mind was set. Hiding his limp as best he could, he approached the young woman with a smile. Inside his pocket, he slipped his fingers around a folded stack of bills. He propositioned her with his eyes while flashing the fistful of cash and extending his elbow. Staring at the bills in his hand the naïve courtesan offered a fire-engine red smile and slipped her arm through his, content to follow his lead.

Proudly, the wolf escorted his sheep through the flock, smiling and nodding as he led her off toward Decatur Street.

Chapter Twenty-One

Nalia was a mess. In one single moment of unrestrained, brutal honesty she laid her soul open on the table. While the revelation afforded her a certain level of release, it was nonetheless crippling. Up until her sudden outburst and admission, she wasn't sure she believed the truth, herself. Now it was undeniable; she wanted the power, and it scared her to death. Fear is paralyzing when allowed to be so, and Nalia could not muster the strength to quash it. How could she entertain the thought of wielding the power held by Mama Lu when her family history predisposed her to self-destruction? The combination was deadly, yet it seemed inevitable.

Nalia's spirit wanted to curl into a ball and cry, but her mind reasoned the notion as foolish and inadequate, availing nothing. Manifesting itself in tight lines on her brow, the conflict spawned equal amounts of anger and frustration. As she sat at the vanity trying to discern whose reflection was staring back, Nalia's world grew precarious and unsettling. Her soul cried out for direction but no answer was readily apparent.

Nalia picked up the polished silver hairbrush given to her by Madame Toulouse. She missed her grandmother and longed for the guidance only her Madame T. could give. "If only you were still here," she thought.

As she ran the brush through her hair, Nalia hit a tender spot on the back of her skull where the sidewalk left its reminder. To Nalia's surprise, pleasant memories sparked to life. Suddenly the theater in her mind was showing clips of a ruggedly handsome young man with a square bescraggled jawline and endless azure blue eyes. The more she tried to put Jack out of her mind, the more difficult the task became. What's more, she found she didn't want to. The thought of his dark hair became like an escape. She imagined running her fingers through it. *What?* Why was she thinking this way? He was pushy, and rude, and somehow adorable all the same. He was intrusive, and displayed distinct characteristics of a stalker. Yet, his eyes revealed a familiar, uncompromising kindness and a gentle nature. He took care of her and seemed genuinely concerned with her well-being. Sure he came off as quirky, awkward, and perhaps socially inept, but what did she expect from someone who made his living with his nose in a book?

The moment Nalia began to consider how lonely Jack's life must be and how he might only need someone to share it, she snapped back to her senses. What was she thinking? She barely knew this man! They met once for a brief awkward moment. He did what any decent, good-natured human would have. He came to the aid of a woman in distress. He called an ambulance. It was really just the expected course of action for any kind individual in the same situation.

But how many people actually would, she asked? How many decent, good-natured, kind humans were still out there, not to mention gorgeous ones? The long lashes framing those beautiful eyes were thick as reeds – definitely magazine material. His lips looked soft, like fresh spring petals. They would feel nice against hers, Nalia thought, their delicate surface contrasting the tingling texture of his trim beard.

"Stop it!" her mind demanded. "This is insane!" The last thing she needed right now was a man clouding her judgment, interfering with critical decisions, whatever those decisions turned out to be. The thought brought Nalia full circle, back to her frustration. Her inner monologue was awash with thoughts and ideas, mapping out conversations and confrontations yet to take place – situations that were unlikely to ever happen at all.

When Nalia placed the silver brush back on top of the vanity, a fragmented memory of Marie Laveau stung her conscience. She could nearly smell the burning incense. Her mind swimming with questions, Nalia stared at the antique piece with newfound fascination. She examined the raised pattern on its handle, trying to recall details of the vision, but her brain would not cooperate. Had she seen what she thought, or had her two worlds simply collided when the paramedics dragged her spirit back to her body? Adrift in a sea of confusion, Nalia decided enough was enough for the night. Perhaps a good night's rest would bring clarity, if either were a possibility. After depositing her clothes in the hamper beside the door and slipping into an oversized tee-shirt, Nalia climbed into bed and snuggled deep beneath her ivory duvet. As she drifted off to sleep, she tried to push all conscious thought from her mind, especially the recurring image of the old man's eyes peering through the blinds. The only notion bringing comfort and rest was the Caribbean blue of her handsome stranger's eyes.

Not long after Nalia drifted off to sleep, the image in her mind began to shift. The brilliant blue of Jack's eyes dissolved into a clear, midnight sky. Stars peeked through a canopy of moss-covered oak trees lit from below by the soft glow of paper lanterns. Drawn, Nalia began to walk, her feet sinking slightly into the dew-kissed path of sand and oyster shell. The lanterns on the ground lit the way to a grand, three-story home, freshly whitewashed and standing out in sharp relief against the darkened tree line beyond.

Soon others appeared on the pathway with Nalia: couples dressed in distinct Victorian attire. Ladies with their hair arranged in a part down the center and bouncy curls on the sides held the arms of their escorts, dashing gentlemen with fanciful walking canes and top hats.

Nalia's fingers stiffened around something in her hand and she realized she was carrying a folded, paper fan. Flaring it to its full length, she admired the floral print gracing its surface. A similar print adorned the silk fabric of her gown.

Nalia stopped in her tracks. She was wearing a long-waisted bodice and full skirt, flared at the hip with petticoats. The couple behind was forced to walk around as she stood in the middle of the path, baffled over her attire. The dress was a lovely shade of ivory, bordering on tan, with light blue ribbon as trim. The neckline dropped far off the shoulder but stopped shy of revealing cleavage. Nalia's neck was bare, but her wrist was ornamented with a tiny pearl bracelet.

The couple who walked around turned their noses with disdain, whispering to each other and glancing back over their shoulders. Nalia could not hear their conversation but got the impression they found her lack of an escort a serious breach of etiquette. Looking around, Nalia saw no one else without a partner. Feeling slightly uncomfortable, she toyed with the fan, rolling it between her fingers as she continued on toward the towering mansion.

Soon, the upbeat swing of a string quartet set her at ease, putting a bounce in her step and a broad smile on her face. As she drew closer, the sound of laughter mingled with the music and the smell of roasted pork filled the night air. Children in formal attire chased each other across the lawn keeping a strict distance from the adult party-goers, and carefully hushing their voices to an uncharacteristically discrete volume.

The large home featured a long porch and a wide gallery on each of the upper floors. Its facade was illuminated by oil lamps, casting complex shadows through its intricate wrought-iron railing. Instinctively, Nalia lifted her skirt as she climbed to the top of the stone steps, making her way past a set of large, white columns and onto the porch. Quietly, she filed into a line of waiting couples near the entryway where two large lamps with tall glass chimneys flickered on either side.

As couples made their way indoors, they were ushered to a small chamber where a servant in a cotton bonnet helped them with their coats and hats. As Nalia needed no assistance, she proceeded on to the main hall. The foyer opened into a grand ballroom, with a vaulted ceiling at least as high as two of the building's three floors. Four tall, sculpted columns formed a large square in the center of the polished, hardwood dance floor. Towering windows trimmed in thick, elegant drapery climbed the walls on either side. Candles and lamps were mounted high around the perimeter with an enormous chandelier hanging low in the center of the room. Nalia was attempting to count the candles on its thick metal ring when a familiar voice caught her attention. "I was hoping my invitation would find you well and agreeable to attend, my lady."

Standing at the entrance to the ballroom, dressed in dark, high-waisted trousers and a tail-coat was Jack. His posture was impeccable, like a military guard. Keeping his hands firmly by his side, Jack bowed low, bending at the waist. Nalia instinctively returned the gesture with a curtsy.

Jack's light blue waistcoat matched the trim of Nalia's gown, as did the wide cravat wrapped around his high collar. The color so accentuated his stunning blue eyes, Nalia felt she might swoon. Without thinking, she flared the fan and began fluttering it briskly beneath her chin. Her cheeks flushed as Jack offered a wide smile.

"Do you have need to freshen up, Miss, or shall I escort you to the dance floor?" As his elbow was extended in charming gentlemanly fashion, Nalia slipped her hand up and through its crook. His arm was thick and powerful, locked in an iron-like rigor. To Nalia, it felt safe. As they made their way around the room, Nalia extended a gentle smile to the smirking couple from the lawn now offering a courteous nod, seeing her on the arm of their host. Under the chandelier, dancers moved and swayed in elegant fashion, gracefully extending their arms in fluid, formal gestures to the rhythm of the stringed instruments. Their movements were synchronized like fine clockwork.

When the festive song came to an end, the hall erupted with laughter and applause. The quartet paused while gentlemen conveyed ladies to their stations and couples prepared to dance the quadrille.

Jack led Nalia to the center of the room, between the sculpted columns where they joined three other couples in a rectangular formation. As the music resumed, Nalia and Jack bowed to the couple across the square, then to the couples at their side, and again to each other. Nalia was not sure how, but the movements that followed came naturally to her. She performed them perfectly, as if she'd been dancing them for years. She did not allow her mind to linger on questions of why or how, but instead slipped into the comfort of familiarity and the revelry of the night. She laughed and danced with Jack among the other couples until her heart raced with unbridled felicity.

When the quadrille concluded, Jack held Nalia at arm's length and squared off for the next dance. Couples took to the floor for a pair's session. Facing Jack one-on-one, Nalia found herself a bit more nervous than before, but when the music started and her eyes found his smile, anxiety vanished like smoke on the breeze. The song was light and bouncy, as was the dance. Jack twirled Nalia around the dance floor weaving quickly in and out of other spinning couples as the tempo of the strings matched the frivolity of the mood.

Nalia's head began to spin and though her feet never missed a step, she became dizzy. As she focused on Jack's crystal blue eyes, the world around them faded and blurred into constant motion. Nalia felt ill. Soon, indistinct voices cut through the music, distorted and muffled as if underwater. Somewhere in the distance a jazzy harmonica joined the strings in a dissonant blend of complex scales. The sound besieged her mind, resonating loudly. Jack was still smiling, apparently unaffected.

Nalia began to look around but found it difficult to focus as images faded in and out of her periphery. The couples around them danced on as if nothing was askew. Their steps remained in perfect rhythm, their faces fixed and jovial.

As the music crescendoed into a high-pitched squeal, Nalia noticed a change. The bouncing locks of the women around her began to grey and quickly faded to stark white. The men's hair did the same. As Nalia was finally able to focus, time accelerated, compressing years into mere seconds. Wrinkles appeared before her eyes and the dancers faces shriveled into skeletal forms with sunken eyes and thin, translucent skin. Muscles, veins, and tissue became exposed as their faces seemed to melt away like dripping candle wax, until only meaty bits were left clinging to their grisly skulls. Locks of hair became instantly brittle, breaking away and flying into the air like seed blown from dandelions. Nalia wanted to scream but could not find her voice.

As the endless dance whirled on, the formations parted like the red sea, clearing a narrow pathway across the room. On the eastern wall, a bright light shone through one of the spire-like windows, spilling a reflection onto the polished floor like a beacon calling to Nalia. She stood stock still as the window rushed through her field of vision until it was close enough to touch.

A looming shadow formed in the light, and Nalia found herself face to face with the image of Madame Toulouse. The elder woman was standing just beyond the glass, staring in, struggling to see. As frightened tears flowed down Nalia's cheeks, Madame Toulouse raised a hand and pressed it against the pane. There was urgency in her eyes and a slight quiver in her lips. The image lasted only a moment before the light faded, leaving Nalia staring at her own reflection. Raindrops slid silently down the window, masking the tears on Nalia's face, but as she peered into the glass, her own hair began to whiten. In a matter of seconds, her appearance grew pallid and withered, but Nalia could only focus on the reflection behind her: the beautiful, clear blue eyes of Jack Haufmann shimmering like perfect pools in an oasis of tranquility.

———————

Gasping for breath, Nalia awoke in her bedroom warmly tucked under her ivory duvet. Her heart was pounding, her cheeks were hot, and her throat was dry as chalk. She was relieved to see the familiar surroundings of her bedroom, but she did not know why. The only memory she could recall was the tranquil blue eyes of her gallant dance partner.

Chapter Twenty-Two

The smell of fresh coffee filled the house like the gentle flood of morning sunshine, and Nalia was anxious for a cup. She couldn't remember the last time she slept so well, or felt so rested. It was invigorating. Perhaps last night's sudden outburst was to blame, she thought. The acknowledgement and admission of her fear drew her one step closer to finding direction. Nalia liked all her ducks in a row.

She also liked the idea of taking Jack up on his lunch invitation. The handsome young man was the first thought on Nalia's mind when light spilled through her window. Though the realization was a bit hard to comprehend at first, Nalia quickly grew comfortable with having a man be her first, waking thought. It was a pleasant change, she decided. Perhaps, she was ready.

She found herself taking a bit more time choosing her attire, even putting two outfits back before deciding on a pair of slim-fitting jeans, an ivory sweater, and a pair of cappuccino-colored, knee-high, leather boots. The combination was classy enough to impress, but casual enough to disguise its intent. A little more attention to her makeup than usual and a slight struggle over which earrings best complimented her outfit gave Nalia pause to consider her motives. She casually dismissed them with a blushing smile, asking the fitting question, "Why not?" A spritz of perfume and she was on her way. Finally, she tucked a lipstick and her silver brush into her bag should the need to freshen up arise later. Exiting her bedroom fully dressed with a spring in her step she headed down the hall toward the staircase.

The smell of sausage greeted Nalia as she descended the stairs. The aroma triggered a memory of roasted pork from… a lost dream. Nalia found her hand grasping strangely at the air, searching for an absent paper fan. A picture formed in her mind of Victorian gowns twirling across a dance floor. Mental puzzle pieces fell into place as she remembered Jack's elegant tailcoat and blue cravat, the confidence with which he offered his arm, and the way his eyes reflected the candlelight. A wild assortment of images and emotions rolled in and out of Nalia's awareness, but the most vivid was the sense of security she found at his side. It promised her peace.

Bounding down the stairs, Nalia found Mama Lu and Mr. John finishing up breakfast and sipping remnants of coffee from their mugs.

"Pretty as a peach," Mr. John declared as Nalia reached the bottom of the steps. Her rosy cheeks deepened in hue.

Placing her hands against the door jamb and leaning into the kitchen, Nalia closed her eyes and took a deep breath, as if she were inhaling life itself. "This has got to be the most wonderful smell on earth," she said with a broad smile.

Mama Lu looked around in surprise. "Well, looks like somebody's in a better spirit," she announced. Her voice was lighthearted, but Nalia sensed a shadow still darkening her demeanor. "There's some Andouille scramble on the stove, chil'. Help y'self. Some coffee, too."

"Yo' Mama Lu outdone herself dis mornin'," said Mr. John, finishing off a bit of toast layered with cream cheese and Jezebel jelly. His words were sincere but his jovial timbre was forced.

Still trying to gauge the room, Nalia ran her fingertips over Mama Lu's shoulders as she headed for the coffee pot. She dropped a slice of whole wheat bread into the toaster before pouring some of the chicory brew into her cup. After doctoring her java with the proper amount of hazelnut creamer and honey, Nalia took a hearty sip allowing the blend of flavors to fully awaken her senses. She had just finished plating a small serving of the mixture in the skillet when her toast sprang from the slot. Nalia joined Mama Lu and Mr. John at the table, surveying her breakfast with tethered anticipation. Mama Lu's Andouille scramble was a blend of scrambled eggs and rice, bits of Andouille sausage, halved grape tomatoes, chopped onion, slivers of jalapeño pepper, and aged white cheddar, seasoned with a dash of celery salt. While Nalia loved the dish, its significance did not go unnoticed. Mama Lu typically preferred a sweeter breakfast of cinnamon buns, French toast, or her favorite pecan-crusted sweet potato pancakes. When Mama Lu deviated from the norm, something heavy was on her heart. Fearing she might be the cause, Nalia spoke up.

"Mama I want to apologize for my outburst last night. I am struggling with my feelings. I was frustrated, and rude. I am so sorry. I hope you understand."

Mama Lu managed a pleasant smile but spoke with a grim intonation. "Dat ain't necessary, chil'. You spoke the truth from yo' heart. You never need apologize for showin' yo' feelin's. I understand yo' struggle, I been there. I shouldn't have been so demandin', shouldn't have pushed you so hard."

"I think your push was the reason I finally saw everything clearly. It's all good." Nalia reached for Mama Lu's hand. When they touched, she felt a ripple in her spirit, a wave of unusual energy. Mama Lu was trembling. "What is it, Mama?"

Mr. John answered, "She been shakin' like dat since yesterday. We still ain't found no trace of Zoe."

"Her house looks like she just walked out to run some errands or somethin'," continued Mama Lu, her voice cracking. "But, somethin' ain't right. I can feel it, but I can't see it." She looked into Nalia's eyes as if seeking guidance. "Why can't I see it? Why can't I see her?"

Nalia had no answer. Dumbfounded by the sudden role reversal, she faltered. Nalia had never seen such desperation in Mama Lu's eyes before. As she watched the tears flow down Mama Lu's face, Nalia realized whatever was happening was breaking her to the core. She felt it in the way Mama Lu squeezed her hand. Nalia's eyes refused to stay dry as Mama Lu rose and turned for the stairs. "I'll be ready to go soon as I'm dressed, John," she said, climbing wearily up the steps.

"Take yo' time, Lu," he called back, his eyes fixed on Nalia and showing the concern he would not permit in his voice.

Nalia turned to him and whispered, "This is serious."

"Oh, you best b'lieve it is," he replied, shedding the veneer. "She had dat dream again last night. Woke up in the parlor starin' at the clock. Sleepwalkin'."

"And no trace of Zoe?"

"She says Zoe always leads her to the same place and dat's where we need to go. Dat's where we gon' find her. It's got her messed up somethin' terrible. I ain't never seen her like dis." Mr. John folded his hands over his empty plate and stared at the table looking lost.

Not knowing what to say, Nalia allowed the silence to linger as she picked at her breakfast. A myriad of ideas assaulted her mind, but one lingered longer. "I want you to do something," she said as Mr. John raised his eyes. "I want you to go next door when you get to the store. Check out the old man who runs the watch shop. I'm getting a weird vibe about him, and I don't know why, but I feel like he might have something to do with these visions."

"What makes you say dat?"

"I don't know, just a feeling, I guess. Maybe more." Nalia did not care to go into detail about the visions she'd seen of the old man and the spire, nor did she want to influence Mr. John's opinion. She trusted his judgment, and if he detected anything amiss, it would confirm her suspicion. She also wanted to spare Jack any implication by association. For some reason, she felt protective of him. "Just check him out and tell me what you think," she finished. "I may go out for lunch today, so if you guys aren't there I'll just lock up for a bit."

"No tellin' how long we gon' be, but I'm sure yo' Mama Lu won't mind." Mr. John leaned across the table, collected Mama Lu's barely-touched plate and utensils onto his and carried them over to the sink. He didn't notice the small box fall from his pocket when he rose from his seat. Nalia wouldn't have noticed it either had it not hit her foot.

"I think you dropped some..." She stopped mid-sentence when she saw the tiny velvet cube. "What is this?" she asked, bending to pick it up.

Mr. John hurried back to the table and took the box from her hand before she could examine it. "Dat's nothin', baby. Nothin' fo' you to concern yo'self wit'."

An excited and smug grin lit up Nalia's face. "What you call nothing looks an awful lot like a jewelry box to me. What exactly are you up to?"

Mr. John was as flushed as Nalia ever saw him. He nervously fumbled the box back into his pocket and tried to change the subject. "I'm gon' go visit wit' dat fella ov'r at the watch shop soon as I get there," he said, hurrying back to the sink and turning on the faucet.

Nalia leaned back in her chair, folded her arms, crossed her legs, and clicked her tongue inside her cheek. Mr. John stole a peek over his shoulder and for a fraction of a second, thought he saw Madame Toulouse sitting in Nalia's chair.

"You know, in just a few minutes Mama Lu is going to walk back down those steps and tell you she's ready to go," Nalia went on. "That means you've got precious little time to explain what's going on before I'm forced to start running my mouth." Her leg was bouncing up and down like a see-saw, and her face was fixed with a look that screamed "Try me."

Mr. John was nearly certain Nalia was bluffing, but he couldn't take the chance. He removed the box from his pocket, opened it, and set it down on the table. "Get a good look, and get it quick," he said. "Befo' she comes back down dem steps."

Nalia immediately uncrossed her legs and sat back up to the table. Lifting and examining the box, she turned her back to the stairwell. Inside was a princess-cut diamond, catching the sunlight in a fiery display of color. It was surrounded by seven tiny gemstones on a band of white gold. Nalia's mouth hung open as she turned to Mr. John. "It's gorgeous," she whispered, immediately shifting her focus back to the ring. Refracted light danced over her face and across the ceiling. Her mouth was still agape when she turned to Mr. John a second time. "This is an engagement ring!" she whispered again with barely contained excitement that threatened to erupt.

"Yes, it is," said Mr. John, steadily watching the staircase. "Now can we put it away, please? Dis is not the time."

Nalia suddenly felt terrible for threatening to spill the beans. She expected jewelry in the box, but an engagement ring never crossed her mind. Everything she knew about Mr. John and Mama Lu's relationship suddenly shifted. She always viewed it as fixed, not as evolving. She never gave it consideration, but now that she did, she found it adorable. "You've loved her your whole life, haven't you?" said Nalia handing the box back to Mr. John.

"Since the moment we met," he replied. The gravity in his tone matched the distance in his eyes. Nalia never saw a look so sincere, a mixture of admiration, joy, and heartbreak. "I don't want you gettin' yo' hopes up dat anythin' is ever gon' come o' dis," he stammered. "Yo' Mama Lu ain't never been too crazy 'bout the idea of... marriage." It seemed to take everything he had to say the word. Like speaking life into a fantasy, suddenly it felt real. "I don't have any expectation she gon' say yes, but I ain't gon' let dat stop me from askin' dis time. Me and yo' Mama Lu ain't gettin' no younger, and it just don't make sense for us to be on our own. Besides, like you said, I've loved her my whole life."

Nalia didn't notice her own tears until they dropped from her cheek. Suddenly her face was swelling, making it harder to breathe. Her chest was heaving with emotion. "When did you *know*?" she asked, her mind briefly drifting to Jack. "When were you sure that feeling was really love?"

Mr. John chuckled in quiet reflection. He sat back down at the table and took Nalia by the hand. "Sweet baby girl," he said. "You got it all wrong. Fo' some reason you got the notion dat love is somethin' dat happens *to* you. Love ain't just some feelin' dat causes butterflies in yo' stomach. It ain't some passin' emotion dat keeps yo' mind driftin' to dat certain person. Dat ain't what love is, baby. It ain't some kind of treasure dat we find, or some trap dat snares us. It ain't somethin' we fall in and out of like some folks say. Dat's all stuff you find in fairy tales and I hate to be the one to break it to you, but dem fairy tales ain't real."

Nalia looked up to see tears threatening Mr. John's eyes now. He squeezed her hand with a tangible honesty. "Real love don't happen *to* you, it happens *from* you. It's action; it's somethin' you do. Love is puttin' others befo' yo'self. It's patience, compassion, and forgiveness. Dat's what real love is. Dat's lastin' love. You asked me when I knew it was love? I know every day, because I start over lovin' yo' Mama Lu brand new each mornin'."

Mr. John's words were nothing more than a simple truth uttered by a simple man, but Nalia questioned whether she ever heard anything so eloquent. By the time Mama Lu reached the bottom of the stairs, Nalia successfully dried her eyes and regained her composure enough to present a convincing front to any reasonable person. Since Mama Lu did not fit that category, Nalia was glad she was still too distracted to notice.

Chapter Twenty-Three

The morning mist was clearing as were the last stragglers of early mass when Mama Lu and Mr. John arrived at St. Louis Cathedral. The sun was shimmering off the white face of the building, and Jackson Square was beginning to show the first colorful signs of spring foliage. The temperature was climbing, but there was still a biting chill on the breeze coming off the river.

Each hair on the back of Mama Lu's neck stood on end. She could still see Madame Zoe in her mind, leather cords stitching her mouth shut, terror haunting her eyes. The burden weighed on Mama Lu's spirit like thick, heavy chains. She found it difficult to concentrate. Her mind stayed fixed on her friend crying desperately for help while she remained powerless to rescue her.

When Mama Lu reached the cathedral steps she stopped and turned toward Jackson Square. The image in her mind came alive before her eyes. She saw Zoe standing near the iron gate surrounded by corpses of young women. Zoe's gurgling moans pierced Mama Lu's brain, her indistinct pleas driving out all other conscious thought.

Mama Lu covered her ears, attempting to silence the noise in her head, but it was useless. Bicyclers whizzed past, couples found seats along the benches, and musicians uncased their instruments, but Mama Lu saw only Zoe, heard only the stifled screams of her tormented friend. She stood in trance-like rigor as the vision continued to assault her senses.

Mr. John quickly came to her aid, taking her by the shoulders and checking her glassy eyes. He spoke to her, first calmly, but eventually shouting, asking what was the matter. Concern, then panic filled his eyes.

Mama Lu saw him standing in front of her. She could tell his mouth was moving, but the noise in her head was overbearing. The world was spinning in slow motion and Mama Lu grew weak. In desperation she turned toward the cathedral and willed her legs forward, one lead-heavy foot at a time. Mr. John helped steady her as she made her way to the door.

A young woman, her eyes as big as saucers, saw them as she exited the building. She held the door open but let it go as soon as Mama Lu and Mr. John crossed into the foyer, eager to depart. As the heavy door swung shut, Mama Lu's vision grew dark, and the noise ceased, like time and space suddenly vanished into a vacuum. The blackness lasted only a moment before she regained her faculties. Mr. John was still holding her when she came around.

"What happened, Lu?" he asked. "It's like you was somewhere else fo' a minute."

"Her energy is strong here," Mama Lu answered. "She's screaming her lungs out fo' me but I still can't hear her. She's in torment."

Mama Lu's mouth was dry. Her forehead beaded with sweat, and she staggered slightly when she tried to walk. "Help me inside, John. I need some water."

Mr. John aided Mama Lu through the doors to the sanctuary. When a friendly parishioner offered his assistance, Mr. John conveyed their need. The man hurried off and quickly returned with a bottle of water, a cool rag, and a short, thin, bespectacled priest.

"Lucia Deminy," the priest said with a smile, kneeling on the pew in front of her, helping to wipe her head with the damp cloth. "You don't look so well. What can I do for you, Mama?"

"Give me a minute to catch my breath," Mama Lu coughed, cracking open the water. "I had a lil' spell jus' now, dat's all."

"Not the kind of spell you're typically known for, hmm?" the priest chuckled, pleased with his pun. The response on Mama Lu's face told him this was no time for jokes. Clearing his throat he continued. "What kind of spell were you referring to, Mama? Do I need to call you a doctor?"

"No Father Carmelo, I'll be fine. But I do need yo' assistance."

"Are you here for confession?" Although his question was sincere, the look on Mama Lu's face said she thought he was still attempting humor. She eyed the priest with contempt as she drank heavily from the water bottle.

"We need some info'mation," interrupted Mr. John, before Mama Lu had the chance to get angry.

"I'm happy to help if I can," the priest said, attempting to work his way back into Mama Lu's good graces.

"It's about one of yo' parishioners, a friend of mine," Mama Lu conveyed, finally able to breathe normally. "What can you tell me 'bout Zoe Lovell?"

"Zoe Lovell," the priest repeated, hoping to gain some recall by speaking the name. His eyes drifted, and he tapped his fingers on the back of the pew until a distant memory struck. "Do you mean Madame Zoe, the gypsy lady? I didn't know her last name."

"I never knew either until I read it on her untouched mail yesterday. She's missin'."

Father Carmelo's face flushed with concern. "I haven't seen Zoe at mass in over a year. I saw her out front one evening a few months ago while locking up after a wedding rehearsal. How long has she been missing?"

"Several days," said Mr. John.

"Days? Are you sure she hasn't simply left town? Gone to visit family or..."

His sentence was cut short by the scathing look in Mama Lu's eyes. "She's missin', and she's in trouble!" she insisted.

Father Carmelo knew better than to ask how Mama Lu came about her information. He knew Mama Lu well and her reputation even better. She attended mass with some regularity for as long as he could remember, even before her practice showed restraint. Father Carmelo remembered the first time they met. Mama Lu came to mass with the strict intent of meeting the new parish priest. He had no idea who she was but found her cordial and cooperative, a pleasant woman of gentle nature. Later that afternoon, a fellow priest and several deacons pulled him into a private office and informed him he just met the reigning Voodoo queen of New Orleans, the great Mambo Lucia Deminy. For the next half hour they regaled him with ghastly tales that made his blood run cold. Though he found most of their stories far-fetched and unlikely, his soul was unsettled. He could not understand why a Voodoo priestess would be attending Catholic mass, so he did what any green priest would – he asked her. Several weeks later, when Mama Lu once again attended mass, he pulled her aside into the same private office. It was there she explained to him the African origins of Voodoo. Father Carmelo learned how slaves brought it to Haiti and eventually New Orleans. He learned about Bondye, the good god, and about the lesser gods known as Loa. Mama Lu explained how slaves were forced to observe their master's religion, made to worship Jehovah and the saints of the Catholic faith. The slave-owners were unaware how closely the hierarchy of saints matched the Loa. The slaves hid their religion in the structure of Catholicism, worshipping their Voodoo gods alongside their master in plain sight. The two soon became intertwined, and to the slaves, interchangeable. Today, Mama Lu explained, the correlation still existed. Father Carmelo was impressed by her candor and her knowledge, and expressed his pleasure to have her attend mass anytime. He explained his job was not to judge, but to simply love God and love people. They remained good friends from that day forth.

He would never forget Mama Lu's answer the day he finally worked up the nerve to ask if the sordid legends about her were true. She offered a cunning smile and a raised brow. "Tell me father," she said, "Do all priests share an affinity for altar boys?" When he adamantly protested she replied, "It's hard to hear the whisper of the saint while the sinner is shouting." Her point made, she chuckled and winked at the young priest. "Folks hear what they wants to hear, father, and they b'lieve what they wants to b'lieve."

Mama Lu attended mass regularly after that day – not regularly according to the mass schedule, but regularly according to hers. She remained a prominent figure in society and within the church. She championed the cause for abused and abandoned children and made several sizeable donations to related charities on the church's behalf. Father Carmelo visited her shop on many occasions, purchased trinkets, and even sought her advice on certain statuary. He knew Mambo Lucia Deminy well enough to believe her when she said someone was in trouble.

"What brought you here instead of to the police?" he asked, knowing Mama Lu had connections in the department as well.

"We done checked the station and asked around the hospitals," said Mr. John. "I gots all my people checkin' 'round and we still turnin' up nothin'."

When Father Carmelo heard the word hospital, he knew the situation was serious. When he heard even "Doctor" John could offer no leads, he feared it bordered on hopeless.

"She led me here, father," Mama Lu said with a tone of desperation, "In a dream. I didn't catch it at firs', but she led me straight here."

Father Carmelo looked as lost as a fallen angel. "I don't understand why she would lead you here," he continued. "As I've said, I haven't seen her for months. I'll check with the other priests and the rest of the staff, but..."

Mama Lu's attention was diverted. Near the altar, another of the parish priests was leading two men their direction. The men were untidy and out of place, but they walked with purpose. The one behind the priest carried a heavy toolbox and kept his eyes forward. The one in the rear could not keep his head from swiveling. His eyes darted around the sanctuary, taking in the splendor of the hall's art, stained glass, and statuary, as if seeing it for the first time.

A fierce chill ripped through Mama Lu's body leaving her gasping for breath. As the men approached, she stared at them with unabashed intent, as if possessed.

Father Carmelo was taken aback by Mama Lu's reaction and turned to see what caught her eye. He acknowledged the priest with a nod and surveyed the two men but found no call for alarm. Pivoting back to Mama Lu he watched her face turn pale. "What is it?" he asked, as the men and the priest passed them, heading for the rear of the sanctuary.

Struggling to find her voice, Mama Lu questioned, "Who are they? Why are they here?"

"Just repairmen, I believe," Father Carmelo replied, "They're here to fix the clock."

"The clock?" gasped Mama Lu.

"Yes," replied the father, "It stopped working a few nights ago. I believe it was Sunday, during the storm."

Mama Lu rose without uttering a word. Digging deep, her determination conquered her fatigue and she ran for the door. Mr. John and Father Carmelo were left staring at each other's blank expressions, but quickly realized Mama Lu was on to something. By the time they reached the cathedral steps, Mama Lu was running across the brick street toward the iron gates of Jackson Square putting pigeons to flight in every direction. Whirling back toward the cathedral, she stared up at the motionless clock, her face a stark mixture of worry and revelation.

"Eight fifty-five, John!" she cried out, her voice booming over the courtyard. "You find me out what was goin' on right here, Sunday night at eight fifty-five!"

Chapter Twenty-Four

It was nearly noon on what Nalia believed to be the longest morning of her life. Since her early arrival at The Doll Maker, she finished updating the website's database of online inventory, rearranged one of the glass showcases to make room for Mama Lu's latest creations, organized the table space she was using as a makeshift office, and spent more time glancing out the window than she cared to admit. In fact, her level of productivity was the direct result of disciplining herself away from the front of the store.

Try as she might, she could not keep her thoughts from drifting to Jack. The more she lingered on the memory of his face, the more handsome he became in her mind. A schoolyard-crush anxiety kept her gazing out into the street, hoping to find him approaching his store or perhaps even popping in to visit. Surely he did not forget about lunch… if he was actually serious. Nalia's mind jumped from one extreme to the next in a vigorous dance of dualities. Would Jack feel the same way she did? Of course he would, she could see the attraction in his eyes. But what if she misread the signals? She was suffering from a head injury, after all. Certainly not, there was something there. He invited her to lunch, for crying out loud.

Finally, displeased with her inability to focus and the lack of a "Jack sighting", she decided to walk next door. A quick trip to the bathroom to check her appearance resulted in another reminder to replace the mirror and a fierce frustration with her newfound fascination.

"Ridiculous," she thought, running the polished silver brush through her hair. "He's just a guy. No need to make a fuss." Setting the brush down on the edge of the sink, Nalia straightened the ends of her hair with her fingertips. Still attempting to convince herself of Jack's insignificance, she touched up her lipstick and left the tube beside the brush. On the shop's bathroom sink, her brush looked strangely out of place. Nalia could not remember ever seeing it anywhere but her vanity. Somewhere in the recesses of her mind, the memory sparked again and ignited just long enough to make Nalia question its validity – the brush sitting on a round table draped in red velvet. Shuddering, Nalia swore she saw the eyes of Marie Laveau in the mirror, but as soon as the image appeared, it was gone, leaving her confused and uneasy.

Eager to shake off the jitters, Nalia exited the bathroom allowing her mind to drift back to her alleged lunch date. She slipped through the workroom to the front of the store, shut down her laptop, and walked outside.

The sky was overcast and a slight breeze cascaded in from the river, but Nalia was not interested in the weather. Nor was she distracted by the fragrance of jasmine wafting across the street from the local florist's sidewalk display. Nalia's mind was fixated on one thing – Jack.

The blinds were still drawn across the window of the neighboring shop and the door's glass panel was covered by the shade, but a distinct change in the shop's facade caught Nalia's attention. Ornate lettering was stenciled on the glass in black and gold. A flourishing font spelled out the business' name: Uhrmacher, Fine Timepieces. Nalia studied the sign briefly, admiring the style. It looked like something found outside an old barber shop, and it complimented the building nicely. "Very nostalgic," she thought. "Classy."

Nalia knocked on the door, but got no reply. There appeared to be no lights on behind the drawn blinds, and no indication of activity. Taking a step back, she finally noticed the small, metal CLOSED sign in the corner of the glass panel beneath the fanciful logo. To Nalia's surprise, her heart sank. For reasons that seemed to defy logic, she felt dismissed. There were plenty of reasonable explanations for the circumstances, she thought:

perhaps business, or some type of emergency. Maybe this was simply his normal routine. Despite all the viable arguments, the result was the same – Nalia felt rejected, and it bothered her greatly. Her mind kicked into overdrive trying to determine why she even cared, but her thoughts always went back to Jack's crystal blue eyes. Did she really have it that bad?

Frustrated and disappointed, Nalia turned back toward The Doll Maker only to find Jack leaning against a post near the door, as if he appeared out of nowhere.

"Looking for me?" he asked with a smile – a calming, beautiful smile, Nalia thought. She wanted to deny her intrigue, to somehow play off her actions as nonchalant and innocent, but words escaped her mouth before her brain could regulate them.

"Oh, umm... yes. Yes, I was."

"How's your head?"

"My head? Oh, yesterday, yes, fine... I'm fine. Doctor says I'm going to make it." She stuffed her hands into the pockets of her jeans, because she couldn't decide what else to do with them. Rocking back and forth on her heels, Nalia searched for words. "You're looking good."

Not those words!

But he was. Standing there in his Italian leather shoes, dark slacks, and freshly-pressed Hugo Boss slim-fit, silver dress-shirt with the cuffs rolled halfway up his forearms, Jack seemed to glow in the midday sun.

"Well, thank you," he said blushing, smiling, and studying the pavement.

"All dressed up, I mean," said Nalia, her cheeks reddening to match his.

"I was hoping for that lunch date. Wanted to look my best. You feeling up to it?"

"I don't know, I seem to remember a previous engagement with a Jack Haufmann. Surely you understand, Mr. Uhrmacher?" Nalia asked coyly, looking back at the sign on the door.

"It's not a name," Jack replied with a gentle laugh and a grin of genuine delight, "It's German for clock maker."

"Hmm," said Nalia, giving consideration to the name. "Dignified, I like it."

"Well, we had to come up with something new. Our last place, in Atlanta, was called The Watch Maker. That just wouldn't do moving in next door to The Doll Maker, now would it?"

Nalia chuckled. "I suppose not," she said as the two exchanged awkward glances.

"So about that lunch..." Jack said.

"Are you sure you can break away from your busy schedule?" Nalia asked gesturing her thumb toward the closed shop.

"Yeah, we aren't quite ready for the public yet. A few more days."

"And tell me why it is I should accompany a complete stranger."

"Well, normally I would advise against it, but in this case it would cause me great disappointment. Besides, I was hoping the whole reviving you and calling you an ambulance was at least enough to break the ice."

"Give me a minute to lock up," Nalia replied with a smirk. She walked casually past Jack and stepped inside Mama Lu's shop, successfully hiding the fact she was bursting with excitement. She took a second to catch a deep breath as the door closed behind her and the bells overhead tinkled to life. Her heart was dancing a tango.

Retrieving her bag and keys, Nalia locked the shop and found Jack staring at the sign next door.

"It does look dignified," he said with a satisfied smile. "Where are we headed?"

"Depends on what you want."

"History," Jack replied without hesitation. "Lead me to history."

"Well, you can't escape that in the quarter. Follow me."

Nalia began walking south on Decatur. Her gait was casual and relaxed, a welcomed change from her typical hurried pace. It would be nice to slow down and enjoy her surroundings on a deeper level. She found it peculiar that her comfort level with this stranger allowed for such ease. Being with Jack felt effortless and natural. Before Nalia could overanalyze the situation, Jackson Square came into view.

"From this side of the park you get a good view of the cathedral," said Nalia.

"And the equestrian statue of Andrew Jackson," Jack interrupted. "There are three others just like it, all cast by the same sculptor: one in Florida, one in Tennessee, and the original in D.C."

"Why do I get the feeling you're taking me on the history tour?" asked Nalia.

"You know they used to hang people here," Jack continued, undeterred. "Criminals, runaway slaves, and basically anybody who pissed off the wrong people. It used to be the military parade grounds. It also used to overlook the river before they built this area up with the levees." He paused for a moment taking in the sights and breathing the brisk air. He was just distracted enough to wish he'd opted for a jacket when he noticed the silence. Nalia's jaw was still open when he spun around.

"No, I'm serious. I feel like I'm in class here," she insisted.

Jack chuckled. "Sorry, I've done a lot of research on this area: the history, geography, demographics, it's all fascinating. It's so exciting to see the places I've read so much about."

"Well, don't stop now, professor," said Nalia, crossing her arms. "Impress me."

Standing tall with his hands on his hips, Jack took another deep breath and looked around. "The French Quarter is so unique in its makeup because it's one of the few places that combines residential and commercial properties and still manages to sustain heavy tourism. I mean, just look around. You've got apartments and hotels, condos and retail shops, restaurants, bars, museums, the cathedral, and the park. This small area is as diverse as the city itself. There is so much history here, so many ghosts just waiting to tell their stories."

"You mean actual ghosts?"

"I was actually using the term as a metaphor for the architecture, but yes, also that. New Orleans is reportedly one of the most haunted cities in the country... the world, for that matter. So many tragedies here: fires, war, yellow fever, storms, so many lives taken by calamity."

"Please tell me you aren't one of those ghost-hunter types who sees orbs in every ray of light and calls it a spirit." Nalia said, her crooked brow announcing a fresh reservation.

"Hardly," replied Jack, defensive but not offended. "Truth is stranger than fiction. I believe enough history will find us if we allow it; when we try and create it, we fall short. Can we go down to the old Urseline Convent?"

Nalia shook her head and smiled. Jack was like a kid in a candy store – a candy store where he studied, in detail, the ingredients of each and every treat sold, but a kid nonetheless.

"Later," she said adamantly. "First we eat. I'm starving." With a bounce in her step, she grabbed Jack by the arm and led him past the square.

They chatted about the buildings as they strolled down Decatur and took a right at Conti. "I'm sure you know most of the architecture in the Quarter is Spanish," Nalia said.

"Yes," Jack replied, "Nearly all the French colonial architecture was destroyed by the fires that burned the city in the late 1700s, which is why I'd like to see the convent. It's one of the only surviving structures."

"The French architecture, huh? You sure it has nothing to do with the legend of the casket girls?" asked Nalia playfully, watching for a reaction. Jack turned red. "I knew it! You do want to check out the hauntings."

"Okay, I admit it, they are intriguing. But I'm mostly interested in the historic sights."

"Sure you are," Nalia said unable to contain her cocky grin. "So since you're all about history, before we see the convent I'll take you by the Dauphine Hotel. It's one of the oldest buildings here. They say it dates back to when the city was founded."

"1718. I'd love to see the Dauphine. I've read the nails used in some of its construction were hand made in Jean Lafitte's blacksmith shop."

"That is the legend," Nalia confirmed. "Let's go this way, I'll show you another spot." The couple took a left on Royal Street and continued on to Iberville where Jack recognized the historic Hotel Monteleone immediately. "I thought you'd like seeing this one because it's historic and haunted, not to mention unique with its carousel bar. It should satisfy your ghost fascination. Rumor has it there are more sightings here than almost anywhere. They say there's an old grandfather clock in the lobby that's visited frequently by the ghost of its maker. I don't remember how old it is, but..." Nalia turned to find Jack staring at the building, awestruck. His mouth was slightly open and his eyes were glazed over with amazement. "Jack?"

"Huh? Oh!" he snapped. "Yes, this hotel dates back to the late 1800s. It went through a major expansion just before the stock market crash. It's a wonder the business survived the depression. Some say it's because the founder had the property blessed by Marie Laveau II."

"You know for someone who is mostly interested in historical sights, I'm starting to see a distinct theme here leaning toward the paranormal."

"No, nothing ghostly, spectral, or creepy! Marie Laveau is the subject of my new book. Lots of research going on in that department."

"Great. Tell me about it over lunch. We're almost there."

A block over, on Bourbon St., the couple found the line for Galatoire's. They would have waited a lot longer had the maître d' not recognized Nalia. Being related to Mambo Lucia Deminy had its privileges on occasion. They were seated at a corner table in the classic dining room where Jack wasted no time ordering a bottle of Sauvignon Blanc from the extensive wine list.

"My grandmother used to bring me here when I was young," confided Nalia, slightly surprised to open up so quickly. "She would show up on Sunday, dressed to the nines and whisk me off to brunch. We would spend most of the afternoon here, and it's the first place I ever tried coffee. She would always order a cup after her meal, and even though she rarely stated her preference, the waiters always remembered to bring it with cream and honey." Nalia sighed as her eyes went distant with remembrance.

"She sounds lovely," said Jack. "Does she still come here?"

Nalia swallowed the lump in her throat and allowed her reservations to hold her tongue. After a thoughtful pause she simply answered, "I think so." Her face relaxed into a peaceful smile, and Jack got the message.

Opening the menu, Jack retrieved a pair of gunmetal-framed Oakleys from his shirt pocket and casually fixed them across the bridge of his nose. When Nalia looked up she was stunned and quickly raised the menu to hide her expression. The addition of the glasses leveled Jack up from incredibly good-looking to insanely hot. With her face flushed, Nalia reached for a nearby glass of water and gulped voraciously. Though each glance made her thirst more insatiable, she continued to peer discreetly over the menu at Jack. Her glass was empty before the waiter returned with the wine.

After uncorking the bottle and allowing his guests to examine the bouquet, the waiter made his recommendations. Nalia ordered the Godchaux salad, a delicious mix of greens and seafood with a Creole mustard vinaigrette. Taking the server's suggestion Jack chose the Pompano. He was intrigued by the description of the Crabmeat Yvonne topping: sautéed mushrooms and artichoke with lump crab and meuniére butter.

"So tell me about this book you're writing," Nalia said, unable to take her eyes off her companion.

Jack blushed. "We are in a one-hundred-year-old dining establishment in the heart of the historic French Quarter in one of the oldest cities in the south, and you want to talk about a book?"

"We are at my favorite restaurant, in my home town, so yes, tell me about the book."

Jack sighed heavily and sipped his wine. "Marie Laveau," he said. "Fantastical legend, woman of mystery, dark sorceress, Voodoo queen of New Orleans, the legend goes on and on. But, who was she really, not according to legend, but as far as actual documented accounts of her life? Do the facts support or disprove her legacy? That's what I'm exploring."

"And that's why you're interested in Mama Lu?"

Jack swallowed hard and stiffened in his chair. "I'm sorry?"

Nalia tipped her glass toward him. A warning light was flashing somewhere in her conscience. "You told me yesterday you were eager to meet Mama Lu. I know I hit my head, but I certainly didn't imagine that part of our conversation, and I'm not stupid or naïve. You're writing a book on the Voodoo queen of New Orleans, you tell me you've done a little research on my Mama Lu, and I'm supposed to believe our lunch date is just a friendly afternoon get-together? If you've shown me one thing this afternoon, it's that you don't do a *little* research on anything. I'm sure you've dug pretty deep into my Mama's past, and you know all there is available to know about Mambo Lucia Deminy and her involvement with the Voodoo culture around here. So, if taking me out is some kind of ploy to get close to her, just tell me now and we can avoid a lot of difficulty." Her voice was calm and tolerant, not at all reflective of its cutting content. She even managed a smile as she lifted her glass, but her eyes were fixed and matter-of-fact.

Jack took another sip of his wine and returned it to the table. He removed his glasses and drew a deep breath. Slumping slightly in his chair, his eyes scanned back and forth along the tablecloth. "Let me try and explain," he said as Nalia sat back. "Yes, I have done a lot of research on Mambo Lucia, and yes, I have uncovered more than a fair share of stories, some more unsavory than others. But I look at your Mama Lu the same way I look at Marie Laveau, with a clean slate. I don't know where the facts branch off into legend, nor am I here to judge should I find out. I am not some news reporter ready to sensationalize a story just to make a buck. I'm a historian. I'm interested in the truth, whatever it may be, and my focus is Marie Laveau, not Mambo Lucia." Jack sat up and fixed his eyes firmly on Nalia's. "Have I done some homework on your Mama Lu? Yes. Am I interested in meeting her? Yes, I find her stories fascinating. But I asked you to lunch for one reason and one reason only, because when we met, I found you absolutely stunning. I had no idea what kind of person you were, but I thought 'Why not take a chance? This lovely woman might just say yes.' And I'm so glad you did, because during the course of this afternoon I've found you to be a genuine delight and even though it frightens me to admit it, I find myself sincerely attracted to you. So if I've done anything to cause you to feel uncomfortable, or to make you think you're here because of some hidden agenda, please accept my apology."

Nalia didn't know what to say. She was merely trying to clear the air and remove any unrealistic expectations. She didn't intend to come across as accusatory, nor did she mean to offend. All the same, she apparently plucked a nerve, and she found Jack's reaction touching. His humility and honesty softened her, and Nalia found herself simply melting. Barely able to speak, she cleared her throat and managed, "I feel as though I'm the one who needs to apologize."

The awkward exchange was cut gratefully short by the arrival of their entrées, and the presentation of the pompano in its steaming parchment packet served as a fine distraction. For the next hour they talked about a great many things while dining on the Quarter's finest cuisine. By the end of the meal, Nalia felt as if she'd known Jack for years. She successfully skirted questions about her past, preferring to learn more about him instead.

Sensing her hesitation, Jack didn't pry. After sharing a slice of sweet potato cheesecake, he insisted on picking up the check. They finished what they could of the wine before continuing their tour of the Quarter.

Nalia led Jack to the Dauphine Hotel as promised, where he regaled her with tales of Storyville, the red-light district of the late 1800s. Afterwards, they walked over to the Old Urseline Convent where, along with architecture, darker subjects returned to the discussion.

"So do you believe the story of the casket girls?" Nalia asked.

"Which one, that they were vampires themselves, or that they brought vampires with them to this country?"

"Either."

Jack thought for a moment. "How about neither," he said finally. "I don't believe in vampires. I've seen a lot of strange things in my life, but nothing to make me believe in undead creatures who walk about in the darkness drinking blood."

"But you believe in spirits."

"Spirits are a different matter altogether. Even though I've never seen one, their presence can be felt." Jack's gaze drifted off in reflection. "Don't you agree?"

If he only knew, thought Nalia. "We'll save that conversation for later," she replied.

Jack's eyes were smiling a deeply satisfied and content smile, one that originated in the very core of his soul. With a soft tone he said, "You know, I feel like I could walk around this town with you all day and never get bored."

A quick phone call to Mama Lu to ensure the shop was covered made it possible.

Nalia could not imagine being happier.

Chapter Twenty-Five

Mr. John's network was alive and working like a well-oiled machine. Cell phones vibrated in pockets all across the city as folks asked questions about what went down Sunday night. So far Mr. John had fielded over a dozen calls. He knew about a fire in the ninth ward, the hushed arrest of two prominent public figures, and the prostitute from the newspaper story who was found dead behind a dumpster just off Bourbon Street. Lightning was to blame for the fire, alcohol for the arrests, but there were no leads in the case of the murdered young woman. It was, however, the closest event in proximity to the area about which Mr. John was concerned. So far, none of his contacts could tell him anything about the mall in front of St. Louis Cathedral, but Mr. John was far from concerned. He was confident with enough time, one of his sources would turn up useful information about Madame Zoe.

He was not surprised when Charlie, whose nephew was a door man at one of the strip clubs on Bourbon, reported nothing out of the ordinary. The spectrum of "ordinary" on Bourbon Street was far too broad to be helpful. He did find it unusual when Tiny had nothing to offer. Tiny was a big man who played piano over at Palm Court and had for many years. He was well known in the jazz circles and played nearly every club in the city over the span of his career. Tiny told Mr. John he knew a sax player named Bobby D. who was playing on the streets down by the cathedral on Sunday night. "Nothin' unusual," Tiny conveyed, "Normal crowd... musicians, artists, card readers, and tourists. Bobby said the storm swooped in pretty hard just after dark and everybody went scatterin' like roaches." Unfortunately, Bobby D. vacated long before eight fifty-five.

While Mr. John kept faith in his network, Mama Lu was in a tizzy. By the time they reached The Doll Maker, shortly after lunch, Johnny the Conqueror was worn ragged. Mama Lu felt as if a thousand tiny needles were pricking her skin from head to toe. She could not relax, nor could she stand still. When she turned her key and opened the door, Mama Lu was surprised to hear only the sound of the overhead bells. Apparently, Nalia forgot to set the alarm when she left. Mama Lu briefly wondered where the girl's mind might be, but quickly turned her attention back to Zoe.

Before entering the building, Mr. John unlocked the panel behind his shoeshine stand. Reaching inside, he retrieved two small sachets, the first filled with a blend of herbs including sage, sandalwood, thyme, and bergamot. The other pouch was with filled with chamomile and lavender tea. The first he gave to Mama Lu, instructing her to tuck it in her bra, close to her heart. The second, he placed in an old, ceramic coffee mug.

After only a moment rummaging through the workroom, Mr. John located the old hot plate Mama Lu used for melting paraffin and certain epoxies that bonded better when heated. He plugged it in near the paint table and used it to brew Mama Lu a soothing cup of tea. He found a packet of raw sugar in the catch-all bin at the end of the table and brought the sweetened cup out to Mama Lu. She was seated on a stool behind the counter keeping an eye on a young couple browsing the displays. Mr. John was glad to see customers keeping her occupied. His gris-gris would work faster with her mind marginally distracted.

He leaned against the counter for a moment while the tea cooled, making sure Mama Lu's spirit settled. While he knew his herbs, strong as they were, could not relax her completely, he was confident they would take the edge off. As Mama Lu sipped the tea, Mr. John fingered the phone in his pocket, turning its ringer off. He could check his messages and return calls a bit later, he decided; Mama Lu did not need the anxiety caused by its incessant ringing. Like a physician monitoring anesthesia, Mr. John watched his gris-gris take effect, but his mind was already next door. He was sure he saw lights on in the watch maker's store and remembered Nalia's request to check the old man out. As soon as Mama Lu was a bit more settled, Mr. John excused himself, stating a desire to snoop around the gadgets at the neighboring shop. He had in truth, been dying to poke about the merchandise ever since his initial visit when the crates arrived.

Exiting The Doll Maker, Mr. John once again stopped quickly at his shoeshine stand to pocket a small pouch before proceeding next door. The lights in the neighboring shop were indeed burning but the shade and blinds remained drawn. Peeking in around the edges of the window, he saw movement on the far side. Undeterred by the CLOSED sign, Mr. John tapped on the glass next to the newly-stenciled lettering. He got no answer.

Determined to get inside the building, Mr. John tapped a little louder, and a little longer. When again no one came, he began slapping the wood of the door with the palm of his hand. The old door rattled in the jamb until finally, the shade was pulled aside, and a distinguished, white-haired man peered out with a less-than-pleasant look on his face. Without a word the old man pointed a thin finger to the sign in the corner of the glass and let the shade drop back into place.

Before the old man could get too far, Mr. John rapped on the door once more. This time he heard the bolt turn and the door opened.

"We're closed," said the old man, obviously aggravated. "Not open until next week."

Mr. John gently placed his hand against the open door and offered the old man an exaggerated grin. "Yes sir, I understand. I ain't lookin' to purchase anythin', not yet at least."

The old man grew even more aggravated. An insistent individual who had no interest in buying was either selling something, or was another of those city officials looking to harass him about proper permits.

Mr. John quickly attempted to deescalate the man's rising irritation. "I'm yo' neighbor, John Barrett," he said extending his other hand. "I run the shoe-shine stand out front. Just wanted to drop by and welcome you to the buildin'." Noticing the old man's expression begin to soften, Mr. John kept talking. "Sure is nice to have somebody moving in over here. Business always seems to do a lil' better when the buildin' is full. I been here for a good many years now and I've seen..."

"It's very nice to meet you, Mr. Barrett," interrupted the old man with a reserved smile, "But if you'll excuse me..."

"I brought somethin' fo' you," said Mr. John, applying pressure to the door. He reached into his pocket and produced the gris-gris bag. "I'll show you what it's fo'." Mr. John gently pushed his way inside, pleasantly chatting all the while. His gesture was forceful, but polite.

The store was quiet, with a soothing ambience. Classical piano music played softly from the speaker system, not quite loud enough to cover the ticking of the vast collection of ornate timepieces.

"Dis here is a special packet I make myself... whoa!" Mr. John stammered, genuinely awestruck by the fine collection of clocks on display. Moving around the elderly gent, he made a conscious effort to keep his jaw in place as he surveyed the inventory of fine pieces. "These are beautiful," said Mr. John, moving closer to a large grandfather clock, ornamented with layers of delicately carved wooden panels along the sides. The piece was richly stained and flamed around the edges to accentuate the distressed carvings. The wooden panels were cut into large, toothed wheels, layered one on top of another and fitted together to form a train of wooden gears. The artwork was exquisite. Years of woodworking gave Mr. John a particular appreciation for the craftsmanship. He approached the clock reverently, gently running his fingertips over the glossy finish. "You do dis' work yo'self?" he asked.

The old man hesitated, discerning whether or not to continue the conversation with his unwelcomed guest. After a moment and a lengthy sigh, he made up his mind. "The design is mine. The woodwork I had done to my specifications, the clockwork I crafted myself."

Mr. John was so taken with the carvings, he had yet to notice the intricacies of the clock's face. Different sized gears were tooled and shaped to form a three-dimensional border around the edge. Polished brass numbers were attached to the frame, and the face was backed with lightly frosted glass, so the clockwork's ghostly image could be seen beyond the hands. Mr. John could not stop staring.

"I don' believe I've ever seen anythin' like dis," he said humbly.

"It'll be for sale in a few days, if you like it," said the old man, his tone easing.

From the small knob on the glass cover, hung a tiny, handwritten paper tag. On it was scribbled the word "Cherry" followed by a staggeringly large number.

"I'm gon' have to shine a few mo' shoes befo' I can afford dat," coughed Mr. John, turning toward the counter. Setting down the gris-gris bag, he admired the extensive display of watches under the glass, paying particular attention to the pocket variety. "How long you been in the watch b'ness, Mister...?"

"Haufmann," offered the old man, moving behind the counter and sliding his hand over a gold pocket watch left open beside a set of jeweler's tools. He closed its cover quickly and casually slipped the piece into his pocket, studying Mr. John all the while. "Elias Haufmann." As he spoke, the old man reached down and flipped a switch on the back of the display. Several lights flickered to life inside the case sending a refracted rainbow shimmering across Mr. John's awed expression. "See anything you like, Mr. Barrett?" the old man asked, more concerned with sizing Mr. John up than his actual answer.

"What's not to like?" he replied with a smile. "I always did have a fancy fo' pocket watches. You got some real beauties, here." Mr. John looked over the pieces, nearly salivating, before turning his attention to the tiny screwdrivers at the end of the counter. "You do repairs, too?" he asked, reaching into his pocket.

The old man stiffened. His expression turned sour as he took a step back, touching the watch in his pocket through the fabric of his pants. "Yes," he said, guarded. "Why do you ask?"

Sensing the old man withdraw, Mr. John looked up curiously. Though the corners of his mouth remained taut, the sincerity of Mr. Haufmann's smile had faded. Presenting his antique silver watch, Mr. John studied the old man's reaction. "Dis thing ain't keepin' good time no mo'," he said, flipping open the cover. "Seem like every day I gots to reset it, 'cause it's lost a few minutes."

The old man stepped back to the counter and took the watch from Mr. John. Turning the piece over in his hand, he examined its intricate patterns while searching for its markings. As he studied the watch, his expression softened, and his mannerisms grew more relaxed. He squinted, struggling to see the tiny lettering found along the edge. Eventually, the old man moved into better light and propped a pair of wire-framed spectacles over the bridge of his nose. With his mouth falling idly open, he moved the watch back and forth in an attempt to focus.

"Dat's been in my family fo' a long time, now," said Mr. John. "B'longed to my great, great, grandfather, used to work the railroad."

The old man shot an inquisitive glance over his spectacles. "When was that?" he drawled.

Mr. John shuffled his eyes, doing the math in his head. "Probably somewhere 'round nineteen-hun'ed."

The old man allowed a smile to creep across his face. "I'm guessing more like 1885," he said. "AWWCo."

He set the watch down on the glass-topped counter and retrieved one of the tiny screwdrivers. With it, he pointed to a miniscule engraving along the bottom edge, inside the case. "American Waltham Watch Company. The marking tells me it was made before 1907 when they dropped the A, shortening the name to simply Waltham Watch Company. Of course, the fact he used it on the railroad already told me it predated 1908. It's a hunter's case, stem-wind, stem-set. In 1908, the railroads standardized their pocket watches to open-faced, stem-wind, lever-set models. It's rare to see one like this in silver. Very unique. You say it's losing time, eh? You mind if I take a look?"

"I was hopin' you would," smiled Mr. John, sheepishly rubbing the back of his neck.

Elias Haufmann went to work on the antique watch. Pulling a soft cloth from his pocket, he flattened it on the countertop and placed the watch in the middle. In a matter of seconds, he had the piece disassembled. Retrieving a loupe from his shirt pocket he examined the clockwork, studying each gear.

Soon, the old man's slumping posture stiffened. Pulling the loupe from his eye, he looked across the counter at Mr. John. "Well your mainspring coil is in surprisingly good condition, but if you'll notice right here," he said pointing to a particular section of one of the larger gears, "A few of your teeth are worn down."

Mr. John looked closely but could not see it with his naked eye. Handing him the loupe, the old man said, "Look through here."

With the magnification of the loupe, Mr. John could see wear on the brass wheel. When he looked back up, the old man was gone.

Next to the door of the shop's back room was a large cabinet with many small plastic drawers. It was old, unsightly, and out of place next to the rich new decor. "I was told I needed to keep this cabinet in the back," said the old man, gingerly tapping on the drawers with his fingertips as he searched for the correct label. "But I like it here where I've got easy access to it. I don't move as fast as I used to, and I need all of my accoutrements close by."

Finding the drawer he was looking for, the old man gave it a hearty thump and removed it from the cabinet. He brought it and another set of tiny tools back over to the counter. Faster than Mr. John thought possible, the old man replaced the worn part, reassembled the watch, wound it, set it, and handed it back. "That ought to do it," he said with a smile while Mr. John stared.

"You mean you had the part for dis old watch right there in yo' cabinet?"

"It's not an uncommon gear, pretty standard for that time period, but yes I've amassed quite an inventory of parts over the years."

"I don't know what to say. How much I owe you?"

"No charge, neighbor," said the old man tucking his tools away. "Besides, like I said, we're not even open yet."

Mr. John could only stammer in refusal, but the old man insisted. Finally, Mr. John accepted the man's generosity and offered a simple "thank you" while tucking the watch back into his pocket.

"You going to show me what's in that bag?" asked the old man.

"Oh, I almos' forgot," said Mr. John palming the gris-gris bag. "You ain't gots to open it up for it to work. You just tuck it into yo' cash register."

"What's inside?" the old man asked.

"Squill root," replied Mr. John. "Draws money to you. Good for business. Keep it in yo' register and always keep a coin next to it, the bigger the better."

The old man raised a single eyebrow. "I don't mean to offend, Mr. Barrett, but I don't see how a little piece of root is going to increase my revenue. Sounds like a bit of nonsense to me."

"I don't take no offense at all, Mr. Haufmann," laughed Mr. John. "You ain't the first person to doubt my gris-gris. I done heard dem same words plenty o' times. You jus' tuck dat into yo' register and watch it work. You'll see."

The old man was unconvinced, but kept the bag all the same. He thanked Mr. John for the gesture and politely asked to be allowed the opportunity to get back to his work. Mr. John obliged.

"I can tell you gon' be seein' plenty o' me, Mr. Haufmann," he said, still admiring the clocks as he left. The old man offered a dismissive wave as he punched the tender button on his antique cash register. He took one last look at the small pouch, turning it over between his fingers before tossing it into the tray and shutting the drawer. Casting his eyes toward the front of the store he caught the shadow of Mr. John through the blinds, moving past the window.

"Good day... doctor," he said, under his breath.

Chapter Twenty-Six

Nalia and Jack's tour of the French Quarter concluded early in the evening with coffee at Antoine's on Royal Street, where they discussed the grisly practices of Madame Delphine LaLaurie, whose mansion stood a few blocks away. Jack wanted to see the three-story, storm-grey structure before dark, so with blue hour dawning, the couple headed north. The two admired the now fully renovated building from across the street, its contrasting stark-white and jet-black trim creating bold lines against the pinkish sky. Speculating how many bodies escaped excavation and were still buried on the property, Jack told Nalia about the first restoration in the eighteen-seventies. Burned and charred floorboards were removed from the upstairs torture chamber uncovering more than a dozen skeletons hidden for over forty years.

In addition to the LaLaurie mansion, Nalia showed him the infamous home of Jacques St. Germaine.

"Once again," said Jack, "Don't believe in vampires. Intriguing story, the man who lives forever, but I'll save the vampire stories for Hollywood."

"I've always found the story and the concept fascinating," Nalia said. "Having the ability to extend your life through centuries. You know, his story is where we get the legend of the philosopher's stone. Don't you think it would be grand, the gift of immortality?"

Jack thought for a moment. "As a historian," he said finally, "I believe I would find the gift of time travel more suiting. I find the mysteries of the past far more interesting than the promise of the future."

Putting his arm around Nalia's shoulder, Jack pulled her into his side. For a fleeting few seconds Nalia was uncomfortable, but quickly relaxed into the moment, pulling her hands into the sleeves of her sweater and tucking herself against Jack's body. He rubbed his hand up and down her arm, warming her with friction.

"It's getting chilly out," he said. "We'd better get back."

As the two turned back toward The Doll Maker, Jack looked down at Nalia, admiring her placid smile. "You know," he said, "You're like a second-hand sweater."

The comment took a moment to register. When it did, Nalia's face crinkled with confusion and offense. "Excuse me?" she said, pulling away from his side. Jack stopped in his tracks.

"Well, you're new. We just met, but there's something familiar about you. You have this wonderfully intimate quality that draws me in and makes me feel like you've been here all along. With you I'm not stiff, awkward, or itchy. I'm comfortable. And, I don't know... I guess I'd just like to be comfortable more often."

A bit shocked, Nalia did not know what to say. The few seconds she stood staring seemed to stretch for hours. "Are you saying you want to see me again?" she finally asked with a playful grin.

"I think so, yes."

"Well, we could always turn this into dinner," said Nalia, surprised at her candor. She was excited by the possibility, but felt Jack's spirit sink at the suggestion.

"I would love nothing more," he responded with regret. "But I've got some business to take care of tonight, a meeting with a consultant."

The corner of Nalia's mouth shifted to the side, the only outward indication of the surprising disappointment swelling inside her. She tried to pass the letdown off as insignificant but Jack sensed her chagrin.

"Please don't think I'm searching for some easy avenue of avoidance. I really do have a meeting this evening, and I truly would like to see you again."

His eyes were honest, thought Nalia. There was something hauntingly familiar about them, warm and understanding. She accepted his reasoning and tucked herself back into Jack's side as they continued their walk to the shop.

Nalia insisted on taking the St. Charles line home, despite Jack's offer of a ride if she was willing to wait until the undetermined time of his meeting's conclusion. After a lengthy goodbye, culminating in a reluctant separation of her hand from Jack's, Nalia headed for Canal Street. Still unsure of exactly what transpired over the last several hours, she could not explain her spirit's thirst.

A thin sliver of light ran the length of the window where Jack peered through the blinds into the darkened street. The natural gas lanterns suspended from the overhanging gallery washed the sidewalk with a flickering glow as foot traffic passed beneath, sending shadows dancing along the uneven pavement. Several sets of headlights passed while Jack watched but as of yet, none stopped. Tonight, he was waiting for the black Lincoln's arrival.

Having given Madame Luciénne's proposal careful consideration, not for the simple benefits she claimed would accompany inclusion in her business league, but for the greater prize of aiding his quest, Jack eagerly awaited their meeting.

A single obsession burned in his mind like an ember refusing to cool. Years of following leads to dead ends left his research pointing directly to a mystery-shrouded woman named Margaret Barronne. A budding socialite destined for New Orleans aristocracy, despite her husband's reclusive nature, the woman simply vanished into thin air one brisk October evening, nearly twenty years ago. Properties were left abandoned, bank activities ceased, and public records disappeared. While the discovery of her wealthy, influential husband's bound and mutilated corpse pointed to a mob vendetta, there existed no such evidence of Margaret's fate. Foul play was never ruled out in the case of her disappearance, and considering reputed ties to the Verelli crime family, general suspicion remained she met the same grisly end as her husband. However, proof in the form of a body was never uncovered, giving Jack cause to entertain a different theory.

Around the same time, the Verellis' two key players also disappeared without a trace, essentially ending the family's regional control. Dark tales of their fate abounded, including hushed rumors of strange Voodoo practices. True or not, the result was the same: the Verelli's vanished, and someone was responsible. In between the facts and the fiction, lay the answers Jack sought – answers to the questions surrounding Margaret Barronne. If his hunch was right, the Verellis never got to Margaret, affording the woman an opportunity to flee and change her identity. All things considered, she could have also stayed in, or around New Orleans under an assumed name. She could even still be living in the area. Whichever scenario was actually true, Jack was certain she had help, and he knew just one person capable of orchestrating such a grandiose deception.

The corners of his mouth curled with satisfaction as Madame Luciénne's large automobile glided to the curb. He watched as the driver's door opened and a wide-brimmed hat tipped out of the vehicle. She was alone, and from the way she slammed the car door, less than even-tempered. Though he watched her approach the entrance, Jack allowed Vivian time to knock. He waited several seconds before pulling aside the shade, acknowledging her arrival, and opening the door.

Madame Luciénne was all business. Her skirt was tight, cut well above the knee, and though her jacket was a bit outdated it complimented her figure well. Her signature sly smile intact, she slunk past Jack looking him up and down as she entered. She walked with purpose to the counter, threw down her bag, and turned with a snap.

"Are we alone?" she asked impatiently.

"We are... confidential," Jack replied. "My grandfather is upstairs. He has no concern for what's going on down here, and even if he did, his hearing isn't what it used to be."

Madame Luciénne stiffened uncomfortably, looking around the shop, her eyes paying particular attention to the door in the rear. "I hope you haven't called me here just to disappoint me, Mr. Haufmann," she announced. "I am expectin' good news."

"Oh, I don't think you'll be disappointed at all," said Jack, locking the door and avoiding eye contact. His pace was relaxed and casual as he turned and made his way to the counter. Keeping his head down in ponderance, Jack continued. "I've given your proposal a great deal of thought," he said. "I'm eager to discuss an arrangement."

Madame Luciénne swelled with pride. She found herself breathing more easily, able to release the wrinkles in her brow she hadn't realized were there. A thin smile of satisfaction conquered her agitated visage.

"I also have some stipulations," Jack continued, moving behind the counter and stiffening to a confident bearing.

Madame Luciénne's smile withered into a stare of disbelief. Her hope for an amicable agreement was quickly waning; Jack's eyes held a stern, unwavering resolve that made her uneasy. The longer she held her tongue, the more control she felt slipping from her grasp. With a deep breath she placed both palms on the countertop and straightened her back.

"Last time we spoke," she began, dropping her chin. "I believe I made certain conditions clear, Mr. Haufmann. I don't see much room for compromise."

"Then perhaps you should broaden your perspective, Madame," Jack quipped, showing no sign of retreat. "Your arrogance limits your vision."

Madame Luciénne's lips parted in shock. Her instinct was to turn and walk away, leaving Jack to suffer the consequences of his unwillingness to cooperate, but the arrogance he spoke of would not allow her to leave without the last word. She lifted a finger, preparing to speak, but Jack cut her off.

"I reevaluated the not-so-subtle threat you made last time we spoke and decided it didn't suit me," he said. "So here's what I'm proposing."

"Mr. Haufmann," interrupted Vivian, boldly, "Survival in the Quarter is becomin' more dependent on my assistance, every day. If you want dis lil' business of your grandfather's to last more than six months before it's shut down, I suggest you refrain from makin' any proposals. My offer is more than generous. The benefits I'm offerin' are well worth what amounts to a minor indiscretion of ethics."

"I don't think you understand," Jack interrupted, nonchalantly.

"I'm quite sure you don't understand," Vivian fired back. Her patience wore paper-thin. "You're gon' list me in that book as a descendant of Marie Laveau or I'll not only shut dis place down..."

"You won't do a damned thing without me," Jack said, his voice slightly elevated. "Now, shut up and listen."

Luciénne bit her tongue. She was shocked and angered, but there was a burning in Jack's eyes she hadn't seen before, like flame dancing over coals.

"You don't get it, I can help you or I can ruin you, but it's my choice. I can sing your praises or I can shape your demise. I will either substantiate your lineage or include you in a chapter on false claims to ancestry, swindlers who use Marie Laveau's name to defraud their clients. I'm willing to negotiate, but I will not be backed into a corner and force-fed terms and conditions."

"There's a word for what you're threatenin'," spat Luciénne. "It's called slander."

"Actually, it's called libel. I'm quite familiar with the term and its legal ramifications. It's not libel if the claims are factual, and I already have enough facts to squash any allegation you might try to bring. I've done enough research on you to fill a novel. Hell, my publisher wants me to submit it as a separate work."

Madame Luciénne's eyes became slits and her brow creased once again. Her face grew warm as anger brought her blood to a simmer.

"Now if you'll take a moment to breathe," Jack went on, calmly, "Perhaps we can discuss some terms that will benefit both of us."

Madame Luciénne hadn't realized she was holding her breath. She tried to release it slowly in defiance, but his crystal-blue eyes saw right through her charade. Jack had her full attention.

"Now I'm willing to scratch your back if you can, in turn, take care of my itch," said Jack, playfully. "I'm looking for someone, and I think you can help me find her."

Madame Luciénne cocked her head to one side. "I don't know, Jack. Yo' tactics are makin' my back itch somethin' fierce."

Jack's expression morphed into a dreamy smile, sending unexpected chills through Madame Luciénne's body.

"Oh come on, Vivian," he said slyly. "Surely an ambitious woman such as yourself enjoys a healthy game of hard ball."

"Talk to me."

Jack laughed. "Blame it on the fact that I tend to be a completionist, but there is a story I've been looking into for years which vexes me to this day. It's become somewhat of an obsession, I'm afraid. As you may be aware, there was more than one Marie Laveau."

Madame Luciénne rolled her eyes. "I *am* from New Orleans."

"I thought as much. Well, history tells us the legacy of Marie the First was continued by her daughter Marie the Second. Some accounts say there was even a third, fueling rumors of her unnaturally long life and even immortality. They all went by the same name and looked just alike, so back then people didn't know the difference. Now, legend paints Marie the First as the more benevolent figure and her daughter, Marie the Second as a real nasty piece of work. My research, however, indicates elements of good and evil in both ladies' character. Like all of us, right?" Jack searched Madame Luciénne's eyes to make sure she was following. She smiled and nodded slightly in agreement.

"However, I did run across some evidence to suggest Marie the Second was the more feared of the two. During the late eighteen-hundreds a branch of the family, the Darcantels, fell from Marie the Second's good graces and moved away to escape her wrath. Marie was gaining notoriety and a fearful reputation, so after settling in Georgia, the Darcantels changed their name to avoid association. Instead of changing the name outright, they morphed it... into Decantrel."

The color faded from Luciénne's face as a tingle of anxiety climbed her spine and settled at the base of her skull. She managed to keep her smile firmly in place but all manner of pleasantry drained from her eyes like sand through an hourglass. Seeing her unsettled, Jack went on.

"I've traced the Decantrels to their last surviving relative, a woman named Margaret from Atlanta. Twenty-three years ago, she married a wealthy businessman named Michael Barronne and moved to New Orleans. The couple enjoyed substantial success for over six years before they disappeared."

"Disappeared?" asked Vivian, feigning surprise and trying not to swallow hard.

"Oh, they eventually found the husband, or at least his body, but Margaret Barronne simply... vanished."

Vivian fought hard to keep her breathing steady as the anxiety crawled across her scalp like marching ants. Her hands trembled as horrific visions raced across her mind: a nearly-nude woman bound with chains, the flash of a ceremonial blade, blood spilling over a ritual table. She did well to suppress the memories over the years, but certain images could not be forgotten; at the simple mention of a name, they blazed fully back to life.

When Jack spoke again, Madame Luciénne wondered how long her silence had lingered while thoughts of Margaret raped her consciousness.

"Don't try and convince me all this is news to you, Vivian. I've got a feeling I know what happened to Margaret Barronne, and the look in your eyes tells me I'm on the right track."

Luciénne gasped, batting her eyes nervously and trying to form words that would not escape her gaping mouth.

"The mob took care of her husband, I'm certain of that, and she was running from them too. From what I've read about the Verellis, you didn't sidestep them easily and you definitely couldn't disappear without help. The kind of vanishing act Margaret Barronne pulled off required the assistance of someone who was well-connected. Like I said, I've done my homework on you. I know you've got the kind of connections that could make it happen."

Jack let his statement linger in the air for a moment while he watched Madame Luciénne sweat. Her bearing was calm but her eyes were squirming and looking for the door. She definitely knew something.

"But, you didn't have all those connections back then, did you? No, not until you escaped the watchful eyes of Mama Lucia Deminy."

Luciénne's squirming became scrambling, and her body language betrayed her. Her fingers twitched involuntarily, and her eyes widened like balloons about to burst.

"Mama Lu, as they call her," Jack went on, "Had a wealth of power and influence back then. According to most accounts, she had the whole city under her thumb. Rumors say she's the most powerful Voodoo queen since Marie Laveau herself, so helping someone change their identity would have been child's play. Or so it seems."

Madame Luciénne's mind was racing like wildfire through dry brush. She did not like being caught off-guard, she hated feeling out of control, and she loathed uncertainty. She could feel the blood surging through her veins and hear her own heartbeat pounding in her ears. Jack was entirely too interested in subjects which needed no attention.

"I know Margaret Barronne is still around," Jack continued, his sly grin widening. "I know Mama Lu helped hide her, probably changed her name and provided protection. You worked for Mama Lu back then; you're bound to have known Margaret Barronne. I need to find her. I need to know where she is."

Madame Luciénne cleared her throat, choking back a sigh of relief. Her muscles cried out in sweet release as the tension holding them captive loosened its grip. If Jack thought Margaret was still alive, it would be much easier to claim no knowledge of her current whereabouts than attempt an explanation of the alternative. In fact, now that she was off the ropes, Madame Luciénne thought, she might even be able to find an advantage in this match. She held her expression, studying Jack. There was urgency in his eyes she hadn't noticed before. He hadn't said he "wanted" to find Margaret; he used the word "need". Some small part of his proposition reeked of desperation. Madame Luciénne relaxed her back and leaned over the glass, display counter. The lights inside twinkled off the polished, precious metals and gemstones throwing a dazzling refraction onto her long neck. She looked down at the artful display in the case, watching the pieces shimmer. They spoke without words, she thought. There was a certain majesty in their silence. Holding her tongue, she tested the limits of Jack's patience.

His restraint splintering, Jack wrung his fingers into fists as a vein on the side of his neck began to pulse. "Vivian, if you want to negotiate any kind of deal with me, I need to know what you can tell me about Margaret Barronne," he said finally.

Finding his insistence telling, Madame Luciénne proceeded with questions instead of answers, toying with him. "Why is Margaret Barronne so important to you? There must be plenty of other descendants of Marie Laveau you can investigate and interview for yo' book. The woman had, what, fifteen children?"

"It's the bloodline," said Jack, resisting the urge to slap the counter. "There are others related by marriage of distant cousins and stepchildren, but Margaret Barronne is the last of the direct traceable bloodline to Marie Laveau. She's the one I want. What can you tell me?"

Madame Luciénne considered the implications of Jack's words, of Marie Laveau's ancestry reaching all the way to Margaret Barronne... and beyond. Mama Lu was good, thought Madame Luciénne. She reflected briefly on what kind of power and pull it must take to make a person completely disappear. If a seasoned professional spent years researching every detail of Margaret Barronne's life, and turned up a cold, dead end, Mama Lu was good, indeed. She recalled the look in Mama Lu's eyes the night they split Margaret's soul, the night she swore to protect the child. It held a promise of swift justice for the disloyal.

Vivian never revealed the child's identity to anyone. It was one thing to betray Mambo Lucia, quite another to endanger her child.

Madame Luciénne weighed her options. She was one of few people alive who had witnessed the vengeance of Mama Lu, seen first-hand the kind of power the woman could wield, even narrowly escaped her wrath. She was not of a mind to cross the line again. Still, circumstances were different now. The child whose identity she swore to conceal was grown and now knew about her past.

"What can you tell me, Vivian?" Jack fired, his impatience swelling.

"I don't know anything about Margaret Barronne, other than she used to frequent the store. She was a vile woman as I recall, but well-financed. I remember wishin' I worked on commission when she was around."

"You're not telling me anything I don't already know, Vivian. What happened to her? Where is she?"

Surely revealing her true lineage would be beneficial, thought Vivian, minimal repercussions, at worst. There was really no one from whom she needed to hide, no one left to harm her. "I'm afraid I don't know anything else," Vivian demanded. "One day she just stopped visitin' the shop. I heard about her disappearance on the news. I assumed, like everyone else, she was dead. If Mama Lu had anything to do with hidin' her away, I never knew. She never trusted me much, anyway."

"Only enough to apprentice you," Jack said with a poisonous tone. He studied Luciénne's reaction, not to gauge whether she was lying, he already knew that, but to find her breaking point.

Vivian bristled. She was no longer simply uncomfortable, she was offended and angry. She felt violated. Her nosed turned up in disgust. How much had this meddlesome writer learned about her? How far into her closet had he reached? "Well, Mr. Haufmann," she said with thick distaste, "You have done yo' homework, haven't you?" Reaching for her bag, Madame Luciénne prepared herself for a dramatic exit. While she was not exactly sure how to combat Jack Haufmann yet, she knew how to categorize him – formidable. "I'm afraid there's nothin' more I can tell you," she said. "Now, if you'll be so kind as to show me out, I really must go. I'm sorry we could not come to terms, I hope dis doesn't end our negotiation."

Jack's nostrils flared as he attempted to stifle his resentment. With a smug expression he stuffed his hands deep into his pockets and rounded the counter. "It's a pity we couldn't reach an agreement. With Margaret Barronne ending the bloodline, there would be no real opposition to your claim of lineage if I were to include it," he said walking to the door.

Madame Luciénne felt an emptiness, like opportunity was slipping through her fingers. She must be certain. There would be no second chance.

"My publisher just informed me today the rights to distribution have gone international. The legend of Marie Laveau has large appeal in Haiti, South America, parts of Africa, even Australia. Sounds like a major deal."

The threat was gone. Surely enough time had passed by now. Protection and secrecy were no longer relevant. The promise was made so long ago.

Jack reached for the bolt and turned it with finality. Shaking his head, he opened the door. "Have you ever considered the possibilities of expanding your interests... globally?"

Luciénne held her breath. Just one more step would finalize her decision. It was a step she could not take. Locking her eyes on Jack, she reached for the door, closed it, and turned the bolt.

"You're never gon' find the woman you're lookin' for," she said resting her back against the door jamb. "Margaret Barronne is dead. I can't tell you how I know, but it's an indisputable certainty."

Jack went silent. His mouth hung slightly open in stunned reflection. His eyes filled with restrained panic, like a lost child trying not to cry. Vivian sensed his weakness.

"But what if told you I'm just as certain, she ain't the last of the bloodline."

Jack looked up in disbelief. For a fleeting second Madame Luciénne thought she recognized hope, but if it existed, it was quickly squashed by denial.

"I don't have time for games, Vivian. Margaret Barronne was the last of Marie Laveau's ancestry. All the records validate that fact."

"Well, of course they do, darlin', they're supposed to," said Luciénne as her catlike grin found its home. "They were altered, hidden, and destroyed to make it look exactly that way."

In a single moment Jack's whole world shifted; every cell in his body reflected it. Completely unaware he was hanging on Madame Luciénne's every word, his facial expression dissolved to a blank slate.

"What are you saying?" he asked, scarcely whispering.

"Mama Lu hid somebody away alright, but it wasn't Margaret Barronne," said Vivian, drawing Jack in with a silky timbre, inching closer with every breath. "Now let's discuss my inclusion and my percentage of yo' book, while I tell you about Margaret Barronne's daughter."

Chapter Twenty-Seven

Mama Lu sat at her kitchen table wearing a house dress and slippers. She was alone, nursing a cup of weak tea and picking at a cold piece of pecan pie. She flaked off bits of crust with her fork as she stared past the pie to the shallow bowl of water behind it. A single pillar candle burned nearby, its flame reflecting off the water's oily surface. Mama Lu was not really hungry. She was picking at the dessert more out of frustration than anything. Her failed attempt to see Zoe in the oil on the water left her nerves standing on end and her spirit nearly broken. Reaching a point where she felt the need to cry, destroy something, or otherwise occupy her mind, tea and pie seemed the most benign option.

The back door was open with light from the porch spilling through the screen. The chirp of crickets filled the air, mocking Mama Lu's inability to view the spirit world. The resulting sense of loss gnawed at her soul like a starving rodent. *The sight* served her so well for so long, she was helpless without it. The revelation of the depth of her dependence was frightening.

Her friend was out there somewhere, trapped between the world of the living and the world of the dead, and Mama Lu was unable to help. If she could not find Madame Zoe, who could? How long would her friend remain in this tortured hell?

Mr. John's network proved just as useless as *the sight*, thus far. All avenues of acquiring information were blocked off, like the world suddenly went dark.

Perhaps *the sight* was spitefully growing cold, thought Mama Lu. After all, she stepped down from her public position years ago and all but abandoned her religion when she took in Nalia. Serious folks with serious issues still knew where to find Mama Lu when they needed her, but that aside, she was not immersed in traditions or practice the way she once was. Perhaps *the sight* finally grew tired of her neglect.

"Certainly not," Mama Lu argued with herself. The spirits still communed with her. She still observed holy days, rituals, and annual traditions. She still practiced enough spellcraft to keep serious followers from having to turn to charlatans like Vivian Luciénne. She served her community and held the religion in good favor before the scoffers and misguided attention-seekers. Still, *the sight* seemed to have abandoned her. She could not see Madame Zoe, nor could she see who was blocking her or why.

As she picked at the pie's crust a bit more, Mama Lu was suddenly struck with an alarming notion. Turning to the clock on the stove, she noticed the hour was late. Nalia should have been home long before now. She called earlier to say she was extending her lunch break, showing a friend around the Quarter. When she did not return before closing time, Mama Lu didn't give the matter much thought, surmising Nalia simply decided to take the rest of the afternoon off. The idea seemed harmless enough. Truth be known, Mama Lu's focus was still on Zoe and not much else. She had casually entertained Mr. John's ramblings about the new neighbor. Mr. Haufmann, the watch maker, came off as a reserved but delightful gentleman. Mr. John was looking forward to having him fit some wood pieces with clockwork. He mentioned Nalia seemed a bit uneasy about the elderly gent, but he couldn't understand why. He talked quite a bit in between fielding fruitless calls from his network.

He'd attempted to hide the phone calls, tried to disguise the subject matter being discussed, but Mama Lu was no fool. She could read between the lines and knew he was trying not to worry her. His gris-gris helped a bit with her nerves, but in the end Mama Lu was still hopelessly preoccupied.

No sooner than her mind turned to Nalia, Mama Lu heard footsteps coming up the walk and then the distinct creaking of the back steps. A shadow from the porch light filled the screen door as Nalia shuffled across the wood planks, but Mama Lu continued to stare at the water in the bowl.

Nalia was a bit startled by the atypical scene. She was not used to seeing the kitchen lit by a single candle. Even less familiar was the worry twisting Mama Lu's face. Noting the bowl of water and the two amber vials beside the candle, Nalia opened the screen quietly and stepped inside. As she set her bag down beside the coat rack, Mama Lu looked up.

"You can turn the light on, chil'," she said, sitting back and rubbing her eyes. "Dis is provin' pointless anyway."

Nalia flipped the switch and the light above the table sparked to life. Mama Lu looked exhausted. Her eyes were sunken and glassy, her expression careworn. Shocked, Nalia sat at the table next to her. "You want to talk about it?" she asked.

"Ain't no use," replied Mama Lu, pushing the barely-touched pie across the table. "Not much to talk about, crust is dry, fillin's a lil' too sweet."

Nalia pursed her lips. "You know that's not what I meant. What's with the divination tools? I haven't seen you use anything like this in ages."

"Can't see nothin' no other way, figured I'd give it a try."

"And?"

Mama Lu shook her head. "Nothin'."

"Still no news on Madame Zoe?" Nalia asked, picking up the fork. "I thought for sure Mr. John would've turned up something by now."

"Nobody's been able to tell him anythin' dat lets me know where she's at, or what done happened to her," answered Mama Lu, tears forming in the corners of her eyes. "I can't see her. Oil jus' sits on top the water starin' back at me like I'm crazy. My sight is failin' me, least where Zoe is concerned. Somethin' is blockin' my vision. Dat makes it even worse."

"When you say 'something', you mean someone?" asked Nalia, taking a bite of the dessert.

"Dat's what I'm 'fraid of," whispered Mama Lu, wringing her hands.

Nalia could not remember the last time she heard Mama Lu say she was afraid of anything, in any context. "I'm sure it's nothing like that," Nalia said, attempting to reassure her. "There's no one alive powerful enough to pull off something like that against you."

"My power will splinter," Mama Lu replied. "As time goes on, it will cling to you; but the more you reject it, the more unstable it will become. I know you don't like hearin' dat, but…"

"You know this is not that bad," Nalia interrupted, taking another bite of the pie and shifting her eyes away. Her complexion went pale with an unexpected wave of guilt.

"You in awfully late," said Mama Lu changing the subject. "You must been havin' a fine time. Wha's his name?"

Color retuned to Nalia's cheeks, reddening them. Rising, she walked to the refrigerator for a bottle of water. "Our neighbor, Jack Haufmann," she said cracking the cap and reflecting on how effortlessly his name rolled off her tongue. "He was eager to see the Quarter, so I gave him the extended tour after he took me to lunch."

"Same fella called the EMTs fo' you?"

"Yeah, him. Really nice guy," Nalia went on, sipping from the bottle. Her eyes drifted dreamily toward the ceiling as she spoke. "There's something about him that feels so right. I can't explain what it is, but I feel like I've known him forever."

Mama Lu's ears perked up. "Dis the fella you jus' met yeste'day?" she asked, red flags waving frantically in her mind.

"I know, it sounds crazy, right? But there's just something about him. I feel comfortable with him. Safe." Nalia went on to tell Mama Lu about Jack's interest in the historic buildings of the Quarter, about how much history he covered in their afternoon together.

"We've grown so close already, just today," Nalia went on, sitting back down with a faraway look in her eyes. "I know it's sudden, but I really feel like this could be going somewhere."

Mama Lu was shocked. "Are you listenin' to yo'self? Have you lost yo' mind?" Her skin was tingling from head to toe. Something was not right, not just with the situation, but in her spirit. Mama Lu sensed danger. "Jus' dis mornin' you asked Mr. John to check out dis man's grandfather 'cause you was uneasy. Now, it sounds like you ready to skip down the aisle. Oh, I don't like the sound of dis one bit."

Nalia tried to explain, but her arguments were not logical. She attempted to settle Mama Lu's nerves by telling her about the book.

"You'll like him when you meet him. He's researching Marie Laveau, and he's anxious to talk to you."

A thousand oppositional statements were on the tip of Mama Lu's tongue when the rapid sound of footsteps caught her attention.

Before she could voice her concern, Mr. John threw open the screen door.

"I think I found her," he said, slightly out of breath.

Mama Lu jumped up from the table. "Where she at?"

"Mercy Hospital," said Mr. John. "Get dressed. I'll fire up the truck."

Chapter Twenty-Eight

"So you're telling me Michael and Margaret Barronne had a daughter that Mama Lu completely erased," said Jack in disbelief. "Just wiped off the face of the earth like she never existed at all?"

"That's exactly what I'm tellin' you," Madame Luciénne replied, tilting her head softly so she peeked from beneath her hat.

Jack turned his back, rubbing his chin and gesturing toward the floor. "That's impossible," he said. "There would be birth records, hospital records, tax records, medical records, vaccines and shots, the list goes on and on."

"The most powerful Voodoo queen since Marie Laveau herself, I believe is how you put it," smirked Madame Luciénne.

"Voodoo queen or not," cried Jack, whipping back around, "You're talking about government documents that would have to be altered." His denial was growing. His speech pattern quickened, and his head shook in disbelief with every comment. "You can't tell me she has that kind of power."

"Ha!" Madame Luciénne laughed, covering her mouth to contain her outburst. "You think there wasn't folks who knew that child? There were teachers who saw her every day, children who grew up with her. We're talkin' about people's minds being altered, memories erased, powerful Voodoo. Getting' rid of the paper trail was like tossin' out a grocery list."

"So she really does have the power," said Jack, his jaw hanging low. Looking at the floor he began to pace a short path across the middle of the store. The wheels of his mind were spinning feverishly.

"Let's not lose our focus here. Just because I possess the information you desire, doesn't mean I'm willin' to give it up without a substantial deal," continued Vivian. Lifting her scarred chin, she flattened her hat against the door and looked down her nose. "A moment ago you were willin' to throw out my offer because you didn't feel it suited you. Now that the tables have turned, what makes you think you can offer a deal sizable enough to procure the goods?"

Jack stopped pacing. He whipped his head toward Luciénne meeting her eyes with a mixture of fury and disbelief.

"Perhaps you underestimate your leverage here, Vivian," he said, arrogantly. "I'm not an amateur. Now that I know Margaret Barronne had a daughter, I believe I can follow the proper leads to find what I need. It's not hard to dig up buried treasure once you know where the X is. What makes you think I need your information?"

Madame Luciénne raised a single brow and permitted a sickeningly sweet smile to linger momentarily before she lifted her back off the door and made a threatening turn to leave. "Well, my apologies, Mr. Haufmann. You've done such a bang-up job so far, how could I have ever doubted you?" She placed her hand on the deadbolt lock and gave it a turn. "I wish you luck in yo' endeavor."

Jack nodded with a gleam in his eye, gambling on her bluff.

Luciénne placed a hand on the doorknob, stopped short, and reluctantly whirled back around. "Have you been listenin'?" she asked with contempt. "You're not ever gon' find her. Her existence has been thoroughly expunged. Mama Lu cast spells over dis city coverin' it like a blanket – powerful spells, the likes of which you ain't never seen. Anybody who goes lookin' for that girl gets redirected and led straight to a dead end. Hell, she didn't even know who she was until recently."

Jack folded. Without breaking eye contact, he breathed a healthy sigh and surrendered his position. The fight was pointless. He was beaten, but not yet defeated. Luciénne let enough information slip for Jack to know, without a doubt, she was there when the girl was hidden and she still kept tabs on her now.

"What can you tell me about her?" he asked quietly.

A glorious sense of victory welled inside Madame Luciénne. Her chest heaved with pride as a sparkle of excitement returned to her eyes. "I can tell you her name and where to find her... for the proper compensation."

Jack's defeated expression faded into a sinister sneer. His azure-blue eyes danced, and his hair stood on end with anticipation. "You hand me the legitimate daughter of Margaret Barronne, and you can name your price, lady."

Madame Luciénne's body tingled from head to toe. She could feel the energy swelling inside her, the power to dominate her adversary. She loved the rush as much as the game. "It seems we may come to terms after all, Mr. Haufmann."

Jack extended a hand to his guest. The corner of his mouth turned in a crooked, satisfied grin. "You know," he said, "I have a fine bottle of aged merlot in the back. Would you care to discuss the details over a glass of wine?"

Madame Luciénne's cheeks flushed around her sultry smile as she took Jack's hand and allowed him to lead her toward the back room. As they made their way behind the counter, Madame Luciénne heard a gentle thud and the obnoxious squeak of rusty wheels just beyond the back door. The hair on her neck bristled momentarily at the sound.

Jack was unaffected, casually leading her by the hand. With a cryptic glare, he opened the door, allowing her through. The horrific scene beyond the doorway nearly sent Vivian straight to the floor.

The old man looked up from his task in surprise, nearly dropping the ankles of the naked, bloody corpse he was attempting to move with a furniture dolly – an ashen young woman with fire-engine red lipstick. Vivian's panicked gasp was silenced as Jack's hand covered her mouth from behind. Overcome by his strength, Madame Luciénne dropped her bag as Jack's other arm immobilized her body. She felt her neck about to snap as he pulled her head back. Hot breath rolled over her shoulder as Jack began to chant softly in her ear. She was familiar with the language, but she had only ever heard it uttered by Mama Lu. Tears of stark terror escaped her wide eyes just before they closed, and the world went dark.

Chapter Twenty-Nine

Nalia polished off a few more bites of pecan pie before climbing the stairs. Her legs were a bit strained from the afternoon's extensive walk, and her head was wearied from the abundant sunshine. A nice, hot soak and a good night's sleep would be heavenly.

As she topped the stairs, scenes from earlier in day drifted into Nalia's mind. Pleasant memories of Jack danced hand in hand with her emotions until she felt absolutely silly. One day with a man was hardly sufficient time to stir these types of feelings, she rationalized, regardless of how wonderful the day had been, or how beautiful the man was.

Pushing open the bathroom door, Nalia took in the relaxing scent of lavender that always seemed to linger in the air. She turned the water on a little extra hot this evening and allowed it to run in the antique tub with a sprinkle of her favorite bath salts.

Retrieving an elastic band from the cup beside the sink, Nalia held it between her teeth and gathered her hair. She pulled it into a short ponytail and wrapped it snuggly with the band as steam from the running water crept up the mirror.

Nalia closed her eyes and breathed deeply, allowing the fragrant vapor to penetrate her nasal passages. The soothing scent calmed her spirit, and though logical reasoning continued to protest, her mind drifted back to Jack. Why couldn't she entertain the thought of a new relationship? Was she so undeserving? Should she be denied the prospect of romantic involvement simply because social convention said it was too soon? Should she continue shutting out the possibility because one situation went south? How long was long enough?

By the time Nalia opened her eyes, fog completely engulfed the mirror, distorting her reflection. A raging memory of the old man in the top hat scurried across her mind, causing Nalia to question if she would ever again be able to look into her bathroom mirror without recalling his ghastly face. She hoped time would dissolve the image.

Deciding the water had reached a suitable level, Nalia leaned over the tub and turned off the faucet. She ran her fingertips along the surface of the water to check the temperature. Feeling the heat, she anticipated slipping into the steaming pool. Before removing her clothes, Nalia turned to shut the door. As she reached for the knob, she froze. Madame Toulouse stood in the threshold.

Questions fired off in Nalia's mind like a fireworks finale. Had she fallen and hit her head? Had she passed out? Was she actually lying on the bathroom floor, or worse, had she drowned?

The figure of her Madame T. looked real, not like a shade or an apparition. She appeared just as vibrant as ever wearing an emerald green dress and opera gloves. A fanciful green hat with black tulle and gold trim rested delicately on top of her head, and her eyebrows were set in a stern, commanding arch.

Nalia instinctively began touching things. She fingered the wall and the sink, unconsciously discerning their tangibility. Finding no indication she was dreaming, Nalia backed away studying the figure. It was as if her grandmother breached the veil of the spirit world and stood before her in bodily form. Were it not for the fact Madame Toulouse's feet did not appear to touch the floor, Nalia would have sworn she was back from the dead.

Questioning the notion of a spiritual visit while fully awake, Nalia nervously approached the door, studying the expression on Madame Toulouse's face, waiting for her to speak. The woman did not smile, nor did she open her mouth, but simply stared directly at Nalia with the gravest of warnings haunting her eyes.

Nalia was at a loss. She felt as though there was something she was supposed to understand, something Madame Toulouse was trying to communicate. "Why are you here Madame T.?" she asked, hoping for a clear answer. Madame Toulouse only stared.

When Nalia inched within arm's reach, Madame Toulouse parted her lips. Before she could speak, a filthy, gnarled hand slipped out of the darkness and covered her mouth from behind.

Nalia screamed as its long nails dug into the flesh of Madame Toulouse's cheek. Her eyes widening, Madame Toulouse sank backward while the leathery, wrinkled face of the old man emerged beside her head. His top hat was pulled down tight and his eyes were bloodshot, glowing red with hatred. A wide, wicked smile slid across his face as he tightened his grip on Madame Toulouse and leered at Nalia.

Nalia found herself more startled than afraid. A stern resolve tightened her stomach and righteous anger inflated her spirit. She planted her feet in a fierce, defensive stance, staring back at the old man with rising confidence.

Then, as quickly as Madame Toulouse and her assailant appeared, they vanished, leaving the hallway darkened and empty. Tension drained from Nalia's body like water through a ruptured dam, but still her eyes darted around the room, scanning in front and behind, mentally preparing for anything. For nearly a full minute she stood motionless attempting to make sense of what happened. Visions never came to her in this manner! Even on occasions where *the sight* revealed itself apart from a dream or a blackout, the images always took place in her mind. Never before had she experienced a physical manifestation. As far as she knew, that type of mastery was known only to Mama Lu.

As her breathing returned to normal, Nalia's speculations were interrupted by the doorbell, echoing its deep chime through the empty house. "Who could be ringing the bell at this hour?" she thought, warily. The hair on her arms bristled as she debated whether or not to answer. Cautiously, she stepped to the doorway and peeked into the hall, not sure what she expected to see. She listened carefully to the quiet, old house. Hearing only the faint ticking of the clock, she moved to the stairs and gingerly began her descent. Had she imagined the doorbell? Was it an echo of the vision, lingering in her mind?

As she studied her surroundings, the doorbell softly chimed again. Someone was undoubtedly on the front porch, probably looking for Mama Lu. Nalia remembered many times in years past, even after Mama Lu relinquished her practice, when her residual clientele would show up on the doorstep at all hours of the night, distraught about this or needing a remedy for that. No matter what the time or the situation, Mama Lu never turned anyone away.

Reaching the bottom of the steps, Nalia turned toward the front door and saw light from the porch spilling around a shadow in the center of the glass pane. A comforting spirit washed over her as she approached, and soon she was close enough to make out a familiar distorted figure. Jack was standing just beyond the glass. Stunned, Nalia searched for reason. After spending the day hearing about his research techniques, she was not surprised he was *able* to track her down, but the fact he *had* was suspect.

No sooner than Nalia began to question Jack's motives, the unusual calming spirit swelled once again, driving away fear and skepticism. Against all logic, Nalia was lulled into a child-like state of fascination as she turned the knob and opened the door.

Bathed in the porch light against the backdrop of the moon-washed front lawn, Jack stood with his hands in the pockets of his cotton slacks, a look of chagrin on his face. When he saw Nalia, his azure-blue eyes beamed with delight, and a genuine smile of adoration formed lengthening his rugged jaw line.

"Okay, right now, I am praying you'll find this charming, not creepy, but I just couldn't stop thinking about you." he blurted out with naked sincerity. "I know this is awkward, and inappropriate, and potentially devastating to furthering this relationship, but there are some things in this world that are worth risking everything for, and I just couldn't stand the thought of ending this evening without you."

From the uncomfortable look in his gorgeous eyes to his less-than-confident posture, Jack's entire presentation was adorable. Nalia melted into the moment. Reaching behind her head, she released her ponytail allowing her hair to fall around her shoulders as she blushed uncomfortably. Leaning against the doorframe, she bit her lip nervously and tucked the hair tie into her pocket. She found herself drawn to Jack, unlike anything she even knew before. It made no sense but she was powerless to stop it.

"So what exactly did you have in mind, showing up on my doorstep?" she asked. "I hope you didn't take me for the kind of girl who..."

"Never," interrupted Jack. "I don't have any expectations, if that's what you're wondering. I just thought you might want to go for a walk in the moonlight, that's all."

Silence hung in the night air for a moment while Nalia analyzed the sincerity of her charming beau's offer. Finally, unable to resist, she smiled in blissful surrender. Closing the door gently behind her, Nalia stepped out onto the porch. Her mind was so adrift she did not even realize she'd forgotten to fetch her shoes.

Chapter Thirty

The ride to the hospital took forever in Mama Lu's mind. White-knuckled, she sat next to Mr. John going over a thousand possibilities, all leading back to the same disturbing outcome. Just yesterday she was at Mercy Hospital for the better part of the day and saw absolutely nothing with regard to Zoe. If the woman Mr. John's network turned up was, indeed, Madame Zoe, she had been in the same building all along. Mama Lu's inner sight was like radar and should have been pinging off the wall with activity, but there was nothing, not a single blip. The only explanation confirmed her worst suspicion: magic was at work – powerful magic. Mama Lu had to remind herself to breathe as the truck pulled into the parking lot.

According to Mr. John, the time of the clock's breakdown prompted his network to search for any events at the police station remotely connected to the cathedral Sunday at eight fifty-five. Police records were incomplete and of little help, but a 911 dispatcher remembered a call for EMS to Jackson Square shortly before daybreak the following morning. Subsequent calls to the area hospitals turned up a Jane Doe brought into Mercy matching the gypsy's description. Mama Lu hoped she was wrong, but her gut told her it was Zoe. Stepping out of the truck, she steeled her mind and prepared for battle. If dark forces were at work, Mama Lu would be ready.

The hospital was a looming sight, like a medieval castle waiting to be breached. Mama Lu walked with defined purpose, her eyes fixed and grave. Her senses were heightened. Seeing, hearing, and feeling everything around her, Mama Lu breathed in the night like never before. Her nerves tingled with sensory overload as she analyzed her surroundings like a supercomputer crunching data. Each person she passed on her way to the entrance was like an open book, their thoughts and feelings laid bare on the pages for her to read; her inner eye saw it all, and still nothing of Zoe.

Mama Lu and Mr. John passed a group of smokers huddled around a designated ash can and entered through the emergency room's automatic sliding door. The scene was nothing short of chaotic. Crying children swaddled in blankets bounced up and down in their mother's arms, wailing from discomfort. A strung-out addict sat on the floor mumbling and vomiting into the base of a ficus tree. An aging gentleman stood at the reception desk, holding his shoulder and shouting swear words at the apathetic nurse on the other side as a security guard stepped in to assist.

Mama Lu seemed to glide through the room unnoticed with Mr. John following close behind. Like a missile locked on its target, Mama Lu approached the desk. She stood next to the elderly gent arguing with the guard and addressed the irritable nurse.

"Excuse me," she said bluntly. "I'm looking for..."

"Just sign in and have seat. I'll call you in a moment," said the nurse shoving a clipboard across the desk.

Mama Lu took the clipboard in one hand and sailed it like a Frisbee just over the young nurse's head. Its papers scattered and floated to the ground as the clipboard struck the rear wall, hard. The nurse looked up, stunned. She looked at the security guard for assistance but he was still engaged in conversation with the bum-shouldered man. He did not appear to have noticed the incident. In fact, he showed no sign of noticing Mama Lu at all. Looking around the room, the nurse concluded no one had witnessed a thing, as if she and Mama Lu were isolated in their own little world.

When her eyes once again met Mama Lu's, the nurse became frightened. She had never seen such purpose in anyone's glare before. Mama Lu's eyes were like tiny windows to another dimension – one in which all subjects yielded to the bidding of their queen.

"I'm lookin' for a Jane Doe, was brought in early Monday mornin', sometime befo' sun-up. I need you to tell me where she is," said Mama Lu, raising a single eyebrow.

Fearful and obedient, the nurse began clicking the keys of her computer's keyboard and within minutes, found the result. "Jane Doe 486," she said. "Looks like she's on the cardiac floor, room 238."

"Thank you," said Mama Lu, "Which way?"

"Oh, I'm afraid visiting hours are..."

With a wave of Mama Lu's hand, the nurse's eyes fixed dead-ahead and glassed over. Her head listed lazily to one side and her mouth hung slightly open.

"Which way to the cardiac floor?" repeated Mama Lu.

Without moving her eyes or her head, the nurse replied in a calm, solemn voice. "Through the security doors behind me. Follow the hallway around to the left. Take the elevator to the second floor. When you get off, the nurse's station will be on the right."

"Dat's a good girl, now clear dat record," said Mama Lu, her eyes glowing like starlight. The nurse clicked away at the keys as instructed while Mama Lu smiled her approval. "C'mon John," she said, turning and stepping around the desk.

Mr. John stared into the nurse's blank expression with amazement. Though he'd seen Mama Lu use the charm several times, it always fascinated him. He leaned over the counter and waved a hand in front of the nurse's face, but the young lady was unaffected. "These ain't the droids you lookin' fo'," he whispered quickly before following Mama Lu into the secure area.

When the door slammed shut, the woman came to, bothered by the escalating argument between the man and the security guard, wondering what happened to her clipboard.

When Mama Lu and Mr. John got off the elevator, tension sparked into the air like electricity. The two nurses at the station watched in awe as Mama Lu walked past. Both wanted to address her, but neither found words. There was a recognizable presence about the woman, like royalty. She walked with a mysterious confidence, like a vapor with purpose. The nurses were overcome with fear and reverence as she passed.

Reading the signs on the walls, Mama Lu proceeded easily to the appropriate wing and found room 238 with little effort. Placing a hand lightly on the heavy wooden door, she cut a look to Mr. John for assurance. He was her rock.

With a gentle push, the door swung open slowly. The light was on, and the room was bright. As the door continued to swing, the bed came into view, its moss-green blankets pulled tight and straight. Mama Lu's heart sank as she stepped over the threshold. The bed was empty. Confused and stunned, she stepped to the bedside. Her jaw slacked open as she touched the blanket hoping to feel something... anything.

Mr. John slipped in behind her. Fearing the worst, he removed his hat and wrung it gently between his fingers. A lump rose in his throat as he searched for what to say. He opened his mouth to speak, but it was not his words that broke the silence.

"You looking for Zoe ain't you?" said a small voice behind them.

Tears in her eyes, Mama Lu whirled around to find a pale young nurse standing just inside the doorway, one hand on the latch, the other on the wall, as if afraid to come in.

Mama Lu's defenses went up, but the nurse's eyes were kind. Her name tag read Edith, and her timid demeanor said she was not a threat. With a careful expression she looked up at Mama Lu, as if seeking permission to speak.

"What you know 'bout my Zoe, chil'?" asked Mama Lu, slowly stepping her direction. "Speak to me, tell me what you know."

"So she is Madame Zoe," replied the young girl, retrieving the gum she stored briefly in her cheek. Chewing nervously, she continued. "I thought so. I've seen her in the square before. A friend of mine got a reading from her once, said it changed her life. She said Madame Zoe was the real deal, not a fake like the others."

Mama Lu and Mr. John were stunned into silence. They had the confirmation they needed, now they waited for the news they both hoped wasn't coming.

"I've been looking in on her. I stopped by every night, whether she was my charge or not. I would talk to her, hold her hand, try and get her to respond. She never came to, just kept starin' off into space. I always felt like her eyes were trying to tell me something, like she was afraid. I've only seen that look one other time before. My ex-boyfriend used to have spells of sleep paralysis, and I saw one once. He woke up, eyes wide open, but he couldn't move a muscle. He told me it was the scariest thing you could imagine, 'cause that's when the demons come and try to choke the life from you. Madame Zoe had the same look in her eyes all the time."

"When did she..." stammered Mr. John.

"Couple hours ago," Edith replied. "Doc Prejean rounded and said there wasn't nothin' left he could do for her. He's like that. If he can't help somebody, or can't figure out what's wrong with them, he wants them gone."

Mr. John's mouth hung open in disbelief.

"You're Mama Lu, ain't you?" Edith continued. "My mom has told me stories about you. You came to help her, didn't you? If what my mom says is true, I figure you're the only one who can."

"Wait. You mean she's still here?" said Mr. John. "She not... she didn't...?"

"Where is she, chil'?" asked Mama Lu placing her hands on the young nurse's shoulders. "Tell me where I can find Madame Zoe."

"Psych ward," replied Edith, nearly swallowing her gum. "Doc Prejean had her moved to the psych ward a couple of hours ago. Two floors up, right above us."

By the time she reached the fourth floor, the energy surrounding Mama Lu was at its peak. Virtually invisible, she and Mr. John slipped past security on the psych ward without so much as a glance their direction. Casually and effortlessly, Mama Lu made her way to the appropriate door and gently pushed it open. Unlike the one on the second floor, this room was dark, lit only by a flickering fluorescent bulb above the bed, and the faint blue glow of chirping monitors. The absence of light, however, was the least of what darkened the room; a sinister shadow shrouded it with a thick, heavy presence. Beneath the dingy bed sheets, its captive lay motionless.

Mama Lu gasped when she saw the figure lying in the bed. Madame Zoe was nearly unrecognizable. Her body was withered and her limbs were drawn up into crooked, unnatural positions. Her eyes were sunken and hollow, more closely resembling a corpse than the woman she used to be.

Heart sinking, Mama Lu approached. "Oh, Zoe," she whispered, "Wha's happened to you?"

Mr. John could only stare, thinking death would be a more desirable fate. Having been involved in the ritualistic dealings of Mama Lu's nefarious past, he was no stranger to bodies in various states of decomposition. This, however, was different. Never before had he seen a living, breathing human in such a state. Pity overwhelmed him.

Gingerly, Mama Lu stepped to the bedside and leaned over her beloved friend, a film-roll of memories playing in her mind. Madame Zoe's eyes did not move or track, but remained firmly focused straight ahead. Just as in the vision, they were full of unconquerable fear.

Mama Lu's blood began to boil. "Somebody doin' dis to her, John," she said in a whisper. "She's trapped. A prisoner inside her own body."

Dark images flashed through Mama Lu's mind. Visions of blood spilling over a ritual table and of life-like dolls sitting high on shelves. A sting of guilt pricked her heart but was quickly vanquished by the still-rising anger. "I want to know who done dis. Zoe you gots to show me who done dis to you."

Mama Lu grabbed Zoe's cold, shriveled hand and focused her mind, sure she would see something now that physical touch was achieved. Still, nothing came! The spirit world grew even darker with shadow; Mama Lu's vision was completely blocked. Desperately, she grabbed Zoe's other hand. "Where are you Zoe?" she said, tears streaming down her cheeks. "Help me find you!"

Sensing Mama Lu's frustration, Mr. John removed his wallet. Tucked inside the billfold were several small bits of paper folded into tiny envelopes. One by one, he removed them, holding them to the light and placing them beneath his nose until he found the one he was looking for. Unfolding the flaps of the envelope, he gently peeled it apart revealing a small sprig of herb and a dark oval-shaped disc. "Here, Lu," he said, emptying the contents of the package into her hand. "Put dat in yo' mouth."

"What is it?" she asked, curiously.

"Dried mango and moonflower," Mr. John replied. "To help you fly. Bite down on it, then hold it on yo' tongue and let it work."

Without hesitation, Mama Lu popped the herbs in her mouth and did exactly as Mr. John instructed. Within minutes, she felt her spirit relax and shift, trying to leave her body. "John is good," she thought as she took hold of Madame Zoe's hand again.

Slowly, reverently, obediently the energy began to wrap itself around their bond like a snake preparing to strike, tightening coil by coil until Mama Lu could feel it binding them together as one. Soon her eyes rolled into her head, and traveling on the influence of the herbs, she slipped away into the dark void of the spirit world.

Mama Lu navigated the astral plane with ease and soon recognized a faint call on the air, the phantom voice of her dear friend. "Lucia," the voice called out, fading in and out of clarity. "Lucia, I'm here!"

Attenuating to the sound, Mama Lu raced across the spiritual plane until a familiar scene emerged. Out of the fog, the rusty iron fence of Jackson Square faded into view. Beyond its border, the dead remnants of neglected foliage appeared alive with watchful eyes. The cathedral steps rose to meet Mama Lu's feet, solidifying beneath her. Cautiously she stepped down onto the brick street as the voice called again.

"I'm here," it sang through the damp night air with a chilling, tortured timbre.

Mama Lu had only just begun to look around for the source when a wispy vapor began to swirl near the tall gates. Churning from the ground toward the sky, the vapor swirled faster and higher until the image of Madame Zoe materialized. She stood alone staring up at the clock, a ghastly skeletal fraction of her former being. Withered and deformed like her physical body, her spirit was darkened, weighted with heavy shadow. The tough leather cord still bound her lips and jaw, but her voice seemed to be speaking through her eyes.

Despite Zoe's gruesome appearance, Mama Lu felt the relief of a thousand lifetimes wash over her spirit as she rushed to finally meet her friend.

A fragile smile fought its way through the heavy, leather cord. "I've been calling for you, Lucia. Day and night I've cried out to you." Though her mouth did not move, her voice was clear and pleading.

"I been tryin' to reach you, Zoe. I been tryin' so hard to reach you. I jus' aint been able to find you. No matter how hard I tried, I couldn't see you."

Pain haunted Zoe's eyes, her suffering evident through the fragile smile.

"You couldn't see me 'cause I ain't me no more," she managed.

Mama Lu's spirit shuddered. Instinctively she backed away, warily. "What you mean, you ain't you no mo'?" she asked.

"Don't leave me here, Lucia. It's still me, just not all of me. I'm a prisoner here, bound to this place. Bound to him."

"Whose prisoner? Who's got you, Zoe?" insisted Mama Lu. Her anger was growing.

"I am unable to reveal," Zoe replied. "He's got me sewn up tight in this spell. He's powerful, Lucia. He has broken me, stolen me. He's trapped part of his soul inside my body, taken part of mine for his."

"He split your soul?" asked Mama Lu, fuming, yet fascinated... and frightened.

"He switched it, without any ritual. He is powerful. He keeps me here, just beyond the veil. I cannot return, yet he won't allow me to cross. I am his secret, a vessel for his deception."

"What do you mean, Zoe? What deception?"

"He took things from me, things he needed. He stole kindness and compassion from my spirit. Anyone who looks upon him will see enough of me to disguise the hatred that rules his heart. So long as I'm alive, his secret is safe."

"Who is he, Zoe?" begged Mama Lu, steering the conversation away from the uncomfortable reality she refused to acknowledge.

"I am unable to reveal. So long as I'm alive... his secret is safe."

"Who is he?" Mama Lu gasped through a cracking voice and flowing tears. "Tell me Zoe," she pleaded, falling to her knees. "I know you can. Jus' tell me and dis will all be over."

"You have to let me go, Lucia," said Zoe, her lips still motionless. "It's why I've been calling for you. You have to set me free. Only then will the spell be broken. Only then will I be at peace." Her eyes were desperate. "I am tormented, Lucia. You must do this for me."

"You want me to kill you?" cried Mama Lu.

"He has already claimed my soul, Lucia. Claim my body. Set me free of this prison, I beg you."

"No," replied Mama Lu, shaking her head. "No, Zoe I can bring you back. I've done it befo'. If I can get you to my ritual..." Even as she entertained the thought, Mama Lu realized its impossibility. Zoe knew it too.

"There can be no ritual. Even if you could do it, my body wouldn't survive, Lucia. I am broken."

Mama Lu could not speak. Her spirit anguished. Gathering every ounce of energy she could muster, she attempted to rationalize her friend's request. "Zoe, you askin' me to do somethin' I can't do."

"You must, Lucia. I'm already gone, darlin'. Put me at peace."

"I can't, Zoe. You askin' fo' murder."

"I'm asking for mercy."

With no more words, Madame Zoe struggled, just managing to lift her hands turning them palm-side up. Laboriously she moved her fingers, beckoning Mama Lu to place her hands on top.

Hesitantly, Mama Lu obliged. When their fingers touched, a force gripped her like high-voltage current biting its unsuspecting victim. Excruciating pain swept through Mama Lu's spirit. It was not physical pain felt by her body, but unbearable suffering fueled by despair, hopelessness, loss, and fear – pain only a soul could fathom. Suddenly, Mama Lu understood.

"This is how I suffer, Lucia. This is what he puts me through. Don't let it continue. End this! The sooner you do, the sooner we will all be out of danger."

Mama Lu pulled away from Madame Zoe. The bond was nearly impossible to break, but when it shattered, Mama Lu's spirit slammed back through the veil so hard her body shook violently. Forced back against the wall, she crumbled to the cold, tile floor.

Mr. John rushed to her side. She was shaking uncontrollably and crying, silent, resilient tears. What Mr. John saw in her eyes, swept a chill through his soul. He recalled seeing that wide-eyed heavy stare once before. His mind shifted back to the ritual room, his baby girl chained to a ceremonial table with a wicked, evil spirit using her body as a vessel. With every alternative exhausted, Mama Lu was forced to accept the harsh reality of what needed to be done. Though it nearly killed her, she prepared to carry out the soul-crushing task. A silent exchange confirmed what Mr. John read in her eyes, as he held Mama Lu in horrified solace.

"She's sufferin', John," Mama Lu whimpered. "Ain't but one way to set her free."

Mr. John knew Mama Lu well, and understood on a level only he could. He felt her heart breaking over the dilemma, and it pained him too. "She asked you to, didn't she?"

Mama Lu nodded.

"Ain't no other way?"

Hesitantly, Mama Lu shook her head. There were many ways to kill a body, but only one method Mama Lu was willing to entertain.

"I gots to call her out," she finally whispered. "I gots to call out wha's left of her life force... set it free. It's what she wants, John. She begged me to do it."

Mr. John had heard of calling a life out of its body but had never seen it or been a party. The painstaking process required three souls: one to be called from the spirit realm, one to anchor the world of the living, and one to bridge the gap between. Even for a powerful, experienced mambo, it was a dangerous technique demanding no small amount of honed energy.

"Can you be my anchor?" Mama Lu asked, trying to set her mind for the task.

"You jus' tell me what I needs to do," John replied.

"You gots to focus on me, hold me in yo' mind. Zoe wants to cross the veil, but there's another spirit in dat body ain't gon' want her to leave. It's gon' fight like hell to keep her even if it means pullin' me across too. You gots to be my anchor. No matter what, you can't let me go. Can you do dat?"

Mr. John was never so sure of anything in his life. He was her rock, and if nothing else, her fierce protector. He nodded in agreement with a grave look.

"One mo' thing," said Mama Lu. "When you feel her spirit drawn out, dat's when you gots to let go. You gots to free yo' mind of every thought, quiet yo' spirit, and let her pass. When the time is right, you gon' know and you can't hesitate, even fo' a second. Too soon and you could lose us both, too late and I lose you."

Shifting his eyes, Mr. John nodded again. He would simply allow his spirit to enter a restful trance, a practice with which he was not unfamiliar. "You can do dis," he told himself. His only reservation was the absence of his drum. His tribal cadences were always so instrumental in aiding his release, he questioned his ability to slip out of consciousness in their absence. Nevertheless, he refused to let Mama Lu down.

"Once the bond is made, I'm in yo' hands, John," said Mama Lu with unexpected surrender. "I'm dependin' on you."

To Mr. John's surprise, the look in her eyes bore confidence, not concern. It gave him strength and courage beyond measure.

Turning toward the hospital bed, Mama Lu beheld the frail form of her dear friend. A familiar lump choked her throat as she whispered calm words and stroked Zoe's thinning hair. Tears flowed until they dried as Mama Lu allowed her mind to drift from fond memories to critical preparation. Her comforting whispers soon became Creole chants as Mr. John joined in the familiar, calming verse. Taking Madame Zoe's withered, rigid hand, Mama Lu focused her mind and her energy on the spirit world. As Mr. John held tightly, Mama Lu allowed the power to rise inside her, strong and resolute. Coiling around and through her body, the energy swelled and wound its way down her arms, around her anchor, and into the spirit realm.

With the sting of the herbs lingering on her tongue, Mama Lu reached back through the veil. She felt Zoe's spirit eagerly tighten around hers, willing and ready, begging for relief. With a commanding lurch of energy the bond was made.

In turn, Mr. John felt Mama Lu latch onto his spirit. She wrapped her energy around him like vines, drawing tight lines and bands, weaving them into a secure net. Mr. John felt the spirit realm tugging at his soul, calling him to surrender, but he held his mind firmly in the world of the living, focusing his will solely on Mama Lu.

The bond was strong, and Mama Lu felt Zoe desperately hanging on with the grip of a struggling swimmer rescued from an angry sea. With an ethereal voice audible only to souls in limbo, Mama Lu called to Zoe, drawing her from the spirit world.

Like a sparrow on the wind, Madame Zoe's spirit glided effortlessly through the veil, soaring on the promise of freedom. The energy of the bond hushed in a tender sigh of relief as Zoe transitioned, and tranquility flowed over the trio like a gentle stream.

Just before Zoe's spirit reached the living realm, Mama Lu felt harsh resistance. Zoe lurched violently, like a heavy chain was thrown around her ankles. Mama Lu held fast, but Zoe began drifting back toward the veil. Something gripped her tightly, drawing her back to the twisted torment.

The baleful shadow over the tiny hospital room thickened like billowing, black smoke rising from a coal stack. The florescent bulb and monitors sparked and shorted out as their glow flashed sporadically in the darkness. Menacing rage swelled in defiance to a tall, threatening presence. The shadow refused to give up the fight.

Mama Lu felt Zoe slipping and could no longer divide her strength. Though her spirit trusted Mr. John, her tenacious flesh held a part of her in reserve. That small piece clung desperately to her anchor, refusing to relinquish control. While the shadow laughed at her struggle, Mama Lu realized she could not hold Zoe with a divided heart. The decision was imminent.

With the shadow licking its foul lips in victory, Mama Lu surrendered her spirit, placing her trust completely in Mr. John. With all the might of her soul and mind, she latched on to her tortured friend, devoting herself wholly to the bond. On one side of the veil or the other, she and Zoe would end up together.

Mr. John felt the jolt like dead weight on his being. Mama Lu's web of energy slipped from around him like a mooring rope released from its cleat. He reacted in an instant. Grounding his spirit to the hospital room, he wrapped his own energy around Mama Lu with the strength of a steel cable. While the veil pummeled him with hurricane winds, Mr. John tightened his bond and fought to stay centered. The battle proved more intense than he ever imagined, straining every fiber of his soul. In the midst of the fight he heard the spirit world call to him, beckoning him over. It offered him peace and rest, promised him comfort and shelter from the raging storm.

The struggle will end. Serenity can be yours. Peace is waiting. Just let go.

His resistance waning, Mr. John focused on the core of his strength – images so solid they seemed to breach the realm of tangibility: the gentle honesty in Mama Lu's eyes when she smiled, the ferocity with which she defended the innocent, the vulnerability she tried so hard to hide. The more he immersed himself in the qualities of the woman he loved, the easier he found it to pull her spirit back through the veil. Relentlessly he tugged, remembering each time he'd brushed his fingers against her cheek, rubbed the tension from her shoulders, or felt the sweet surrender of her tender lips.

He would not lose her. Not now. Cementing his spirit in the living realm he held strong, pulling with all his might.

With a rippling tremor, the shadow's chain let go, and with it, all power the spiritual plane employed. Mr. John felt Mama Lu's spirit rush back to him as her body collapsed in his arms. Her heart was racing. Mr. John could feel it beating heavily against his flesh like the thump of his ritual drum. Steeling his mind and centering his soul, he prepared to receive Zoe's spirit. With Mama Lu's heartbeat aiding his abandon, Mr. John let go of all emotion and made himself a vessel.

Like a peaceful, gentle wind, Madame Zoe's spirit moved through Mr. John's body creating little more than butterflies in his stomach. A sparkling joy bubbled inside him, working its way upward until it took leave through the soft flesh at the base of his neck, an easy portal for spiritual travel. Mr. John felt the hairs of his neck stand on end and tingle as the spirit broke free.

Mama Lu came to just in time to see a slightly crooked, Cheshire grin overtake Mr. John's face for a fleeting second. Knowing Zoe was at peace, she melted into her anchor's embrace.

The tranquility lasted only a moment. Without warning, the energy of *the sight* slammed Mama Lu like a wrecking ball. Images assaulted her mind hard and fast, stiffening her body with death-like rigor. Mr. John panicked, wrapping his arms around her frame and squeezing with all the strength he had left. As her limbs began to twitch in violent convulsions, Mama Lu's mind soared back to the brick streets of the cathedral square.

A cool, biting wind blew in from the river and the smell of rain filled the night air as the scene unfolded. Mama Lu could just make out the sound of raindrops on the foliage behind the fence but could not yet feel the drizzle. She found herself seated at a weathered card table in the flickering glow of several candles, directly across from the cathedral's entrance. Her hands were not her own and her wrists were heavily adorned with hoop bracelets. There was a silk scarf tied around her head adorned with thin gold chains and tiny coins. On the table before her rested a well-worn deck of tarot cards. Her vision was hazy, slightly out of focus, but she could see the crowd dispersing, taking cover from the gathering storm. Other card readers were packing up their belongings and folding up their tables, but

Mama Lu sat quietly, staring up at the clock as if it was not yet time to leave – as if waiting for someone. She trembled, not from the cold but from anxiety. An eerie paranoia crawled across her skin, yet her eyes remained fixed on the clock.

In the distance, she heard the distinctive tap of a cane against the brick. Faint at first, the sound grew louder as it approached. Mama Lu's suspicion swelled.

As the cane's steady tapping slowed to a stop, a spindly man in an overcoat and top hat hobbled into Mama Lu's field of vision. His face was hidden beneath the brim of his hat, but he stepped up to the table with confidence. Reaching into his coat pocket, the man produced a fifty dollar bill and dropped it onto the table in front of her.

Mama Lu felt the muscles of her arms begin to move, though she was not willing them to. With hesitation, she took the bill and folded it twice before slipping it into a small beaded coin purse hanging from a chain around her neck. Mama Lu recognized the purse; it belonged to Madame Zoe.

Her hands began to shake as she moved a tall candle from the edge of the table to the center and slid the tarot deck across to the stranger. Bending low, she tried to see the man's face, but was unsuccessful.

The stranger tugged his hat down a bit more, cut the deck, and relaxed his posture. Mama Lu felt strangely drawn to him. Though her instincts said drop the cards and run, she could not. There was something curiously familiar about the strange man in the top hat.

While Mama Lu watched the scene play, her hands dealt the deck into Madame Zoe's signature eight-card, Celtic cross pattern. After setting the rest of the deck aside, she turned over the first three cards. Opening her mouth to speak, Mama Lu was surprised to hear Madame Zoe's voice interpreting the meaning of the overturned cards. "You've lived a long life," said the voice. The man's uncanny familiarity caused Mama Lu to shudder as the words were spoken. She tried again to see his face, but his hat served as an ample shield. Mama Lu listened closely as Madame Zoe interpreted the rest of the meaning: talk of great wealth, suffering, and lost love.

After the next three cards were turned over and explained, the man grew increasingly agitated. Mama Lu became uneasy when talk of business and travel turned to a darker subject. Something hunted this man with fierce determination, but he was also the hunter, cunning and resilient. Every fiber of Mama Lu's existence crawled with anticipation.

As the last two cards were revealed, lightning split the night sky, washing her field of vision to a brilliant white canvas. Struggling to see, Mama Lu squinted and strained. Soon a whirling image danced across her mind, materializing in the distance on the field of white – a woman, spinning around in a serpentine fashion, her body engaged in a familiar ritualistic dance. Her movements were fluid, her presence commanding, her energy bright and powerful. Closer and closer she danced until her smiling face filled the canvas. It was Nalia. She parted her lips to speak, but before she could make a sound, her face burst into flames. The blinding light faded to darkness as Nalia's face was consumed in fire leaving only a smoldering, tortured skull in its wake.

Mama Lu was terrified. As the card table returned to clarity, she beheld the tarot's final revelation: the high priestess and the death card. Mama Lu gasped and looked up at the mysterious stranger, his eyes now fully visible and staring her down.

"No!" she said, hearing her own voice echo inside her mind. "Dis can't be! You can't be here. You can't be..."

The stranger's beautiful, azure-blue eyes were filled with hatred. Mama Lu recognized those eyes. A fleeting memory from her youth assaulted her consciousness: the pleading, blue eyes of a young man, desperate for help. The same blue eyes stared back at her now, across the tiled cards.

As Mama Lu stiffened in disbelief, the man hobbled around the table, slipped his hand around her neck and whispered a powerful, ancient Haitian chant into her ear. She felt a presence wash over her, consuming her mind, wrestling with her spirit. Her eyes drifted upward toward the clock as the man's charm paralyzed her body.

Mama Lu did not sense the man slip away, but felt the cold rain begin to fall. Unable to move she stared at the motionless clock as the downpour extinguished her candles. The gusting wind intensified, scattering the contents of the table into the street.

As rain pooled on the table's naked surface Mama Lu felt Madame Zoe's muscles stiffen with determination. Energy flowed through her body, raising one arm and extending a withered gypsy finger to the table. Mama Lu watched as a final message was scrawled in the gathering raindrops. The letters disappeared almost as quickly as they were written, but the word was unmistakable, the warning undeniable – BOKOR.

A fresh terror swept through Mama Lu's body as thundering rain washed away the vision, and the dead-steady tone of Zoe's flatlined heart monitor filled her ears.

Chapter Thirty-One

Her head dizzied with a strange elation, Nalia walked to the edge of the porch and drank in the moonlight. The bluish glow cascading over the lawn reminded her of Jack's crystal eyes. A blanket of cotton stretched across the night sky as she stared at the silver orb hanging high above.

Jack approached from behind whispering in Nalia's ear. "It's beautiful, isn't it?" he asked, his warm breath falling gently on the soft skin at the base of her neck.

A tingling sensation filled Nalia's body, growing like a spring flower. She took in the moment, never wanting to forget the moonlight's play of light and shadow, the peaceful sound of nocturnal insects, the smell of magnolias on the night air mixed with the lingering scent of Jack's cologne as he wrapped his arms around her waist. In gentle surrender, she placed her hands on his and leaned into his body, resting her head on his shoulder. A spark of desire burned inside her as Jack continued to whisper in Nalia's ear. His words seemed inconsequential next to the ecstasy of his lips brushing against her neck.

The spark grew to a brilliant flame, prompting Nalia to turn and meet his lips. Yielding to her desire, she tried, but Jack's arms slid over hers and held her fast, forcing her hard against his chest. Instinctively, she tried to struggle free but Jack's grip proved too strong.

Panic took hold of Nalia's body as she recognized Jack's speech pattern. He recited a rhythmic dialect she only heard uttered by one other – Mama Lu. The language was Haitian Creole, and the message was dark. Before she could to resist, Nalia felt a shadow fall over her spirit, dragging her down like weighted chains. Slowly, her consciousness slipped away as the world grew dark and cold.

———————

Vibration shook Nalia to coherence, along with the deafening sound of iron grinding against stone. A forceful wind whipped around her body, cold and cutting. Vertigo threatened her mind causing her body to sway freely in the breeze. Feeling she might fall, Nalia looked to the ground only to find it drastically out of reach.

The tiny surface on which she balanced was little more than a meter wide, spinning slowly like a dial, high above the earth below – the top of the stone spire. Looking down, Nalia recognized the large, round courtyard with its sidewalks radiating out from the center. At the edges, near the fence line stood the carved, stone benches, shaped like roman numerals. "XII," Nalia thought eyeing to the largest set. "Twelve."

From her lofty perch, the numbers made sense and Nalia saw the courtyard for what it was… the face of a giant clock. "The world of the living," echoed the words of Madame Toulouse inside Nalia's head. The old man's soul was trapped here.

As the spire continued to turn, Nalia saw him. The old man stood on the ground near the fence beside a pair of long benches forming the Roman numeral two. His red eyes glowed with anger as his laser-keen vision fixed on Nalia. He moved with lightning speed to the base of the spire. Gripping the stone with his sharpened nails, he climbed quickly, like a cockroach up a wall. Beneath him, fog rolled in from the edges of the courtyard, covering the ground like a blanket. The thick vapor consumed the lawn as the old man scaled the side of the spire, rapidly approaching Nalia at the apex.

Fear gripped Nalia's throat. Her mouth went dry, and her skin grew clammy. The old man's bright red eyes were gaining ground at a feverish rate. Within seconds, he would be upon her. Refusing to stand idle and be overtaken, Nalia made the only decision she could. Without a second thought, she faced the old man and jumped from the top of the spire. Feet first, she dropped like a bomb toward its target. The old man's eyes widened in terror. Digging in his claw-like nails, he held fast to the side of the spire and braced for impact.

Nalia did not feel it when her feet connected with the old man's head, nor did she feel the impact of their bodies hitting the ground below. This last sensation she could remember was falling into the blanket of fog, her vision lost in the haze.

———————

The dank odor of dust and incense stung like smelling salts on Nalia's conscience, jarring her violently from the darkness. In an instant she stood face to face with Marie Laveau. Nalia was neither nervous, nor afraid. She grew weary of *the sight's* callous way of tossing her spirit from one plane to the next. Aggravation fueling her resolve, Nalia refused to bow to fear and intimidation. She stood firm and stared unwaveringly into the eyes of Marie Laveau.

Marie looked Nalia up and down, scrutinizing her, analyzing her motives, and finally dismissing her with flared nostrils. "You gon' see what you came to see dis time, chil'?" she asked. "Quit barging into my parlor, uninvited?"

Nalia took a deep breath, wondering whether to speak or keep silent.

"Yo' lyin' tongue done found you out," Marie continued in a booming voice, cutting her eyes and turning to reveal the scene behind her. Two large, muscular henchmen with the strength of oxen stood on either side of a small chair with a dark-haired man lashed to its seat. The man struggled and squirmed against his bindings, sweating profusely and gnashing his teeth in anger. "What have you done with her, you evil witch?" he shouted. "Where is she?"

"Evil? Witch?" Marie said, clicking her tongue in disdain. "Strong words comin' from a deceiver and a devil like yo'self." She walked slowly back and forth beside the table, fingering a length of coarse twine with several bones and charms attached. "And I guess you talkin' 'bout yo' blushin' bride-to-be," she continued. "Or I guess we should call her yo' mistress, since she married to the man you claimed was her father."

The man stopped fighting. He looked up through his sweat-soaked bangs like a child caught with his hand in the cookie jar. Though the flickering candlelight cast deep shadows across his face, Nalia recognized some resemblance. His was beaten and swollen, worked over by Marie's brutes, but the prisoner in the chair had features oddly similar to Jack's. His eyes, however, were distinctly bloodshot-red, identical to the old man's. His square jaw was set in defiance as he stared up at Marie Laveau.

"I cast yo' spell," she said, removing the polished silver brush from the sash of her robe. Holding it in front of her face, Marie curled her lip in disgust. Her eyes were angry, but Nalia noticed something else – a hint of regret. With a heavy sigh she tossed the brush on the red, velvet table and leaned over it. "I gave you the protection you asked fo'. I gots to hand it to you. You was very convincing, you and yo' lil' tramp." Slapping the table, she shook her head and continued to pace.

"What have you done with her?" the man demanded.

"Shut him up!" shouted Marie pointing a rigid finger at her captive. One of the gargantuan servants at his side removed a heavy cord from his waist and wrapped it around the man's head, through his mouth, forming a gag. Grabbing a handful of sweaty hair, he jerked the bound man's head back and lashed the rest of the cord to the back of the chair. The rope kept the man's head still and his neck exposed. Looking down his nose he continued to stare at Marie Laveau.

"Dat po' man," she went on. "You had me set a curse on dat po' man after you stole his wife, stole his money, and tried to pay me off wit' his watch."

The charm-laden length of twine in Marie's hand stretched so tightly Nalia thought it would snap from the tension. The woman's knuckles were white and raw.

"Well, I cast yo' spell and I hope you proud. You done accomplished a feat dat's hard to achieve, deceiving Marie Laveau. Hell, most folks too scared to even try and pull dat off. I'm gon' show you why dat is."

The eyes of the Voodoo queen rolled languidly into her head as she released the tension in her rigid muscles and unwound the twine from her bulging fingers. Momentarily blocking out the world, Marie focused solely on the bones and charms, thumbing them along the twine in a manner not unlike Mama Lu and her twisted root. Her eyelids trembled, and her lips moved in a silent, rhythmic pattern as she calmed her nerves, honing her rage into a powerful, terrifying weapon.

Tying the charms around her neck, Marie turned and walked to a tall cabinet against the far wall. As she opened the door, the flames of the candles on the table behind her grew tall and straight, fueled by power and energy.

When Marie whirled back around, she was holding a familiar double-edged ritual knife. Nalia recognized the blade instantly. The scars on her torso began to tingle in its presence.

The blade's mirror-like finish gleamed in the candlelight as Marie nodded to the other guard. Crossing the room, the large man slipped into the corner and positioned himself behind a wide drum with an oiled, leather head. Its tone was rich and deep, resonating through the parlor as the bull-like servant struck his palms rhythmically against the bearing edge.

"The man you runnin' from don't hunt you no mo'," continued Marie, her tone cold and grim. "His heart gave out while ridin' into the city. Keeled over and fell off his horse. They tell me his boot got hung up in the stirrup. Horse trampled him to death straight down the neutral ground fo' all to see."

The captive's eyes widened. News of his lover's husband had already reached him, but until now he was not privy to the details surrounding his death. Marie was indeed powerful, he surmised – a terrifying realization to have while staring down the point of her ritual blade.

Marie held the knife over the man's heart, poking him gently with the tip. She moved it from side to side sticking him in various places until she finally struck a hard surface. With a baneful grin she gripped the handle tightly and sliced horizontally across the bottom of his breast pocket. The gold pocket watch fell into his lap.

A barely-audible chuckle revealed the Voodoo queen's twisted satisfaction as she trailed her knife down the prisoner's chest and past his abdomen. He squirmed and trembled, wetting himself when Marie toyed with the blade dangerously close to his manhood. Finding its chain with the knife's razor-sharp tip, she lifted the watch and dropped it onto the table.

"I cast yo' spell," she repeated. "I granted yo' wish. I gave you the protection you wanted from dat man. You came to me askin' only to live and to love." Her stare set like concrete as her voice hushed to a hateful whisper. "Well, I'm gon' let you live alright, but you ain't never gon' know love."

The energy of the room swelled as the sound of the drum grew louder and faster. Nalia recalled scenes of Mr. John and Mama Lu in similar settings. Her mind warped around the concept of déjà vu compounded on déjà vu, analyzing time and space, wondering which scene begat which.

"You want to know what I done wit' yo' lil' woman?" Marie's voice boomed with new resonance, her body jerking in time with the pounding cadence. "The answer is nothin'!" She moved terrifyingly close to her captive, whirling the ritual blade wildly about his face and neck as she danced. "Not yet, anyways. Didn't have to. She took off an' left you when she heard I found out 'bout yo' lil' scheme. You see, she got enough sense to be 'fraid. But, don't you worry none, honey, she gon' get her due soon enough."

The man's eye filled with a mixture of anger and shock, fear and sadness. As he continued to struggle against his bindings, Nalia saw tears break through the sweat and roll down his cheeks.

Allowing her head to roll back onto her shoulders, Marie closed her eyes. Nalia could see them twitching beneath the lids like a deep REM sleep. The drum grew louder as the servant bloodied his hands against the head. Marie's body pulsed with the rhythm. Energy filled the room to bursting until suddenly, all sound and motion slammed to a halt and the Voodoo queen collapsed to her knees, sweating and quivering in mild convulsions. The terrified man's labored breathing was the only audible noise.

Silence lingered for what seemed like a lifetime before Marie opened her eyes and fixed them on the shaking, bound man. With her gaze undeterred, she stood and walked calmly to her high-backed chair. She motioned for her muscle-bound brute to push her captive closer to the table. With a thump, she laid the heavy ritual knife beside the watch, pointing the tip in the man's direction. Raising a single brow, Marie stared at his exposed neck, rested an elbow on the table, and pointed a thin finger at the man's throat. She moved her fingertip in small circles, toying with it in the air. Soon, he began to writhe in pain, screaming through his gag. A small trail of blood appeared on his sweaty, heaving throat, as if a phantom blade were making a surgical incision.

"Don't you worry none 'bout yo' lost lover," said Marie with a calm and soothing timbre as she moved her fingertip slowly across the air. "I'll find her. I'm gon' make sure she meets a quick, painless death. I ain't 'bout to bring prolonged sufferin' on dat chil' she's carryin'."

The man squirmed with increased vigor, struggling to break free, but the brute behind him pulled the bindings even tighter, wrenching his neck backward and exposing the cut.

As Marie moved her finger, the gash on his throat grew to a gaping wound from one side to the other. Blood poured forth like a river, shining black in the candlelight and soaking his shirt.

"You, on the other hand, are a diff'rent story; death is too good for you." As casually as Marie drew the line with her finger, she traced it back the other direction. Though the blood remained on the man's neck and chest, the wound began to close. "You 'bout to find out what a devilish curse I can really fix. Dere are fates worse than death, you know."

She finished her motion, completely closing the laceration, and picked up the ritual blade. Opening the cover of the pocket watch she brought the knife's handle down hard against the face, smashing it to pieces. "You gon' live a good long life while I let yo' justice fall on the ones you love. I'm gon' curse yo' seed in dis generation, the next, and on, and on."

Laying the ritual knife across her palm, Marie Laveau uttered a powerful incantation and drew the blade swiftly. As blood flowed between the fingers of her tightened fist, she held it above the table and let it drip into the broken face of the pocket watch.

"But don't ever let it be told dat Marie Laveau was unfair," she said in a wicked, mocking tone. "I ain't gon' leave you wit'out a fightin' chance. I love a good game jus' like anybody else."

Standing up, Marie held the ritual knife to the man's throat. After sadistically playing with it for a bit, she severed the cord, releasing the gag. The weakened man gasped for breath, but his efforts were short-lived as Marie grabbed the watch and stuffed it violently into his mouth. Watching him gag and choke on its cold metal and her still-warm blood, she leaned over his face.

"You find a way to get dis watch workin' again, you'll break the curse," she said with a sinister grin. "'Til den... have a nice life."

Her cackling laughter echoed through the parlor as Marie turned and strode through the curtained doorway. Just before she disappeared, she cut a pointed look in Nalia's direction and winked.

Chapter Thirty-Two

The room was dark, and Nalia felt ill. Somewhere in the pit of her stomach was a knot the size of a grapefruit. The urge to be sick held a promise of relief, but none came; the knot lingered, fueling her nausea. Her head ached and her body was sore. If she didn't know better, Nalia would swear she was suffering from the flu.

In the darkness she tried to right her mind, grasping for any thought or image she could remember. Scenes faded tauntingly in and out of her conscience, clarity just out of reach. Visions of hot, running water, Madame Toulouse, and the old man in the top hat toyed with her senses. She remembered a doorbell, and then... Jack.

Nalia's head began to clear as her thoughts became lucid. Jack stood at the door with his beautiful smile and his crystal eyes. She remembered standing in the moonlight when she heard the voice in her ear... the language... a spell... a curse.

Nalia shuddered from the inside out. Her blood never felt so cold. The realization Jack could, and did, put a curse on her raised frightening questions, and she wasn't sure she wanted the answers. Who was this man? He seemed so kind, so genuine. How could he have manipulated her that way? Why? Of all the mysteries flooding Nalia's brain, the question disturbing her most was the one defying logic: why did she not seem to mind what Jack had done?

Nalia's aching head raged on, but it soon became insignificant compared to the burning pain in her wrists. As cognizance continued to creep through her fog, Nalia realized her hands were bound together with what felt like a plastic zip tie. The binding was tight, cutting off her circulation. Her shoulders were sore from their awkward position and a heavy wooden beam pressed firmly into her back. Splinters scraped her spine and forearms as she struggled against the binding to no avail.

The dark room smelled of dust, spices, candle wax, and death. The odor was powerfully familiar, permanently etched into the recesses of Nalia's mind. Even before the single lightbulb flickered to life overhead, Nalia knew she was in The Doll Maker's upper room – Mama Lu's ritual chamber.

The lightbulb brought the room dimly to life, and all at once, Nalia realized she was sitting on the floor, secured to one leg of the heavy, oak table. Mama Lu's altar was before her with its many stumps of used candles, vials of oil, and other ritual items.

Distant sounds began to ebb and flow like an angry tide in Nalia's head, beginning with a high-pitched whine intermingled with mumbling voices. Nalia soon identified other noises: laughter, crying, and footsteps.

Her body quivered as the footsteps grew louder. She could turn her head only so far and from her vantage point on the floor, she could see next to nothing, but someone was approaching. As the heavy steps rounded the table, Nalia heard Jack's voice speaking in the same Haitian Creole.

"Bélantre dife," he said in a breathy whisper as Nalia felt a wave of power flow through the room. One by one, the candles on the altar flashed to life, their tiny flames growing and dancing in harmony. Soon the room was well-lit, and Nalia felt a dry lump gather in her throat. The picture of the nude woman dancing with a snake above the altar seemed to move with life as Jack's lower body entered her field of vision. He still wore his casual cotton slacks and carried a glass of red wine.

Crouching before her, Jack placed a hand to Nalia's chin and moved her head from side to side. Her headache intensified, and her vision, still a bit blurry, grew worse from the motion. The only points that stayed in focus were Jack's eyes. His crystal clear, azure-blues looked straight through Nalia with stern purpose. Their fire danced like the candles.

"You in there?" he asked, as buoyantly as if he were knocking on a bathroom door. His tone was out of place and awkward, but it jarred Nalia's senses. Shaking her head she finally came around.

"There you are," Jack continued. "Hated to have to put that little charm on you, but it seemed the easiest way to get you here and, well... tied up. You're a pretty strong-willed woman, I didn't think it was going to be that easy."

Nalia fumed with rage, but almost instantly, the anger quelled leaving only tranquil adoration for Jack in its wake. Her emotions made no sense. She could not understand why she still felt enamored with the man currently holding her prisoner.

Jack rose. Tucking his free hand comfortably into his pocket, he raised the glass to his lips and looked around the room. A sip of wine and a deep breath later, he turned his attention back to Nalia.

"It's a shame, isn't it?" he said, his eyes darting from Nalia to the runes and symbols covering the walls. "This room was once a hub of ceremonial activity. Elders gathered here under the watchful eye of Mambo Lucia Deminy, casting extraordinary spells, wielding unbelievable power, performing unspeakable acts." Jack's body shuddered as a shiver of excitement ran its length. He shook it off and took another sip from his glass. "Now, it's nothing but a sad reminder of an era that's faded away. Its energy has grown stale. If you put your hands on the table, you can still feel it, but it's more like a gentle breeze than the rushing wind it once was."

"Energy binds itself to people, not places," Nalia said.

"Oh that's where you're wrong, young one," Jack replied. "Energy can be bent and bound to most anything." Pulling his hand from his pocket, he removed an antique, gold pocket watch. Nalia recognized it from the vision. Gasping, she wondered if this haunted heirloom was handed down from one cursed generation to the next. Flipping open the cover Jack's expression turned sour. He tossed the watch toward Nalia's head. She winced and closed her eyes as it clattered across the table above her.

"Why did it have to be you?" Jack asked, crouching again to face his captive. "I was really starting to like you."

Nalia's face screwed in confusion. "I don't understand. Why did what have to be me? Why am I here?"

Jack allowed a crooked grin to break through his stern presentation. "You really don't know who you are, do you?" he said. Shaking his head, Jack stood slowly. He walked around the table in the direction from where he appeared. Nalia squirmed, twisting her body around the table leg, following Jack with her eyes. The zip tie cut deep into her wrists as she shifted, but she managed to turn just enough to see.

Jack was standing in a newly formed entryway between Mama Lu's upper room and his own. Jagged bits of wood, brick, and plaster still hung around the edges where a stud had been cut and wall panels removed. Instantly, Nalia knew how he'd bypassed the alarm system. No sensors were ever installed upstairs.

Beyond Jack and through the opening, was a room lit by work lights casting long, moving shadows up the wall. The moaning started again, coupled with the sound of frightened, rapid gasps.

"She tried to tell me you didn't know," said Jack, nonchalantly sipping his wine. "But I didn't believe her. She lies, you know. Not very trustworthy."

Turning his eyes back toward Nalia, Jack stepped out of the way to reveal Madame Vivian Luciénne. Lashed to the beam of what used to serve as the building's freight elevator, Madame Luciénne sat piled on the floor in front of the bright bulbs. Her hands were bound behind her back, her clothing torn to scraps. A gag filled her mouth, and sweat poured profusely down her face from the heat of the lamps. Worst of all, was a large cut on the side of her neck, bleeding heavily. Her eyes met Nalia's, terrified and pleading.

Walking back around the table, Jack continued. "Well, surely your Mama Lu had to know. Why else would she keep you a secret for so many years? Even from yourself as I understand."

Nalia still had no idea what Jack was talking about, but a sting of betrayal resurrected itself. Mama Lu allowed Nalia to live the better part of her life believing she was someone she wasn't. Last summer straightened all that out. Was Jack saying there was more to the story?

"I can't imagine why she wouldn't want you to know, unless she was afraid you would overpower her."

"What do you mean?" snapped Nalia. "What would she not want me to know?"

Jack cocked his head to one side and grinned. A patronizing softness filled his eyes, like he was going to share the truth about Santa. Nalia's gut knotted anxiously as she waited for Jack's answer.

"You are the last of the bloodline," he said with certainty. "The sole living heir to the throne, so to speak. Direct decendant of the Voodoo Queen of New Orleans, Marie Laveau herself."

Nalia's entire essence slowly left her body, draining out through her feet. A sickeningly familiar feeling of betrayal washed over her. Her identity was lost once again. A lonely, distant glaze covered her eyes as she shook her head in confusion. She shuddered with angst, and then... relief. Searching her spirit, Nalia realized she already knew the truth. Somehow she knew, all along.

Jack went on explaining her mother's connection to the Darcantels. He recited, from memory, generations of her ancestry all the way back to the early 1800s, but Nalia was no longer listening. Her mind revisited the visions of Marie Laveau: her light skin, her caramel eyes, her ability to see through the veil. Nalia was certain Marie could see her through time and space; now she knew why. She was family. Had Mama Lu known? Had she really kept this secret, after all that happened?

"Well, don't think for a second your newfound 'royalty' is flattering, Ms. Deminy... Barronne... whatever it is you go by," Jack continued. "Being related to that witch is nothing to be proud of. Vile, nasty woman is what she was. She's the reason I'm here today. She's the reason for all of this."

"She cursed your family, didn't she?" Nalia asked.

Jack whipped around, hatred shining in his eyes. Nalia knew that hatred. It was the same blend of anger and fear haunting the old man in the top hat.

"'Cursed' does not begin to describe what she did to me," Jack fumed. "Damned me, that's what she did! But we're going to end that tonight, right here." Setting his glass down on the altar, Jack examined the ceremonial items on display, paying particular attention to one relic. Desperate to divert his attention from the table, Nalia searched her memory, recalling the vision.

"What happened to the child?" she cried out.

Jack stopped dead. His entire body went rigid as he straightened his neck in stunned silence.

"The man with the watch... his lover was pregnant. What happened to the child?"

Cutting his eyes, Jack turned and stared in amazement. "So her sight has found you," he said. "What else has she shown you?"

Nalia watched Jack's eyes redden, reminiscent of the old man on the tower. His looming presence moved her to silence, and for a moment, she was five years old again. Withdrawing into a ball, she breathed deeply, trying to calm her racing heart.

Instantly, Jack was upon her. Dropping to a knee, he gripped Nalia's face and squeezed hard, lifting her chin and straining her neck. Shaking with anger, he brought his face so close Nalia felt his spit when he spoke.

"What else did she show you?" he demanded, his face reddening.

As Jack's grip tightened, the fear drained from Nalia's body, replaced by a growing resentment and ultimately, acceptance.

Unnerved by her inability to control her emotions, Nalia grew restless and agitated. She wanted to hate Jack for his actions. She wanted to be angry. She should be angry, but something was in the way. Jack's blue eyes held a secret he did not want Nalia, or anyone else to know. She saw it just as clearly as she had in the old man's eyes – Jack was terrified.

"I've seen the courtyard," she said finally. Jack's grip lost its strength. His hand trembled and folded at his side. "I've been to the clock-faced prison where your grandfather's soul is trapped. I've seen his pain. I know his fear."

Jack's jaw dropped. Behind his eyes, a gaping wound lay bare and bleeding. As he stood, Nalia saw a tear gathering at the edge of his eye.

"You still don't see it, do you?" he said, returning to the altar and palming his glass. The silence was deafening as Jack stared at the candles, sipped his wine, and finally steadied his voice. "My grandfather died in 1822."

Jack's words hung in the air like paper lanterns floating across the night sky. Nalia's mind struggled to understand what she heard. All the pieces of the puzzle were there, but she was unable to put them together fast enough.

"The old man I call my grandfather," Jack explained, "Is my son – the most recent of many." He was breathing deeply now, pacing a solid line between the altar and Mr. John's worn set of congas. Wringing his fingers around the wine glass, Jack studied the room, determined to look anywhere except at Nalia. As his voice softened to a whisper, Nalia struggled to decide whether he was speaking to her or to himself.

"Clever woman, she was. You have to hand it to her. Brilliant, really," he said, running his fingers roughly through his hair. "Immortality! Who wouldn't want to live forever? It's a grand idea until you start working out the details. Oh, but Marie Laveau was a crafty conjurer, she was. She knew how to spoil the fruit from the inside out. You see, an apple can have a brilliant red flesh and still go bad on the inside. Looking at me,

who would guess I was born over two hundred years ago."
Holding up his glass, Jack studied his reflection in its curved
surface, turning his cheeks from side to side. "She was so good,
she made it so my face and skin retain their youthful glow... all
while my body rots away on the inside, feeling every ache,
every pain, every crippling disease."

A deranged look fell over Jack's eyes as he fixed his gaze on
Vivian. "Oh, but Jack is crafty too. I figured out ways to
circumvent the pain," he said.

"You never quite get used to it," Jack continued, staring into
his glass and swirling the red liquid. "The wine makes it
palatable, but you still never really get used to the bitter,
metallic taste. It's the iron content that spoils it, but that's what
makes it work. Sort of a... necessary evil, I guess you could say.
You see, I discovered long ago, the blood of the young helps
alleviate the pain." He raised his glass in Vivian's direction.
"This one's not as young as I prefer, but she was an easy catch."

The nausea returned. This time Nalia was sure she would
vomit. Scrambling to achieve a position where she could expel
the contents of her stomach, Nalia writhed against her binding
and the table. The pain in her arms flared as the zip tie bit her
tender flesh leaving a trail of blood dripping down her fingers.

Noticing the scuffling noise, Jack finally looked at her.
Watching her retch and grimace, his voice softened.

"Oh don't think I enjoy it," he said, as if trying to regain
some degree of dignity. "I don't want to kill. It's not sporting or
pleasurable. It's a necessity. I kill for the elixir. I kill because
without blood, the pain is excruciating. Over the years I've
become adept, but that doesn't make me a monster. It simply
makes me a master of the craft. You'd be surprised how well
you learn an art when you practice for centuries. With time, it
becomes quite normal."

Nalia tried to sit up. Once again she found herself struggling
to define "normal". Visions flashed through her mind of Marie

Laveau pointing a ritual blade at a dark-haired terrified young man.

"It was you," said Nalia, recalling the fear in the young man's eyes. "It was you that tricked her into cursing that woman's husband."

Jack reached a deeper level of silence. His gaze was lost in reflection, his eyes misty. "I loved her," he said, gulping the last of the blood-red liquid from his glass and wiping a dribble from his chin. "I loved her more than life itself, and she felt the same, or at least that's what I believed. I wanted nothing more than to take her away from her abusive husband. Turned out she wanted freedom more than she wanted me." Jack's head hung so low Nalia thought it would slide off his shoulders and fall to the floor.

"I wasn't the only one she tried to con into ferrying her away from that savage she married. I was just the only one crazy enough to actually do it. Turns out the baby she was carrying wasn't even mine, but that didn't change the fact that I loved her." Jack's voice cracked and shook softly as he went on. "I was young and foolish. I never meant for Marie's curse to kill her husband. I was just trying to get us to safety... to get *her* to safety."

Nalia watched as Jack's demeanor changed again. The muscles in his neck went rigid and his grip tightened around the wine glass.

"But that woman," he went on, through clenched teeth. "That woman couldn't let it go. She couldn't bear the thought someone made a fool of her… said no one deceived her and got away with it." Jack paused, centuries of reflection flooding his mind. A single vein in his temple began to throb and he spun on Nalia.

"Tell me, did the witch show you what she did to me?" he demanded hotly. "Did she show you how she snuffed the life from the woman I loved? How she laughed as my lover died in my arms? How she cursed me to watch every single person on this earth I care about, die in front of me... for centuries?" The glass shattered under the pressure of Jack's grip. A few broken pieces fell to the floor with a crash, while others imbedded deeply into his flesh. Jack grimaced, wailing in pain, but Nalia suspected it was not from the cut in his hand.

Opening his palm, Jack stared at the broken shards lodged in his palm as tears pooled in the corners of his crystalline eyes. In a sobering display, he removed the pieces one by one, casually tossing them aside. Not a single drop of blood dripped from his hand. As Nalia watched in amazement, the wounds in Jack's palm slowly closed as if stitched with an unseen suture. In a matter of moments, his skin was as smooth and beautiful as ever.

"It's a grand idea until you start working out the details," Jack whispered, looking at his hand but focusing nowhere.

Nalia's eyes widened. She hoped Jack didn't notice her surprise, but feared her gasp was far too audible.

When Jack's gaze caught hers, his expression was devoid of all emotion, stale and lifeless. He held up his hand and turned it from back to front for Nalia to examine. "Pretty wicked, huh?" he said, with a catch in his throat. Jack drew a single, rapid, ragged breath before he turned away and crumbled into tears.

Nalia's spirit stirred. The reality of an eternity spent watching your loved ones die hit her hard in the gut. While in high school, the loss of a dear friend shook her world to its core, causing Nalia to question her very existence. She shut the door on relationships, family, and religion, building walls not easily toppled.

Not even a year ago, she lost one of the closest members of her family. The pain was still gut-wrenching. She recalled elderly women from her childhood, friends of Mama Lu, Voodoo elders. She remembered the sadness in their eyes that came with outliving their families. Nalia could only imagine how it must feel to live two centuries carrying such pain day in and day out. She searched her spirit for words, anything that might bring a hint of comfort to the crumpled man on the floor.

"I saw her give you a chance. Tell me about the watch."

Jack's laughter rose through the tears. "A chance? Ha! That wasn't a chance, it was just another way for that sadistic woman to torment me," he said, shaking with renewed rage. "It wasn't enough to damn me to an eternity of misery, she wanted to drive me mad, as well." Jack stood. Resuming his path, he paced the floor again. "'Fix the watch,' she said. For the first few months I tried desperately, thinking I could save Emily. I thought if I could break the curse before that witch found her, she would live. I took that watch to every smith I could find, even studied the craft myself. Every gear, spring, and cog was perfectly restored. No one could explain why the watch wouldn't work."

Jack stopped pacing. He stood behind the congas staring into the corner. He scanned the runes on the wall like an astronomer studying the night sky, lost in a memory.

"I found her before Marie did. I knew where she would be, and I sought her out. I found her in a small settlement ten miles east of the Mississippi. She told me the baby died in childbirth, but I knew better. I tried to convince her to flee with me, thinking if we ran far enough we could outrun the magic. She refused to go. Wouldn't have mattered anyway, because I wasn't aware Marie's brutes were tailing me. I led them straight to her. They captured us both and dragged us right back to New Orleans. You should have seen the satisfaction on that witch's face when they brought us in. I swear, I was looking at the devil himself."

Nalia sat in awe listening to the story. She did not feel the pain in her wrists or the aching in her shoulders. The nausea subsided, and her anxiety vanished. She was transfixed.

"She took the watch from me, stripped us both, and locked us in an iron cage in her cellar, like animals. Only, no animal should ever be treated the way we were. The water table is so high here along the coast, the floor was always wet and cold. No place to sleep or rest. There was a pipe hanging overhead that dripped water into the cage. It was the only meager sustenance we were allowed. Soon our muscles began to ache and after some time, Emily grew weak and rigid with cramps."

Jack turned around, but his eyes remained lost. He dropped his gaze to the congas and ran a single finger along the bearing edge of the largest drum, tracing its round shape and speaking lazily, disconnected in a haze of remembrance.

"Your stomach hurts at first, but after a week or so, you start to get used to it. Of course the curse was on me, so I was in no danger of dying, but Emily was wasting away. She started having hallucinations, seeing demons and fairies and what-not. Pretty soon she stopped drinking the water altogether. She got so dehydrated she didn't even realize she was thirsty. After three weeks she started gnawing on her own flesh, biting what was left of her nails and chewing her fingers down to the bone. She didn't even stop when her teeth started breaking and falling out. She hung on with no food for thirty-seven days before she died in my arms. That was the day Marie came down to the cellar. She stood outside the cage and laughed the deepest belly laugh I've ever heard. She tossed the watch into the cage and told me to keep trying."

Nalia swallowed the lump in her throat.

"You would think that would be enough, but no. She had one of her brutes drive a spike into the cellar's support beam about six feet off the ground. After that she hung Emily's body up for me to watch it decompose. They rammed the spike right through the base of her skull. She just hung there staring at me, rotting away. I would have died from the smell and the methane if it wasn't for the blessed curse. It took nearly two weeks for the maggots to devour the rest of Emily's flesh. For two weeks I sat there holding that watch knowing I had to find a way to break the spell. After that, the brutes brought me up, put me out on the street, and let me go. People in town thought I was some kind of monster – naked, emaciated, cold, shaking, and smelling of death. I was so overcome with grief I couldn't even form words. I just staggered around vomiting bile for days. Not a soul would get near me. They knew I'd been cursed by the Voodoo Queen. I never saw Marie Laveau again, but through the years, each time someone close to me passes, I still hear that belly laugh... and I know it's my fault."

Jack moved to the altar, with a solitary look in his eyes. In the midst of the candles lay Mama Lu's ritual blade. Nalia never discussed its origin with Mama Lu, but remembering the vision, she realized it must be handed down from queen to queen through the years. Its mirror finish still shined brightly as Jack turned it on its point in the candlelight. A glimmering display of refracted light filled the room and spun hypnotically, like a slow-rolling disco ball.

Nalia could only speculate as to Jack's intentions. Feeling returned to her screaming body and panic rose in her throat once again. Her breathing accelerated and her heart rate climbed. Just when she began to feel the nausea tighten her stomach again, a piercing, high-pitched tone assaulted her ears. The buildings alarm was tripped.

"That'll be the great mambo," said Jack, spinning around and holding the blade with a devilish grin.

Jack moved swiftly to the floor beside Nalia. Holding the ritual blade to the side of her throat, he permitted the steel edge to taste Nalia's flesh.

"Don't you move," he said with absolution in his eyes. "I don't want to have to cut you too soon, but I will if I have to. You just keep your pretty little mouth quiet, and hope your Mama Lu is in a mood to cooperate."

In no time, the high-pitched tone died, replaced by the booming sound of footsteps on the stairs. Jack tightened his grip on the blade as three separate deadbolt locks turned in their casings and the door flew open in a fury.

"Don't even try!" yelled Jack as Mama Lu stepped over the threshold. His eyes showed no hint of compassion. The knife was cutting Nalia's skin ever so delicately. "If you so much as think about raising a hand I will slice this young lady's head clean off."

"Mama, don't listen to him," cried Nalia, but the blade cut deeper before she could finish her sentence. As a thin trail of blood flowed down her neck, her eyes bulged with uncertainty.

"I thought we were all going to play nice," spat Jack angrily in Nalia's ear.

Mama Lu did not move. She surveyed the scene, trying to take in as much information as she could. She noted the hole in the wall and saw Vivian in the next room collapsed in a heap, but she could not take her eyes off her own ritual knife at her daughter's throat. Jack was crouched beside her, his familiar azure-blue eyes sparkling in the candlelight.

"You haven't aged a bit Jack, if that is indeed your name," she said, presenting her palms in surrender.

"Au contraire, Mambo. I am old as the hills," said Jack. "And yes, Jack is my signature calling, although I have gone by many names throughout the years: Jack, Jackie, Jackson. Jacques St. Germaine was one of my favorites, but that was long before your time Mambo. It's the last name I tend to vary. I believe I was going by Thatcher when last we met."

"Wait! You two know each other?" cried Nalia.

"Femen," whispered Jack in the Haitian Creole dialect, waving his free hand toward Mama Lu. The door behind her slammed shut with a loud bang and the locks clicked themselves closed. "Know each other? Hell, she practically made me."

"Impressive," said Mama Lu, eyeing the door behind her. "But not much more than a glorified parlor trick."

"Oh, I have so much more to show you," said Jack slyly. "But that can wait. For now, I have a lovely pair of shackles for you, and I would so appreciate you sparing me the trouble."

Jack nodded at the table where Mama Lu's own heavy iron manacles lay chained to another one of its legs. Nalia tried again to stop her, but Mama Lu was not listening. Her eyes never left the blade, but she moved forward slowly and picked up the restraints.

"That's it," said Jack, "Around the back and clasped in front."

Mama Lu followed the instructions. Kneeling beside the table, she wrapped the chain once around her back and closed the cold shackles over her wrists pinning her body to the heavy leg.

"Well, that went well," said Jack, removing the blade from Nalia's neck and rising to greet Mama Lu properly.

"He wouldn't have hurt me, Mama," Nalia said. "He needs me for something."

"She's right you know," offered Jack, pursing his lips at Mama Lu. "I wasn't really going to hurt her. Not yet. But you knew I was bluffing. Your cooperation had nothing to do with my little ruse. You were just the diversion. You were supposed to keep my attention while the good doctor rushed in to save the day."

A long shadow darkened the room as a tall figure stepped into the newly formed entrance, backlit by the massive flood bulbs.

"Well hello there, Doctor John," Jack mocked. "So good of you to join us. Allow me to clear you a place at our table."

Anguish paled Mr. John's face as he stepped through the opening, followed by the old man holding a twelve gauge shotgun.

Chapter Thirty-Three

"I'm glad we could all be here together for this special occasion," said Jack presiding over the ritual table with Mama Lu chained to one leg and Mr. John and Nalia zip-tied to two others. Mr. John was regretting the pride he took years earlier in securing the table to the floor with seven-inch lag screws, assuring Mama Lu it "wasn't goin' nowhere."

"I can't help but revel in the irony," Jack went on, twirling the ritual blade on the table like a game of spin the bottle. "The very blade that set the curse and the woman who ultimately sent me looking for it."

"Mama, what's he talking about?" asked Nalia trying to fit all the pieces into their boxes. Her mind was swimming with possibilities, none of which held the promise of a simple explanation.

"He's a bokor," replied Mama Lu, "A dark sorcerer, one who dabbles in practices dat ought to be left alone."

"Dark sorcerer?" interrupted Jack. "You flatter me Mambo. And here I simply thought of myself as a keeper of the craft. Darkness, light, good, evil, it's all just a matter of perspective really. I mean, according to the demons, the angels are the evil ones, right? Regardless, I hardly think the infamous Mambo Lucia Deminy is one to determine what affairs should or should not be dabbled in."

Mr. John was fuming. Though he was careful not to move his arms and shoulders, he struggled like crazy to loosen his wrists from their plastic binding. His protective instincts were working overtime.

"I'm saddened, however, by your refusal to acknowledge your role in all of this, Mambo," Jack went on. "If it wasn't for you, I'd still be trying to fix that watch with a set of jeweler's tools and a pair of pliers, going mad from the inability to make it work." Jack let the blade spin freely another time before picking it up and circling the table. He stopped in front of Nalia and knelt, staring her straight in the eyes. "You see, it was your Mama Lu here who clued me in to the fact that breaking a blood curse was about more than just repairing an ancient time piece. Marie Laveau said in order to break the curse, I must fix the watch. Mama Lu enlightened me to the true nature of the spell: to fix the watch, I must break the curse." He cut a sharp eye at Mama Lu and went on. "Then she sent me on my way, refusing to help."

"You told me Marie Laveau cursed yo' family wit' dat watch, generation after generation. It wasn't so much as I wouldn't help you, as dat I couldn't. You 'spect me to break a curse put on yo' family by the Voodoo Queen herself? I didn't have dat kind of power."

"Don't flatter yourself Mambo, you still don't," snapped Jack. "But don't be disheartened, no one here in the States does, except me. What you have here in New Orleans is a milk-toast, watered-down version of the pure form of religion practiced elsewhere. I had to go all the way to the Congo to find a suitable mentor. That's where you find the purists who live and breathe the craft, who *are* the craft. Here everyone is too preoccupied with themselves to truly devote their life to the art." He gave a dismissive nod to the next room where Madame Luciénne lay barely clinging to life.

"I really have you to thank for it, Mambo. The twelve years I spent there were some of the most rewarding of my existence, and that's saying something, considering how long I've been around. I studied under a Makayan shaman who wields more power than you could ever fathom. I could have spent another hundred years in his service and not learned all he knows about the worlds around us: religion and science dancing in harmony, the nonlocality of quarks defining the anatomy of the spiritual realms, and most importantly for me, how to transcend this physical life for the next. Of course, first I have to break this heinous curse. I learned a lot about curses: how to cast them and how to break them. They're tricky, delicate things, especially the good ones. The ones born of Marie Laveau are especially complicated, crafty witch that she was. Even my shaman was impressed with her talent for blood curses. He taught me when a blood curse is fixed only blood can lay it waste. In this case, the blood of Marie Laveau." Jack brushed Nalia's chin with his fingertips. "It was smart of your Mama Lu to hide you away, you being the last of the bloodline."

"Mama, did you know about this? Please tell me you didn't know about this," Nalia pleaded.

Mama Lu kept silent while Jack sat down on the floor between them and reclined.

"Well go on Mambo, tell her you didn't know," he said, enjoying the moment. He folded his arms over his knees and waved the blade back and forth between the two. "You're not going to try and convince her you were ignorant, that you didn't know where her ancestry led? Of course you knew, why else..."

"I didn't know for sure!" shouted Mama Lu hotly. "Nalia, don't you let him do dis to you. I'll admit I had an idea, firs' time yo' mother told me her maiden name, but I didn't know fo' certain. I never traced yo' family history. Truth is I didn't want to look into yo' mother's past 'cause I couldn't take a chance on turnin' up somebody who'd want to take you away. I made a promise to a beaten, broken lil' girl dat I would never let anyone hurt her again. All I wanted was to know you was safe from harm. Dat's why I hid you away. You know dat's the truth, chil'. Don't you let him turn us against each other."

It was Nalia's turn for silence. Jack tried to watch her eyes but she turned away. Her spirit was wounded. Jack sensed the ebb of energy and felt his own spirit stir.

"You gots to believe me, chil'," Mama Lu pleaded. "I wouldn't keep nothin' from you. Not no mo'. Not after all we been through."

Mr. John sat quietly, listening to the exchange and struggling against his bindings. Using the tension of the room to his advantage, he focused his energy on his body. In a well-honed meditation, he concentrated on increasing his heart rate and perspiration. The more sweat he willed down his arms, the more slippery his wrists became. Just when he thought he might be close to slipping free, he caught the old man's gaze. Standing before Mr. John with shotgun in hand, the old man noticed his struggle. He did not move, but tightened his grip on the twelve gauge.

Mr. John froze, pleading with his eyes. His lungs refused to work. He watched the old man carefully, trying to discern his intentions. Elias Haufmann stared him down for well over a minute, before Mr. John saw his resolve break. For a split second the old man glanced at Jack, then turned back to Mr. John with the faintest flicker of compassion in his eyes. Reading the opportunity, Mr. John hesitantly resumed his struggle, watching for the old man's reaction. Elias turned away and did not look back.

"While I'd love to sit here all night and discuss the delicate fabric of your mother/daughter relationship," said Jack, tiring of the silence. "I have a curse to break." Rising to his feet, Jack cut a scathing look at the old man and nodded toward Mama Lu. "Let's make sure the young lady knows I'm serious."

Without hesitation, Elias Haufmann moved around the table and stood near Mama Lu, placing the barrel of the shotgun firmly against her temple.

"No!" Nalia screamed in protest. "Don't hurt her! I'll do whatever you want."

Mr. John jumped, losing all progress he'd made on the zip tie. With his back turned he could see nothing, but sensed the situation's urgency. "Lu, wha's he doing? You alright?"

"Fine, John," came the shaky reply, as Mama Lu stared up into the old man's face. "Don't you worry 'bout me, I'm fine."

Mama Lu swallowed hard. As a frightened, angry tear rolled off her cheek, the old man turned his eyes away.

Once again Jack knelt in front of Nalia. "Now sweetheart, do I have your attention?"

Nalia nodded.

"Good, so you'll be disinclined to do anything foolish." Moving in closely, Jack put his arms around Nalia in an awkward embrace. He felt behind her back until he found her delicate wrists, still bleeding from the tension of the zip tie.

"I really was starting to like you," he whispered in her ear as her chest heaved against his. Slipping the blade under the binding Jack drew it back, careful not to cut Nalia in the process. Once the zip tie was broken he backed away, leaving Nalia free to rub her wrists where the binding dug into her flesh. Circulation returned to her fingers as Nalia stared into Jacks crystal clear, azure-blue eyes.

"One misstep," Jack warned, "And he pulls that trigger."

Mr. John panicked. Mention of the word trigger had him scrambling from side to side, trying to see what was happening.

"I'd keep still if I were you, Doctor," said Jack. "My son isn't as steady with that shotgun as he used to be. His age is catching up to him. Wouldn't want your girlfriend to lose her head because you couldn't keep still." While Mama Lu had already pieced together the truth, Mr. John was confused by the familial reference.

"You can kill me if that's what you're planning," assured Nalia, gritting her teeth. "Just don't hurt them."

Jack laughed. "Oh, darling you misunderstand. I don't want to kill you, I just want you to break the curse."

"And what if I can't," Nalia asked sheepishly. "What if it doesn't work?"

"Well, that's another story, entirely," replied Jack, throwing a glance to Madame Luciénne who lay slumped, barely breathing, in a pool of her own blood.

Reaching down, Jack gripped Nalia firmly by her bruised and bloodied wrist, jerking her up harshly. With swift motion and brute strength he spun her around and pushed her down onto the table, putting her face-to-face with the antique gold pocket watch. With his hand gripping the back of her neck, Jack held Nalia's head firm.

The hands of the watch were set stone still with fierce determination. Nalia thought she never saw anything appear so rigid, as if the delicate hands were anchored to the face, an immovable part of the world around them.

Jack slammed the ritual blade onto the table beside her. For a moment, Nalia considered grabbing it, turning on her captor, and stabbing him through his tortured heart. The thought of the old man holding the shotgun to Mama Lu's head stopped her, but something more stirred her spirit. Even if Mama Lu was safely far away and Nalia could manage to overpower Jack, she still could not bring herself to drive the blade. She was intrigued by him, drawn to him.

Reaching down, Jack grabbed Nalia by the forearm and slammed her hand down onto the table with her palm toward the ceiling. "You keep real still, now," he whispered in her ear. "This will be over before you know it. You keep your eyes on that watch and wait for those hands to move."

With one hand gripping Nalia's arm and the other on the ritual knife, Jack raised the blade and turned his face toward the altar with a crazed look in his eyes.

"This is it, Marie!" he shouted, laughing maniacally. "It all ends here! You are beaten! Your blade, your blood, your bond!"

Mr. John struggled furiously. When trying to slip free of the bond proved futile he resorted to brute force. Straining with all his might, he pulled feverishly against the plastic strap, but the gauge was too thick. His effort earned him only injury and exhaustion.

Lowering the ritual blade to Nalia's open palm, Jack brought his lips to her ear and began to whisper in a broken, forgotten dialect.

Ede mwen Loa.

Ede mwen Bondye

Slowly, he pulled the razor sharp edge across the soft flesh of Nalia's left palm, spilling her blood onto the ritual table.

Pote san.

Pote lajistis.

Pote v alimante.

The wound was deep. With Nalia's hand open and bleeding freely, Jack stabbed the knife into the oak table beside the watch. Shaking with anticipation, he held Nalia's arm high until blood from the wound trickled into the open face of the ancient timepiece.

Kase mwen tauhe.

Gratis mwen lespir.

Ban mwen lapè.

Pain seared Nalia's hand, climbing all the way to her shoulder, but she did not take her eyes off the watch. She stared intently as blood pooled on the face and along the edges. A large drop fell onto the hour hand and slid its way from the center, out to the edge. The energy in the room swelled. Mama Lu and Mr. John felt the pressure of the spirit world bearing down, like a crushing weight. The flames of the altar candles rose tall and bright, burning the fuel of the spirit realm.

Mr. John swung his head around until he could barely see the crazed look in Jack's pained eyes. Mama Lu watched the grimace on Nalia's face while the old man pushed the barrel of the gun further into her temple.

Energy rose, power swelled, and tension raged like a bonfire as Nalia's blood filled the face of the watch. Jack was on his tiptoes with excitement when a soaring wind blew through the room, whipped around the table, spiraled high into the air, and fell with a hush.

In an instant it was over. Like the eye of a storm, the room, and everything in it, fell silent. Jack could hear his own heart beating as he waited breathlessly to hear the first blessed tick of the watch announcing the curse was over. Quietly he watched to see the slightest motion of the hands over the face. Desperately, he waited, listening for the sound of a lifetime without love to come to an end. To his horror, the only sound Jack heard was the steady-rolling, belly laugh of Marie Laveau inside his tortured mind.

With the rage of two hundred years, Jack threw his head back and screamed. His piercing bellow echoed through the ritual room and even briefly roused Madame Luciénne from her languid state.

With fear and anger coursing through his veins, Jack grabbed Nalia by the hair and lifted her from the table. Violently he flipped her around and gripped her by the shoulders.

"What did you do?" he cried. "Why didn't it work? It was supposed to be over!"

Casting Nalia aside he leaned over the table and grabbed the ancient timepiece. Nalia fell to the floor beside the altar and watched as Jack's appearance began to change. As if suddenly seized by intense pain, Jack grimaced and held his stomach. His mouth hung open, locked in a crippling convulsion. Moaning loudly, he doubled over at the waist, holding the watch to his gut.

The old man removed the gun from Mama Lu's head and watched his father in horror as Jack fell to his knees.

Quietly, Jack began to whisper. "This was it. She's the last of the bloodline. It was supposed to work."

Nalia looked from Mama Lu to Mr. John as Jack continued his mantra of denial. Their eyes held as much confusion as hers. The room fell silent as Jack began to sob.

"I can't do this anymore. I can't stand it. She was my last hope. What went wrong?" Pain hit Jack hard again in the stomach as reality struck. The watch was his only saving grace, his only hope that one day the curse would be lifted, finally granting him release. With that option gone, he stared into the cold face of an eternal existence devoid of peace. In disbelief he looked up at Nalia.

The wound in Jack's soul was now laid open for Nalia to see, for everyone to see. As Nalia stared into his beautiful, tear-filled eyes, she no longer saw pain and rage, but only the fear underneath. She remembered seeing it before, masked in his stare. It haunted his soul in the form of the old man in the courtyard – Jack was terrified. He lived more than two-hundred years, traveled the world, found riches and tremendous power, but was paralyzed by the promise of existing forever without love. His eyes reflected the fear of a lost toddler, unable to decide what to do or where to go. In the moment, Jack was crushed.

Silently, Nalia crept forward, unsure of whether she was approaching a frightened child, or a cornered animal.

"Jack, it's not over," she said, not quite sure where the words originated. "I love you."

Mama Lu and Mr. John were shocked into silence, but shot looks of warning to their baby girl. Nalia never saw them. Her eyes were fixed on Jack. With her hand still bleeding, she left a trail of blood across the floor as she crawled toward her blue-eyed captor.

Staring up from his crumpled heap, Jack looked like a different person. The agony of two hundred years, plus eternity, weighed on his heart. His face was red and swollen, his beautiful, blue eyes bloodshot and tearful. He looked at Nalia in disbelief. "What did you say?"

"I said, I love you," replied Nalia, "And we're not finished here."

Jack began to laugh. "You still don't understand, do you?" he said chuckling and summoning the strength to stand. "You don't realize how crafty the woman was."

Leaving Nalia on the floor, Jack walked back to the ritual table. A threatening glare at Elias warned the old man to train the shotgun back on Mama Lu.

Nalia noticed Jack's defeated posture and mannerisms as all emotion drained from his body. Emptiness filled his eyes as he picked up the ritual blade and turned it over in his hands.

"Talent, the likes of which was never seen before, or since – that was Marie Laveau. See, there's one thing the woman could do that I've never been able to match, nor have I known anyone else who could." Tapping the flat edge of the blade against the side of his head, Jack stared straight through Nalia. "She gave life to the curse. She not only cast it, she made it a living, breathing, entity with a mind of its own. Now that was clever. You see, I thought I found a way to beat the curse. After sixty years of traveling the world, seeking out master craftsmen to fix that damned watch, I gave up. I changed my tactic. I thought if the curse was going to kill off everyone I loved, I'd show it. I taught myself how to loath, and given my circumstance it wasn't difficult. I gave my heart over to hatred. I became practiced and proficient at avoiding love. Still am today. Hell, the only reason Elias is still with me is because I'm so adept at loathing. I've hated that worthless heap since the day he was born. He's more of a slave than a son, which is to his benefit, really. It's prolonged his life so far."

All eyes in the room turned to the old man. The tension in his body collapsed and the look on his face reflected the sting of Jack's hurtful remark. A lifetime of pain and rejection suddenly showed in the way his shoulders seemed to crouch like a beaten animal.

"So thumbing my nose at Marie Laveau, I *became* hatred," continued Jack. "I withdrew myself from society and everyone I once loved or even knew. I did well for about a decade. I became a new person, completely focused on selfishness and abhorrence, an abomination of human existence. I reveled in the belief the curse couldn't touch me. Then it happened: the curse took on a life of its own. It's like Marie reached out from beyond the grave to show me I didn't have it licked." Jack chuckled in self-reflection as he returned to pacing the floor. "The curse," he said loudly, "Started drawing people to me. It decided if I wasn't going to love anyone, it was going to make them love me. Young women were its prime focus. It even targeted my type. Soon women were throwing themselves at me, and not just sexually. The curse was working so well, it found women to connect with me on a spiritual level. It *made* me love them, then ripped them away. Sometimes they would last long enough to have a child before the curse snuffed them, adding to the misery. I had no choice but return to the watch. That's when I came to you, Mambo."

Pushing the old man aside, Jack toyed with the ritual blade around Mama Lu's neck. Flame danced in his eyes again as he trailed the blade from one ear to the other.

"A certain young gypsy woman told me of a powerful Voodoo queen, one whose talent rivaled the legendary Marie Laveau. She said if anyone could remove the shadow from my soul, it would be the great Mambo Lucia." Barely able to bridle his anger, Jack permitted the blade to prick Mama Lu's flesh just below her ear. He was impressed when she didn't flinch.

"But you sent me away," he continued, curling his lip. "You cast me aside with no concern and no remorse, just like Marie when she turned me loose in the street. So while the curse continued drawing women to me, I poured myself into finding a way to break the spell, to make the watch work. I have to admit Elias here gave it his all. He's devoted his life to trying to fix that thing. Picked up a slight obsession from his old man."

Jack finished with Mama Lu and sauntered back across the room to where Nalia sat on the floor, steadily holding pressure on her wound.

"So you see, sweetheart," he finished, "You don't love me. What you're feeling is simply the byproduct of a powerful curse cast by a very talented Voodoo queen. Didn't you find it strange having such intense feelings of adoration for a man you just met? Didn't you find it unusual your mind was so easily wrapped up in this fairy tale?"

"Fairy tales have nothing to do with love," Nalia spat back, sitting up. Ignoring the pain in her hand, she cut an eye at Mr. John. Remembering his words, Nalia thought about his relationship with Mama Lu. Through good times, troublesome situations, and events hardly definable as fairy tales, they never left each other's side. Even now, chained to a table, uncertain if they would live to see morning, they were together, and they would have it no other way.

"Love is not some feeling that causes butterflies in your stomach," Nalia went on. "It's not some flippant physical attraction that gets your blood pumping. It's not some passing emotion, or even a spell that causes your mind to keep drifting back to a certain person."

Hearing Nalia's words, Mr. John looked up from his exhausted state. Though his body was slumped and fatigued, his eyes reflected only adoration.

"Real love is action," Nalia continued rising and staring at Jack. "It's something you do. It's putting the needs of others before your own. It's patience, compassion, and forgiveness. That's real love. Now, I told you I love you, and I told you this isn't over. Give me the watch, I can break the spell."

Chapter Thirty-Four

"Nalia, what are you sayin' chil'?" cried Mama Lu, baffled. She couldn't tell if her daughter was playing for time or legitimately delusional.

"I can do it. I can break the spell," she replied.

Jack took a step backward, clutching the watch with one hand and pointing the blade at Nalia with the other. Breathing heavily he stared in disbelief. "How can you possibly break the curse, you've got no knowledge... You can't possibly... "

"I know how to reach Marie," Nalia said, her eyes laser-fixed on Jack.

Mama Lu gasped. No longer caring about the twelve gauge pointed at her head, she refused to keep silent. "You talkin' out yo' head chil'. What you mean you can reach Marie Laveau?"

"He knows exactly what I mean," Nalia replied, answering Mama Lu but keeping her gaze targeted on Jack. "He knows I've seen her. He knows she showed me his past. She showed me the curse and how she fixed it. What he doesn't know is... she's seen me."

Jack and Mama Lu had the same, simultaneous reaction: their jaws dropped in awe. While Mama Lu's expression remained one of shock, Jack's swung quickly to skepticism. The concept was foreign. In all his study, Jack never heard of a memory springing to life.

"A vision is simply that, nothing more," he insisted. "To tell me she can see you is like saying actors on the television can look into your living room. It's preposterous!"

"She's seen me," Nalia insisted. She looked right at me, even spoke to me. She didn't take kindly to my presence in her parlor. I don't have to tell you the kind of threats she can make with her eyes; you've seen them, and so have I. Surely you remember the way she can look right through you, see your soul, and take you down like a gator in a death roll."

Jack's defenses dropped. His face became lost in reflection, and his body shuddered as Nalia continued.

"She can bring life to a vision just like she can breathe it into a curse. Tell me you don't believe the Voodoo Queen of New Orleans can pierce the veil between the worlds. You know she can. That's why you hear her laughter so clearly."

Jack dropped the blade to his side and stared at the watch, speechless and inanimate. His mind swimming in disbelief, he did not notice Nalia move until she was upon him. Startled, Jack raised the knife, but Nalia quickly cupped her hands around his, and the watch. Her left palm was still bleeding, making a dark-red mess of the union, but her touch gave Jack pause. His muscles released their tension, and his spirit began to yield.

Looking up into his eyes, Nalia pleaded. "I can do this. You've got to let me try. I can reach her."

Nalia could see Jack's spirit splintering, his conscience struggling between the terrified child desperate for release, and the hate-fueled persona he created in order to cope.

"How will you do it?" he asked, his eyes a mixture of the personalities. "How will you..."

"I don't know that yet," interrupted Nalia. "But I'll figure it out." Looking down at the watch, Nalia unfolded her hands. Blood covered the timepiece, Jack's palm, and hers. Feeling him tremble, she stepped closer until their bodies touched. "This is where you trust me," she said, turning her eyes back to his.

Timidly, Jack tipped his hand and let the watch fall into Nalia's. A piece of his spirit dropped with it.

"I can do this," Nalia assured him again before turning around and walking to the table. "But, *you've* got to help me," she said to Mama Lu.

Elias, having relaxed his stance, gripped the shotgun more tightly as she approached. By the time Nalia knelt face to face with Mama Lu, it was once again raised. Elias shifted his aim from one to the other as Nalia pleaded with the fatigued Mambo. "I can't do this by myself. I need your help."

Mama Lu knew this was the decision she'd waited for Nalia to make, but now the circumstances were all wrong. "You can't do dis fo' me or fo' anybody else. If you ain't doin' it fo' you, it'll never work. It might even backfire."

"I've made up my mind Mama. This is what I want," Nalia replied. "I won't let fear rule my life," she said with a gentle nod to Jack. "I know now, the sight can't take me where I don't want to go. It will walk with me down the path I choose. It will listen to my will, like a loyal friend. It won't take me to a dark place if I don't allow it. I'm ready."

Mama Lu nodded. A weight lifted from her soul. Nalia finally knew the truth about *the sight* – a truth she could only learn for herself, one that would live in her heart, not her mind. "You are wise fo' yo' years, chil'," said Mama Lu with a grim smile. "Yo' Madame T. would be so proud."

"She is, Mama. I know she is."

Nalia turned back to face Jack, holding the watch tightly in her hands. "I need you to release my Mama Lu," she said, watching for his reaction.

His malevolent side took the battle, like a demon rearing its head. Twisted with rage, Jack gripped the blade firmly. "You expect me to fall for that?" he roared. "You want me to turn Mambo Lucia Deminy loose against me in her own ritual room, her own hub of power? I believe we've covered I wasn't born yesterday."

"You saw me when I blacked out," Nalia fired back. "You think I did that on purpose? The visions come to me, not the other way around. I can't fly on my own." Nalia turned back toward Mama Lu, her chest heaving in desperation. "Even if I could, I'm not confronting Marie Laveau without backup."

Jack raised his brow. He studied Nalia and Mama Lu carefully. More than a lifetime of dealing with women he couldn't trust instilled no confidence in the situation. He looked for the angle, trying to find their ulterior motive. They could easily take the watch and destroy it, but given the present circumstance, the piece was useless anyway. The more he scrutinized the situation, the more Jack realized they were his only hope. Still, he would not be bested by trickery.

Eyeing Mr. John, he moved alongside him and knelt. With raging strength, he wrapped his arm around Mr. John's shoulders, palming his head and yanking it back. Jack stared coldly at Nalia and Mama Lu as he held the ritual knife tightly to Mr. John's throat. Sweat fell onto the blade and ran its length as Mr. John trembled with anger.

"Just in case," Jack said.

He motioned for Elias to release Mama Lu who now shot a scathing look in Jack's direction.

"You hurt him and I swear, I'll... "

"Kill me?" Jack taunted, his eyes alight with enmity. "Do your best, Mambo."

Elias leaned the twelve gauge against Mr. John's congas and searched the altar for the key to the shackles. With Mama Lu shouting instructions he quickly located it among the ritual items and tossed it within her reach. Retrieving the shotgun he resumed his position.

Mama Lu's hands shook with rage as she unlocked the restraints and removed the chain from her body. Her knees and legs ached as she stood. She massaged her wrists and stretched her back, never taking her eyes off Jack.

Nalia tried desperately to calm her, but the tension in the room was running hot. "Focus on me, Mama," she pleaded, placing a bloody hand to Mama Lu's chin and physically turning her gaze away from Jack.

"Look at me, Mama," she repeated. "I need you with me, you've got to focus."

"Listen to her, Lu," shouted Mr. John. "Ain't gon' do no good to worry 'bout me. You go on, do what needs doing', I'll be fine. I got him right where I want him."

Jack tightened his grip and pressed the blade a little harder for good measure. "This should give you plenty of incentive to learn what you need to end this curse. If you try anything foolish, or if you fail, the good doctor will end up like your pompous little friend in there." He nodded to the other room where Vivian lay motionless on the floor beside the freight elevator. Nalia tried reasoning with Jack, insisting her intentions were true, but his will was unyielding. The demon was completely in control now.

"One other thing, Mambo," Jack called out, removing the knife from his captive's throat. Placing the tip against Mr. John's side, Jack drove the blade smoothly through his flesh. With a wicked, empty stare, he turned to Mama Lu. "You might want to hurry."

Chapter Thirty-Five

Mama Lu was sick. Weakened by the sight of her ritual blade in Mr. John's side, she fell to her knees like a stone. With Elias and his shotgun following close behind, she crawled toward her wounded man, trembling.

"Keep your distance!" shouted Jack, gripping the handle of the knife tightly and threatening to twist. "You focus on that watch, not him."

Mama Lu could barely breathe. Throughout her life, many circumstances cast heavy shadows over her soul. She knew and lost many friends, family, and elders. She witnessed the effects of horrible abuse and terrifying violence. She was no stranger to grisly spectacles and heart-wrenching despair, but nothing matched her present state of desperation.

"Do what he says, Lu," wheezed Mr. John, trying to suppress the pain as blood began to seep through his shirt. "Take Nalia and go."

Elias Haufmann stood over Mama Lu with the shotgun leveled at her back. His face and palms grew sweaty. For brief periods he released his grip to wipe perspiration from his eyes as his lungs heaved with strained breaths. His control of the weapon waned.

"Idiot!" screamed Jack. "Hold the gun on what she cares about." Whipping his head to the side, he indicated Nalia.

The old man hesitated, lost in a trance.

"Christ! Have you gone deaf, you addle-minded ass?" yelled Jack, mocking the old man's blank expression. "Point the gun at her!"

Shaking his head, Elias snapped back to the present, shifting his aim to the bleeding young woman with the watch. Though his gun was on Nalia, his attention was on Mama Lu and Mr. John.

"You hang in there, John," Mama Lu said, sobbing. "I'm gon' see you in jus' a bit. We gon' fix dis, and it's all gon' be over. You hang in there."

"Hurry back to me, Mama," replied Mr. John with a peaceful smile. "I'll wait right here for you."

"I know you will," cried Mama Lu, stretching a hand toward his face. He would wait, she thought. He was always right there waiting for her.

Jack pulled Mr. John back before Mama Lu's hand could reach. "Get going now, Mambo," he said, "Before I remove this blade and let him bleed out."

With a pointed stare at Mr. John and a nod of affirmation, Mama Lu channeled her fury into energy. Turning to her altar, she raised her chin, extended her hand, and motioned for Nalia to follow. Without a word, she stepped up to the makeshift table, home to relics of a previous world long since abandoned. With Nalia following closely, the energy of the room folded around them like the wings of a raven, shielding them from outside influence.

The rest of the room watched in awe, most notably Jack, eager to see the great Mambo at work. The old man lowered his weapon, staring back and forth from the ladies at the altar to Mr. John who was doubled over beside to oak table, wincing and sweating profusely.

Mama Lu reached over the candles to the back of the altar and retrieved a small, iron apparatus. The object resembled a tripod with a thin, flat disc suspended horizontally between the legs. Blowing off the dust, she placed it over the barely-burning stump of a red candle in the center of the altar.

Nalia watched diligently, taking in every detail of the ritual, studying her Mama Lu's craft. She noted the way Mama Lu cupped her hands around the candle and watched as its flame rose to meet the bottom of the round, flat plate. It burned hot, licking its quick, fiery tongue around the edges.

Silently, Mama Lu plucked two glass vials from a small wooden box. Neither vial had a label or markings of any kind, but each was capped with a cork and sealed with a different color wax. Thumbing the blue wax of the first seal, she broke it and popped the cork. After lifting the small glass container to her nose and examining its content, Mama Lu grabbed a thin, wooden stick from the altar, near the candle and ran its tip through the flame allowing it to char. When the black coating was sufficient, she dipped the tip into the vial and twirled it through the oily substance inside.

Still with no words, Mama Lu turned to Nalia, nodded, and opened her mouth wide. Nalia followed suit, as if taking communion, and Mama Lu rolled the oily stick across her tongue. Its taste was the bitterest sensation Nalia ever experienced. Only the charred flavor of the wood kept her from gagging as she lifted her tongue to the roof of her mouth. Closing her eyes and tensing every muscle in her face and throat, she struggled to draw her mind to anything but the rancid taste on her tongue.

Surprisingly, Nalia found refocusing her thoughts an easy task. Her mind shifted and began to float, bobbing up and down on a current of energy. By the time Nalia opened her eyes, her vision was blurry and her head was spinning, ever so slightly. She could barely focus on Mama Lu running the oily stick across her own tongue.

Just when Nalia felt she would black out, she heard the voice of Mama Lu inside her head.

Don't worry, chil'. Let go.

Nalia's physical vision darkened, but somehow she still saw Mama Lu crack the plug of white wax on the second vial and spill several drops onto the hot, iron disc. Within seconds, the oil began to burn allowing thick, pungent smoke to fill the energy-charged area around the altar.

Breathe.

Nalia inhaled deeply, taking the smoke fully into her lungs. Her chest began to burn. Nearly panicking, her lungs screamed with the urgent need to cough but Nalia's mind would not allow it. Instead, Mama Lu's voice instructed her to exhale slowly, and Nalia listened. The bizarre sensation of the mind separating from the body took her by surprise, but Mama Lu's voice calmed her spirit.

Come.

Nalia retained no feeling in her physical form as she followed Mama Lu across the room. Her consciousness hovered somewhere near the ceiling, and before she knew it, she was looking down at the ritual table. She and Mama Lu were flat on their backs, lying head to toe. Their hands were joined in the center of the great oak table with the ancient gold pocket watch cupped between them.

Come.

For a moment Nalia couldn't tell if the voice belonged to Mama Lu or Madame Toulouse, but followed nonetheless and found her spirit racing through time and space. The sensation was purely exhilarating. Nalia had no body, no physical means of feeling, but she recognized each and every atom of her existence, individually and simultaneously. She was still aware of her extremities: head, arms, legs, even fingers, but felt no tangible existence at all. Her energy vibrated in distinct repetitive waves as she floated between planes of the spiritual realm.

Without warning, another set of waves appeared alongside her, interrupting her vibration – a pattern she instinctively recognized as Mama Lu. Soon, their wavelengths stretched and bent until their frequencies became one, mother and daughter flying through the spirit world, dead-locked on the energy of Marie Laveau.

———————

The demon berating his brain retreated and Jack rubbed his eyes, squinting. His face drooped with amazement as pulses of energy fanned outward from the center of the oak table, like heavy bass rattling a speaker. The two ladies glowed with visible white light, a reflection of the spirit world beyond.

Allowing Mr. John's body to fall limp, he stood slack-jawed at the edge of the table as two, thin wisps, like bright silver smoke, rose from Nalia and Mama Lu and climbed toward the ceiling. Revolving and criss-crossing, they wove a complex pattern like DNA, swelling to thick, strong cords. With flashes of energy charging their length in waves, the silver cords ascended, tethering the insensate bodies somewhere beyond the ceiling, beyond the sky.

Fascinated, Jack fought the urge to touch the pulsing cords. The world around him faded from his conscience as he watched the energy flow, his mind adrift in silent prayer that Nalia would accomplish her goal and somehow bring peace to his tortured spirit.

As Mama Lu and Nalia crossed through the dark void between the spiritual planes, the smell of Marie Laveau's earthy incense drifted into existence. Resistance, like a rushing wind, pushed powerfully against their spirits, increasing as their surroundings began to settle. Clearly, they were unwelcome and unwanted.

Nalia felt Mama Lu's energy cradling her tightly. Willing her spirit in return, Nalia held on to Mama Lu, forming an impenetrable bond against which the intruding force fragmented and dissolved, soon replaced by a predominant air of displeasure.

The hollow sound of an empty chamber filled their senses as Marie Laveau's parlor faded into view. Though the room was barren, Mama Lu and Nalia sensed a thousand eyes watching. With their illuminated, astral beings occupying the parlor, they examined their surroundings.

The vision was just as Nalia remembered: the velvet tablecloth, the burning candles, an ancient cabinet, and a curtained doorway. The smell of sweat and blood tainted the fragrant air, and the fresh energy of a struggle lingered heavily in the room. Noticeably different, was her own tangibility. Though she possessed no physical means of doing so, Nalia felt as if she could reach out and touch the objects on the table. She dared not; a foreboding presence was gathering strength, preparing for confrontation.

The curtain fluttered as heavily-ringed fingers pushed it aside. Mama Lu felt a spark of anxiety spiral across her being. Nalia sensed the fluctuation in her energy and tried to calm her spirit, but Mama Lu was awestruck. So many times she'd stared at the painting of Marie Laveau in her secret room, watched the woman with the serpent dance above her altar, meditated on the image of the benevolent figure holding the Guinea peppers. Mama Lu spent hours at her shop, staring at the once prominent doll fashioned in Marie's likeness, communing with what she was sure was the spirit of the famed Voodoo queen. To finally lay eyes on her in this capacity was thrilling and terrifying.

"Relax, Mambo," rolled a thick Creole tone as Marie Laveau emerged from beyond the curtain. "You, I know. It's the other one who rattles my cage."

Mama Lu's spirit bowed in respect. She recognized the pattern of Marie's energy, a strong, familiar vibration. While Nalia allowed her spirit to yield respect, she did not bow. Instead, she stood resolute, firm in her purpose.

"I've felt yo' callin' befo' many times, Mambo. I've greeted you, granted you council, shown you favor. Why now, do you barge into my chamber unannounced, uninvited, and stringin' along dis foreigner. Dis' one's been steppin' over her grounds fo' some time now. Wha's the matter, girl, didn't see enough las' time?"

"I saw what I came to see," Nalia replied with a humble tone. "I didn't force my way in, I was drawn here. I meant no harm, and I had no control. I was drawn by the spirit of the man with the watch."

Marie's eyes widened as she followed Nalia's arm down to her hand where a phantom image of the ancient timepiece was cupped in her palm. Smiling a wicked grin of satisfaction, she chuckled.

"So he's still at it, eh?" she laughed. "Still tryin' to make dat ol' watch tick. How many years he been at it now?"

"Far too long," answered Nalia.

Marie Laveau stammered, affronted. Nalia felt the banishing wind again, but held her ground. She would not be shunned. She might not be convincing, but she would be heard.

"You done worn yo' welcome way past thin," said Marie as her two brutes appeared in the doorway.

"I want only your attention," said Nalia firmly. "I've come here to ask a favor. Isn't that what you do, grant favors? I ask no more than anyone else."

Marie was intrigued. She looked at Mama Lu for affirmation, seeing the severity in her eyes. With a flip of her hand, she waved off her goons and stepped to the middle of the room, so close she could nearly be touched.

"Wha's dis all about, Mambo? Why dis chil' think I'm gon' help her?"

"Jus' listen to her, please," said Mama Lu. "Hear her out."

Folding her arms, Marie stared at Nalia and waited, her demeanor prepared neither for latitude nor negotiation.

"I need you to take back the curse," said Nalia, bluntly. "I need you to release Jack from the prison you put him in."

Marie belly-laughed. Holding her stomach, she turned for the curtain.

"Wait," cried Nalia.

Marie turned around with a smile awaiting the punch line, but saw no humor in Nalia's expression. "Oh, you were serious? Fo' a moment I thought I was havin' an amusin' dream, so I was goin' back to bed."

"I need you to undo it," repeated Nalia, stiffening. "And I'm not leaving until you do."

Marie's expression flipped like a switch, revealing the full scope of rage building behind her eyes. She glared at Nalia with an intensity that burned her spirit. "I don't know who the hell you think you are, waltzin' in here makin' demands of Marie Laveau, but I got a mind to help you understan' my position, in a painfully unnatural way," she spewed. "Dat man got what he deserved, and ain't no way I'm takin' back dat curse. He cheated me. He lied to me. He caused me to cast a spell dat killed an innocent man!"

"You're right," agreed Nalia. "He did all those things. He was a liar and a thief, and he got what he deserved."

Marie breathed deeply. The intensity in her eyes diminished, as Nalia continued to speak.

"I'm not going to try and defend him, because he doesn't deserve it. Even though his intentions were only to rescue the woman he loved, his methods were wrong and unjust. He was duly punished."

Nalia's voice was smooth, like heavy cream. She watched Marie's reaction as the situation deescalated. Taking Marie's side against Jack gave them a common bond. Jack's curse was about vengeance, for sure. But more than that, it was about justice for the wronged: Marie and the slain, innocent man. Justice was a noble cause, worth championing. Somewhere beyond Marie's raging eyes, shined a tiny light of humanity. Nalia latched her energy onto it and began to pull.

"He has known the suffering of two lifetimes and more," she continued. "His mind is splintered in two: one still weeps for that which is lost, the other rages violently against all that will never be. He has done his penance. It's time to let him go, not just for his sake, but for the others."

Skeptical, Marie looked from Nalia to Mama Lu and back again. Her spirit settled to a guarded, but more reasonable temperament. "Somethin' familiar about you, girl," she said. "Some energy inside you dat speaks to me, but I still can't grant yo' wish. Even if I..."

"There's a reason our energies harmonize. The familiarity you see... is you, Marie," Nalia broke in. "I'm your flesh and blood, ten generations down and the last of the family."

Marie stiffened with shock, studying Nalia's face and features. Now with the truth revealed, the resemblance was striking. She stepped forward extending a hand, running it across Nalia's cheek. Nalia felt the energy bond with her spirit, and saw Marie's rough visage soften.

"The sight has chosen me, *your* sight," Nalia continued. "I'm to be the next Mambo, the next queen. The power of your line still reigns today, but sadly, it will be lost."

Marie stepped back, placing a hand to her chest. Her spirit cried out, wounded. A puzzled look of disbelief surfaced in her eyes as her mouth dropped lazily open.

"The line will end with me," Nalia explained. "The blood, the power, the legacy will all be gone. You see, the curse has come back to you. Like a spinning wheel, it has drawn in the last of your family. It's targeted me, and if you don't undo it, I will become its next victim. The line will be lost, the legend forgotten. Your mother passed the power to you. Your daughters, in turn, received it from you, and on down the line all the way to me. All I ask is for a chance to pass your sight to my daughters, someday – to continue the legacy of Marie Laveau."

Marie grew pensive. "No matter how long it takes," she thought. "Truth always comes to fruition. Everything you do comes back to you."

Nalia steeled her eyes, locking them with a resolve Marie had no choice but to respect. "I want nothing more than to carry on our line, but the hate ends with me. The name Marie Laveau is synonymous with power and villainy, but it's also known for compassion and charity. I will not pass on a legacy of vengeance. The world beyond me will know the beauty of your sight, not the fear."

Marie was moved. With the weight of Nalia's words heavy on her soul, she sat down at the round table. Folding her hands, she stared into the flames of the candles in solemn reflection. The gravity of the curse and its consequences wreaked havoc with her spirit as she pondered her decision. "I can't take it back," she said, finally. The tremor in her voice conveyed absolution, and a hint of regret. "Even if I was willing," she continued. "I can't reverse a curse dat I fix, it's got to run its course."

Nalia's fear became reality as Marie confirmed her suspicion. Her hope was crushed. All light drained from Nalia's spirit as the words rolled off Marie's tongue. She looked at Mama Lu in desperation.

"What if we can break it?" Mama Lu asked. "You say it's got to run its course, but you gave dat man a way out. How do we fix dat watch? How can we break the curse?"

Marie's eyes slowly began to dance as thoughts connected like a chain inside her head. "You can do it," she said, looking to Nalia with revelation. "I set dat curse wit' my blood to make a point, to let dat man know he would have to best me in order to undo it. If you truly are my flesh and blood, you can break it. A blood curse can only be broken by blood, in dis case my blood, the blood dat runs in yo' veins. You watched me set dat curse, you can break it if you remember. Spill fresh blood on the ritual object, recite the charm and the spell will be lifted."

Nalia's spirit fell. Opening her palm, she revealed the watch and the cut in her palm. "Your blade, your blood," she said. "It didn't work."

"Oh chil'," replied Marie with a wicked grin. "I'm 'fraid dat was jus' another piece of my twisted lil' puzzle. You can't make dat watch work again by spillin' the blood dere. Dat timepiece only indicates the state of the curse. What you need is the real ritual object, the one dat truly houses the spell."

Turning to the ancient cabinet Marie retrieved Jack's other article of payment, the polished silver brush. "Dis is the item you need. Dis is the relic dat can break the spell," she said, her eyes growing grave. "But I can't simply hand it over to you through the void."

"I have it!" shouted Nalia. "That's my brush, I know where it is."

Marie was shocked. Her mind ran wild, analyzing possibilities and probabilities. "You tellin' me dis is yo' brush? Dat it belongs to you in yo' present time?"

"Yes!" insisted Nalia, taking note of the raised pattern on its handle. "That's the same brush my Madame T. gave to me. I can break the spell!"

The energy of the room fell heavy with desperation, and Marie's complexion sallowed. "Oh, if only it were dat easy," she said, her eyes going distant. "You have it dere in yo' time, because I can send it to you in dis one. I can enchant dis brush to make it find you through time and space, but dat depends on you and dis very moment."

Nalia was confused. She had the brush, it was right there on the sink in the shop where she left it. The outcome was already finalized; what could it possibly depend on?

"Let me explain, darlin'," Marie continued. "I don't take payment fo' my spells jus' to pad my pocketbook. I got plenty means of doin' dat on the side. I take payment because magic has a price. All life is a balance and when you tip the scale you have to compensate. I can cast a spell to make dis brush find you, but dere's got to be payment made. Now since you say you have the brush, I know the spell *will* be cast. Dat, my darlin', is a certainty. My question is, wha's yo' sacrifice?"

Nalia was baffled. She understood the concept: the spell must have been cast because the brush came to her on her twelfth birthday. But what payment could she possibly offer here and now? She had nothing to give. Before she could voice her confusion, Mama Lu spoke up.

"I have the payment," she said. "I'll make the sacrifice. Cast yo' spell."

Chapter Thirty-Six

Marie Laveau raised an eyebrow in a way only she could. She studied Mama Lu in disbelief, discerning her intentions. She could feel her will and sense her decision. Her spirit sank like sand through a sieve. "You sure 'bout dis, Mambo?"

Mama Lu affirmed with a barely visible nod, and a tearful eye.

"Mama, what are you saying?" asked Nalia with a sudden shiver of unease.

"Ain't no turnin' back, you know," said Marie, paying Nalia no mind. "Wha's done is done."

"I realize dat," said Mama Lu. "Let's get dis over wit'."

"What's going on, Mama?" Nalia insisted. "What sacrifice are you talking about?"

Mama Lu tried to speak, but when she choked on her words, Marie conveyed them for her.

"Her power, chil'," she said with no indication of levity. "She's givin' up her power."

As Nalia's world screeched to a shuddering halt, her spirit cried out in opposition. "No! Mama you can't. I won't let you."

"Ain't yo' decision to make, baby. Dis between me and Marie Laveau. My mind is made up."

Nalia would not be silenced. "You can't do this, Mama. If you hand your power over to her..."

"Ain't you been listenin', chil'?" asked Mama Lu, shaking her head. "Like the brush, I can't jus' hand dis over through the veil. I can't pass my power to Marie Laveau, but I can pass it to her bloodline."

Stunned for a moment, Nalia's face finally contorted with recognition. "No! Mama you can't... I can't... I won't let you make this choice."

"You said it yo'self," insisted Mama Lu. "Love is puttin' the needs of others befo' yo' own. Right now, the man I love is bleedin' out on my floor, and the woman I raised from a chil' is next in line to be claimed by dis monstrous curse. There is no choice to make. We must simply do what needs doin'."

"But without your power, without the sight, you'll be..."

"Jus' fine," said Mama Lu. "I'll be jus' fine." She offered Nalia a smile filled with sadness and acceptance, but a smile nonetheless.

"It's settled, den," said Marie, "When yo' spirit flies along dis tether back to yo' body, it will be done. The spell will be cast and the sight will shift. The power will be transferred to you, young one. Are you ready?"

Nalia cut a look to Mama Lu, her eyes both asking the question and affirming the answer. Reaching a tearful understanding, they joined hands and nodded to Marie.

"Tell me yo' name, chil'," said the Voodoo queen.

"Nalia," she said, strong and proud.

"Nalia," repeated Marie, "Such a beautiful name. I should have known. It fits you. Do you know what it means?"

Nalia looked at Mama Lu. Finding only a blank stare she swiveled back to Marie and shook her head.

"It means 'the stem'," she answered. "A grand new legacy gon' stem from you, chil'. I'll be watchin'. I 'spect I'm gon' be seein' a lot more' of you in the future."

"Indeed you will," said Mama Lu before Nalia could answer. She looked at her daughter with a grin of anticpation. "Jus' because I won't have the sight, don't mean I can't teach you the art. We got a lot of work to do, chil'."

Nalia blushed.

"I will make sure dis brush finds you, young Nalia," said Marie Laveau. "You do what you will wit' it. You know how, and you have the power."

Just then, Nalia felt Mama Lu's spirit lurch with urgency. Darkness, pain, and fear all flooded through the veil, calling her back across the bridge between the worlds.

"We gots to leave," she said. "Somethin' ain't right. I feel John callin' to me. We gots to go now!"

Mama Lu enveloped Nalia in her spirit as they heard Marie's final words calling to them. "Fly Mambo, do what needs doin'. Fear not, young Nalia, the brush will find you."

With Mr. John's urgent cry screaming in her head, Mama Lu led them back through the void, traveling like lightning along their silver tethers.

Chapter Thirty-Seven

With the thundering pressure of a crashing wave, Nalia's spirit returned to her body. Slightly groggy, she raised her head, trying to focus. The scene in the ritual room was chaotic. Mr. John, freed from his restraint, was huddled over the body of Madame Luciénne. A wide trail of blood stretched from her present position through the opening in the wall. Elias Haufmann held a blood-soaked rag to her neck, firmly applying pressure while Mr. John attempted CPR.

On the floor beside the ritual table lay Jack's motionless body, face down, limbs flailed in various directions. The twelve gauge was at his side.

"What happened in here?" cried Mama Lu, rushing to Mr. John's side.

He did not answer. His attention was focused completely on Madame Luciénne. With one hand covering the other he pressed firmly and repeatedly in the center of her chest, counting as he went. Every thirty compressions he lifted her neck and blew twice into her mouth, but Vivian was not responding. He yelled at her not to give up, as he continued to work feverishly. With painstaking effort he tried to revive her, sweat pouring from his body.

Mama Lu sensed the end was nigh when she noticed John crying. His strength was failing, his effort waning. After one final attempt, he felt for a pulse, looked at Mama Lu, shook his head and doubled over. The ritual blade was still in his side.

"She's gone, Lu," he wheezed. "I can't get no pulse. We tried, but we was jus' too late."

His breath was ragged and his muscles were exhausted. If there was one person in the world Mr. John never expected to mourn, it was Madame Vivian Luciénne. Now, having fought to save her life and failed, he could not contain his remorse. He sobbed uncontrollably repeating the phrase, "I'm so sorry," and stroking her hair.

Mama Lu had no time to mourn. Mr. John needed attention. She was about to run for the first aid kit when Nalia burst back into the room and tossed it to her. She was so involved with John and Luciénne she never even noticed Nalia slip downstairs.

Elias held Mr. John's head while Mama Lu examined the wound.

"He saved me, Lu," said Mr. John. "Cracked ol' Jack in the back of the head wit' the butt of dat gun and cut me loose. I told him we needed to work on Vivian, but I couldn't walk. He dragged her in here fo' me but I couldn't..."

"Hush, John," said Mama Lu, coming to a grim conclusion. "Jack was right, I can't pull dis blade or you'll bleed out. We got to call you an ambulance. Where's yo' phone?"

Mr. John feebly tapped his chest pocket, and Mama Lu retrieved the ancient apparatus only to find its battery dead. She looked at Elias.

"Our phone line isn't connected yet," he said.

"You'll have to go get mine," said Mama Lu. "Downstairs, on the counter, by the register. Go! I'm not leavin' him."

Elias agreed. He laid Mr. John gently onto the floor and made for the stairs. Before he was even across the room, Jack groaned and stirred.

"Did she do it?" Mr. John asked. "Did she break the spell?"

"No, but I can," said Nalia, presenting her polished silver hairbrush.

Mr. John looked up in confusion. He turned to Mama Lu for an explanation as Jack moaned again.

The three turned to the center of the room as Jack sat up to one elbow and rubbed the back of his head. Before they could stop him, Jack reached for the twelve gauge, but he was a second too late. Nalia scooped the weapon from the floor, held it like a shovel, and drove the butt into Jack's head again. With a thud, he dropped like a stone.

"He ain't gon' be out fo' long," said Mr. John, groaning from the pain of the blade. "So if you can break dat curse, you best get to it."

Standing over Jack with the shotgun, Nalia couldn't pull her worried eyes from Mr. John, lying on the floor, his energy spent. Mama Lu huddled over him in desperation, holding his hand. His situation was grim, but his face was stern. His voice was raspy, but commanding. "I said hurry up, girl," he managed with urgency. "Get it done! If he comes to, it changes everythin'."

Mama Lu nodded in agreement, as Nalia heard the voice of Madame Toulouse in her head.

It's time fo' you to face yo' fears and do what needs doin', befo' it's too late.

Images of the courtyard flashed through Nalia's mind: blood on her hands, her throat slashed, Jack in his top hat with his bloodshot eyes and his hungry stare. The memories were terrifying, but no image made her shudder more than the knife in Mr. John's side. She needed the blade for the ritual.

Realizing the dilemma at the same time as Nalia, Mama Lu sat shell-shocked staring at her daughter's tears. Pain hit her gut with renewed vigor as she realized a choice must be made. Her power was gone. She could not draw energy to help Mr. John and Nalia's power would be spent with the ritual.

"What are you waitin' fo'," asked Mr. John as Jack began to groan and stir again. "Get to it."

"She needs the blade, John," said Mama Lu, her voice faint and cracking. "If I take it out..."

Mr. John's moment of reflection was so brief, it was nearly non-existent. With all his remaining strength he reached to pull the knife from his side.

Mama Lu stopped him, wailing. "No, John! If you pull dat blade out you ain't gon' make it."

"If she don't break dat curse, ain't none of us gon' make it,"
John replied, struggling against her.

Mama Lu fought hard. "I can't let you do it. I can't..."

Mr. John removed his hands from the handle of the knife and
placed them tenderly on top of Mama Lu's. With earnest eyes,
he drew her gaze. Through her frantic tears and his determined
stare, they spoke without words, making a pact between their
spirits.

"I'm gon' be fine, long as you hold pressure," he reassured
her. "It's gon' hurt like the devil, but you got to put yo' weight
on it. No matter what, you can't let go."

Mama Lu nodded, sniffling and turning her eyes away.

"Look at me," said Mr. John, drawing her back. "Once dis
blade is out, I'm in yo' hands, Lu. I'm dependin' on you." His
eyes conveyed confidence, not concern, giving Mama Lu the
strength she needed. With a heavy heart and a quivering lip, she
instructed Nalia to remove the blade.

Jack groaned again as Nalia stepped forward and wrapped
her fingers around the handle of the knife. She looked back and
forth between Mr. John and Mama Lu, both resolute in their
decision, but both tearing and anxious.

"Go on, do what needs doin', baby girl," said John with
finality.

Holding her breath and closing her eyes, Nalia pulled the
knife swiftly from John's side as he moaned uncontrollably in
agony. As quickly as she could manage, Nalia flipped Jack onto
his back and laid the brush on his chest.

Mama Lu continued to weep as she sat to her knees, putting
all her body weight onto Mr. John's open wound. Despite her
efforts, blood began to pool underneath her rigid palms.

Nalia coupled the intensity of the room with the adrenaline
coursing through her body to hone her spirit like a surgical
instrument. Blocking everything from her consciousness, she
focused on the memory of Marie Laveau and the ritual that set
the curse. She smelled the incense of the dusty room, saw the

intensity in the Voodoo queen's eyes, heard the beating of the ancient drum. As Nalia's spirit took on a new and otherworldly existence, her heartbeat kept time with the pounding of the drum until she could feel the rhythm pulsing in her veins. Scenes from the vision strobed through her mind with each strike of the drum: the mixture of emotions in Jack's frightened eyes, his struggle against the bindings, sweat rolling down his cheek. Holding the ritual blade across her right palm, Nalia felt the presence of her departed grandmother, the natural strength of Marie Laveau's bloodline, and the newly-acquired energy of Mama Lu – a perfect trifecta of power surging through her body.

Mama Lu felt the pulse. Energy emanating from Nalia physically pummeled her body in waves. Looking up, she saw a halo of light around her daughter's form as Nalia slipped effortlessly into a deep, dream-like trance. Mama Lu watched her eyes twitch rapidly under their lids as her head rolled back onto her shoulders.

Entirely unaware of her body's movement, Nalia's mind joined the spirit world as her soul walked between. The sound of the drum grew louder and faster, as Nalia's rhythmic convulsions increased to mirror the tempo. The energy in the room swelled to bursting until, finally, the sound of the drum ceased.

Nalia opened her eyes, not quite in the world of the living, but neither fully given over to the spirit realm. The room took on a strange and unnatural appearance. Souls became visible, glowing like heat signatures on an infrared display. Every object in the room lit up with palpable energy before Nalia's eyes. She felt the vibration of every seemingly-mundane item separately, but all together at the same time. A new universe emerged as Nalia instantly realized all things vibrated on their own frequency, but came together in harmony with their surroundings. The flames of the candles, the wooden beams of the wall, the memories housed within the ritual table all glowed with their own unique signature.

A quick glance at Mr. John revealed his spiritual struggle, wanting to fight for life but longing for peace. Without hesitation, Nalia centered her energy on the ritual. To her surprise the dialect began to roll off her tongue naturally, though she barely recalled the words of the incantation.

Ede mwen Loa, ede mwen Bondye

Pote san, pote lajistis, pote v alimante.

Kase mwen tauhe, gratis mwen lespir, ban mwen lapè

Drawing the blade swiftly across her palm, Nalia closed her fist and squeezed, allowing blood to seep between her fingers.

Jack stirred, jarred by the pulsing energy. His bloodshot eyes found Nalia like a lost boy finding his mother. He watched in bittersweet release as Nalia held her fist over the polished silver hairbrush and allowed her blood to spill across its shining surface, over the raised pattern and into the grooves.

As the crimson trail flowed over its decorative curves, a shockwave of energy like an atom bomb burst from the brush, whipping through the room and beyond the walls, shaking everything in its path. Mama Lu struggled to maintain her balance and keep pressure on Mr. John's bleeding wound as the force nearly knocked her over.

Alone in the eye of the hurricane, Jack reached a gentle hand to Nalia's face. His bloodshot eyes turned crystal clear and filled with adoration.

"I really was starting to like you," he said. "In another time and another place, under different circumstances, I could have loved you."

Nalia simply smiled. She had no time to ponder what could have been, what should have been, or what would never come to pass. She focused on the curse and releasing Jack's spirit.

"Thank you," he whispered as his last breath escaped his parted lips.

Nalia watched his glowing spirit separate from his body and drift toward the ceiling like a wispy summer cloud. He hovered only a moment, as if turning to say goodbye. In an instant, he was gone.

With the brush steadily releasing its torrent of energy, Jack's body withdrew and shrank. His perfect, baby-smooth skin began to wrinkle and crack. Nalia heard a sound like the scream of a distant banshee as Jack's flesh dried like desert sand in seconds. Tissue flaked into ash and scattered on the raging wind of power, eventually dissipating into nothing, until all that remained was a blood-soaked silver brush lying on the floor in front of Nalia. With a final, powerful pulse, the energy of the brush faded into oblivion, and the golden pocket watch, for the first time in ages, began to tick. The curse was broken and the sound of approaching sirens filled the street outside.

With his strength vanquished, Mr. John's eyes rolled into his head. Through her sobbing, Mama Lu called his name and yelled at him to hang on. He tracked her voice with his eyes for a brief second before they rolled back again.

"Don't you die on me, John Barrett!" she yelled. "You stay wit' me!" Taking a hand away from the wound, she beat him on the chest with her fist. "Don't you die on me, they almost here!" The flow of warm blood alerted Mama Lu to her mistake. Refocusing her attention, she increased pressure on his side.

Through the desperate scuffling and weeping, the faint sound of a cough rose across the room. Though barely audible, Nalia's heightened senses detected the feeble sound. Madame Luciénne was wheezing in quiet, tiny convulsions. Rushing to her side, Nalia placed a bleeding hand on her wounded neck. With inhuman effort, Madame Luciénne whispered gasping words into Nalia's ear.

"Don't help me... help John," she managed. "Too late for me... got what I deserve. I'm the reason all dis happened... I told him who you were... tell Mama Lu... I'm sor..."

The final word never escaped Madame Luciénne's lips, but whether fueled by remorse, guilt, or gratitude, her message was clear.

Still walking between the worlds, Nalia watched Vivian's spirit glow and separate from her body. Gently, it gathered above her corpse and started its journey toward the sky, like lingering smoke from a snuffed candle.

In that moment, Nalia felt the trifecta of power swirling inside her once more, coursing through her veins like a team of thundering horses. Unaware of its origin, a notion appeared in her mind and instinctively she acted on it, trusting her spirit, trusting her sight. Arching her back and stretching her arms wide Nalia inhaled more deeply than ever before. With blood pouring from the stinging wounds in her palms, Nalia drew the spirit of Madame Luciénne into herself, filling every atom of her body. Acting as a benevolent host, Nalia charged Luciénne's spirit with the surging energy of the trifecta. The sensation was electrifying, exhilarating, and draining all at once, leaving Nalia spent in an exhausted state of elation.

With a final effort, Nalia leaned over, pressed her mouth against Vivian's cold lips and breathed life back into her body, giving her frail form enough strength to hang on as bag-carrying paramedics raced up the stairs followed by a humbled and shaking Elias Haufmann.

Chapter Thirty-Eight

The dew was thick and the bricks were slippery on the morning Nalia and Mama Lu visited St. Louis Cathedral. Father Carmelo agreed to open the doors early so the ladies could have a moment to themselves. With clear minds and heavy hearts, they made their way to the entrance.

Before opening the heavy wooden door, Mama Lu turned and cast a mournful eye toward Jackson Square. She saw no grisly image of Madame Zoe, no ghostly apparitions of slain young women, only the peaceful, dew-kissed flora of the budding foliage. Remembering Zoe's crooked, Cheshire smile, Mama Lu sighed and breathed in the clean morning air. Nearly two weeks had passed since the events in the upper room. Madame Zoe's body was laid to rest in Mount Olivet Cemetery, with a small ceremony honoring her life and memory. Zoe would be missed, but she was at peace, and there was comfort in that.

Jack was also at peace, thought Mama Lu, beaming at her beautiful daughter. She knew no words to express her pride in Nalia's wisdom and maturity. One is never truly enlightened until they can show compassion to those who wrong them, understand their situation, and react with kindness instead of vengeance.

Elias Haufmann currently sat behind bars, awaiting judgment for his role in the disappearance of Jack's victim's. Mama Lu and Nalia would use their influence to make sure his sentence was as lenient as possible. The man already knew a lifetime of punishment, brainwashed and enslaved to a twisted, tortured master ruled by hatred and pain. His shop would be looked after until such time as he could return to live the rest of his days among the springs and gears of his beloved clocks, the only real love he'd ever known.

Madame Luciénne was nearly ready to be released from Mercy hospital. After five hours in surgery and two blood transfusions, she spent a critical few days in intensive care. She currently occupied a room on the surgical post-op floor where Edith had been re-assigned. Mama Lu and Nalia kept regular tabs with the young lady about Luciénne's condition. Nalia even sent an arrangement of white tulips and yarrow, with an unsigned card simply reading "Life is like a spinning wheel."

With Mama Lu's encouragement, Nalia considered attending mass on a regular basis. It was important, she noted, to maintain a healthy connection with the spirit world, recognize the saints, and acknowledge deity. As they entered the foyer of the cathedral, Nalia felt a peaceful energy surround her, wrapping her in a blanket of warmth and serenity. It was a feeling she could abide.

Nalia resigned herself to the notion of giving greater weight to Mama Lu's advice. She would be under her strict instruction until time for the official transference of power ritual, at which point she would attain the title of Mambo, High Priestess of the order.

"I've got so much to learn, Mama," Nalia said, "Patience, discipline, timing, and technique. I have so far to go."

"Not as far as you might think, chil'," replied Mama Lu as they made their way to the prayer candles. "Yo' wisdom far surpasses yo' age, and yo' natural ability is unmatched. It's in yo' blood, chil'."

Reverently, they approached the candles and retrieved matches from the holder. A single flame was already burning, letting Mama Lu know Father Carmelo already offered a prayer of his own. With words of thanksgiving, and petition to the saints, Mama Lu and Nalia lit their matches and held them each to a separate candle. They stood for a moment in silent reflection, listening to the voices of the past, accepting the present, and hoping for the future.

Mama Lu slipped a hand inside her bag and produced a small, flat, silver plate and a heavy piece of paper. She placed the dish in front of the candles and handed the paper to Nalia. It was approximately four inches by six, heavy cardstock, with a detailed pattern. Flipping the card over, Nalia saw the pale horse with the skeletal rider from her vision – the death card of the tarot.

With a nod from Mama Lu, Nalia dipped the corner of the card into the flame of Zoe's candle. She held it in her hand as long as she could, watching the edge of the flame march across the image, swallowing death in its path. When the flame reached her fingertips, Nalia dropped the card onto the silver plate and watched it burn to ash.

As the last of the smoke dissipated, Mama Lu heard a cough echo in the hall behind her. Turning around, she and Nalia saw a well-dressed man standing in the light of the open doorway, removing his Fedora. It was Mr. John dressed in his very best suit and freshly polished shoes. With his hat in his hands and a shy, nervous smile, Mr. John shuffled toward Mama Lu in the way only an aging man can – with reservation, but undeterred purpose.

In that moment Mr. John was part gentle old man, part cocky adolescent, part innocent child, and every bit a confident gentleman, wholly in love with the woman before him.

"Please, don't say nothin'," he asked of Mama Lu. "I got somethin' weighin' on my mind, and I can't live another second without sayin' it. Lu, I know you pride yo'self on bein' a strong, self-sufficient woman, and I can't begin to tell you how much I respect dat. You've made a wonderful life for yo'self, Lu, and it's admirable. But, I want you to know 'bout the life you've made fo' me."

Nalia's eyes began to tear, and her throat swelled, making it difficult to breathe as she tried to step back silently, unnoticed.

"You the sun and the moon fo' me, Lu. You the breath I breathe and the life in my veins. Everythin' I am is because of yo' influence on my world. Because of you, I'm wise when I need to be, compassionate when I should be, and strong when I have to be. I didn't get dat way on my own, and I hate to think of the man I'd be if it wasn't fo' you."

Reaching into his pants pocket, Mr. John produced the small, velvet box and opened it. Having waited far too long, the ring inside finally met Mama Lu's eyes. She was trying desperately not to cry. With anxious breath and a humble stare, Mr. John looked up to see Mama Lu bewildered, holding a gentle hand to her chest. His nerves permitted only a moment's gaze before diverting his eyes to the floor.

"I thought long and hard 'bout what to say," he continued in a quiet, reverent voice. "How it makes good sense, how we ain't gettin' any younger, and how we need to be able to take care of each other. I got a whole lot of logical arguments in my mind on how to convince you dis is right. But truth is, Lu, logic don't have a thing to do wit' it, 'cause even if I had a thousand, logical reasons *not* to love you, they still couldn't sway my heart. I'm standin' here today fo' one reason, and dat's 'cause I can't deny dat truth anymo'. Now, if you can't see dat, and you won't have me... well, I guess we jus' gon' have to work somethin' out 'cause I don't plan on taking no fo' an answer." Gritting through the lingering pain in his side, Mr. John dropped to one knee in what he believed was the only appropriate position for the question at hand. "So I'm askin' you dis, Lucia Deminy," he said, slipping the princess cut ring onto her finger. "Will you honor me, by being my bride?"

His voice was steady, but his hands were trembling. Silently, Mr. John waited with hope in his heart and adoration in his welling eyes.

For a long moment Mama Lu could not speak, and silence hung thick as molasses in the empty hall. Nalia managed to find a far wall and watched, casting her eye back and forth from Mama Lu to Mr. John. She thought nothing was ever so perfect, but as the silence lingered, she began to fear the outcome.

Finally, Mama Lu conquered the lump in her throat. She looked down at John, her eyes revealing nothing but sincerity.

"I saw dis comin' a long time ago," she said. "I gave it plenty of thought, and I made my mind up. I ain't never needed no man, long as I've lived, and I still don't today."

Nalia gasped, placing her hand over her lips. New tears formed in the corner of her eyes as she watched Mr. John's spirit break.

His heart heavy with despair, Mr. John barely managed to stand. He could not turn his eyes away from his reflection in the polished floor.

With a gentle hand, Mama Lu touched his face and lifted his gaze until his glassy eyes met hers. "But what I need, and what I want is two different things," she said with an adoring, wide smile. "So my answer, John Barrett, is yes, I will have you."

In a single moment, the weight a lifetime lifted from Mr. John. He felt light enough to fly past the stars. Taking Mama Lu in a firm embrace, he vowed in his heart to hold her for as long as life allowed, and beyond.

Nalia couldn't contain her happiness. It leaked from her eyes like rain through a spout as she rushed over to embrace them both.

A small clap echoed through the hall as the group realized Father Carmelo was standing in the corner, smiling and silently praying for a long and blessed union.

Pushing away from John's embrace, Mama Lu looked him square in the eyes with stern resolution. "So what took you so long to ask me? You been carryin' dis ring around in yo' pocket fo' months now," she said. "It ain't like I ain't been droppin' hints, doin' my part to coax it out of you."

Mr. John looked like he'd been slapped in the face with a fish. "What you mean doin' yo' part? What hints?"

"John Barrett, why you think I been feedin' you weddin' chicken every Monday night fo' the past two months."

Recognition hit Mr. John like a hammer. "Is dat what dat was? Wait, you ain't put no spell on me, have you?"

Mama Lu raised an eyebrow. "Would it matter if I did?" she asked, with a sly grin.

Not knowing how to respond, Mr. John slipped his hat back on his head and turned for the door in disbelief. "I'm gon' be in the truck if y'all want to ride. Don't keep me waitin' all day, now."

"You jumpin' on my las' nerve, John Barrett," called Mama Lu, barely able to disguise her elation. "My las' nerve."

With a final, reverent nod to the candles of Madame Zoe and Madame Toulouse and a wink to Father Carmelo, Mama Lu and Nalia exited St. Louis Cathedral with the morning sun shining on their smiling faces. The days to come would be marked with transition, adjustment, conflict, and compromise, but they would all brave the new frontier together with honor, remembrance, and fierce anticipation of many great things to come.

- The End -

About the author –

L. E. Gay is a recreational author from Southeast Texas, where he lives and writes beneath a canopy of 150 year-old oak trees with his wife Carol, their English shepherd Treble, and their cats Timmy and Sasha. He is blessed to be supported by his family and friends, and is currently working on the next chapter of Nalia's life in New Orleans.

For more works by L. E. Gay, visit www.legayauthor.com

Also by L. E. Gay

The Doll Maker

When a casual date with a college classmate takes an unexpected turn, Nalia Deminy is plagued by disturbing visions that threaten her sanity and her life. Desperate for answers, she returns to the heart of New Orleans and the only mother she has ever known. Clues to the mysteries of Nalia's past lie with Mama Lu, a world-renowned porcelain crafter and owner of "The Doll Maker" – a French Quarter storefront with a notorious history of its own. With the ceremony of St. John's Eve imminent, and pressure from a rival practitioner reaching aggressive levels, Mama Lu will stop at nothing to protect her daughter, including a return to the dark world she gave up in order to raise her. Together with her mentor, Madame Toulouse and her mysterious friend "Doctor" John, Mama Lu must begin the delicate process of ritualistically returning the memories hidden inside her daughter's mind. As Nalia's visions grow more violent, the trio struggles to reveal the truth about her shocking past, while protecting the one secret she must never learn.

Available as an eBook from smashwords.com, barnesandnoble.com, amazon.com, and other sites where eBooks are sold.

Paperback copies are available from Lulu.com

Praise for **The Doll Maker**

***** One of the "Best Read Books of 2013"
"Delicate, loving, unnerving, suspenseful, and hopeful all
when it needed to be... a very multi-dimensional book."
-Lesleigh Nahay, *Of Words and Writing.*

***** "...nail-biting, stay-up-all-night-to-finish suspense. A
great book with wonderfully drawn characters."
-smashwords.com

***** "Incredible read! ...that rare novel that leaves you
realizing late into the night you've run out of pages to turn
because you kept telling yourself, 'just one more chapter.' I
would recommend it to any reader seeking thrill, a little bit of
history, and characters to hold in their heart."
-barnesandnoble.com

***** "Great read with a nice twist on New Orleans' voodoo
culture. I am so invested in the characters that I am hoping for a
sequel."
-amazon.com